HER ABUNDANT JOY

Also by Lyn Cote

BLESSED ASSURANCE
THE DESIRES OF HER HEART
HER INHERITANCE FOREVER

HER ABUNDANT JOY

TEXAS: *Star of Destiny*

BOOK THREE

LYN COTE

AVON
INSPIRE

An Imprint of HarperCollins*Publishers*

HER ABUNDANT JOY. Copyright © 2010 by Lyn Cote. All rights reserved. Printed in the United States of America. No part of this book may be used or reproduced in any manner whatsoever without written permission except in the case of brief quotations embodied in critical articles and reviews. For information address HarperCollins Publishers, 10 East 53rd Street, New York, NY 10022.

FIRST AVON PAPERBACK EDITION PUBLISHED 2010.

Designed by Diahann Sturge

Library of Congress Cataloging-in-Publication Data
Cote, Lyn.
  Her abundant joy / Lyn Cote.
    p. cm. — (Texas, star of destiny ; bk. 3)
  ISBN 978-0-06-137342-8 (pbk.)
  1. Frontier and pioneer life—Texas—Fiction. 2. Women immigrants—Fiction. 3. Germans—Texas—Fiction. 4. Texas Rangers—Fiction. 5. Texas—Fiction. I. Title.
  PS3553.O76378H44 2010
  813'.54—dc22

                                                      2009044958

10 11 12 13 14   OV/RRD   10 9 8 7 6 5 4 3 2 1

To my editor, Cynthia DiTiberio, thanks for all your "right on the nose" editing and encouragement. Also thanks to my publicists, Joanne Minutillo and Kendra Newton, who went above and beyond, and everyone else at Avon Inspire/HarperCollins who worked so hard to the benefit of this series.

Trust in the Lord, and do good;
so shalt thou dwell in the land,
But the meek shall inherit the earth; and
shall delight themselves in the abundance of peace. . . .
Mark the perfect man, and behold the upright:
for the end of that man is peace.

Psalm 37:3, 11, 37

One

Texas, April 1846

Gazing ahead through the pouring rain, Carson Quinn tried to take a deep breath but couldn't. A searing tightness in his chest kept reminding him; he hadn't been able to blot out the images. Images from the past week with Blanche had blistered into his mind, knotted around his lungs. Late on his second day in the saddle, all he was looking forward to was a hot bath and a warm bed at one of Galveston's inns, comfort for his body, if not his spirit.

Draped within the dismal mist, he nudged his horse to churn quicker through mud and murky puddles over the last half mile into the seaport. Amid the jumble of buildings, strange people clogged the streets. He pulled up on his reins. Something had happened here. Something out of the ordinary. Something that might force him out of his own misery into the misery of others.

People huddled under dripping trees or canvas; they stood under the overhanging roofs of stores. Everyone was drenched. Rainwater funneled down Carson's leather hat as he steered his horse through the throng. Those who peered up at him looked pale, forlorn and sickly. They weren't dressed like Texans, or even Americans—

He inhaled a shallow breath. He still thought of Americans as separate from Texians, from him. But Texas was part of the United States now. Had been for months.

Who were these people?

He scanned the crowd and could not pick out any man who appeared to be in charge. Not that he could tell—they weren't speaking any language Carson spoke.

Finally, he saw someone he recognized. He hailed the man, a former Ranger named Tunney, and drew up beside him. "Hey!"

Tunney, a tall, big-boned man with weathered folds on his tanned face, halted, then waved in recognition. "Come!" He motioned for Carson to get down and accompany him inside the nearby cantina. Carson complied, tying his horse to the hitching rail. He realized he could breathe a bit deeper. It was good to see a face he knew, a man he'd patrolled with.

Inside, Carson found Tunney waiting for him at the bar with a mug of ale ready for him. Tunney smiled—a real smile of welcome. Nothing like the false ones Carson had endured these past few days . . .

Shaking phantom memories off, Carson drank deep, then got down to business. "Who are all these people?"

"They're from Germany, from what I hear. Only they don't call themselves Dutch but doit-cha." Tunney's mouth twisted as he tried to pronounce the word. "Been here over a week now."

"That's fine and good, but what are they doing hanging around town, clogging the streets?"

"All the drivers and their freighter wagons are off supplying the U.S. Army."

"All of them?" Carson paused, his cup right under his nose. He drew in the yeasty smell of the mild home brew. He'd known the U.S. Army had come to Texas but not that it had caused this.

Tunney chuckled. "You didn't expect the Mexicans to be happy that Texas has been annexed by the United States? I guess Polk is letting the Mexicanos know that the U.S. won't stand for them invading Texas, now it's U.S. territory. General Zachary Taylor is at the Rio Grande. Haven't you kept up?"

Carson drank some more ale. He'd been busy fighting Comanche this year, far from newspapers. And then at the wedding, his misery had sucked away most everything else and left behind only consuming pain. "I've been out patrolling and then . . . some family business came up." He shut his mind to the taunting images. "I didn't see a newspaper till I got to San Felipe." *And I didn't pay too much attention to it then.* Nothing much else had mattered to him at San Felipe.

"That's right." Tunney raised his voice, talking over an explosion of laughter at the end of the bar. "Your mother has family there."

Yeah, family. Carson nodded but refused to elaborate. "So these people are just stuck here?"

"Yeah, they aren't happy about it, and neither are the townspeople. The Germans don't seem to have money to buy shelter or food. Some of them speak English, but most don't. A bad business."

Carson shrugged, feeling suddenly flat inside. It was as if he'd reached the point where he couldn't muster any more emotion.

This past week he'd experienced too much, but all under cover. Pride had forced him to hold it all back in silence. This made the emotions somehow more powerful, more devastating. Even now.

Ignoring this, he chatted with Tunney about the whereabouts of other mutual friends. When he'd gleaned all the information Tunney had, Carson bid his fellow Ranger good-bye and headed back out into the soggy day to find an inn with a bath and a bed for him.

He'd just stepped out the tavern door when he was met by a commotion. A mere two feet from him, a woman obviously in the family way collapsed. Carson darted forward and lifted her limp body from the muddy ground.

"Ma'am? Ma'am?" He shook her a little, but she didn't react.

By then he was surrounded by people, all shouting at him in what must be German. He didn't waste any time. Barreling across the miry street with the woman in his arms, he entered the nearest inn. "I need a room!" he bellowed at the potbellied innkeeper who was just coming down the stairs. "Now! I'm a Ranger!"

That last bit worked. What a Ranger wanted in Texas, he got. Within minutes, Carson was laying the woman down on a bed upstairs. Another woman had followed him and wouldn't let the innkeeper push her out.

Carson turned. "Let her stay. Send for a doctor!"

The innkeeper left, grumbling loud and long, but Carson didn't doubt that he would do what he'd been asked.

He took a moment to eye the woman standing bedside the bed. She was very small and thin and reminded him of his mother and foster sister, with her flaxen hair and pale skin.

The woman bobbed several curtseys. *"Danke. Danke, mein herr."* Then she inched toward the unconscious woman and took her hand.

Still dripping, Carson stepped back and took off his hat. He slapped it against his leg, sending droplets everywhere. Then he said, making each word distinct, "I am Carson Quinn." He pointed to himself. "I am Carson Quinn."

The pale woman bobbed again. "*Ich bin Mariel.*" She pointed to herself, then toward the unconscious woman. "*Sie ist Frau Heller.*" Then she colored. "I am Mariel. I speak little English."

He repeated the names in his mind and nodded as footsteps came up the stairs. He leaned out the door and saw a doctor, complete with black bag. The man must have been just down the street. "In here."

The white-haired doctor, clad in a black frock coat, came in and went immediately to the woman's side. He felt her forehead, took her pulse, and then unstoppered a bottle under her nose. After a quick jerk, the woman gasped and opened her eyes. Once she focused, her confusion turned to alarm. She looked at Mariel, and the two women jabbered to each other in rapid speech.

The doctor turned to Carson. "Isn't this woman one of the stranded Germans?"

"Must be. She collapsed in front of me across the street. I didn't know if she was seriously ill or just fainted." Carson watched the woman trying to sit up. "Lay back," he ordered and demonstrated with hand motions.

"I think this woman is just weak from the journey here. These immigrants are in danger of disease every day they stay here. Typhus, malaria, all manner of contagions," the doctor said. "I've tried to encourage them to leave, but . . ." He shrugged.

"I heard. They want to leave, but there aren't any freight wagons for them to transport their goods." Carson folded his arms and tried to figure out what to do. "What do I owe you?"

"Nothing. All I did was wave smelling salts under her nose. What we need is someone to take action." The doctor eyed him.

This was not the first time Carson had been on the receiving end of an appeal for help. Since the age of eighteen, he'd been a Ranger—six years of taking action to protect others. Judging from this situation, he'd be doing the same here.

The bath and bed he longed for slipped further away.

"Thanks, Doc." He shook the man's hand. "I'll take it from here, then."

The doctor left, and Carson turned to the woman who'd said she spoke English. "Who is in charge of the Germans, miss?"

She looked confused and shook her head, coloring.

"Who is your leader?"

"Leader?" she repeated, looking like she was thinking.

"Who's the man who runs everything?" He tried a different set of words. Again the woman shook her head.

He paused and studied her. Under different circumstances—and with a lot more food under her belt—she might have been called pretty. But she looked half-starved, and the gray shadows under her eyes were deep and dark.

She suddenly smiled, her lips losing their pinched look. "Herr Meuserbach lead us."

"Meuserbach?" he repeated, seeing a ghost of what she would have looked like happy and well fed.

"*Ja.* Y-yes," she stammered.

"Stay here." He pointed down. "Stay here."

She nodded and curtseyed.

He pulled on his soaked hat with some regret and headed out into the relentless rain again. Though half of him had died this week, he could still do his job. Some of his fatigue melted away as he headed straight to the wharf, where all the warehouses were. Within a few minutes, he located the owner of several of them. "I need a warehouse. What do you have that's free?"

The older man eyed him from under bushy gray-and-white brows. "Who're you?"

"I'm a Ranger. Carson Quinn." He shook the man's hand.

"With the freighters all off to the Rio Grande, I'm pretty full. I got only one warehouse that's mostly empty. What do you want to store?"

"Which one is it?" Carson asked, looking at the line of large, shabby, waterfront buildings.

The man pointed. "What you storing? And how long?"

"People—"

"Hey! This isn't an inn—"

Carson turned and gave him a look that brooked no denial. "The people will be in the warehouse just for tonight, and then they'll be storing their large heavy cargo in that warehouse until they can get everything transported to their new settlement." Carson didn't mention the fact that he hadn't even talked to the newcomers.

Someone had to take action before they all sickened and died of disease. And since Tunney had retired from the Rangers, that meant Carson had to be the one. As soon as these people had stepped onto Texas land, they had become his responsibility, like every other Texian.

He pulled out his wallet, paid the man the price he named, then turned back toward the inn. On the way, he stopped at another warehouse to pick up the spices and books that had brought him to Galveston. He'd left San Felipe early to get some peace, but Galveston wasn't proving to be a haven where he could lick his raw wounds in peace. Shaking his head, he strode off, hearing the squishing sound of mud and water with every step he took. The unpleasant sound heightened his desire for a hot bath and bed, and he quickened his pace. Perhaps he'd soon be done with this situation and could tend to his own needs.

When he came to the inn, a large crowd of immigrants milled around the entrance. They hushed and parted as he walked in and up the stairs to the room. When he opened the door, he found a man with the two women.

Carson looked the gentleman up and down. The German was over a head shorter than Carson, but he looked warily confident. He didn't have the same starved look the two women had. And in spite of the dampness, his wool clothing looked well-tailored and expensive. Carson offered his hand.

"I'm Carson Quinn."

"I am John O. Meuserbach." The men shook hands. "Frau Wolffe called for me." He nodded toward the blond who'd called herself Mariel. "Mariel said you had asked who was in charge."

Mariel colored again and looked at the floor. A shy little thing, Carson thought. His instinct to protect nudged him again. He looked away. "I'm a Ranger."

"A Ranger?"

"Yes, Rangers are the law in Texas." *Or have been.* Would that be changing now that Texas was no longer a sovereign republic?

"The law? Have we done something wrong?" Meuserbach asked.

"No, but you can't just sit around here waiting for freighter wagons and drivers to carry your cargo inland. The Rio Grande River is where the freighters have driven with the U.S. Army supplies. And the Grande is weeks from here. And there's no telling how long it will be before the freight wagons are empty and the drivers head north again. I assume you are heading west toward some new settlement?"

The man looked as if he was having trouble keeping up. "Yes, we have purchased land west of here near the Colorado River—"

"How many of you are there?" Carson slowed his speech to be more easily understood.

"Nearly hundred."

A hundred. Carson cast a grimace at the floor. *Great.* "I'm heading west in the morning. I'll lead your group at least to Montezuma, where I'm meeting my family. We can talk all about this in the morning."

"But I—"

Carson suddenly ran flat out of patience. He just wanted to be done with this. "I've secured a place for you and your people in a warehouse on the wharf. The owner is waiting for you. Get your people under cover for a dry night's rest, and then we'll leave in the morning."

"But we don't have any wagons for our—"

Carson's impatience dug into him like spurs. "Tell your people to pack up just what they can carry. They'll need guns if they have them, shovels, axes and hatchets, cooking pots, and all the food they can carry. Just what they can carry. Everything else will be left at the warehouse until you can send someone back to get it."

"But . . . but," the man sputtered, "it is miles and miles to our land."

Carson fixed the man with a stern look. The German might as well get the plain truth and decide if he could stomach it. "My mother came to Texas in 1821 and she walked all the way from New Orleans to San Antonio. You won't be the first to walk to your new home. Now this is the choice. You can sit here and watch your people get sick and die one by one. Or you can let me lead you out of Galveston and get to your land with most still alive. Which will it be?"

The foreigner gawked at him, then swallowed. "You will lead us?"

"Yes, I'm a Ranger. Have been for years. I spend my days ranging around, protecting the people of Texas from marauding Indians and from Mexican *bandidos.* I'm heading west tomorrow morning, and you better be ready to follow me." Carson made his voice more forceful. "Or who knows when *or if* you'll reach your destination. Do you understand me?"

"I understand." The man looked flustered.

Thank heavens. "Then get your people out of the rain. I've been riding for two days and need a meal and some sleep."

"Of course." The man bowed. "Of course." He went to the door, then waited.

Carson looked at the two women. The expectant mother was on her feet and looking a little better. "Are you able to—"

"She is fine," the blond replied, "and she thank you."

"*Danke*," the pregnant woman said, dropping a curtsey.

"Don't need to thank me. It's my job. I'm sworn to protect the people of Texas, even new ones. I'll see all of you in the morning."

The pregnant woman walked past him and exited with Meuserbach, who took her arm. The smaller one—Mariel— gave him one last fleeting glance before she closed the door.

Carson sat down heavily on the side of the bed and rubbed his face with his hands.

In the sudden return to solitude, the deep heart-wound he'd sustained this week rebounded on him, nearly crushing the life from him. He drew a shallow breath, and the act caused him physical pain.

How could disappointment hurt that bad?

He closed his eyes, then forced himself off the bed. He'd done all he could for the immigrants. And now, though he had no appetite, he would go down and eat a hot meal. A man had to go on living no matter what happened to him. And he had people to lead tomorrow.

Mariel followed her mistress and Herr Meuserbach out into the chilling, miserable rain. Her English was rusty. Thanks to her father, who had taught modern languages at a boy's academy, she had understood the main points of what the tall American had said. This man, this . . . . "Carson Quinn," she murmured the name to herself. When someone talked about Americans, this was the kind of man they were talking about. He was so tall and straight. His leather clothing had been strange to her. So had that wide cape of brown wool without any fastenings that shed rainwater. And even wet and muddy, she could see that his boots had been well made.

More important than his clothing, he looked a person right in the eye. And he took action without hesitation. He didn't ignore or brood and delay.

When Frau Heller had fainted, he had scooped her up as if she'd been a downy feather and taken her out of the rain, ordered a room, and summoned a doctor with quick, sharp orders. Mariel had seen the respect that the innkeeper and doctor had shown him.

What had he called himself? "A Ranger." She whispered the word to herself as if it had been a new title of nobility, even grander than *Prinz*, prince. *Ranger.*

Herr Meuserbach stopped on the corner and began calling, "*Achtung, bitte!* Attention, please!"

The people gathered around, and her employer, Herr Jorg Heller, sought out his wife. Mariel didn't know where he had been when his wife had fainted. Or why he hadn't come to the room. He wasn't a very good husband. Now Mariel stepped back, putting as much distance between them as she could without calling attention to the fact that she didn't want to be within the man's reach. His objectionable conduct had started just recently. He'd been unpleasant before but not offensive.

As Mariel listened to Herr Meuserbach, she understood all that the Ranger was doing for them. *And he doesn't even know us.* The Herr was explaining that this man, this Carson Quinn, was evidently an official of Texas, a Ranger. Someone asked what that was. And the Herr explained that a Ranger must be like a constable who protected people from warlike natives and bandits.

And he repeated what Carson Quinn had said about his mother walking from New Orleans to San Antonio. He ended by telling them to spread the word that they must all go to the warehouse that the Ranger had rented for them for the night. There they would pack for the trek that would start tomorrow.

When Mariel looked at the faces around her, she observed various reactions. Some people looked shocked, others relieved, most doubtful. Herr Meuserbach waved his hand in a sweeping motion. "Let's get under cover! Now! Come!"

And because they were all tired, wet, and miserable, they followed him. What choice did they have?

Mariel trailed behind her employers, slogging through the mud. She had thought that nothing could have been worse than seasickness and the two-month voyage from Bremerhaven to Galveston. But after a week of rain and no shelter and scant food, that was debatable. She closed her eyes against the chilling, sapping misery and forged on, cold rainwater and mud squishing through her stockings, in and out of her shoes, with each step.

She opened her eyes. How much could one person bear? She had the unpleasant premonition that she would find the answer to that terrible question here in Texas—this Texas that was not the paradise others had predicted.

She took a deep breath as she shivered in the cold rain. Not paradise. Yet there were Rangers in Texas, men who took action and were willing to lead. That was good, very good. The image of the tall Texan with his confident ways lifted her, gave her hope. And for so long, there had been no real hope for her future. Only regret over her past.

* * *

Early the next morning, Mariel watched the Texas man, the Ranger, stride up to the warehouse, leading his horse. He halted, gazing at the people who gathered in the warehouse doorway. She tried not to stare at him. But since everyone else was doing just that, perhaps her not staring at him would be noticed.

She could not help registering the way he looked them over, his roving eyes taking their measure. When his gaze skittered over her, she blushed and looked down. Her pale skin as always announced her embarrassment plainly. She pressed her hands over her cheeks. *I will stop blushing.*

Meuserbach hurried to him. "Herr . . . I mean, Mr. Quinn. We are ready."

Mariel glanced up, wondering if this man sensed that many in the group did not want to leave this morning. Most had only reluctantly filled packs, which now sat at their feet.

"Has everyone eaten breakfast?" Carson Quinn asked.

"*Ja. Ja.*" Herr Meuserbach bobbed his head.

"Do you have a map or description of the land you're heading to?"

"*Ja.*" Herr Meuserbach pulled out a document written in German. "I translate for you." He did so.

Mariel was pleased that she had brought along the English grammar and dictionary to review again on the voyage. She'd understood most of the Ranger's words today—more than she'd thought she would recall. Her father and Dieter had been wrong. She could and had learned.

Thinking of Dieter and his scorn brought a dip in her spirits. She shook these off. The Ranger was here. He would lead them.

Mr. Quinn appeared to consider the geographical description of the land purchased by Prince Carl. She noted that his mouth was drawn down and his brows pulled together. Did he know something about the land they didn't?

"I know where you're headed." He paused. "You know there are Comanche there?"

"Comanche? *Ja.*" Herr Meuserbach nodded. "I have presents for the *Inderin.*"

Mariel's heartbeat sped up. She had heard that these *Inderin*—some said savages—who lived here killed newcomers. She glanced around and saw the same fear in other faces.

"Here. Look." Mr. Quinn lowered himself onto his heels. With his knife point in the wet sandy dirt, he sketched in large bold strokes what must be a map of Texas.

"Here we are on the coast. We're here," he said, pressing his knife tip into the coast. Then he pointed to the lines he had traced. "These are the Colorado and Guadalupe rivers." Then he made two more impressions. "I'm to meet my family here in Montezuma. And we're on our way home to our ranch southwest of San Antonio here," he said, indicating each in turn.

"Where is our land?" Herr Meuserbach asked.

"Here." Carson pressed his knife at a place just north of the impression that had been San Antonio. "Your land's in the Hill Country."

"How long to go there?" Herr Meuserbach pointed to the impression where their land was.

"If it was just me on horseback, five or six days. With all these people on foot"—Mr. Quinn motioned to the crowd pressing in around them—"twice that at least. Plus there's been a lot of rain, so the rivers and creeks will be high and running fast."

Meuserbach started to stand, his chin low. "You think the freight wagons will not come back soon."

Mr. Quinn held up a hand, stopping him. The Ranger traced another line far south of the other two lines, another river it seemed. "Here's the Rio Grande, where they've all gone. Who knows when they will get back here? I don't. Do you?"

The distance from Galveston to the Rio Grande River looked vast. Mariel wondered at a land this big and with so much openness. What would it look like, feel like? In Germany, towns and villages were close, and one did not usually travel far from home. This new land, with its overflowing rivers and vast miles, was unsettling. Uncertainty prickled over her skin. She rubbed her arms with her hands.

Herr Meuserbach suddenly nodded several times. "We go. *Ja*. We go."

The Ranger rose and looked around at the crowd in the doorway. When Herr Meuserbach turned and began giving orders, Mr. Quinn held up a hand. Meuserbach fell silent. Every eye turned to Quinn.

"I need to make a few things clear first. Will you translate what I say to your people?" Without waiting for agreement, the Ranger went on, "Texas is a good place to live, but it's not an easy place to live." He paused and listened to his words being relayed.

"There are very few towns," he continued. "As we walk to your land, we will have to hunt for food. There won't be many inns or places to shelter for the night."

The faces around Mariel drew down into grim lines or widened in surprise.

"Some of you will probably die on the way."

When they heard this reluctantly translated, a few people gasped.

"You are weak from a long sea journey, and now you face an even tougher one overland. The rivers are high and swollen with spring rain. You need to decide if this is what you really want to do. You have choices."

There was no sound but the falling rain, the Texan's strong voice, and their translation.

"You can stay here in Galveston, find work, and get a place

to live. Or you can get on a boat and go back to New Orleans. There are jobs there. You don't have to go to this land if you've changed your minds."

Mariel looked at Herr Meuserbach's face. He didn't like translating this, but he did it.

Mr. Quinn perched his hands on his hips. "Now does anyone have any questions?"

Silence.

Then her employer Herr Heller raised his arm. "You have see our land, *ja?*"

"Yes, I've been there," the Texan replied. "It's a beautiful place, good fresh spring water in abundance. But you'll be farming in the valleys, not the hillsides. It won't be easy there."

Another man raised his hand. "*Inderin?* They take off hair truly? And kill?"

Mr. Quinn nodded. "They take scalps."

Mariel felt a shiver of common fear go through them all.

"I want to take a vote, a canvass," Mr. Quinn said, folding his arms over his chest. "Everyone fourteen and over, man and woman, must decide for themselves if they really want to go farther west."

Herr Meuserbach interrupted, "These people signed a document with the *Adelsverein*—"

The Ranger cut him off. "Yes, but they signed in Europe, not here in Texas. I've already told you that you are facing a life-and-death decision. Do you want to be responsible for forcing someone to go forward—only to bury them in a lonely grave far from home and family?"

The Ranger's words silenced the German.

Mr. Quinn continued, "So only the ones who really and strongly want to go on should be held to their agreement. Everyone needs to make this decision—men and women."

Mariel's heart began to hop and skip. Vote? This Ranger

would let her decide—in fact, insisted—that she give her opinion? Women voting; she had never heard of such a thing.

"The husbands will decide," Herr Meuserbach objected, looking stubborn.

The Texan stood straighter and looked directly into the faces turned to him. "Everyone gets a vote. When a man is living out on the frontier, his family has to be behind him one hundred percent. A man depends on his wife and the wife on the husband, because usually that's the only one near enough to help. It's time to decide which way you want to go—west, east, or stay here. It's time to find out if the whole family agrees. If not, it won't work. At a crucial moment, it could mean life or death."

The Texas man took a step back. "You all talk it over, and then we'll take a vote. That's how we do things here in Texas." He amended, "In America."

Two

You all talk it over and then we'll take a vote. That's how we do things here in Texas. In America. The Ranger's new and amazing words replayed in Mariel's mind.

Until Herr Heller slapped her cheek. She gasped. "Stupid girl, listen. Now when the vote is taken, you will vote to go on, just like my wife. I'll have none of this nonsense of servants and women telling men—" The man's voice stopped. He looked over her head, wide-mouthed.

Mariel whirled around. The Ranger was standing right behind her, his arms folded and his eyes boring deep gouges into Herr Heller. Her breath caught in her throat. As the Ranger continued to stare, the people around her all fell silent.

Herr Heller was no match for Carson Quinn. He nodded, then lowered his eyes, chastened.

The Texan walked on, and Heller muttered curses under his breath. Mariel moved away from him, but she remained near enough to respond to her mistress if she should be needed. Mariel tingled all over with the shock of what had just taken place. Herr Heller had never struck her before. She had been so surprised that she hadn't been able to say a word. Would he try it again? And the Ranger had defended her, a servant. Her father had been an educated man. She had lowered herself to a servant because that had been the only way she'd been allowed to come on this voyage. No women had been allowed unless they'd been under the protection of a husband or master. And staying in Germany had not been a choice, not after her husband's shameful death.

Her mind came back to the present. Did she want to stay here and be free of Heller?

"Okay!" The Ranger held up both hands. "Time to vote!" Herr Meuserbach translated, and there was silence.

"If you want to stay here," the Texan called out, "raise your right hand!"

It seemed that everyone was suddenly sober, glancing around to see whose hands rose. Hands began to rise all around. Her own hand twitched, as if it wanted to rise also. But here she would be a defenseless woman alone in a strange land. The thought froze her hand to her side.

Herr Heller stood, his arms folded over his chest, looking disdainful of those who were signaling their desire to stay. What would he do if she voted to remain in Galveston? She almost wanted to do it to see his reaction.

"Okay!" Mr. Quinn shouted. "Come toward me. And I'll tell you where to go and look for work."

Those who'd decided to stay behind moved forward. One by one, the Ranger and Herr Meuserbach dealt with them. Then they began saying good-bye. And soon they were walking away into the mist. As Mariel watched familiar people departing under the gloomy sky, a lonely, gray mood slithered into her heart. The pull to follow them tugged at her. Mariel went to her mistress, who squeezed her hand.

The Ranger lifted his hands again and silence fell. "I want to make sure that everyone gets a vote. All those who want to go on, raise your right hands."

Until that moment, Mariel hadn't realized that the act of voting was not as easy as she'd thought. No one before had ever asked or cared if she'd had an opinion. Not even when it had come to her parents choosing her husband. Now she was in Texas, where she was asked for her opinion. She found she wanted to go on for the same reason she had boarded the ship in Bremerhaven. She wanted to put as much distance between her and Germany, between her and the past, as possible.

She looked up and saw that the Ranger was looking straight into her eyes. Awareness of him splashed through her, a warmth that combated the relentless rain outside the warehouse. This man was sworn to protect the people of Texas. She trusted this man, this Ranger. She took a deep breath. Slowly her hand rose. *I am now a woman of Texas, or I will be if I vote to go on to our land.* A woman of Texas—she liked the sound of that. It was good and strong. Hopeful.

Carson looked over the raised hands and nodded, disgruntled. He drew breath bit by bit. "All right. Those of you who are going, you need to look in your packs and take out anything that you don't absolutely need. We need canteens, tools, guns, knives, axes, extra clothing, mending thread and needles, cooking utensils and food."

He rubbed the back of his taut neck. These people didn't understand what would be asked of them over the miles to come. How many of them would die along the trail? He gritted his teeth. "If you take unnecessary items, in the miles ahead you'll only find that you discard them along the way."

He'd seen evidence of this on every trail he'd ever traveled. "If you leave items here, at least they will stay safe in a dry and locked warehouse. You're going to be walking at least two weeks, and every pound, every ounce will grow heavier every day. Understand?" He hoped this warning would cause a few more to stay behind.

After the translation, the remaining immigrants nodded. Many bent to sort through their packs again.

"Hey!"

Carson turned and through the mist and rain saw Tunney ambling toward him leading his horse. Carson raised a hand in welcome. "Tunney, what can I do for you?"

Tunney walked up and grinned. "I'm bored to tears with weeks of rain and thought I'd travel with you as far as Montezuma. I got a cousin there, and I'll rest a spell with him."

Carson wasn't fooled. Tunney was lending him a much-needed hand. Carson grinned, suddenly able to breathe freely. "I guess I can stand your sorry face for a little while, at least, till Montezuma."

"Same here," Tunney joked.

Shouldering the weight of these nearly sixty lives depending on him, Carson drew himself up straighter. Tunney was a godsend. "Okay, let's get going, then." Everyone swung their packs over their shoulders. Two men were carrying a plow between them. It hung on a long rod that rested on their shoulders. Another two men were carrying what looked like a length of sturdy canvas, rolled-up and tied, one man at each end. Even the children shouldered packs. It grieved Carson to see young backs bearing such burdens. Children should be allowed to roam free. But this was the way it had to be. On the frontier, a child grew up fast. He had.

Carson turned to find the owner of the warehouse at his elbow. "These people are leaving, then?" the man asked.

"Yes, and they will send for what they've left behind. If the money runs out, just put it on their tab." Carson shook his hand.

"Godspeed," the man said, nodding. "You'll need all the help you can get leading a bunch of greenhorns to the Hill Country."

Carson swung up into his saddle. "No doubt. *Adios.*" He turned back and looked over the crowd, his eye straying to the frail blond. Did she have the grit to last on the frontier?

* * *

Dusk finally came. Mariel's every bone ached from the day's walking. And after being soaked fording a stream, her flesh was chilled. Still, she forced herself to help her mistress settle onto a fallen log. Suffering a difficult pregnancy, Frau Heller needed her more and more and was grateful for any small kindness. Mariel took her place behind the Frau, leaning against a tree. The Ranger called out, "Women and children, gather moss from the trees, and twigs and sticks for a fire! Men, come help put up the tent and cut wood!"

Petrified in her fatigue, Mariel watched as others began moving around doing what he'd ordered. She tried to marshal her strength to join them and failed. It suddenly occurred to her that this was her first night in the wilderness. She looked up through the tree boughs to the clouds that scudded overhead. *I am here. I am in Texas, far from civilization.* The thought tried to overwhelm her.

Herr Heller took her by surprise. From behind, he touched her in that nasty way that made her feel dirty. She fled the few feet to his wife and sat down on the log beside her. This insulting behavior had begun when they'd landed in Galveston. Before that he had only been overbearing and ill-tempered. "Stupid girl!" her master shouted. "Go gather twigs like the American said!"

Mariel jumped up, her face burning from both the assault on her person and his shouting. She didn't want to make a scene and embarrass his wife, a poor woman who had enough to deal with already. There had to be some way to get out of this situation before reaching their land. Maybe she would be able to find other employment with another family or somehow set up her own business, perhaps sewing.

Fear had broken her stupor. She began gathering twigs and downed branches. The Ranger, with the help of several men, was stretching the large canvas over the boughs of an ancient spreading oak and then, with pegs and a hammer, fastening it to the ground on one side. The canvas would be both roof and a windbreak.

The other American was chopping down a tree outside of camp with amazing speed. In a practiced rhythm, his ax caught the wood. *Chunk . . . Chunk . . .* The tree gave way with a crash. The other men bent into the work of chopping the felled trunk into logs for the fire.

Some of the men had started a bonfire just beyond the spreading oak tree that provided the structure for their canvas "inn." Despite the weary camaraderie of her companions, Mariel's heart ached. The numbness that Herr Heller's unwanted touch always summoned was claiming her. She blinked away the tears that threatened to come as she fought to hold onto herself. She would not become deadened, frozen again.

I am a Texas woman now. I will be free of Herr Heller. Soon. I'll find a way.

That thought stopped the creeping numbness. Gave her hope. Things would turn out differently here if only she clung to that belief. She just had to hold on. She had come to Texas to get away from the past, but now she realized that she might find more than a haven here. If Texas had men like this Ranger, perhaps she would find that she had a future here with a man who would love her and give her children to love. It was a dangerous temptation to hope.

* * *

Riding her horse beside the buckboard, Sugar Quinn wondered for the thousandth time why she hadn't refused to go with the family to east Texas for the wedding. Behind the buckboard rode Emilio Ramirez, the only person who made the trip bearable for her. And he had suffered for it. Why couldn't she let him know how much that meant to her?

Sugar forced herself to look straight ahead rather than repeatedly glancing back at Emilio. If only it was easy for her to speak, to let him know how much it meant to her that for her sake, he'd endured slurs and insults with unmatched aplomb.

Little Erin, who was sitting behind Sugar's saddle, said without preamble, "I can't stand Cousin Blanche. Why did that nice man marry her? Why would anyone marry her? She's so mean."

Sugar sighed with envy. Her ten-year-old sister could put into words what Sugar could only think.

"Erin," Dorritt said, "you are of course entitled to your opinion of people. But I hope you will not say anything like that about any person except in the privacy of your family's bosom."

"Yes, Mama, I know that, but why does she act so . . ." The little girl with two braids the color of her father's dark hair seemed unable to find a word to describe her cousin's behavior.

Sugar didn't have the same problem. Erin's cousin, Blanche LaCroix, was spoiled and demanding and had a nasty tongue. And worse yet, Blanche reserved her nasty tongue for servants and unimportant relatives like her disreputable shirttail family from west Texas. And *Tejanos* like Emilio, who was a Texian of Mexican descent. Anyone with darker skin.

To other whites, Blanche was sweet as . . . sugar.

Sugar wrinkled her nose. She hated that phrase—even when people used it as a compliment. To her, it was a painful scar. She was called Sugar because no one knew her real name, not even she. She shook off the persistent feeling of not being real because she had no past. Instead she let herself savor the memory of the very first time she had seen the Quinn Ranch and Emilio. He was the son of the foreman at the nearby Rancho Sandoval. Emilio had been the first to run out to greet her. She'd only been around seven and he had been nearly a man, twice her age. He had seemed so big to her, so kind. Sugar had been entranced by his welcoming smile and the way he had softened his voice to speak to her, and how it had felt when he'd so gently swung her down from behind Carson's saddle.

"I don't know why we even had to go to this stupid wedding," Erin grumbled, interrupting Sugar's happy turn of thought.

"Family is family," their father, Quinn, spoke up. "While your Grandmother Kilbride lives, we will visit the plantation."

Sugar picked up on the reverse truth—that they would cease visiting once Dorritt's mother was dead. Sugar sensed Emilio riding up closer behind her. Emilio had always made her feel special, from helping her make a piñata for her first birthday as a Quinn, to later, when she'd been eleven, letting him teach her how to dance the fandango, and he'd teased and chuckled throughout the lessons. Two years ago, when she'd donned her first grown-up dress and put up her hair, she had savored the way he had looked at her. Ever since then, he'd treated her like a lady, one he admired, no longer as a little girl. Emilio Ramirez was one of the finest gentlemen she knew.

"Señorita Sugar," Emilio said, "your horse is starting to limp."

Although the sound of his voice rippled through Sugar like warm water, his words chilled her. Today they should reach Montezuma, where they'd meet up with Carson and then head home. She didn't want anything to hold them up. She pulled on her reins, halting the horse. Guilt stung her. Why hadn't she noticed her horse was limping?

She slid from her saddle and helped Erin climb down. The buckboard drew to a halt. As Quinn and Emilio examined the horse's hoof, Sugar stood to the side, watching, listening. The two men decided it must be merely a stone bruise. The horse would need rest and shoeing in Montezuma. If there wasn't a farrier there, perhaps they'd find one in Gonzales.

"Well, Sugar, you won't be riding any longer," her father said. "We need to let him walk without any weight."

"I'm sorry. I should have . . ." Her voice failed her—not because she was afraid of being scolded but because Emilio had looked up and smiled at her. She wanted to smile in return, to speak. But she was unable to make her mouth work as it should.

She wished Carson had been there. When Carson was near, she could speak . . . a little. And she was never happy to be away from the Quinn Ranch or Rancho Sandoval if Carson wasn't with them. Somehow, even after ten years had passed, Carson had always been the one who'd made Sugar feel safe. But Emilio had always been there too, helping her learn Spanish, teaching her how to ride, making her feel as if she mattered. And, in the past two years, gazing at her as if he thought her pretty, special. Tonight they would meet up with Carson in Montezuma and maybe he could help her, teach her how to speak of love to Emilio—

Her heart stuttered just like her contrary tongue, which could never voice her feelings. How could she be so unfeeling as to speak of her love for Emilio after the humiliation Carson had suffered at Blanche's hands?

* * *

Three days after leaving Galveston, Carson glanced around the party. The sun was lower in the western sky. Without the party he was leading, he'd already have arrived at Montezuma. But he was a Ranger, and it was his duty to take care of the people of Texas. At least, that's the way it had been. How would this change when the annexation actually took effect?

Tunney was riding in the rear as usual while Carson led. Carson itched to be at Montezuma. Actually, he longed to ride up to the sprawling hacienda where he'd been raised. Maybe now that Texas was a U.S. state, he'd be able to quit the Rangers, settle down, stay home, and be a help to his father. Quinn would never admit it, but he was nearing his fifties, and he didn't have the strength he'd had when Carson was a boy. Still, Quinn was stronger than most men—

A child screamed.

Three

Carson whirled his mount around. Galloped toward the continued screeching. Ahead, he glimpsed people clumping together. "Let me through!" he shouted, his heart pounding in his ears. He slid from his saddle. He pushed his way through the gathering. Tunney was right behind him.

"*Hilf mir! Hilf mir!*" a wild-eyed woman shouted as she hugged a wailing, weeping child to her.

Carson saw at once what had happened. A snake with its head cut off lay at the child's feet. A foot-long copperhead. He cursed under his breath. "Where was the child bit?" he shouted. When no one answered, he jerked the child from the mother's arms. "Where—"

"His finger!" Mariel the frail blond called out, crouching beside the mother. "His little finger!"

Carson grabbed the child's ankles and swung him upside down. Without a word spoken, Tunney snapped off a string of leather from his shirt. He tied it as a tourniquet around the finger with the bleeding snake bite. Then, with a quick stroke of his Bowie knife, he sliced off the finger.

The mother fainted. Shouting curses in German, the furious father caught her. That alone evidently stopped him from attacking Carson.

The crowd roared with anger. With shock. The child sobbed, screamed for his mother. Yet Carson knew he was doing his best.

Tunney untied the tourniquet and let the blood flow freely from the wound. He and Carson exchanged sickened glances. It had been a rough remedy, but what else could they have done?

The father, whom Carson now recognized as the man who had slapped the frail Mariel, was still shouting angry German at him as he held his pregnant wife.

"Why have you done this?" Meuserbach demanded, standing, white-faced, beside the parents.

Carson looked at the father, the horror of what they had just been forced to do pawing through him with icy fingers, threatening to weaken him. He gathered his nerve and said as gently as he could, "Not because we wanted to. Copperheads are poisonous—especially to a child this little—"

"The child could still die," Tunney interrupted in his deep, gruff voice. "We got here as fast as we could and acted. The child might still die."

Looking nauseated, Meuserbach translated their words about the copperhead being deadly. Then there was one of those dazed, horrified silences that Carson had experienced before and hated as much as ever. The sobbing child was getting dangerously red-faced from being hung upside down, and he appeared to be losing consciousness. "Should I hold him like this a little longer, or has it been long enough?" Carson asked Tunney in a lowered voice.

"A little longer to be safe."

Mariel came forward and began talking to the child in a soft, soothing voice. She stroked his tear-wet face with a handkerchief and continued murmuring calming words. The child's sobs ebbed into a kind of subdued hitching breath.

"I think it's going to do more harm than good if we hang him any longer," Tunney said finally.

Carson nodded. Gently, he turned the child right side up. The boy lay in his arms, stunned and tear-stained. "Mariel, I'll need bandages and iodine. Do you understand?"

She nodded. "Bandage. Iodine."

"There are some in my saddlebags. Would you get them, please?"

Mariel bobbed and hurried to his horse. Soon she returned with a cloth sack full of clean bandages and iodine, which Carson's mother packed for him every time he left home. The child's mother was reviving, gasping for breath. The father looked to Meuserbach and rattled off more heated words.

"But why would you need to cut off his finger?" Meuserbach asked in a strained voice.

After the rush of peril, Carson was experiencing the letdown. His muscles were loosening, and he wished he could sit down. "A snake bites and shoots his venom, his poison, into the flesh, where it mixes with the blood," Carson explained while Mariel busied herself bandaging the child's hand.

"If the venom gets to the heart, the person dies," Tunney added. "That's why Carson swung him upside down to make it harder for the blood to reach his heart. Doctors all think they got antidotes to snake poison, but I never seen one that works like this does."

Carson was glad to let Tunney take care of the explanations. Holding onto his self-control, Carson cradled the child close, trying to reassure him with his strength and tight grasp.

"Carson's parents are the one who taught us Rangers what to do about snake bites. His pa is half Cherokee, and his ma is a very knowin' lady. We're lucky the snake bit the boy's little finger. That was easy to take off, and most of the venom would have still been in that finger."

"I'm sorry, ma'am," Carson spoke, looking toward the mother, the woman he recognized as the one he'd rescued in Galveston when he'd first met Mariel. "But better to lose his little finger than his life."

Mariel turned and, without waiting for Meuserbach, evidently translated his words to the mother. The woman staggered to her feet. Followed by her still-glowering husband, she came to her son's side. Mariel stepped back. The mother took over crooning and stroking the boy's still-flushed cheeks, then began weeping in a way that troubled Carson. She was nearing hysteria.

Again Tunney came to the rescue. "Meuserbach, does anyone have any strong drink? A little whiskey or somethin' strong would calm her nerves a bit. And a few drops would put the child to sleep for a while. They both suffered a bad turn." The child's hand was swollen, of course, but so far, he was not having trouble breathing, nor was there any other unusual swelling.

Many people scrambled to help. Soon the mother sipped some dark red liqueur, and a teaspoonful was given to the child. The little boy fell asleep almost immediately in his father's arms.

Carson took a deep breath. "Okay. We have several more miles to cover before we camp for the night. Let's get moving again!"

He approached the father and held out his arms, wordlessly asking for the child. "Give me the child. I'll carry him in front of me."

The man glared at him.

Carson didn't take offense. Nodding toward the woman, he

said, "You need to help your wife. I'll take the child." Again, he held out his arms.

The man muttered angry-sounding words, but he nodded, evidently understanding Carson's intent. Carson gingerly mounted his horse, then accepted the sleeping child, laying him across his lap. He glanced down and saw Mariel hovering in the fringes of the crowd. He pulled the brim of his hat toward her. Then he rode to the front again.

He hadn't held a small child for a long time. How could a child so small survive what had just happened to him? But Carson knew that they could face worse than this in the miles to come.

With lowering light, evening had finally come. Mariel rubbed her forehead, then stretched her neck. The uproar over the snake bite had made her feel sick and tense for the rest of the day. Mariel's heart went out to the two Texians also. They had been forced to take quick and brutal action to try to save a child's life. She recalled their expressions—so grim, sad, sickened.

After several nights on the trail, Mariel knew what her chores were in setting up for another night under and around the canvas roof. She carried these out in silence. The whole party seemed subdued. Voices were quieter than usual. No spontaneous laughter sounded as the sun lowered more toward the horizon. She recalled the Ranger's stern warning in Galveston: *Some of you will die.*

When all her chores were done, she wandered around the camp, unable to settle down. She wanted to do something for the men who were leading them, protecting them in this unfamiliar wilderness. But what could she do for them?

She found herself pausing some distance from where the two Rangers sat by a smaller fire near the edge of the camp. Then she thought of a service she could do for the two men. Did she have the nerve to approach them with her shaky English and make the offer?

She forced herself to walk toward the Rangers. Pausing beside them, she silently waited to be acknowledged.

The one called Tunney saw her first. He nodded toward her. "What can we do for you, little lady?"

Mr. Quinn rose.

His politeness made her look downward. She gestured toward the collar of the handsome Ranger's shirt, which he wore under his leather coat. "You have tear," she said, pointing at it. "I sew for you." She made a sign showing the moving of a needle.

Before Quinn replied, Tunney grinned. "Why, that's real nice of you." He went to his saddlebag and pulled out two shirts, obviously in need of washing and some mending. "Thanks a lot, little lady."

Mariel accepted these from him, then turned to Quinn. "*Bitte*, please, I sew for you?"

"Go on, Quinn," Tunney said in a voice that teased. "Let the little lady sew your shirt."

Quinn gave her a look she could not read. Then he shrugged out of his jacket and shirt, revealing his chest. "Thanks. It's not necessary, but thanks."

Seeing him without his shirt left her mute. She hated her shyness. Blushing in hot, unwelcome waves, she hurried away.

Unfortunately, she bumped into Herr Heller.

"What are you doing, you stupid girl?"

She looked at him, noting how ugly his angry eyes looked. "I am sewing for the Rangers to thank them—"

"I know what you're doing," he interrupted her, gripping her arm, tight and hurtful. "He won't have you. You're nothing. He's a Ranger, an official of the government. You're nothing. Just a servant girl."

Mariel made no reply; she just stared into the man's face, refusing to lower her eyes. When the Ranger had stared at him for slapping her in Galveston, Herr Heller had shown cowardice by backing down and then cursing the Ranger behind his back. And she liked Heller even less for it.

And I know what you're angry about, Herr Heller, what you want from me. And as long as the Ranger is here, he will not let you get away with it. And before he leaves, I will think of a way to leave your employ.

Mariel yanked herself away and walked toward the fire, where her mistress and her little son sat. The woman greeted her with a wan smile and a plea for Mariel to relax. Mariel nodded. A sense of victory over her master's nasty remarks strengthened her even as sudden tears threatened. She blinked them away, however, and got out her sewing basket. No one in Germany had thought she was worth much—not her father, not her husband. Only her *grossmutter* had told her she was special, a child of *Gott*. A verse she had often quoted came to mind: "Trust in the LORD, and do good; so shalt thou dwell in the land." Mariel hadn't known then that the land would be Texas. She whispered, "Now I am a Texas woman. I will trust *Gott*, do good, and dwell in this land. This land with men like Carson Quinn."

* * *

Under the warm afternoon sun, Sugar stood to the side of the one dirt street that made up Montezuma. The town was barely big enough to be called a town. Besides the one muddy street, it had a ferry over the Colorado River, a blacksmith, and a small general store. Tufts of wild grass, wildflowers, and cottonwood trees provided the only touches of beauty.

She and her family had arrived late yesterday, expecting to find Carson waiting for them. However, Carson had yet to arrive. She rubbed her forearms, worrying.

An older woman sitting in a rocking chair in front of her house kept eyeing Sugar. It made her uneasy. Why was the woman watching her so closely? The woman, whose face was shadowed by her unstarched bonnet brim, continued rocking and smoking a long wooden pipe, a habit some Texas women had, a habit that still horrified her mother. But then, Dorritt had been born a lady.

"You must not worry, señorita," Emilio said.

She involuntarily jerked at the sound of his voice. She had been so focused on the woman that she hadn't heard him even though he wore spurs on his boots.

"I'm sorry I have surprised you," he apologized in that rich, velvety voice she loved.

As she turned, her bonnet, only loosely tied, slid back on her neck. Then she was looking into the face that to her was the best in all of Texas. Emilio's skin was a rich tan, his eyes coffee black. His dark hair waved and curled around his ears, and his generous mouth was curved into the special grin he reserved for her alone.

She tried to smile back, but her lips felt tight.

"You must not worry, señorita," he repeated. "Your brother Carson will come soon. He is just delayed."

This time she managed a smile. She glanced over her shoulder. The woman had left her rocker and gone inside. "I know," she murmured, but the anxiety was still there. She didn't like to be away from the Quinns' rancho and without Carson. The old, unnamed fear lingered, always there just under the surface. Without Carson here, she felt exposed, defenseless.

That's foolish. Emilio and my father would protect me.

"I am going to the blacksmith to see if our horse is reshod. Would you like to walk with me?" Emilio coaxed her with another, even richer, grin. "I know the town is busy with people, and we don't like crowds, do we?"

She scanned the lone street, empty now except for a sleeping sow lying out on her side on the mud and a few chickens walking and bobbing their heads. She chuckled, her tightness relaxing. "No, I don't like crowds . . . like this."

Emilio offered her his arm. "Perhaps we will stop at the store on the way back. We could pretend we're children and buy peppermint."

She took his arm. He was teasing her. Everyone knew that she loved peppermints.

She leaned a bit closer and tighter to him. Walking beside Emilio gave her such a splendid feeling of—

"Hey, lady!" a loud voice interrupted Sugar's thoughts. "Is that Mexican bothering you?" A large man in buckskin and linsey-woolsey had stepped out of the general store. He took a menacing step toward them.

Sugar wanted to shout her anger at this insult to Emilio. Her breath rushed out, but she couldn't form a word.

"Hello, señor, I am Emilio Ramirez, a Ranger." Emilio held out his hand.

The stranger looked him up and down, finally gripped Emilio's hand, then swept his hat off to Sugar. "Sorry. Didn't know you were a Ranger. Some Mexicans are pretty nervy. Think they're as good as Texians."

"I have relatives in Mexico, I suppose," Emilio drawled, "but I have never met them. So yes, they probably think they are better than Texians."

The stranger's face twisted with concentration. Emilio's mild tone and friendly smile appeared innocent. Emilio knew how to disarm rude people and, at the same time, poke fun at them in a way they couldn't object to. Indeed, though the man appeared to know he was being put in his place, he couldn't find any way to protest without looking a fool. He finally asked, "You two with the family that's waiting in town?"

"*Sí*, we are waiting for Carson Quinn, another Ranger and this señorita's brother."

Nodding, the stranger put his hat back on and walked away, whistling. Sugar looked away from Emilio, ashamed that her face was burning. The rude encounter had distressed her too deeply for words, disgraced them both in some way.

Emilio began leading her, but not to the blacksmith's forge. He guided her to a nearby grove of cottonwood, showy with white spring blossoms fluttering with the breeze, and away from the dismal town. Bluebonnets carpeted the surrounding open pasture with a deep violet blue. Emilio let go of her and bent down to pluck a few. He gave them to her and said, "I am sorry if that *gamberro*, that lout, upset you."

Sugar accepted the flowers, cool and smooth in her hands, but continued to stare down. Biting her lower lip, she gathered herself together, then looked up. "I hate it . . . when people say such . . . rude things."

"Rude people say rude things. Good people speak good things. It is as Señora Quinn says. What a man speaks reveals his heart."

For once, she found herself able to reply. "When I go to San Antonio, people I barely know walk up to me and say, 'Oh, you're that orphan girl the half-breed Quinn and his New Orleans lady took in after San Jacinto.' It's like by using those words, they . . ." Her voice faltered.

"They make you less than you are? Make the Quinns less than the good people they are?" Emilio suggested.

She nodded. It had cost her a great deal to say that aloud; now her breath came fast. She had thought it for years but had never been able to put it into words. "It's hard for me . . . to speak." In the distance, she heard the sound of the rocking chair on the wooden porch resume, and she glanced over her shoulder.

Was the older woman with her pipe back on her porch, still staring hard at Sugar? This thought gave Sugar gooseflesh.

Emilio took one of the bluebonnets and tickled her nose with it. She shivered at this delicate touch even though it was meant to tease her into smiling. Then he grimaced and pushed the flower back into her hands. "I know it is hard for you to speak." His voice was distant now. "You are still so young."

"I am not a child. I'm a woman," she insisted, goaded.

"But still a young woman." His voice had become very brisk, and he half-turned from her. "Let us go to the blacksmith and see if he's finished with the horse."

His words drenched her like a pail of cold water. And she found herself tongue-tied again. Why couldn't she ever speak what was in her heart for Emilio?

And as they approached the one street town, why wouldn't that woman stop staring at her?

* * *

Carson approached Montezuma with unexpected qualms. Leading the large party of immigrants had kept him busy every daylight hour and so exhausted that he had slept without dreaming, a boon. But as he came around a bend, he glimpsed Sugar and Emilio walking down the muddy street toward him. The sight of them unleashed every turbulent emotion from the days at Buena Vista. Every miserable, mortifying moment burst inside him like fomenting wounds.

He fought back.

Emilio, one of his best friends, had gone off with him six years ago to serve in the Rangers. Emilio and he were near the same age, and they had ridden many rough and dangerous miles together. Walking with a newspaper folded under his arm, Emilio saw him too. He evidently told Sugar, who looked up. She blushed, as though caught in an indiscretion, like a cat in an upturned cream pot. Then Emilio was hurrying Sugar forward and shouting in welcome.

Carson grinned. Emilio, a friend indeed. Carson held up his hand in greeting and slid from his saddle. Then, remembering his duties as leader, he turned his back on Emilio and called out, "Halt! We camp here tonight!" He turned back in time to receive Sugar's welcoming hug.

"We were worried," she said, rosy pink, and then her usual self-consciousness took over and she couldn't continue.

"Hey, *amigo*." Emilio slapped Carson's back. "You get lost without me to guide you?"

Carson grimaced and nodded toward the people crowding behind him. "Some more pilgrims for the promised land."

Coming out of their wikiup at the edge of town, his parents and little Erin hurried forward. Seeing them again stirred every sad, awful emotion Carson was feeling from the family trip east for Blanche's wedding. Carson was having a hard time keeping everything in, but he was managing. Just. Little Erin threw her arms around his waist.

Then, interrupting his mother's greeting, distressed shouts came from behind. Pulling away from Erin's hold, Carson turned and hurried toward the familiar babble of German and the tight knot of gawkers and moaners.

He found that a woman had collapsed. Her husband was gripping her hand, saying her name. Carson turned back, but he didn't have to call out. As always in times of trouble, his mother Dorritt was there. She knelt beside the woman and felt her forehead. "She's burning up." His mother checked the woman's pulse at the wrist. Then she bent her head to listen to the heartbeat. Erin held back, under her father's arm.

Dorritt rose. "We need to get her under cover. There aren't any inns. We've set up our tent. Bring her there. I must bathe her face and wrists with alcohol and bring down that fever."

Before Carson could speak, Meuserbach was explaining this in German. Carson moved forward to help the woman's husband pick her up and carry her toward Dorritt and Quinn's campsite at the edge of town. He ducked inside their tent and followed his mother's instructions to lay the woman down on bedding his father had quickly unrolled.

Mariel moved forward through the crowd and positioned herself so that she could see inside the strange tent, which looked as if it was made of animal hide. Their odd-looking tent was round at the bottom and narrower at the top,with a peak where smoke curled up. These people must be the Ranger's family they were to meet.

Tunney suddenly appeared in front of her. "Come on." He took her hand and drew her toward the strange dwelling. She stumbled forward, keeping up with his long strides over the uneven ground.

"Carson," Tunney said, "I brought Miss Mariel to help your mother. She can interpret too."

What? Mariel's whole body tightened. She was to interpret?

Carson greeted her with a distracted smile. "Mother, this is Miss Mariel. She has acted as a nurse for us already and speaks some English."

Mariel was startled again by the fact that they didn't treat her differently because she was a servant. She found herself staring at the Ranger. As soon as she was aware that he was gazing back at her, she turned her face away, trying to act as if she hadn't been staring at him.

"Hello, Mariel. I'm Dorritt Quinn. And this is my husband, who is called Quinn."

Bending because of the low ceiling near the entrance, Mariel curtseyed. When she forced herself to look up, she found herself being given a quick, but thorough, scrutiny. Mrs. Quinn was an imposing woman. It wasn't just that she appeared very tall for a woman; it was more about the force of her person. Mariel sensed this woman did not do things in halves.

Mariel received the same impression from the man Quinn, who was kneeling and gazing up at her. He wore his hair in a long tail. She had never seen this style on any man before. Or heard of a man who was called only by his last name by his own family. A fair-haired young woman with a dark-haired little girl stood near the entrance with a young man of darker skin.

"Please come closer. I need you to translate," Mrs. Quinn invited with a tight smile.

"I will help. *Bitte,*" Mariel managed to murmur. *Please, God, don't let me do anything wrong.*

"What is this woman's name?" Mrs. Quinn asked, gesturing toward the patient, who had just opened her eyes. "And will you please ask her what her symptoms are?"

"Symptoms?" Mariel didn't know this word. Her stuttering heart began to thud.

"Yes, what different types of sickness is she feeling besides the fever?" Mrs. Quinn added.

Mariel's heart slowed its thudding. She could do that. She came forward and knelt beside the woman, asking about her symptoms. Then she turned to Mrs. Quinn. Before she spoke, she swallowed once, twice. "Frau Braun say she started fever last night. She hope . . . be better in morning. But she feel weak and weak all day. She hurt in all her body. Aches. And feel cold and hot." Mariel was aware that the Ranger was watching her closely, as was his mother.

"Good job." Mrs. Quinn sat back on her heels. "It sounds to me like Frau Braun has what's called influenza, or the grippe. Men, all of you leave and shut the flap behind you. This young woman . . ." She motioned toward Mariel.

"Miss Mariel," the Ranger prompted, already obeying his mother and backing away to the door.

Mariel's nerves were calming, her heartbeat nearing normal. Hearing the Ranger say her name again and with the polite title of Miss brought the same embarrassing warmth to her face and neck. Noting this, his mother paused to look to her son and then back to Mariel, once, twice, as if weighing and measuring.

Then Mrs. Quinn smiled and asked, "You don't mind, Miss Mariel, remaining to help nurse and translate for me?"

Mariel nodded but said no more. Mrs. Quinn's gaze had been penetrating. Mariel only hoped she hadn't given the wrong impression. There was nothing between her and the Ranger.

After the men left, Mrs. Quinn and Mariel remained beside the ailing Frau Braun. The young woman and little girl Mariel didn't know still lingered just inside the tent.

"Mother, what can we do?" the older, very fair girl asked.

Mrs. Quinn turned her head. "Mariel, these are Carson's sisters. The eldest is Sugar, and the youngest is Erin. Girls, this is Miss Mariel."

Mariel smiled, taken by the sensitive eyes of the older daughter and her obvious concern over a stranger. The younger daughter looked intelligent and curious. Mariel smiled at her too.

"Sugar, please ask your brother to bring me buckets of well water. And then please keep Erin with you and away from the other immigrants. I don't want her exposed. There might be more coming down with this." The two of them left then. Mrs. Quinn smiled at Mariel.

Mariel nodded her willingness to do whatever was asked of her, yet she wondered why they had named their daughter Sugar, a very unusual name. Or maybe that wasn't true in Texas.

Setting to work, Mariel soon became too busy to think of much more than trying to understand the American woman's instructions and requests as together they nursed Frau Braun. Then two more patients, Mrs. Braun's two little boys, also feverish, were carried into the odd-looking tent.

Mrs. Quinn sighed and began to bathe their faces and wrists with alcohol. She then wrapped them in blankets. She was about to speak when Mariel heard the voice of Herr Heller, loud and argumentative, demanding that she come and serve her mistress. As Mariel didn't want him to make more of a scene, she rose, stammered an apology to the American lady, and backed outside, closing the tent flap behind her.

"There you are, you stupid girl," Herr Heller barked. "My wife needs help. You are to obey her, not these Rangers." His face reddened with anger as he lunged forward to backhand her.

And then he was on the ground, looking up at the Ranger and his father. It had happened so fast that Mariel gawked in surprise.

Four

Mariel choked, gasping for air. The Ranger's father was standing over Herr Heller, his fists clenched as if ready to do battle. "Stand up, coward," the man said. "Come on. Hit someone who can strike back."

Herr Meuserbach hurried forward, his hands held in front of him. "Halt! *Bitte!* Halt!" He stepped between the two men. "Why has begun a fight?"

Herr Heller rose, glaring as he wiped blood from his lip. The Ranger's father maintained his stance, ready to continue the fight. "No man strikes a woman in my presence."

At a soft touch on her shoulder, Mariel turned to see Sugar and her little sister. Sugar put an arm around Mariel and murmured that she mustn't worry. Erin stood in front of Mariel as if ready to protect her. Their support was unexpected, but so welcome. And heartening.

The Ranger moved to stand side by side with his father.

Carson said, "I don't know how you people do things in Europe, but if I see that man try to hit Miss Mariel or any woman again, I'll show him again how it feels."

"She is my servant," Herr Heller spat out.

At his contemptuous tone, Mariel bristled. Sugar flushed angrily. Erin growled, and her hands became fists too.

"That makes no difference to us," the Ranger's father said. "I will not permit any man to abuse any woman or servant in my presence."

"Neither will I," said the other man with darker skin, the one who had welcomed the Ranger first. She had heard his name, Emilio.

"Me, too," Tunney joined in.

Mariel was caught between shame at this very public scene and awe at being defended by people she barely knew. Would her parents have defended her like this? She doubted it.

Looking irritated, Herr Meuserbach turned to Herr Heller. "I must agree. This is a new land. In Europe, life was different. Even there, I never agreed with striking servants or other inferiors. This must stop."

"I am my own man," Herr Heller insisted, sneering. "No man can tell me how to treat my servant. I pay her."

Mariel wrapped her arms around herself. Two very different reactions struggled within her. She wanted to tell Heller she was no longer his servant, but at the same time, embarrassment shamed her. Sugar hovered nearer and Erin stepped closer. Mariel wanted to speak, but a lifetime of being told to be silent was hard to leave behind.

"You are free to strike her whenever you feel like it," the Ranger said. "However, I'm also free to beat the stuffing out of you."

"You would try," Herr Heller jeered.

The Ranger made a sound of amusement. "You think you are

better at fighting than me? I've been fighting and killing for six years. That is my job. I fight to protect the people of Texas. I'll even protect you, though I think you're a sorry sort of man. A bully."

Mariel hoped this confrontation would end soon. She must decide how to stop working for this man. There was more to consider than just wanting to distance herself from this bully. Would she be allowed to travel as a single woman now that the Ranger led the party?

"Son, why don't you just let me finish the lesson this newcomer needs to learn so bad?" the Ranger's father asked. "He looks like the stubborn kind."

And then Herr Heller proved just how cowardly he was. He cursed the Texans in Low German, then stalked away.

Mariel sent grateful looks toward the men who had defended her.

The little sister murmured, "You're safe now." Sugar nodded in agreement.

Mariel tried to smile but failed. She was glad of their support, yet humiliated that she needed it. "I must go . . . help my mistress. But I come . . . if Mrs. Quinn calls."

Sugar frowned and looked to her brother. "Shouldn't Mariel stay here?"

Mariel shook her head. "No, I—"

"Yes, Miss Mariel should stay as long as Mother needs her," the Ranger interrupted her.

Mariel closed her eyes, pressing down her continuing embarrassment. *I must find a way to get free from Herr Heller. And soon.*

* * *

Deadened with fatigue, Dorritt was grateful that deep night, with its promise of rest, had come at last. The tent was silent except for the labored breathing and restless sleep of her three patients. Her two precious daughters slept in the tent too. She had sent the young German woman called Mariel away for the night. Carson had escorted her. Dorritt shook her head. Even before Carson had confronted the big German, she'd noted his interest in the girl. Was this a blessing or a curse?

She sighed, the sound loud in the peaceful tent. Ever since she had arrived at Buena Vista, her family's plantation, she had been weighed down by bone-deep guilt. Why had she put her family through the torment of visiting her family plantation, where they were always treated as inferiors? She pushed a stray hair away from her face. Why had she put them all through this?

Now, through the slightly open tent flap, she glimpsed Carson sitting at the campfire with Emilio and Quinn, engaged in low conversation. The camp around them was quiet. The canvas shelter was several yards away, and the German families had all stilled, having settled in for the night.

Emilio rose. "I think I will turn in. Will we try to travel tomorrow?"

Quinn snorted. "Doubt it. My wife won't budge till the woman and her sons are well enough to travel. We're not in any hurry to get back to the ranch. Ash has everything in hand. I just miss my own bed."

Why did I insist on my way? Sitting on the ground, Dorritt wrapped her arms around her bent knees. She hoped Quinn would linger by the fire with Carson until it wasn't obvious how upset she was. Her family had caused Quinn enough trouble over her in recent days.

Emilio wished the other men a *buenas noches* and left. Quiet fell again. In the wikiup, Dorritt blew out the oil lamp. All alone, she rested her head in the nest of her arms. She didn't have to see her son's face to feel his dejection, his hurting.

Before they'd gone to her niece's wedding, she hadn't known that Carson had been the object of Blanche's flirting. Blanche had the same vain and selfish character as her mother, Jewell. And Carson had let nothing slip at home of his fascination with Blanche.

"Son, how long are you going to stare into that cup?" Quinn asked, breaking the silence.

Dorritt looked up, as did Carson.

"Spit it out, son."

The frogs in the nearby creek were singing their night chant, and a mourning dove was cooing overhead in one of the trees. All human sounds had ceased. Dorritt hoped her husband could offer some comfort to their son. But what of Sugar, who'd also suffered because of Dorritt's insistence they go to her family? How could she also make it up to her daughter?

Carson cleared his throat. "I've had a lot to think about since I left Buena Vista—"

"Don't you mean *escaped*?" Quinn said with a touch of humor.

"I'm glad I went to the wedding," Carson said, surprising Dorritt.

Why had he said that? Being glad about going to the wedding made as much sense as being glad about upsetting a wasp's hive. Dorritt didn't usually eavesdrop, but she needed to know this.

"I don't know how Henri LaCroix stands his family," Quinn said. "He's the best of men. We see eye to eye on most things except for his owning slaves."

Dorritt nodded to herself. Her sister's husband, Henri, was a good man and an exceedingly patient one. Yet his wife and daughter were the kind of women who could drive any sane man crazy.

"What's eating you, son?"

Dorritt knew what was eating her son. She also knew that she had unwittingly fostered his trouble. If she had broken with her family years ago, when she'd married Quinn, her children would never have been exposed to such contempt and small-mindedness. Like a hawk tearing, shredding its prey, this realization ripped apart Dorritt's accustomed peace.

Carson tapped his coffee cup on his knee. "Everything. I mean, now Texas is part of the U.S. I know most Texians wanted this, but I'm not sure."

Quinn grunted in response. "You know how I feel about becoming U.S. territory. Your mother and I settled in western Texas to keep our distance from the Anglos. Most of the time I'd rather deal with renegade Mescaleros, Comanche, and the odd Mexican *bandido* than slave-owning whites. Yet what can we do about the annexation? It's fact now."

Dorritt listened harder; Quinn rarely spoke this much at one time. She pressed her wet cheek against the top of her knees, resting her head.

Carson said nothing, just stared at the low orange flames.

Quinn went on, "Texas doesn't have two gold *reals* to rub together. Without Sam Houston, we'd be in sorrier shape than we are. If we hadn't gotten annexed by the U.S., Britain or some other nation would have snapped us up like a gator swallowing a stray hog. In '36, you and I fought and defeated the Mexicans only because Santa Anna was a bad general and the government in Mexico City was so unstable. Even now it's the same."

Carson said, "Mexico isn't going to like the annexation."

Dorritt had lived too long not to know where Texas was headed—toward another war. In Texas, there were three main peoples. First were several Indian tribes like the Comanche, Karankawa, and Apache. Then came the *Tejanos*, descendants of the Spanish colonists and native tribes. And last to arrive were the *Angloamericanos*. It wasn't a happy mix, since Anglos saw all darker-skinned people as inferior. A few *Tejanos*, like Joseph Navarre, had won the respect of the Anglos, but that was rare. Now war would burst upon them again. Mexicans south of the Rio Grande River had never forgiven Anglos or the *Tejanos* who'd fought with Sam Houston for beating Santa Anna and "stealing" Texas from Mexico. Mexican pride spurred them to fight against any incursion of Anglos or Americans. Dorritt squeezed her eyes shut, then opened them. Shutting one's eyes to truth was never wise.

Quinn shrugged. "Mexico hasn't liked anything about Texas since your mother and I came in 1821. We try not to take it personal," he teased. "The Mexicans still think they can push the Anglos back." He shook his head, the low light gleaming on the gray hairs among the dark ones still worn in one long tail.

Dorritt recalled the scornful glances the Anglos at Blanche's wedding had cast at her husband's "Indian" hair. So why, when Carson had become a Ranger, had she encouraged her son to stop at the family home whenever he was in that part of Texas? That had allowed Blanche to work her mischief.

The pull of family ties was one of those funny things in her life. Why had it been so important to her to display her family in their best to her sister's family and their friends? Especially when being with her family gave Dorritt no pleasure? And her family didn't have the wit to recognize that the life Dorritt had was superior to what they possessed.

Dorritt shook her head at her own pride. Had it just been her conceit, her desire to show off? Had she put those she loved most through a week of veiled ridicule for her own vanity?

"Do you think it will mean war with Mexico?" Carson asked.

"Didn't you listen to those West Point graduates at the wedding?" Quinn's tone was sardonic. "They were champing at the bit to kill a few Mexicans for America. Get their pretty white gloves red with blood."

Blanche had married a graduate of West Point. Images of their blue uniforms with their gold buttons, the drawn sabers over the wedding couple, squirmed through Dorritt's mind, troubling her. *We should have stayed at home and enjoyed the last of our peace together.*

A nearby bullfrog began bellowing his mating song. "So are we going to discuss Blanche or not?" Quinn said the words matter-of-factly. He had put into words the matter that tortured Carson most, Dorritt feared.

Carson didn't reply right away. And then he asked, "Why did she play up to me, Pa?"

His father made a sound that was half chuckle, half snort of derision. "Just for the fun of it. Cutting her teeth on a Texas Ranger."

Quinn's words cast all the past images of Blanche in a blinding and unflattering light. And the worst of it was that Blanche, as heartless as her mother Jewell, didn't know and didn't care about the suffering she caused. Didn't know and didn't care that the man, that soldier she had married was far beneath Carson, whom she'd ensnared and then scorned.

"Was that it? Because I'm a Ranger?" Carson asked.

His father nodded, sipping more coffee. "And I'll bet none of her fine friends were around when you visited . . ."

Dorritt pressed her temples, wishing she could rub out the memories of the troubled faces of those she loved. *Father, forgive my pride. My sister and her daughter are beyond comprehending how sad, how wrong their behavior toward others is.*

The bullfrog, mourning dove, and the rush of the water in the nearby Colorado River filled in the silence as Dorritt let regret roll through her.

"I'm going to turn in, Pa. I'm sorry I've involved you in my leading these Germans to their land. I mean, my ma shouldn't have to take care of these people."

"Your mother's good heart is the joy of my life." Quinn also rose. "And, considering the family she came from, a true miracle from the God who loves us and can save us, even from annexation."

Dorritt smiled. Then she thought of the woman Mariel, whose face was sweet and so pretty. And whom Carson appeared to be protecting. Had God already provided a consolation for her son?

Carson turned and hugged his father. Quinn embraced him tightly, slapping him twice on the back. After years living among mostly *Tejanos* southwest of San Antonio, her family had adopted their fondness for embracing and showing affection. Neither she nor Quinn had been raised to show such emotion. Heartened by this show of affection, Dorritt scrambled toward her bedroll so the men wouldn't know she had been observing them. Quinn would be coming in now.

She lay on her side and feigned sleep. Quinn came in and slid down beside her, folding her into his arms. His breath tickled the nape of her neck. And slowly his embrace strengthened her, relaxing her so that she fell into sleep.

Sometime later she awoke. Something had alerted her. She sat up and instantly realized what had happened. Across from her, the feverish woman twitched and moaned.

Quickly Dorritt got to her knees and crept to the woman's side. A touch told her that the fever was worse than ever.

"What is it?" Quinn murmured. "Is she worse?"

"Yes. Pray." Dorritt began loosening the woman's clothing and reached for the alcohol, all other thoughts driven from her mind.

* * *

Two days later, Mariel stood with the whole party and watched Frau Braun's pine coffin being lowered into a grave in the prairie outside of town. No one spoke.

Mariel had not been a close friend of this poor woman. Yet

her death affected Mariel like an amputation. This was the first death in their party. It diminished them all in some indefinable way. Was it because they feared that they might be the next to lie lifeless in a rough greenwood coffin? Maybe that was why no one could speak.

Mariel did not know why, but the Quinn family had chosen to cluster around her. Sugar and Erin stood near, one on each side of her. Erin took her elbow. The little girl was endearing and a bit lonely, the only child among adults. And even facing forward, Mariel was aware of the Ranger's presence behind her. She willed herself not to betray her awareness to anyone.

Surprisingly, Tunney spoke. "Father in heaven, receive the soul of this lady. It's hard to understand why she came so far just to die. It's a hard life here. Yet we know that the dead will rise first when your Son returns for us. The Lord giveth; the Lord taketh. Blessed be the name of the Lord. Ashes to ashes. Dust to dust."

Then he began shoveling the dirt onto the coffin. A few of the other men joined in, while the rest watched as if numb. When the last shovelful of dirt had been tossed in, everyone began to drift away.

Hesitating, Mariel made a point not to look for Herr Heller. She knew that she couldn't bear him to be close to her now. The thought of his vulgar touch or boorish manners made her queasy. Worse, she feared that she would no longer be able to hold back the words that expressed why she despised him— *bully, coward, rogue.*

Sugar took her hand as Mrs. Quinn said, "You must feel no guilt, Mariel. You did everything you could to help me try to save her."

Mariel nodded, unable to speak. Why was she so near tears?

"Why don't you come and share a cup of coffee with us?" Mrs. Quinn invited.

"Yes, come with us," Erin agreed. "I like to hear you talk."

Their kindness and friendliness undid her. Mariel didn't know how long she could hold back the tears that weren't for Frau Braun but for herself. She must not allow herself to become attached to these Texians. They would leave her with her own people soon enough. "I wish . . . be alone. I come later. *Bitte?* Please?"

Mrs. Quinn nodded, and Sugar released her hand. The Quinn family and Tunney walked back toward the caravan. Erin trailed behind them, looking back at Mariel with unhappy eyes. Tears began dripping down Mariel's face. She hurried farther into the surrounding grove of oaks and lush evergreens. Leaning against the rough trunk of an ancient oak, she let herself feel the sorrow, feel the pain of being alone, always alone. She wept for Frau Braun and the husband and two little boys the woman had left behind. Wept for herself, for the forlorn life she had lived in Germany even before her husband had died. She wept over the hard life here, hard miles still ahead.

Would she also die along the way? Or would she find what she had always been looking for—a place in the heart of some good man and a home of her own and children to love? It was difficult to keep hoping when—

Without warning, she was grabbed from behind. A hand clamped over her mouth. She clawed at it but couldn't pry the fingers off. A voice she knew well growled in her ear. "No one is coming to help you this time, *Liebchen*." Herr Heller. His tone was an insult. "Now I'm going to make you pay for your disobedience, your making eyes at that Ranger. And I'm going to enjoy doing it."

He began pulling up her skirt as he forced her down to the earth. She screamed into his hand. He grinned when no sound came forth. She struggled, but his strength overpowered her with ease.

It was hard to breathe. She began to feel woozy, queasy. The haze of terror returned. She couldn't see clearly, and . . .

With a groan Herr Heller released her. Her half-closed eyes flew open.

The Ranger had come out of nowhere. He yanked Heller up by the front of his shirt and flung him back against the tree behind them. Heller bounced against it, then rushed him.

The Ranger moved out of the way. As Heller stumbled past him, the Ranger struck a blow. Heller groaned again. Still, he turned and charged again. The Ranger shoved a fist up under Heller's chin, knocking his head back. And then the Ranger rained blows onto Heller—chin, eye, gut, chin, eye.

The sound of bone striking bone jarred Mariel. Sickened, she wanted to call out, "Stop! Please!" She shrank back, shaking with the horror of what she was witnessing.

Heller tried to protect himself. Even so, he wasn't able to fend off most of the blows. He dropped to the ground but fought his way to his feet again. In spite of his large frame, he didn't know how to fight as well as the Ranger. That was clear. Blood smeared his face, already red from exertion.

Mariel clamped both hands over her mouth to keep from crying out. She pulled up her knees and crouched as though trying to hide herself. Repugnance shrieked through her every nerve.

Heller lunged at the Ranger, who stepped neatly out of reach. Then, as if tired of the fight, the Ranger finished it. One more powerful fist slammed into Heller's middle. Then one more crunch of his knuckles to the German's chin, and Heller crumpled, unconscious.

The Ranger stood over him breathing in loud gasps, his hands on his hips. After a moment he turned and knelt beside her. "I got here in time, didn't I? He didn't hurt you? . . ."

The shame of what Herr Heller had almost done to her hit

her, and she hid her face behind her hands, shaking with silent weeping.

"This isn't your fault. Don't be ashamed." He touched her shoulder, just the barest touch. "This isn't your doing."

"No one must know." She grabbed his hand, pleading, "They will say I . . . encourage him. They will talk of me . . . in bad way."

The Ranger's face hardened. "Heller deserves to be horse-whipped in public."

She clung to his hand. "Please no. I don't want everyone . . . look at me." And then she thought of her sweet mistress, who had been forced by her own parents to marry this awful man. "His wife is good to me. I don't want . . . there to be bad talk." She implored this man to understand.

He nodded, then sat down on the grass beside her. He handed her a handkerchief from his pocket. "Wipe your eyes. You don't want to go back into camp looking so upset."

She obeyed him, drawing in deep breaths and wiping her face. His words calmed her. Slowly she stopped shaking. Still, she couldn't look toward Heller. She crushed her agitation, drawing up her composure. "No one will think my tears . . . wrong. People will think I cry over Frau Braun." She couldn't meet the Ranger's eye.

He took her chin in his hand and forced her to look up into his face. "This is not your fault. I will not speak of it because you don't want me to. But know that this is not your fault."

His touch coursed down her neck, awakening sensations she had never known before. She held very still so he wouldn't drop his hand, so she wouldn't miss any of this indescribable pleasure.

"You will no longer work for this man. I will tell him that. And I will tell him what I will do to him if he ever tries again to hurt you or any other woman this way. He will not bother you. Or he will find out what Texas men do to a man like him."

The Ranger rose, taking his fingers from her chin. She missed his touch immediately. Then he offered her his hand. She took it and let him help her to her feet. It was as if he had lifted her out of shame, out of fear. Freed her.

Trying to take it all in, she shook out her skirt and petticoats and smoothed back her hair, avoiding his gaze. The Ranger picked up her bonnet, which had come off. She accepted it, put it back on, and tied its strings.

I must say something, must let him know I appreciate . . . She looked up then. "*Danke.* Thank you. I have been afraid of him."

Heller moaned. She let herself gaze down at the man, bloodied and already showing bruising around both eyes. "How will you explain why he is . . . ?"

"I'll take him to the river and he can wash the blood off. I'm not telling how this happened, and he won't either. People will wonder but they won't say much."

She did not know if she believed that. People always talked. When her husband had been arrested, even those she had thought of as friends had not hesitated to spread the news of his treasonous crimes. Still, she nodded. How could she explain?

"Now you go back into the camp and wait near Frau Heller. I'm going to ask Frau Braun's husband if he would like you to help him with his boys now that he's lost his wife. And then you won't be working for this"—the Ranger cast Heller a disdainful look—"sorry excuse for a man."

She curtseyed, still tingling from this man's gentle touch. "I will do what you say." She paused. "I thank you." She suddenly ran out of words and the power to speak them. She could only stare at this man, so good who watched out for her.

"You'll be fine now. This is over. It stopped today. Don't worry over this anymore."

She nodded again, though she had no feeling of this being over. Herr Heller was a stupid sort of man, a bully and a coward.

She walked away, gathering strength as she put distance between her and the place where Heller had tried to abuse her in
the deepest way a man could demean a woman.

She had little doubt that Heller might try something again—
maybe not to her but to another poor woman. Nonetheless, she
also had no doubt that next time the Ranger would horsewhip
the bully in public.

A sudden lightness lifted her. Her silent prayer had been answered. *I am free of Herr Heller. I am free.*

* * *

From the other end of the town road, Sugar watched the old
woman smoking the pipe and rocking on her porch. Today they
would leave Montezuma and head west toward the land the
Germans had bought. Her parents had, of course, decided to go
along and help out the newcomers. All Sugar wanted was to get
out of this town before that old woman with the pipe caught
up with her. Sugar had been avoiding the woman ever since
that first day when she had stared at Sugar. The old woman had
called to her a few times, but she'd ignored this and hurried
away. Sugar couldn't put into words why she didn't want to talk
to the woman. *But I don't*, she admitted to herself.

Sugar turned her back to the woman and marched over to
see what was keeping them from getting off early. The sun had
risen over an hour ago. How long did it take these Germans
to get ready? She found her mother at the buckboard, loading
little children into the back with the help of the mothers. To
move things along, Sugar began lifting the children until all of
them were sitting in the wagon bed.

Now they could leave. Relief gushed through Sugar, yet before
she could voice it, several people came forward, stopping Quinn
from helping Dorritt onto the buckboard seat. Sugar wove her
fingers together and hid her nervous hands behind her back.

The German named Meuserbach was speaking. "We have three families who want to stay here."

Everyone stopped talking and stared at the three men who had come with Meuserbach. "They have talked to some of the people here and decided they don't want to go any farther."

The German girl Mariel came up beside Sugar and smiled shyly. Sugar returned the greeting. Erin hurried over to take Mariel's hand and began chattering, asking her to say different words in German, a pastime the two had enjoyed often the past few days.

Quinn nodded to the German. "That's their business. Let's get started. We have many miles to cover today. I don't know about the rest of you, but I want to get home." Quinn slapped the side of the wagon, showing his impatience to leave.

Sugar grinned. Now they would get out of town.

As the party started down the road, everyone wished the families who were staying good-bye. Sugar allowed herself to be drawn along with Mariel and chattering Erin, who wanted to find the Braun boys to play with. This suited Sugar, since within the midst of the Germans, she would be shielded from the old woman's gaze. She kept her eyes toward the muddy ground underfoot. She didn't want to look at the woman.

"Hold up!" an old voice called out. "I been wantin' to talk to you."

Heart pounding, Sugar looked up. The old woman with the pipe had left her porch and was standing next to the wagon. "I want to know the name of your gal. The tall pretty one in the blue dress. She's the spittin' image of Ida Rose."

Five

Sugar couldn't move. The Germans around her didn't appear to understand that the old woman was asking about her. But Mariel looked into her eyes, and Sugar saw the question in them. Erin looked around, as if she didn't know why Sugar had stopped walking. Sugar stood very still, not wanting to hear what the older woman had to say, hoping that she could go on unnoticed. To do that, she would have to put her hands over her ears, and that would call attention to herself. Still, concealed among the Germans, she left her arms at her sides, clearly hearing the woman's words and her foster mother's reply.

"I beg your pardon," Dorritt said, "are you speaking about my daughter?"

"Is she the tall pretty one?" the old woman said, glancing around.

"That's our daughter, yes."

"You call her your daughter." The woman jabbed the air with her long-stemmed pipe. "But is she your blood kin?"

Sugar blinked her eyes. Something peculiar was beginning to happen inside her ears. It was as if someone had been stuffing cotton into them. Mariel took a step nearer her. Erin asked, "What's the matter?" Mariel replied with a finger to her lips. Sugar slipped closer to Mariel.

"No, she isn't our blood," Dorritt said. "But we've raised her as our own since she was just a little thing."

The old woman stood, squinting in the bright sunshine up at Dorritt on the buckboard bench. "Where is she? I've tried to catch her eye these past days so I could talk to her in private. But she just turns her head and walks away."

"Who is Ida Rose?" Dorritt asked.

Erin looked up, asking with her eyes what was wrong. Sugar squeezed her eyes shut. That didn't stop the low buzzing—like a hive of bees inside her ears that began to distort, obscure the voices. She felt the touch of a hand on her shoulder and knew it must be Mariel. She put her hand over Mariel's.

"Ida Rose has passed, but she was the daughter of a friend of mine. Ida Rose's ma and me grew up in Kentucky and married friends. Around '23, we brought our families to Texas together. Lived hereabouts around the Colorado ever since. My friend, her mother, died in '24. Ida Rose, now she was only fifteen when she up and married Ernest McLaughlin from Missouri. They moved over onto the Guadalupe River. Then after their pa died, Ida Rose's sister Violet went to live with them."

"And you think that my foster daughter is this woman's child? Ida Rose's?"

Sugar opened her eyes. Erin was clinging to her arm now. The sound in her ears was nauseating her. Making her unsteady on her feet. Breathing fast, she looked around for a place to hide. Why was terror crawling up her throat? Weren't the words this woman was saying what she longed to hear? Hadn't she always wanted to know who her blood kin had been? *I should want to know who I'm from. Why am I so afraid?*

The old woman cleared her throat. "Well, I watched your girl the past few days. It's a funny thing, but what first caught my eye was the way she walked. You wouldn't think that was something one could pass down by blood, but it is. She walks just like my friend and both her daughters, Ida Rose and Violet. Kind of elegant like, as if they were always getting ready to dance. Now another thing that your girl does like . . ."

Sugar pulled away from Mariel and Erin. She had to get away. And then Emilio was there on his horse. He swung down and offered her his hand.

"No," she whispered, stepping back.

"I will protect you." Then he gestured as if challenging her, saying wordlessly, "Take it. You are safe if you are with me."

Sugar took his hand briefly. Then he put his strong hands around her waist and lifted her onto his saddle. He climbed up in front of her and murmured, "Trust me. You are afraid, but you will be better to face your fear." He glanced over his shoulder. "Do you trust me, Sugar?"

"With my life," she whispered back. Her words made her tingle all over, because for once she had actually said to Emilio what she was feeling, what she meant.

Emilio nodded, then nudged his horse and took Sugar up to the front of the caravan to the old woman. Her ears humming louder, Sugar watched as the old woman came closer and closer. And then something very odd happened.

She could see the old woman's mouth moving, but she couldn't hear the words. The same happened when her mother, Dorritt, spoke. The two women and her father were talking, but still, Sugar could not hear a word of what was being said.

Feeling queasy, she tried to force herself to understand. Now the buzzing and humming had given way to a roaring sound, something like listening to a Gulf shore shell. It filled her head, along with panic. Their mouths were moving. What were they saying—about her, to her?

Finally, the old woman backed away from the wagon. She looked up into Sugar's face, examining her one last time. Then waving her hand behind her, she turned and walked back to her porch. Sugar looked toward her mother. Dorritt had turned away too and had sat back down. Her father slapped the reins, and the caravan started forward. Rather than let her down, Emilio directed his horse to follow.

Moments passed. After a time Sugar faintly heard the jingle of the harnesses and the hooves hitting the dirt. She tightened her arms around Emilio, pressed her face into his soft buckskin shirt. Would she be able to hear voices normally now? Or not?

All those years ago, when she had first been found by the Quinns, she had been unable to hear their voices. Then one day, their friend Alandra had taken her to pick wildflowers. On that day, Sugar had begun hearing what people were saying to her.

Tears filled Sugar's eyes. She didn't want to recall that frightening time. There had been a war then. She gripped Emilio tighter. If he spoke, would she be able to hear his voice? She squeezed her eyes shut against the tears.

Emilio began to sing softly, a Mexican song. She heard him. She understood the words. Relief caused her tears to spill. *I love you, Emilio. Protect me from this deafness.*

What would Emilio say or do if she told him about the deafness? Was she in some way unhinged?

* * *

Later in the afternoon, Carson rode far ahead of the Germans, pleased that Tunney had decided to continue on with the caravan. Carson wondered if it was because of a certain widow whom Tunney always seemed to drift toward. Arriving at a good hunting spot, Carson halted, tied up his horse, and began to prowl around a narrow creek. He would try to get at least three bucks for a hearty supper and teach the Germans how to prepare pemmican. The caravan would catch up with him later.

Carson heard the rustle of grass and looked around. A black bear had wandered out of the brush to drink at the creek. Slipping silently up into a leafy oak, Carson held his breath. Bear didn't usually attack humans. However, they would if suddenly surprised. The irony of the situation was not lost on Carson. He'd come hunting. But on the frontier, there was always the risk that the predator could become the prey.

Sitting there, feeling the rough bark against his back, he recalled Mariel, hunkered down against a tree trunk as he'd laid Heller out flat. Predators that walked on two legs were just as dangerous as this bear. The bully Heller still griped him. Beating the man up had not been enough punishment for what he'd tried to do to Mariel. Women on the frontier faced a hard life head-on, so one thing decent women needed to count on was respect from men. What kind of place was Germany? Did men there get away with assaulting women? *How can I protect Mariel from Heller when they reach their destination and I leave?*

He heard a second rustling, and his tension heightened. A doe with two very young fawns had come to drink just across the stream from the bear. Bear usually preferred wild berries, roots, and honey. Sometimes, though, they did kill and eat fawns or stray calves. Carson wished that there was some silent sign he could send to the doe to warn her that she was exposing her offspring to possible peril. The bear rose up, standing, manlike, on two feet. If Carson had wanted to, he could have touched the bear's head with the butt of his rifle. The bear sniffed the air, pointing his nose skyward. Did the bear smell him? Or the deer? Carson felt strangely protective of the doe and her young. If he shot the doe, the speckled fawns, still sucklings, would die. He'd already decided to let all three go on.

The three deer continued drinking across the stream. As the bear had, the mother kept lifting her head, wary of possible attack. Only death would separate the doe from her fawns. Most women were the same about their babies. So how had Sugar and her mother become separated? Who would leave, abandon a little girl in the midst of a war? The bear thunked back to earth and resumed drinking.

The old woman had said that this Ida Rose McLaughlin, who might have been Sugar's mother, had died. Was that true? Did Sugar remember anything? Strangely, she'd refused to answer the woman's questions this morning, instead turning her head into Emilio's shoulder.

The bond between Sugar and Emilio had been evident to everyone for a long time now. But Emilio held back from speaking his intentions. Why?

Finally, the doe and her fawns wandered away into the bushes. The bear turned in the opposite direction and waddled off on all fours again. Carson relaxed with a silent sigh. He realized that worry over the bear, deer, Sugar, and Mariel had ousted Blanche from his mind. A momentary relief.

A fine big buck strode into sight. Carson lifted his rifle and shot. Then he slid from the tree to the ground, his mind focused on the promise of venison steaks sizzling on the fire tonight.

* * *

Sugar had a feeling of being only half-present. Or was she really half-gone? The caravan halted for the night, and Sugar and Emilio dismounted. As she hovered near him, he helped Quinn unharness the team of horses from the wagon. Then he began checking their hooves after the long day. He murmured to the horses, and she felt his gentle, loving words also flowing through her. He and her family had respected—never ridiculed—her silence. Now, she wanted to put her hand out and touch him, just feel him, know that he was real.

Everyone else around them was hurrying around preparing for the warm evening meal and getting the canvas roof up for the night. Nearby, Carson, who had gone ahead and brought down two bucks, was showing a few of the men how to butcher a deer for tonight's supper and then how to cut strips to make pemmican. Her father was pitching the wikiup, while her mother and Erin had gone off with the mothers of small children to wash up in the water.

Sugar knew she should be with her mother . . . or to be exact, the woman who had been her mother for as long as she could recall. She pressed her hands together in front of her mouth as if in prayer. Words didn't come. Only feeling came—waves of wet, cold fear of the past washed through her.

Emilio straightened up and looked into her face.

Oh, Emilio, please don't ask me anything.

He took her hand. "Come, señorita. We will take the horses to the creek and let them drink."

His gentle words blessed her, yet like a wild bronco being tamed, her emotions still reared and charged. Sugar clung to his hand. In his other hand, he held all the reins and led the way to the creek. There many of the German mothers, as well as Mariel and Dorritt, were already bathing small children and washing diapers. Erin was wading in the water, picking up pebbles. Emilio led the horses along the shore to the water upstream of the children and camp. The horses moseyed up to the stream and began drinking and wading into the water.

Emilio edged back from the horses and drew Sugar under a willow tree. The trees and shrubs around the stream were very thick and green. The lush growth of the canebrake shielded them from the others. Emilio draped his arm over her shoulder, and here, in this private place, Sugar felt better than she had all day.

Yet that wasn't anything near to normal.

What had the old woman said about her? The question repelled and tempted her at the same time. And why hadn't she been able to hear the woman when everyone else evidently had? *Am I losing my mind?*

She glanced sideways at Emilio and got another jolt. His face was twisted with some strong emotion.

"Have I displeased you?" The words flowed from her mouth before she was aware she was speaking.

He glanced her way. "You never displease me, but I have much to think about." He stroked her cheek with one finger. "Much."

His words did not reassure her; his touch did. She pressed closer to him.

"There is much I want to say to you." He paused and stroked her cheek with the back of his hand. "Can you tell me if you think that you could be the daughter of this Ida Rose?"

She looked down and shook her head. A sudden sob shook her.

"*Querida*, do not cry. It is of no importance. I merely wondered if she had stirred up . . . unhappy memories. Calm yourself. No one will be allowed to upset you. I promise."

Sugar didn't try to speak. She merely pressed her face into the crook of Emilio's neck.

* * *

The night exploded with the sound of shots. Mariel jerked up in the blanket wrapped around her. The two little Braun boys sleeping near her didn't stir. All around Mariel, people were

waking too. And the sound must have frightened—no, terrified—them all, not just Mariel. She knew this because no one
was exclaiming or even asking questions. There was a level of
fear that brought only strained silence; that dread hung over
them now.

As her eyes adjusted to the low moon and starlight, she
looked around, trying to see what the problem could be. Then
she glimpsed Herr Meuserbach hurrying toward where the
sound of the shots had come from.

When he returned a few minutes later, he was accompanied
by the Ranger's father. Herr Meuserbach said in a voice loud
enough to be heard but not loud enough to disturb the still
sleeping children, "The Ranger thinks that *Inderin* tried to steal
horses. The Ranger shot to frighten them off. He was wounded
in return."

Many around Mariel gasped. She pressed her hands over
her mouth, almost unable to breathe. Then Herr Meuserbach
shocked her more. "Mariel Wolffe, the Ranger's mother wants
you to come to help her."

Mariel rose, shaking out her skirts, and came forward. She
didn't look around, knowing that this request for her would
elicit suspicious expressions. No one had missed the fact that
she no longer worked for the Hellers. She had heard women
whispering, but no one had said anything to her face. Yet.

The Ranger's father said, "I'll take you." And then he was holding her arm, hurrying her along to that peculiar tent. When they
reached it, she saw that the Ranger was sitting outside, without
his shirt, near the low fire. His mother was with him. The light
from the flames flickered over his tan skin. Mariel halted.

Mrs. Quinn turned and motioned toward Mariel. "I'm afraid
I need you to help with the nursing. Sugar somehow slept
through the shots. But I must go comfort Erin. And I don't
want her to see Carson till his wound is bandaged."

Mrs. Quinn pointed to the Ranger's arm, which was bloodied above the elbow. "I've laid everything out here for you. You need only clean the wound, treat it with iodine, and then bandage it. Can you do it?"

Mariel nodded, wondering why the woman wanted her to be here alone with her son. Mrs. Quinn gave a half smile and turned to her husband. He lifted the tent flap, and Mrs. Quinn lowered her head and shoulders and slipped inside. Quinn followed and closed the flap behind them.

So Mariel was left alone near the fire with the Ranger. Why had the lady asked her to do this? Mariel hadn't been the only one to help nurse poor Frau Braun. So it couldn't be her nursing skill alone.

Mariel's mind stuttered, refusing to accept that Mrs. Quinn had sensed Mariel's fascination with the Ranger and was fostering it. She drew in a deep, steadying breath. "I will help you, sir."

"I'm not a sir," he said, sounding a bit irritated.

"I am sorry. What do I call you?" She took his arm in hand, trying in the low light to see how badly wounded he was.

"My name is Carson."

"I know, but I cannot call you that. You are a . . . Ranger. You are with . . . government."

He gave a half laugh. "I'm just a Ranger, not in Congress."

She couldn't make sense of his words, but she had come to nurse him. That was all. She turned his arm farther toward the firelight so that she could see the wound. Something had sliced a shallow path through the outside of his upper arm. She tried to concentrate on the wound, not his substantial chest so near. "Is this from . . . a gun?"

"No, arrow."

She looked up into his face. "Arrow? What is arrow?"

He showed her a broken wooden shaft with feathers at one end.

"Oh, *Eisen*." She swallowed, realizing what this might mean. "It was *Inderin*, then?" she whispered, finally able to put her fear into words.

"I think it was Comanche. We're getting close to the *Comancheria*, their land."

She tried not to think of Comanches with arrows. The thought that any stranger would seek to hurt her, kill her. *No. No.* She took one of the clean sponges left by Mrs. Quinn and began to wipe away the blood, focusing on the feel of the man's arm—hard with muscle, not soft, like her late husband's had been. She stopped her mind there, refusing to let her thoughts drift back to lonely Germany.

"If it weren't so high on my arm, I could do this myself," he said in a tone that let her know that he didn't like to be dependent on anyone.

"I am . . . happy to do it." She looked up, and that was a mistake. The moonlight had silvered his face, casting shadows and highlighting angles. So handsome. "For you." She stopped herself before she said "sir" again.

She lowered her eyes. After cleansing the shallow wound, she applied the iodine. He drew in air. She looked up. His face was less than an inch from hers. Her breath caught in her throat and she found she couldn't move. The frogs in the creek—some were chirping and some were bellowing. The wind played with the tops of the trees, making the leaves sound as if they were laughing softly.

He brushed her cheek first. Then, as if he were blind and was seeing her face with his touch, with his index finger, he traced her lips, the center of her nose, and then up to her eyebrows—one and then the other. Shivering at his touch, she closed her eyes and drew in the scent of him—wood smoke, leather, and honest perspiration.

"You're so pretty," he whispered. "So pretty and sweet." And then his lips were on hers, warm and gentle.

She kissed him in return, digging her fingers into his shoulders as if afraid he would vanish. The skin was smooth under her palms, the man beneath solid.

Mariel had been kissed before—yet perhaps not. Perhaps this was the first kiss she'd ever been given. It was certainly the first kiss she had ever wanted.

The first kiss ended and the second began. He pulled her closer and began to stroke her hair. She clung to him, not sure where the earth below her had gone. The kiss deepened, and she clutched him, becoming weightless, fearing she would float away.

The sound of a scream interrupted them.

Mariel cried out too, but her outcry was swallowed by Carson's intake of air. He dragged Mariel up as he rose. Emilio, the other Ranger, came running from somewhere in the dark.

Mariel knew she should step away from Carson. Yet her surprise was so deep that she couldn't move, could barely breathe.

"It's inside the wikiup," Carson said. He released her but took her hand in his. "Come on."

She resisted. "Your father, mother won't—"

"Emilio!" Mrs. Quinn's voice came from inside the tent. "Carson!"

Carson turned and hurried into the tent, followed closely by Emilio. Mariel didn't follow. She watched as the lamp inside flickered and flared to life. They left the flap open, and she could hear the low voices, overshadowed by an hysterical voice, rising and falling. It sounded like Sugar, the Ranger's sister.

Mariel heard the parents and the two Rangers trying to calm Sugar down. They had no effect. Mariel remembered something then. She bent down and picked up the bucket of water she had dipped from while attending to Carson's wound. She hurried into the tent. Once there, she took out a dipper of water and flung it into Sugar's face.

Sugar's eyes flew wide open and she breathed in air.

"Sugar, you are with family. You are safe," Mariel said in as firm a voice as she could manage with her heart beating and jumping so. "You are safe." The others stared at her. Abashed, Mariel drew back into the shadows.

Sugar drew another breath and hiccupped. "Carson!" Then she threw her arms around him and clung to him. And extended her hand to Emilio. He looked very worried, yet almost angry, as he gripped her hand.

Mariel suddenly felt even more the intruder, and she retreated nearer the tent flap. She waited uncertainly, unable to leave completely, yet feeling so out of place. A family together, a brother and sister who loved each other and a friend and parents who also loved. What was that like? Having someone to turn to in the night when bad dreams woke one?

Silently she left the tent.

Carson wished Mariel hadn't drawn back. She'd looked upset. And she'd had a right to be upset. Carson wanted to explain why he had kissed her. He was suddenly at a loss. Why had he kissed her?

I didn't plan to kiss her.

But he realized he had wanted to kiss her—and for a long time too. How could that be so soon after his feelings for Blanche?

Sugar was weeping against his shoulder. He was having trouble understanding what she was saying. He looked to his mother, who gave a slight shake of her head. Did that mean she didn't understand this either?

"I couldn't . . . I couldn't hear this morning," Sugar stammered. "I couldn't hear what that woman was saying. And tonight in my dream, another woman, a taller and younger woman, was shouting at me, and then there were a lot of people all around us, crushing us, pushing us down, stepping on us . . ."

She stopped to catch her breath. "Everyone was shouting so loud, and . . . I knew that they were shouting but I couldn't hear any words at all. Why does my head do that?" Sugar paused, then hit her head with her fist. Carson grabbed her hand and pulled it down and held it.

Sugar took in a rattling breath. "Why do my ears start buzzing and I can't hear? That's how it was when you found me all . . . those years ago." Sugar turned her head into his shoulder, hiding.

Carson looked to all the faces turned toward him. Then he looked at Sugar, her head on his shoulder. For a moment, no one spoke.

Then Quinn said, "Sugar, we don't know. Maybe only God knows. We will not let anything happen to you. No one, no one can take you from our family. You are our daughter and have been since '36. We won't let anyone take you away. Do you believe me?"

Sugar peeped out from her hiding place. "I believe that. But my ears filled with those buzzing and roaring sounds—am I going loco? It frightens me when I can't hear like that. It's scary."

Emilio looked down. Carson saw the way his jaw worked. Something more than this nightmare was working in him. What?

Dorritt dug into a bag and pulled out a bottle and a shot glass. "Yes, but you can hear us now. Maybe it won't happen again. We left that woman behind and we're not going to go looking for anyone who might be your blood kin."

"The past doesn't matter. We're your family," Quinn said.

His mother nodded. "I am going to give you a dram of whiskey, and I want you to sip it slowly and let it calm you."

"I don't like whiskey," Sugar whimpered.

"I don't either. This is only for medicinal purposes," Dorritt coaxed.

Emilio reached over and touched Sugar's shoulder. "That's right, señorita. And you know how it is—medicine never tastes good." He forced a grin.

Carson was bolstered to see a smile trying to tug the corners of Sugar's mouth upward as she looked into Emilio's face. Sugar accepted the small half-filled glass and began sipping it. He looked out through the flap and saw Mariel pacing there.

Warmth flooded him as he recalled holding her and kissing her. *What was I thinking? I barely know her. And after all that cad Heller put her through, what is she thinking of me kissing her? Or had she felt she'd owed him because he'd stopped Heller? I don't want that.*

Then Tunney came into view, motioning for him to come out. "Carson, I got bad news," he said in a low tone.

Carson rose and walked outside. Mariel was backing away into the night. He wanted to go to her and explain, apologize—no, kiss her again.

Stop.

Carson turned to Tunney. "What do you mean, bad news?"

Six

"We thought we scared the thieves away, but they still got away with two of our horses," Tunney growled.

The experience of kissing Mariel still overshadowed everything else in Carson's mind. He needed to concentrate. His brow creased as he sorted through his muddled thoughts and marked reactions. He then focused on the very simple topic of stolen horses. "Comanche?"

"Who else?" Tunney grumbled.

Carson was aware that Mariel lingered nearby, listening. And again he was nearly overwhelmed with the urge to draw her close. He turned his back to her. "Which horses did they get away with?"

"My horse." Tunney glared. "And Quinn's. Leaving Emilio's, yours, and the draft horses."

Carson cursed under his breath. Didn't they have enough to contend with? Still they should have expected this type of welcome so close to the *Comancheria*.

His father came out of the tent. "So they didn't take us seriously when Carson fired a warning shot? We'll have to go after them. We need those horses. And no man steals my horse and gets away with it."

Quinn's straightforward words were a relief. Right now all Carson wanted to do was get away from all the confusing emotion and turmoil caused by Sugar's nightmare and the German woman still so close by. He looked skyward. "The moon's high. We have time and light enough. We'll track them on my horse."

He reached down and grabbed up his shirt. He'd taken it off because of his wound, which wasn't bleeding now. As he pulled it on, he relived the sensations from Mariel's touch on his bare chest and arm. His whole body tightened.

Quinn went back inside, spoke quietly to his wife, and came out buckling on his holster, with its two Colt .45s. Then, pausing, he reached just inside the wikiup and brought out his rifle and bag of shot. "Let's go."

Carson hurried after him, calling back to Tunney to start out in the morning as usual. Unfortunately, Carson glanced over his other shoulder and there was Mariel, her face white and strained in the moonlight. He resolutely turned his head forward. When he had the opportunity, he'd apologize to her.

What was I thinking?

Even as he said this, he admitted the truth that if he came within kissing distance of Mariel Wolffe again, he'd be tempted to kiss her. The delicious feeling of holding her washed over him in a fresh warm wave.

Then his father was prowling around the area where the horses had been stolen. Carson did the same and spied impressions where the horses had been led away. "Here, Pa," he whispered. They mounted his horse together bareback. Eyes downward, they began tracking the horses and thieves.

Hours passed as Carson and his father moved silently and

painstakingly over the miles of faint trail left by the horse thieves. Sensations and images of kissing Mariel kept flashing in and out of Carson's mind. Finally, in those chill morning hours just before dawn, they approached the edge of the camp where the small band of thieves slept.

The thieves, who looked to number about six, must have been very young and cocky. They had underestimated Carson and his father. The Comanche had only set one man to watch. He was easily overpowered, gagged, and tied up. With sign language, Quinn told Carson that they wouldn't attack the Comanche, who outnumbered them three to one. But he singled out the horses that had been stolen, then chose the best of the thieves' horses for retribution. Silently, he led the three animals away.

Carson walked his horse beside his father, who had the other leads in hand. The suspense of sneaking away from an Indian camp tightened Carson's perception of the sights, sounds, feel of that dark, forbidding hour.

Finally, when they had put over a mile between them and the Comanche camp, they mounted. Leading the extra horses, they began to make their way back to the trail. "We should catch up with our party just about time for breakfast," his father said.

Carson murmured assent. But he wasn't thinking about breakfast. He was thinking about Mariel's soft, willing lips. Had she really kissed him back? He thought so, but with everything that had happened, he couldn't be sure. *Mariel, why did you let me kiss you?* His unruly mind added, *Will you let me kiss you again?*

* * *

Hours after supper that night, Emilio braced himself for what he knew he must do. For Sugar's sake, for his own. The Quinns sat around the fire outside the wikiup. It was the quiet time in camp, just before everyone found their beds. The sound of low voices created a barrier of sound between their fire and the many German fires. The surrounding prairie had begun the climb to the Hill Country where they were headed.

Emilio cleared his throat and said in a low voice, "I have something to say."

The easy conversation around him ceased, and every eye turned to him. Consciously he made himself look calm, but his pulse raced of its own accord. He looked to Sugar, trying to express his concern and love for her without words. "And I want to say it here in front of everyone." He paused to say a silent prayer, then lifted his chin. "Sugar will never have peace," he said, "until she faces the past."

Sugar made a sound of pain.

Emilio stared into her eyes, hoping she would not freeze up, become deaf or run. "Sugar, a bad time is coming."

He pulled out the newspaper he had bought in Montezuma and held it up. Since he'd first read this newspaper, a heavy weight had sat at the bottom of his stomach. "War is coming soon. This is why I am speaking up. We must all prepare for what is coming. You, Sugar, must prepare."

Sugar half-rose, but her mother pulled her back down onto the log where they sat. With her lower lip quivering, little Erin looked back and forth between Emilio and Sugar.

"This isn't just about the war, is it?" Dorritt said with a knowing look.

Emilio shook his head, smiling his chagrin at her insight. "I am a *Tejano*. So I think of marriage as Mexicans do. It is not just about two people in love. It concerns the whole family. I think you must know that I love and wish to marry Sugar—"

Sugar rose and rushed away into the surrounding shadows. Erin started up, but her mother restrained her. Emilio rose and hurried after Sugar. He caught up with her easily and drew her farther away into the shadows. "Sugar, do not run from me. Do not run from you, run from us."

She let him take her hands. Still, she would not look him in the eye. "Sugar, I love you."

Then she did look up, but she said nothing, merely opened and closed her lips; her cheeks became rosy. She had never looked more beautiful to him. "Sugar, I love you. I want you to be my wife."

Then she closed the distance between them and came into his arms, demonstrating the love that evidently would not come to her lips. He held her close and stroked her hair, whispering words of love to her. *"Estoy enamorado de ti. Mi amor, mi dulce."*

"I love you," she finally whispered into his ear.

"Will you be my wife?" He pulled back so he could see her pale, lovely face in the faint moon and starlight.

"Yes." She was blushing darker pink. *"Sí."*

Emilio pulled her close again and kissed her. He had waited years for this moment, years for this lovely girl to become a woman. He began their first kiss gently, persuading her lips to part. He savored this moment of triumph, of coming together.

When he finally ended the kiss, he clasped her to him and whispered the words he knew she did not want to hear, the words he was forced to say. "There is one thing we must do first."

* * *

Two days later, Mariel was walking behind the wagon where the little Braun boys were riding for a rest. Ever since Carson had kissed her, he had avoided her. She wanted to tell him that she knew it had meant nothing, that she knew he, a Ranger, was above her. But he never came near. And she missed that. She hadn't realized that she had become so accustomed to his walking near her, watching over her. She must face reality—he was not for her. Admitting this left her cold and empty inside.

A shout came from the front. She looked up. Usually a shout set her heart to racing; this time the shout sounded different. It was not filled with fear.

"What is it, Frau Wolffe?" one of the little boys asked.

She smiled. "I don't think it is something bad this time."

Carson and his friend Tunney came walking their horses down the line. "We've made it! You're here!" Tunney called out. "We're just entering the land your Prince Carl bought."

The news raced down the line from one end of the caravan to the other. A babble of voices sprang up all around Mariel. And then everyone was walking faster. Around the next bend the party halted to look out on their new home. It was very different from the prairie they had been walking over. She had not noticed it much; now, she realized they had been walking upland for a time.

She looked out over a striking land, no longer a gentle prairie or coastal plain but a land with low mountains in the distance. The mountains were etched with river valleys, and cypress trees grew along the shores, while spreading oaks and firs grew in the valleys and up the craggy hillsides. Mariel felt uplifted, transported out of her normal self. *Schön*. Beautiful.

"They expect us to farm here?" Herr Heller's voice rang out, strong and vehement. "The soil is thin and stony."

Herr Meuserbach leaped up on the back of the buckboard and waved his arms. When all had fallen silent, he began to speak. "*Ja*, we will farm here. Herr Quinn, the Ranger's father, has told me that the land is hilly, but the soil in the valleys is *gut*. Prince Carl of Solms-Braunfels chose this land and bought it for you with the funds from the *Adelsverein*. You did not think this would be like Germany, *nicht wahr*? Now we will thank *Gott* for bringing us safely here. Herr Quinn says that it is a blessing from *Gott* that more of us did not die on the way here." He removed his hat and bowed his head.

Mariel bowed hers and folded her hands. All through the prayer, however, she had trouble keeping her mind on the words and phrases. She kept peeking up to take one more look at this beautiful place. Something deep inside her opened, stretched, and now sighed with deep joy. This land would be a good place to live.

The prayer ended and the people chattered on. Mariel gazed around, silent. Ahead, Carson sat upon his horse, staring at her. She knew she should look away. She couldn't. She drank in the picture he made—so tall in the saddle, sitting with easy poise, the master of the situation. His leather hat cast his face in shadow. But she had memorized his features and could imagine them with ease.

In the days since he had kissed her, she had been unable to shut out the memory of the sensations or the thrill of being intimate with him in that way. Yet they had not spoken, and he had avoided her. She knew that kissing her had just been a momentary impulse on his part. On the other hand, she knew that it would take time for her to get over the fact that she was attracted to a man who could not be a part of her life here. Yet at this special moment in her life, she let herself savor looking at him. Soon he would leave and she would begin to seek her future here in this lovely place. She would have thought that the beauty around her would have eased the pain of knowing he must leave her. It didn't. It made it a sharper, a keener pain.

What is, is. And I must accept it.

* * *

On the first morning, the second day of May, at the new settlement named New Braunfels, named for Prince Carl, who had chosen it for them, Mariel set out. She stayed a little behind the other women on their way to the fast-running Colorado River in the valley, cut out of the rocky landscape. They carried weeks of laundry in long cloth sacks. All around them was the sound of axes biting into wood. The men were felling trees to build cabins. At the bank of the stream, the women pulled the back hems of their skirts forward between their legs and tucked them firmly into the front of their waistbands.

Mariel shed her worn shoes and socks and walked out ankle deep into the cool water. The difference from Germany was startling. She couldn't have gone wading in May there. The other women were chatting away about the scenery, about family left at home and how to possibly send letters. She had noticed recently that the other women in the party were treating her with a bit more reserve, so she kept her distance, hoping that whatever tales were being spun over her leaving the Hellers would blow over. She began washing the Brauns' clothing.

Among the little boys' shirts and underwear, she found some of Frau Braun's clothing. She halted for a moment, holding the clothing of the woman they had buried in that little town, so many miles back. She saw herself at the graveside.

Then the stark memory of Herr Heller's attack tried to intrude, grab her and drag her into misery and loss. She shook it off. She found a rock, wet one of the shirts, and rubbed it with the yellow bar soap. Then she slapped the shirt on the rock and began rubbing in earnest, working out the dirt the boy had ground into the shirt, not thinking of anything, just the rock, water, soap, and cotton clothing.

"Hello."

Startled, Mariel looked up to see that Carson's mother, Sugar, and Erin had joined them. "*Guten Morgen,*" Mariel stuttered. "I mean, good morning."

"*Guten Morgen!*" Erin called out cheerfully. The little girl was picking up German easily and seemed to enjoy learning the new language as an interesting game.

"I came to do a bit of laundry too." Mrs. Quinn folded up her skirt in the same way that Mariel had, then shed the leather moccasins she wore. Erin followed Mrs. Quinn's actions and waded into the water behind her mother, who carried a sack of clothing tied over one shoulder. The little girl bent over and began picking up rocks, worn smooth from the water.

Sugar hung back and leaned against a tree. Mariel wondered why Sugar seemed so crushed, listless. She knew it must have something to do with her nightmare and that old woman in Montezuma, but Mariel didn't quite understand it all.

Mrs. Quinn chose a large flat rock nearby and began to wash feminine underclothing. "I'm looking forward to getting home."

The mention of her leaving brought a sharp pang to Mariel. When this woman left, her family and no doubt the Ranger would also depart. A pit of loneliness opened within Mariel; she couldn't say anything more than, "Oh?"

The woman nodded, beckoning Erin to come learn how to scrub an undershirt. "I can't wait to be in my own house again."

Mariel could only imagine what it felt like to have a real home to go to and a family there. She shook this off. Life was what it was, and there was no use crying. Isn't that what her mother had told her over and over?

Then Mariel gazed around, letting the beautiful, rugged landscape rising from the valley draw her eyes heavenward. Fresh spring water poured from rocky hillsides. Still, the feeling of impending loss dogged her. She added more soap and scrubbed the underarms of the little shirt. And she tried to rid herself of the low current within her, the current that wanted to drag her into gloom. She hoped she didn't appear as downhearted as Sugar.

"It's a lovely place, isn't it?" Mrs. Quinn commented.

"*Ja*, but . . . it is so wild, so empty." Mariel grasped this topic, a distraction. At home, she had taken for granted the centuries that had shaped the town and the surrounding valleys. Here she felt as if she were among the first people to ever walk these hillsides or use this creek to wash clothing. Mariel struggled to find the words to express this. "I see no sign people . . . live here. Do people live here?"

Mrs. Quinn didn't look up from her washing. "Yes, Comanche have lived here, and probably Waco and Kiowa bands. Indians live on the land without leaving a trace. They wander, following the herds of buffalo."

Mariel tried to imagine life wandering from place to place, living in that strange type of tent the Quinns had. It was not easy. Then she realized that she would probably live and die without leaving much of a trace herself—just a gravestone that would eventually list and crumble into the earth. Ashes to ashes. Dust to dust. Her mind repeated her *grossmutter*'s verse that had been just at the back of her mind since leaving Galveston. "Trust in the LORD, and do good; so shalt thou dwell in the land." Her mind added more this time: "But the humble shall inherit the earth; and shall delight themselves in the abundance of peace. . . ."

She shoved these thoughts aside, trying to concentrate on their conversation. She couldn't imagine living a life following buffalo. "I would not like to live, never stopping or staying."

Erin piped up, "Our house is not like the ones in east Texas and not a cabin either. It is a ranch house, a hacienda, only one floor high, and it has stone floors, not wooden." Erin looked up from the chemise she was scrubbing and grinned broadly. "And at home I don't have to do the laundry. Conchita does the laundry while I do my lessons."

"It doesn't hurt you to learn how to do laundry," Mrs. Quinn said, shaking her finger playfully at Erin. "Someday you might not have Conchita to help you."

This didn't surprise Mariel. Of course the Quinns would have servants. Without much success, she tried to imagine the kind of house Erin had described.

Mariel had finally rubbed the perspiration stain out of the shirt when Mrs. Quinn said, "I'm hoping you'll come home with us for a visit. Erin will miss her German lessons."

"*Ja!*" the little girl said, grinning, "*Bitte.* Please come with us. You'll like our hacienda. Please. *Bitte.*"

Surprised by the invitation, Mariel straightened up. And froze in place by what she saw.

On the top of the rise above the creek was what must be *die Indianer.* He sat upon a horse. His black hair was long and tied into tails. "*Oh,*" Mariel said with a gasp, pointing toward him. And then she blinked and he was gone.

Then she heard the babble of voices around her. Carson had warned them that this land belonged to Comanche. The women around her gathered their wet clothing and raced, shouting, toward where the men were felling trees.

Mariel remained where she was, ankle deep in the cool, rushing water. Mrs. Quinn and Erin did not look frightened, merely interested. There had been nothing to prevent *die Indianer*'s doing something to them had he wanted to, but he had merely looked curious. Mariel turned toward Mrs. Quinn. "What does this mean?"

"It means that the Comanche have just let you know that they know you are on their land."

"They will come and . . ." She tried to imagine what a fight with *Inderin* would be like, but she couldn't. She had just been thinking about how beautiful, how peaceful this valley was. And that she might live in this land with peace.

"Don't be frightened," Erin said. "Carson and Emilio and my father will protect us."

Mariel forced a smile. *Yes, but they will not be here forever.*

* * *

That evening when Mariel tucked the two Braun boys into their blankets, they begged to hear more about the Indian she had seen. "I only saw him for a moment. He had black hair and wore it in two tails like horse tails, and his chest was bare."

"Did he try to scalp you?" one asked, looking horrified and fascinated at the same time.

"No, of course not. We are going to make peace with the Comanche. Now go to sleep, *Kinder*." She patted both their heads. Since their mother's death, she had tried to show a bit of affection to each child. Not much, because she did not want them to become attached to her. Their father would probably remarry as soon as was proper. Mariel had noticed that some of the other unmarried women who had come with their families had taken to chatting with him along the trail.

She rose, turned, and found Herr Braun right there. "Oh! Excuse me. I didn't see you."

"We must talk," he said in a low voice.

She didn't try to hide her surprise. Had she done something wrong with the children? She let him draw her aside under a nearby tree.

"Frau Wolffe, I think that we better marry. Soon."

Mariel looked at him, dumbstruck. "What?" she whispered finally.

He grimaced. "I will need a wife. You are good with my sons. And when I build my cabin, how can you live in it with me and not be my wife?"

"I thought I could live with another family but work for you." She didn't like how agitated the man seemed. "Is everything all right?"

"No." He looked even more uncomfortable. Then he admitted, "There has been talk. About why you left the Hellers' employ."

Though this is exactly what Mariel had dreaded, it was still an unpleasant shock, a jolt to hear it said aloud. "What do they say?" she asked, her mouth dry.

The man appeared to be in pain, his face twisted so. "They say that you must have . . . made overtures to Herr Heller or you wouldn't have been dismissed."

"I was not dismissed." *I left because Herr Heller did more than make overtures to me.* Of course, she couldn't say that. No one would believe her. It was always easier to blacken the name of a defenseless woman without a family to defend her than to confront the man who could strike back. Wolves always went for the weakest.

"I know that," Herr Braun agreed. "And I know that you are not the kind of woman who would do . . . do anything of that nature. So I think that we should marry. Though how to do that out here in the wilderness, I don't know." He threw up his hands, demonstrating his ignorance in this setting.

Mariel tasted blood and realized she'd just bitten her lower lip. "Herr Braun, you have been a good employer, but I don't wish to marry any man now." She ignored her lie. "Why can't we just continue as we have—"

"I've just told you why. It isn't fair. It isn't right. But you must marry me or someone—before you have no reputation left to lose." He shook his head, then walked away from her.

She turned and looked over the people in the encampment around her. Many looked away.

That told her all she needed to know. Her spirits tumbled. She nearly groaned aloud. So the gossip had become more than whispers. And the gossips had twisted the bare facts into a story that she had tried to seduce Herr Heller. How could people believe such rubbish? And what could she do to stop it? Herr Braun was a good man, but she had no desire to marry him. And not out of necessity. But what could she do?

* * *

The day after the Comanche had shown himself to the women, Carson, Quinn, and Meuserbach rode out to make peace with them. Or at least try. And survive. Leaving Tunney and Emilio to guard the Germans still building cabins, Carson and his father had picked up the Comanche trail right away.

Tracking always made Carson's neck tense, his nerves taut. His eyes began their accustomed scanning, his ears tuned to catch the whisper of an arrow slipped into a bow notch.

Quinn was explaining the Comanche to Meuserbach: "When dealing with any tribe, you must take nothing for granted. Comanche, Apaches, Waco are not like whites in how they think, in what they consider important. The main thing you must understand, especially with Comanche, is they live in war."

And that keeps us at war all our lives. That made me a Ranger. Carson let his horse fall behind theirs. He didn't want to be distracted. His father was counting on him as his extra eyes and ears. Both of them knew they could be leading Meuserbach into a trap. Carson's rifle rested across his lap, at the ready.

"What does that mean, that they live in war?" the German asked, looking puzzled.

"It means that the young men can only advance in rank or respect by how good they are at stealing horses, taking scalps, or counting coup—"

"What is that coup?" the German interrupted.

"Counting coup is touching one's enemy in battle and then riding away without being caught." Quinn looked downward, still tracking.

The German gave Carson's father a startled look.

I've never counted coup. Or took a scalp. Many Rangers sported a scalp or two on their belts as a warning not to be taken lightly, but Carson had not been forced to use this tack. All he had to do was mention that he was the son of Quinn.

Meuserbach shook his head. "That is no way to live. Killing people."

Carson let a bleak, cold breath whistle through him. He felt empty, hollow. *It is how I live, how Emilio lives. Or how Emilio has lived. Will he quit the Rangers now that he has proposed to Sugar?*

Quinn's voice became harsher. "On the frontier, killing is more common than probably anywhere else you have ever encountered. I have never been farther east than New Orleans. Yet I think I speak the truth." Quinn shook his head. "In Texas and Mexico, white men take scalps too. In Sonora, the Mexican government pays one hundred dollars for a brave's scalp, fifty dollars for a squaw, and twenty-five dollars for a child under fourteen."

Meuserbach looked horrified.

Glancing skyward, Carson watched a lone eagle riding the warm air high, high above them. Carson thought back to images from his Ranger life—of tracking, then shooting, the enemy, their shocked faces and their bodies falling. These images melted into a stream of black gun smoke, sand, and gore. *I don't even know how many lives I've taken.* The realization desolated him.

A flock of squawking crows lifted from nearby dogwood trees. Carson gripped his rifle. What had spooked the crows?

His mother predicted that a time would come—within his life—when all native tribes would be forced out of Texas, just as Jackson had forced the Cherokee out of Georgia in '38. To Carson, that still seemed far-fetched. Nevertheless, Texas wasn't Texas anymore. It was U.S. territory now.

Carson shifted in his saddle, still tracking the flight of the soaring eagle along with the black cloud of crows. If all the tribes were forced out of Texas, would Texas need Rangers then? Did he want to spend the rest of his life Ranging?

Quinn went on attempting to explain. "This way of life, getting respect from being good at fighting, stealing, and killing, causes the Comanche—all western Indians—to live in a constant state of warfare. Not only against the whites but against other tribes as well."

Carson strained, trying to see what might have set off the crows. And was that a cloud or a wisp of smoke ahead, a sign of a Comanche camp?

"The Comanche first lived farther north. They learned to tame and ride Spanish horses. Became buffalo hunters and horse thieves." Quinn glanced up at the eagle too. "Then they came to Texas and were even able to force the Apache farther southward into Mexico. And if you knew the Apache, you would know what a feat that was."

"Does that mean that they will not make peace with us?" Meuserbach asked.

Carson heard the fear just under the surface of Meuserbach's words. This man didn't want to live like Carson had, always keeping a rifle by his side. Uneasy about the crows and the wisps ahead, Carson gripped his rifle with one hand, ready to swing it up. What would that feel like, to live in peace? *What would I do if I weren't a Ranger?* The question gave him an odd sensation, a feeling of loss, of loneliness.

"No, peace is possible, at least for a time," Quinn said, scanning the surrounding area and acknowledging the wisp with the barest of nods to his son. "I think we might be able to get an agreement with this band of Comanche, the Penateka, the honey-eaters. But you must remember that different bands of a tribe don't all follow the same treaties."

The wisp wasn't a cloud; it was faint mesquite smoke from a camp. They were close now, close to parlay or fight. If they were attacked, would the German know how to use his rifle?

"You mean like in Germany we have many princes but no king?"

Quinn looked at Meuserbach. "What does that mean?"

"Germany is not like England or France, with a central government. We have many small princedoms though we all speak the same language."

"I didn't know that," Carson murmured.

Ahead of them, on one of the craggy hillsides, a lone armed Comanche had stepped out to be seen. Carson straightened in the saddle, staring at the Comanche. Out of the corner of his eye, Carson saw Meuserbach stiffen.

"Now," Quinn said in a lowered voice, "follow my lead. Say nothing, do nothing unless I tell you to." Then Quinn greeted the brave in Comanche and asked permission to meet with the chief of the band. As they followed the sentry toward the Comanche camp, Quinn added, "Also do anything I tell you to without hesitation."

"*Ja.*" The German's voice was tight.

Carson let Meuserbach precede him, and the three of them rode single file into the camp. It seemed that they had been expected, leading Carson to understand that the Comanche's appearance before the women at the river had indeed been an invitation to parlay. The Comanche were curious, but, as always, dangerous.

The head of the band was waiting for them outside his teepee, his arms folded, his expression proud and forbidding. The warm sun was high overhead now. Carson focused on what they had come to do: Make peace. Survive the parlay.

The tribe swiftly gathered around to watch the show. Quinn greeted the chief in solemn tones. His greeting was returned with curtness, a show of superiority. Quinn tried to introduce himself, but he was cut off. The chief had heard of the half-breed Cherokee Quinn. Carson thought dryly, *I'll bet they all have.*

The matter of the horse Quinn had stolen came up. Quinn dismissed it, saying that the marauders had been foolish to steal from him. It should be a lesson to the young braves to first find out who they were stealing from.

There was a tense pause after this. It ended with the chief's agreement that young men were often heedless.

The chief invited Quinn and his companions to dismount and sit with him. After the smoking of the ceremonial pipe and other courtesies, the chief asked about these new people who had come onto Comanche land. Just this winter, the Comanche had signed a treaty drawing a line between the *Comancheria* and Texas. Was Sam Houston allowing that treaty to be violated so soon?

Carson let the wind stroke his skin as he gazed at all the intent faces grouped around them. As usual, he couldn't stop himself from choosing which of the braves around him he should strike first if negotiations suddenly turned sour.

Quinn explained that the newcomers had come not from America but from a distant land over the far eastern sea, and that they wanted to live on the edge of the *Comancheria* and be good neighbors to the Penateka.

The chief looked thoughtful. Carson's hand didn't leave the rifle across his lap.

Then Quinn told the chief that this man Meuserbach, the leader of these people, had with him a sample of the many gifts he had brought to the Penateka from far away.

At his father's nod, Carson rose and went to the horses. He brought back two bulging saddlebags. Quinn said, "Meuserbach, please open the right one and draw out the shawl first. That will make a good impression."

The German drew out a fringed shawl made of fine red silk. The cloth caught the light and shimmered. Then, at Quinn's nod, Meuserbach drew out several intricately carved pipes, more fabrics—many of them intricate tapestries—and a few well-made knives. Each gift was greeted with increasing murmurs of approval. Then he pulled out a tightly bound wooden box. Opening it, he lifted out of the straw and paper packing the finest gilded wineglasses Carson had ever seen. The chief took one in his hand and marveled at it.

Then Meuserbach looked into the chief's eyes. "Quinn, I want to speak to the chief about why we have come. Please tell the chief that we have come this long way because life in Germany is too hard. There are too many people, not enough land or food. We have come all this way to find a place where we can live and raise our families."

Meuserbach waited until Quinn's translation ended. "After coming so far, we just want to settle down and farm the land. We do not live like the Comanche do, roaming free on horses, hunting buffalo. That is not our way. So that should make us good neighbors. But the Comanche were here first. So we must meet them and make an agreement to live side by side. In peace."

Listening to Quinn's translation, the chief studied Meuserbach and said nothing.

The German continued, "When I was young, I was a soldier. I commanded many other soldiers against the French, who attacked us. I won many battles. Not long ago I decided that the best way to protect my people was to find a better place for them."

Quinn nodded in agreement as he translated. Even Carson was impressed with the newcomer's argument.

Meuserbach gestured toward the articles he'd brought out. "If we can come to an understanding, I will bring many more gifts like these. The Comanche will go on living as they do. All we want is to live nearby in our way, but with respect. And, I hope, friendliness for our neighbors. Can this be?"

Seven

Soon Carson, Quinn, and Meuserbach mounted their horses and bid the chief a formal farewell. The chief had promised to consider the matter. At Quinn's suggestion, Meuserbach had packed up all the gifts, leaving only the knives and a few pieces of cloth as tokens of friendship. Carson rode out in the rear position, feeling the gazes of the band on his back like hot sun.

When they were out of earshot, Meuserbach asked, "What do you think? Will they decide to make peace with us?"

Quinn said, "Maybe. Maybe not. We did our best. I think the quality of the gifts and the fact that they were different from anything the Comanche had been offered by whites before made an impression."

"Yes," Carson joined in, "and your speech about how Germans live differently and how you had been a soldier was very good. It explained much to them but informed them that you shouldn't be dismissed as harmless." *A good fighter is the only kind of man they respect.*

The trip back took less time. They weren't tracking, and they wanted to get back to the settlement fast. The thought of a well-prepared meal beside a fire beckoned. Twilight had settled over the horizon when they sighted the smoke from many cooking fires. Finally, all Carson's tension slid down his neck and shoulders and vanished.

Just before they reached the camp, Meuserbach turned and looked Carson in the eye. "I will come to talk later. With you."

With me? Carson lifted an eyebrow. *What now?*

* * *

That evening a touch of spring dampness drew Carson nearer the fire. He sat motionless on a downed log, waiting for Meuserbach to come. He tried to calm the churning of his stomach. What did the German want to talk to him about?

Her face smudged from a day of play, Erin came out of the wikiup. She sat next to him and murmured, "I think Emilio, Mother and Father are discussing Sugar and him getting married. They told me to go outside and play. Why? I want Emilio to marry Sugar. I love weddings. Our *cocinera* will bake a special cake and cookies. And we'll have dancing and music."

Carson shrugged, trying to look interested in the wedding. Erin chattered on, discussing the possibility of a new dress for Sugar's wedding. The fire crackled. Carson added another log and a few branches. From a distance, he glimpsed Meuserbach coming toward the wikiup, working his way through the campfires, pausing here and there, answering greetings.

Mariel was of course by the Braun fire. Carson forced his gaze from her. Nearby, Tunney was flirting with the widow he'd taken a shine to, cutting wood for her fire and grinning. Carson wondered if this former Ranger, who must be near his father's age, would finally give up war and settle down here in this valley. For a moment, he imagined doing that himself. Yet that was not possible now with a war about to begin.

Meuserbach reached him. "*Guten Abend, mein Herr.*"

Carson waved the man to sit on the log beside him. "Erin, why don't you get your book from the wagon and read here by the fire. There are matters I need to discuss with Mr. Meuserbach." Lifting the kettle from the trivet at the edge of the fire, Carson poured a cup of coffee for himself and one for the German.

Erin looked as if she wanted to argue. However, she did as she was told, though he noted that she moved nearer the wikiup, probably trying to eavesdrop.

"I appreciate much your help and your father's today." Meuserbach accepted the cup. "We are much in your father's debt."

"My father is always ready to help." An owl hooted in the distance.

"He is a special man. He knows much. He does much."

The German's unexpected words hit Carson with a snap. This was a rare occurrence. White men rarely appreciated Quinn's expertise; they usually resented both it and Quinn unless they needed him. Somehow Meuserbach's words uncapped a well of words. Carson couldn't stop from saying, "When I had barely learned to walk and talk, my father began teaching me—how to track men and game, how to fight with my fists and sword, how to shoot a gun and bow, how to navigate my way by knowing the stars. He taught me sign language along with my first words of English. Then he taught me to speak Cherokee, Comanche, and Spanish." Recalling this, Carson's love and respect for his father warmed him, strengthened him.

Meuserbach shook his head ruefully. "Next to you, I am *ein Kind*, a child here."

"I know what you mean." Carson glanced at Erin, whose lips were moving as she read. "This land changes so swiftly that a man must know more, always learn more. In the thirty-five years since my parents settled here, Texas has gone from a Spanish colony to independent Mexico with a constitution to a Mexican dictatorship to free Republic of Texas and now a U.S. state. And a war may be about to start."

Meuserbach made a noise of surprise. "*Krieg*? War?"

"Yes, another war with Mexico." The word was a knot in Carson's chest. "Because of all this change, both my parents said I must be ready for anything. My mother taught me white manners, the Bible, and some Latin, along with history and Shakespeare. She told me I must learn both ways—the way of whites and the way of the frontier. You have just come here. I warn you don't expect this land to stay the same as it is now. It doesn't."

If war did come and Mexico won, would his parents lose their land, their home? *I won't let that happen*, Carson thought to himself.

Meuserbach sipped his hot coffee pensively and nodded.

Though worries of war gnawed Carson, he sensed that Meuserbach had something more he wanted to say, dreaded to say. Carson waited, listening to the muted voices rising and falling all around.

Finally the words came. "I hear there is a rumor about the widow Frau Wolffe."

Jolted, Carson forced himself to keep a straight face. "Oh?"

"Yes, some say that Frau Heller accused her of trying to . . ." The German had been speaking quickly before; but now he groped for words. ". . . lure her husband into . . . *Indiskretion*, indiscretion. Others say that she caused a fight between Heller and you over her favors." Meuserbach stared into his face.

Anger flamed up inside Carson. "That's ridiculous. Anyone can see that she is a good woman."

Meuserbach shrugged. "I think the same. Still, this will be a problem. I suggest to Herr Braun that he marry her and end the rumors. She seems to have become friends with your family."

The German studied Carson, as if wanting something, an explanation, a suggestion.

Carson didn't respond outwardly by so much as a blink. But chaos ripped through him. Why should Mariel have to marry a man she barely knew just because people liked to gossip? And the idea of Mariel belonging to another man . . . The sensation of kissing Mariel seared through him like the heat of an adobe oven.

"I thought you should be told," Meuserbach said as he rose. He handed Carson his empty cup, bid him an abrupt good night, and ambled away.

Carson gripped his tin cup tighter. In the shadowy distance, he watched Mariel bed down the two little Braun boys. Braun hovered nearby, casting worried glances toward Mariel. She rose from the children and gazed around. Everyone looked the other way. Carson felt the tin cup in his hand give; he'd squeezed it too hard. Lukewarm coffee splashed on his hand. He stood but halted. He almost went to her.

But he was still a man who served Texas. His Ranger captain would expect him back soon. His leave to go visit family was nearly spent. A possible war loomed. Perhaps, whether Mariel liked it or not, he should tell the truth publicly about what Heller had tried to do to her. Would that help or damage her reputation more?

Glancing over, he saw that Erin had fallen asleep with her book in her lap. He turned to the wikiup. What were his mother, father, Emilio, and Sugar discussing in there? If it had just been wedding plans, both he and Erin would have been included.

Though he'd turned his back, the image of Mariel flickered in Carson's thoughts. The memory of the kisses shared with her still gleamed inside, a private treasure. A fierce desire to do something for her flared within. Was there any way he could help Mariel, protect her?

* * *

When Mariel rose the next morning, which dawned warm and bright, she heard immediately that the Quinns would be leaving that day. She'd been anticipating their departure, trying to prepare herself to bear Carson's leaving. Yet tears still simmered just under the surface. Carson's departure would leave her alone to face the predicament that gossip had caused.

As she went through the motions of preparing for another day of caring for the little Braun boys, she tried to think of a solution. Only one occurred to her. *I must act. I must find someone who will let me room in their cabin when it is built.*

One by one, she considered each of the women in the party, trying to decide who would be most apt to show her kindness. She finally settled on Gretchen, one of the younger women in the party. Gretchen and Mariel had talked many times, and Mariel thought of her as more than an acquaintance but not quite a friend. After all, this woman was not a servant, as Mariel was.

Mariel said a prayer, then made her way through the encampment to Gretchen. "*Guten morgen*," Mariel said, trying to keep the quaver out of her voice.

Gretchen did not return the greeting.

Mariel's heart began skipping, and her face stiffened. "I have come to ask a favor." She hurried on before she lost her nerve. "May I room with you when your cabin is finished? I will work for—"

"*Nein.*"

Mariel stared at the woman. "Please. I—"

"You know why I cannot," Gretchen said. "Everyone is talking about what you have done to poor Frau Heller. And your shameless behavior—getting two men to fight over you. Do you want to ensnare my husband too?"

I did nothing. Mariel could not bring words up to her lips. She hurried away from all the merciless faces watching, glaring at her. Why did people believe nasty gossip? Had Frau Heller spread this tale to protect her husband? Or had it been Heller? Or was it just the maliciousness of people?

"Mariel! Frau Wolffe!" Mrs. Quinn's voice coming nearer stopped Mariel.

For a moment, Mariel just held herself still, composing herself. Then she turned, and Mrs. Quinn was there in front of her. "Yes, Mrs. Quinn?"

"I know we never had a chance to discuss this, but my husband and I would like you to come with us to our ranch and stay. We want you to teach Erin some German and about Europe."

At first Mariel couldn't believe what she had heard. Her ears rang. She nearly shook her head to clear them. "Truly?"

"Yes, you've been very kind to Erin. And we would like you to come home with us. You'll be paid, of course, and we'll provide for all your needs. There are very few teachers in Texas. I'm sure you would be able to find others who will wish you to teach their young when Erin's instruction is complete. Will you come? We are leaving within the hour."

Mariel gawked at the woman, shock vibrating through her. An hour? Less than an hour to decide to leave this place, this valley she had traveled from Germany to reach? "But I am not a teacher," Mariel objected, her mind racing.

Mrs. Quinn smiled. "I've listened to you speak and watched you. It is obvious that you weren't born to be a servant. You have received a good education somehow."

Yes, listening to my father tutor students in our home and sneaking into his library to read books—though he never guessed I was doing so. Mrs. Quinn patted her arm. "I'm sorry, so much keeps happening. Please. I would be so happy if you would say yes."

Mariel could barely breathe. "I will think on it."

"Good, but not long. Come to the wagon with your belongings as soon as possible." The woman smiled, then hurried away.

Mariel stood there near the surrounding fir trees, not moving, her mind in a whirl. Did she have a choice? If Gretchen, whom she'd thought of as almost a friend, wouldn't take her in, who would?

And what of Carson Quinn? Mariel couldn't look at him without recalling those stolen moments beside the fire not many days ago. How could she stay near him and not betray the fact that she was drawn to him?

Herr Heller came by, walking backwards and carrying one end of a newly notched log. He was heading for one of the cabins under construction. He sneered at her.

That was it. She turned away and walked to where she had been camping with the Brauns. She gathered up her meager belongings and headed toward the Quinns' wagon, her pulse speeding.

Herr Braun must have seen what she was doing, because he appeared beside her. She didn't slow her pace. She said, "I'm sorry, Herr Braun. Mrs. Quinn wants to hire me to help with her daughter and to teach her German."

"Are you sure this is what you want?" he asked, panting from running to catch her. "My proposal still stands. You can stay here with your own kind."

Mariel looked sideways, catching his eye. "My own kind?" *You mean the people who do nothing to protect me from a brute and mean-spirited gossip?* Her mouth twisted, but she could not stop herself from saying, "I will be better off with strangers."

Herr Braun pulled his purse out of his pocket and handed her several pieces of silver. "Here is your pay. I thank you for how good you've been to my sons."

Mariel paused, then accepted the payment. Herr Heller owed her money. But now all she wanted to do was to get away from this place, these gossips, even from this lovely valley where she had hoped she would make her home. "I wish you luck, Herr Braun."

"And I wish you the same." He bowed and then hurried away.

Mariel reached the Quinns, who were climbing onto the buckboard. "Mrs. Quinn."

The woman beamed at her. Before Mariel could say anything, Quinn jumped down from the buckboard seat and helped her up onto the back of it beside Erin. Sugar was riding behind the Ranger Emilio on his horse. Carson sat on his mount nearby. He pulled the brim of his hat toward her. Her stomach fluttered.

After the farewells ended, Mr. Quinn slapped the reins on the team. The buckboard started with a lurch, which mimicked the one Mariel's stomach took. As she looked back at the Germans she had traveled from Europe with, they became more and more distant. And then, as the wagon turned around a steep bend of trees, the people she'd known disappeared. She had experienced this sensation before. As she'd stood at the rail onboard the ship, watching the German shore recede and then disappear, she had felt the same way. Now again this feeling of no turning back rocked her, sucked away her breath. Tears flowed down her face.

Erin must have seen them, because she patted Mariel's arm and said, "Don't worry. You'll like our rancho. You will."

Mariel tried to smile, but she could only manage a weak imitation. Her ears were sharp enough to catch the jingle of Carson's spurs as he urged his mount forward. Would she always be so aware of him?

Closing her eyes, she drew in her tears and blinked away the moisture. Being near Carson Quinn and not showing her dawning feelings for him would be an exquisite torture. She had finally found what she was looking for: a good man to love. But he was the son of a landowner, and she would be a servant in his family's home. How could she have allowed this to happen? Yet when had hearts ever been obedient?

* * *

A few miles outside of New Braunfels, Mariel watched as Carson rode beside his friend. Emilio didn't look as pleased as a man who was going to be married soon should look. Emilio looked deeply worried.

Then, unexpectedly, Quinn slowed the team and stopped. "We need to talk."

Carson halted and looked to his father and mother. They looked somber also. "I can't do this," Sugar whispered.

Emilio slid from his saddle to the ground. He held up his hands to lift Sugar from her mount. She reached for him but with reluctance. Mariel couldn't help herself. She discreetly turned her attention to Carson, who was looking concerned. At Erin's insistence, Mariel also climbed down from the buckboard bed.

"Carson, we didn't have time to discuss this with you," Mrs. Quinn said. "Or to mention it to Mariel. But we are going to go back to the cabin near the Guadalupe River where we found Sugar as a little girl."

Sugar was staring down, muttering, "No, no, no."

"Sugar," Emilio coaxed, "this is for our good. You must face your fears. Or you will never be whole. Don't you see that?"

Sugar didn't reply; she merely stared at the ground.

"I love you, Sugar." Emilio took her hands in his. "I have asked you to marry me. You have said yes. Your parents have given us their blessing. As I am sure my parents will. I want you whole and free of the past."

Sugar tried to bolt. Emilio caught her wrists firmly, yet with obvious regard. "Don't run, *mi dulce*." She struggled only a moment, then pressed her face into Emilio's shoulder. "The war is coming, *mi amor*, and I'm sure the Rangers will be wanted and needed. No Anglos or *Tejanos* know Texas and northern Mexico better than we Rangers do. The fancy American general will need us—even if he does not realize that yet. I cannot leave you if I fear that you are not whole, not ready to face whatever comes."

Mariel knew what he was saying. He was telling Sugar that he might be killed and he did not want to leave her in this fragile condition. And that meant that Carson might have to go to war too. War. Mariel had known unrest but not outright war. The thought of Carson riding into battle clutched her lungs, almost squeezing the breath from her.

Quinn cleared his throat. "Sugar, Emilio is right. We are all going with you, the whole family and the man who will make you his wife. You will not face this alone."

Mariel captured her lower lip with her teeth. Did Sugar know how wonderful it was to have her family care about her?

Sugar lifted her eyes to her father's. She gazed at him solemnly for a long time. "I'm frightened."

Dorritt took her husband's hand. "We know that, but the fear you carry is from the past. What happened then cannot truly hurt you. It won't change the way we feel about you—"

"Or the way I feel about you," Emilio cut in.

"Sugar," Carson said, "I've been back there many times—"

Sugar glanced up, eyes wide. "You have?"

"Yes, and from the day I carved those words about you into the tree telling where you could be found, I've never discovered anyone there. Or any evidence that anyone has been there—except for wayfarers or squatters. I don't think your family survived the Revolution."

"Yes," Dorritt spoke up, "that woman in Montezuma said that your mother is dead. Your father may have gone to battle with Houston—"

"Or with General Fannin to Goliad," Quinn added.

"If any of your family had survived, wouldn't they have come looking for you at Rancho Sandoval?" Carson asked. "You're afraid of ghost memories of people who have passed on. They can't hurt you from the grave."

"Memories can hurt you only if you let them," Dorritt said.

"Yes, it is best to face the truth." Mariel heard herself say these words, then she pressed a hand over her mouth. What was she thinking—speaking like a member of the family? "I beg pardon, sir and lady." She lowered her eyes to the ground. Her face flamed.

"You don't need to apologize for speaking the truth," Carson said.

"And we're not 'sir' and 'lady,'" Quinn said. "I'm just Quinn and Dorritt is plain Mrs. Quinn or Señora Quinn. We aren't fancy."

Mariel nodded, still looking down, more puzzled by this unusual family.

"Sugar, will you try?" Emilio asked. "Will you do this for me?"

* * *

They rode southeast all that day, camped overnight, and reached Gonzales on the Guadalupe River. After some shopping in the small town, they set out again. The morning sun was warm and glinting all around. Riding behind Emilio, Sugar tried to brace herself for what was to come. Each mile towed her closer to the cabin, to her shadowy past. Each mile affected her like a rock dropped into a well, a well with no bottom. It was like being pulled down, falling through air and never landing.

That dreadful distant, disconnected feeling began creeping over her. Only Emilio's touch brought her back, linked her to today, to the dirt trail they rode over together. Sugar concentrated on the present—the clip-clop of the horses; the cloud of fine dust kicked up by their hooves, which got into her eyes and up her nose; the heat from the high sun on her shoulders. The spring rains had abated, and now the dry summer had begun.

A high, sweet voice was singing a strange but pretty song. Sugar glanced over at Mariel, who must be singing to Erin in German. The two of them were riding in the back of the buckboard. Sugar caught Carson looking at the pretty woman. The inclusion of Mariel on this journey shouldn't have surprised her. She'd seen her mother speculating while observing Carson watch Mariel. Could Mariel heal Carson's broken heart?

The momentary distraction ended. The meadow and trees felt familiar, perilously familiar. She took in a deep breath, or tried to. Her lungs seemed to have shrunk.

They turned a bend. There, through the trees, was the cabin. As she stared at the abandoned cabin, Sugar's ears began to fill with the familiar humming. The cabin's roof had given way in places. The door hung on one hinge. Here in the yard wild chickens screeched and ran from them.

"Sugar," Emilio spoke to her in a stern voice, "do not let your ears close. Tell yourself that you must do this. For me. For you. For our life together."

She heard his words; they didn't work. The buzzing grew as she let him help her down from his horse. On the ground, they faced each other. He murmured comforting phrases in Spanish and English. Sugar clung to the sound of Emilio's voice as if it was a lifeline, trying to let it overcome the buzzing.

Emilio took her arm. "We will walk around and see if there is anything here that causes you to remember—"

A sharp voice in Sugar's head began chiding her. Sugar couldn't catch the individual words, just the feeling of being scolded as a child. The woman was angry with her. Little Sugar wouldn't do what the woman wanted. Sugar put a hand to her cheek, feeling the sting of a long-ago slap.

The cabin reached out and drew Sugar in. She pulled away from Emilio, walking toward it. As she stepped to the open door, she began to hear more voices of people who weren't there. The words were muffled, and the voices told her they were Pa and Auntie. "No, no, don't go. Don't leave me." Sugar heard her own voice. It shocked her. She tried to turn and run again.

Emilio caught her. "I won't leave you."

"Not you. *He's* leaving me." She pressed her face into Emilio's broad shoulder. Images, voices jumbled in her mind, and the buzzing tried to shut them out.

"Who's leaving you?" Emilio murmured next to her ear.

And she knew the answer. "Pa. My pa is leaving me."

"Left you, you mean," Emilio gently corrected her. "This is from the past. You are not the little girl whose father left her. You are Sugar, daughter of Quinn and betrothed to me, Emilio Ramirez. You know that, *si?*"

Sugar nodded. Clinging to Emilio and listening to his firm, honest voice was keeping her from slipping into the numbness, the deafness. She swallowed, clearing her throat and ears. "I'm feeling the sadness . . . the feeling of losing, being lost. This wasn't a happy place for me." Sugar looked over Emilio's shoulder to the buckboard.

Her father helped her mother down from the bench. "Of course it wasn't," her mother said. "That year, 1836, was not a happy year. Texas won its independence, but many people died, lost loved ones. It was a hard year."

Sugar nodded. Her father Quinn had fought in that war, and so had Carson. She wanted to plead with Emilio to let them leave now. She had no desire to go any further into the past. Her parents walked closer.

Dorritt gently stroked stray hair away from Sugar's face. "Do you think you can go inside?"

Eight

"Do I have to?" Sugar asked, sounding like a child again.

Hating how this was distressing her, Carson slid from his horse. He resolutely turned his back to the buckboard, where Erin and Mariel had just alighted. Even with his back turned, he felt the pull toward the delicate but resilient widow. He forced himself to concentrate on his younger sister. And her pain. It tugged at him.

"Sugar," Emilio replied for Dorritt, "*sí*, you must go in. I will stay beside you. You may leave any time you wish. Still, I think it is important for you to go in."

Sugar looked into Emilio's eyes, then nodded. "All right," she whispered.

Carson joined his parents as they escorted Sugar and Emilio into the abandoned cabin. The dirt floor was thick with dust, dried leaves, old mice nests, and shattered branches that had been blown inside. Carson halted just inside the door. The decayed cabin smelled of animal droppings and was distinctly un-welcoming.

Ahead, Sugar stood in the center of the small one-room house with its sagging loft. Carson shifted on his feet, ready for anything. Sugar had always been fragile.

His mind drew him back a decade ago to that terrible journey here. He'd only been fourteen when he'd found the *vaqueros* from the Rancho Sandoval murdered. His insides tightened at the memory. He'd become a man that day—like it or not. His path had been set. He'd become a man of war, not a man of peace.

Within hours of finding the *vaqueros* dead, he and his mother had set out to find his father, right when all of Texas had been racing toward the eastern border, fleeing before the Mexican Army. At Santa Anna's orders, the army had been burning and looting along the way. Carson and his mother had happened upon this empty cabin their second night.

Then Carson gulped air as he recollected the panicky sound of his mother calling him. He'd burst into the cabin to find only a little girl cowering in a corner. Sugar had looked up and run to him. She'd thrown her arms around him. And suddenly he remembered.

"You called me 'Pa.'"

Everyone turned to him. He blinked. "Ma and I got this far and decided to rest here. She was expecting Erin then and was real tired. She lay down, and I went to gather firewood and see if I could catch one of the chickens left behind to cook for supper. I heard Ma yell, and I ran in here. Sugar, you were crouched over there," he said, pointing toward the corner farthest from him. "When I picked you up, you said, 'Pa,' just once, and then you didn't speak again till weeks later. Do you remember?"

Sugar faced him, looking stunned. "Yes, I remember. I thought you were my pa, then I realized you weren't." She paused to swallow. "And when I couldn't hear what you were saying to me, I just froze up. I thought something had happened to my ears . . . because I was bad."

"You were bad?" Dorritt repeated.

Sugar's face contorted. "That's what I remember. I had been bad. She . . ." Sugar looked away. "She said I'd been bad."

Like Carson, no one pressed Sugar about who "she" was. Sugar's agitation and fear were plain to all.

"And I saw," Sugar continued haltingly, "that Carson wasn't pa, and the buzzing in my ears came. I couldn't hear." She shivered. "Please, can I leave this place? I don't like it here." Her voice became fretful. "I can't see anything that has been left behind here that might tell us about me."

Quinn and Dorritt nodded. But Sugar waited until Emilio nodded. Then he led her out. Their parents looked around some more. Finally, shaking their heads, they walked out. Carson stood alone in the musty wreck of a cabin. As he turned to go, out of the corner of his eye, something made him stop.

Something wasn't right. He stared at the crumbling hearth. It looked like someone had taken away some of the smooth round river stones. And around one corner of the fireplace, just barely visible where the mortar had cracked, was something that looked like it might be a piece of paper. Carson walked over and began chipping out the rest of the mortar with the butt of his knife.

Then he lifted out one river rock, and there was a packet of letters tied together with a faded pink ribbon. He held the slender bundle in one hand. It was light, but it might hold the power to heal or wound his dear younger sister. He debated.

On the one hand, he couldn't withhold something like this— even if it caused Sugar pain. The truth must always be faced. He had faced the truth about Blanche—at last.

On the other hand, that had wounded him deeply. He didn't want what might be in these letters to injure, to scar, Sugar.

Undecided, he scanned the hearth and the remaining walls with deliberation to make sure that he had not overlooked anything else the original dwellers might have left behind, any clue that might be of significance to Sugar.

At a call from his father, Carson walked swiftly to the door. Shoving the packet inside his buckskin jacket, he hurried out into the warm, fresh sunlight.

"Find anything else?" his father asked.

To avoid lying, Carson shrugged. "Let's go." The packet rubbed against his chest and against his conscience. He'd deal with this soon, after some thought.

Quinn nodded and helped Dorritt back up onto the buckboard bench. Carson swung Erin into the back, then turned to find Mariel standing there. He lifted her into the wagon just as he had Erin, then he strode toward his horse. He could walk away from her, but he couldn't shake the feel of her small, soft waist within his palms.

Carson swung into his saddle and headed down the rutted trail to the main road. He didn't look back. He decided it would be best to show the letters to his parents privately and let them decide what must be done. Emilio and Sugar were happy now, in love. Ready to start their lives together. But for how long would they remain untouched by the world?

Carson kept thinking of Zachary Taylor's U.S. troops camped along the Rio Grande. The Mexicans had never recognized that river as the boundary between Texas and Mexico. They had always insisted that the Nueces River farther north was the boundary.

An American army on the Rio Grande could be there for only two reasons: either to provoke an attack or to prevent one. Which motive had prompted President Polk to send troops? Whichever it had been, fresh hostilities were ahead. Waiting for them to begin was like watching someone set a match to a firecracker with a long, but concealed, fuse.

* * *

Asleep in the wikiup, Mariel opened her eyes. It was deep night, too dark to see anything clearly. She lay beside Erin. What had awakened her? Then she heard low voices just outside the tent. Carson was speaking. All that evening near the fire, Carson had been agitated—restless and hard-jawed—about something. Now he muttered, "I didn't want to keep anything from Sugar, but I didn't want to upset her more."

"We can understand that," Mrs. Quinn replied.

Mariel turned her face toward the voices. The low campfire still glowed enough to cast four standing shadows—Carson, his parents, and Emilio. Did this discussion have anything to do with their visit to that deserted cabin?

"You found these letters tucked into the stones of the fireplace?" Quinn asked. He was holding something out in front of him—probably the letters he was talking about, letters from the cabin.

"Did you read them?" Mrs. Quinn asked.

"No." Carson's answer was sharp and short. "They are not my letters. You are our parents. I wanted you to decide whether and when to give these to Sugar."

"They might have nothing to do with her," Emilio said, his tone brisk, his hands settling on his waist.

"That's true," Mrs. Quinn said, but so low Mariel barely heard her. "I will read one letter and see if they are connected with the McLaughlins or that Ida Rose or Violet that woman in Montezuma mentioned." Mrs. Quinn moved toward the fire. Again, Mariel marveled at this family's love for one another, as well as the fact that they did not treat people differently because of their station or skin color.

After reading for a few moments, Mrs. Quinn rose. "This letter is addressed to Ida Rose, and it's from her sister Violet. It was written in April 1834. That was two years before the Revolution."

"So these do concern Sugar's *familia*," Emilio said, sounding aggrieved. Their loving acceptance of this man was more evidence of how they differed from the common way. In Germany, no parents would have agreed to such a mixed marriage.

"I will pack these away," Mrs. Quinn said, her voice stronger. "I will then give them to Sugar when she wants to read them. I think we've forced her to go as far as she can right now. Some memories are so painful that people block them out as if they didn't happen."

The men nodded. The four of them turned back toward the wikiup. Hastily Mariel turned her head the other way, not wishing to be caught eavesdropping. And just before she closed her eyes, she saw that Sugar's eyes were open, shining in the darkness. Had she heard, or was she only half awake? Mariel waited, but Sugar closed her eyes without speaking.

The other four entered the tent and, with little noise, slipped back into their bedding. Mariel pretended to be asleep. Would what the letters contained hurt or heal Sugar?

Sugar made Mariel feel both sympathy and envy. Mariel had known her parents, but she had never felt close to them. Sugar had a loving family and a man who loved her. Mariel drew in a deep breath. She had no right to feel envy. The Quinns had saved her from a very nasty situation. She was so grateful not to have been forced into a second loveless marriage. Yet what could she do to help them in this difficulty? Nothing.

Here she lay on the unrelenting earth beside the little girl, knowing that she could do nothing for Sugar, nothing for Carson. He avoided being alone with her. He must regret kissing her. That was the worst of all. Tears slid from her eyes, and she let them flow. Her mother's voice came to mind: *"Life is what it is, Mariel."* But her grandmother's words took the sting from those words with, *"The humble shall inherit the land . . . and an abundance of peace."*

* * *

At the end of the next, even warmer, day, Mariel glimpsed San Antonio ahead. Weeks had passed since she had been in Galveston. Now the sight of a town bigger than one lone street made her uncomfortably aware of her tenderness from days spent bouncing over a rough trail in the back of the wagon. It also made her aware of her bedraggled appearance. Her shoes were nearly worn through, top and sole. Her clothing was wrinkled and shabby. Fearing her cheeks might be smudged with dirt, she wiped her face in vain with a soiled handkerchief.

Telling them that he would meet them soon at the *posada*, Carson turned away from his parents' buckboard, then went down a side street. What was a *posada*? Mariel forced herself not to watch Carson ride away. Or wonder why and where he was going. Instead, she looked down at the little girl beside her, trying to focus on her.

Erin began to point out the sights. "That's the Alamo, where the Mexicans killed Jim Bowie, Davy Crockett, and Colonel Travis. That was before I was born. That's where the Spanish, then the Mexican, governor used to live. And that's St. Fernando's church. And this is the shop where we buy . . ."

Once again, Mariel glanced at Sugar riding with Emilio. She looked the same today as she had yesterday—very subdued, seeking support from Emilio. Last night's overheard conversation had repeated and repeated itself in Mariel's mind. Mariel wished she hadn't woken and heard it. All day she'd tried to decide whether Sugar had overheard what had been said or not. This question had kept Mariel somber all day. Yet her stomach had not settled down since she'd left New Braunfels. Was there peace anywhere?

The buckboard turned into a street that was especially pretty with many pink, white, and blue flowers hanging in baskets and growing in window boxes. How soon flowers blossomed full and lush here! It was only the first week of May. Already the plants looked the way flowers did in summer in Germany. Mr. Quinn pulled up in front of a building that looked like it must be an inn. It was covered in something she had never seen, which looked rather like dried mud painted a dark yellow. Mr. Quinn went inside while Mrs. Quinn stood under the overhanging roof of the inn, out of the sun. Was *posada* an inn then?

"Mama, are we going to go shopping tomorrow?" Erin asked.

"No, we probably should, but all I want to do is go home tomorrow." Mrs. Quinn sounded weary.

"You said we would shop in San Antonio on our way home from the wedding," the little girl complained as she climbed down from the wagon and went to her mother.

Following the little girl, Mariel could see that Mrs. Quinn was very tired. At last, a chance for her to do something for the lady. Helping her new mistress was difficult, because the lady behaved as if Mariel was just another member of the family. "Erin," Mariel said, bending and cupping Erin's chin, "your mother said this before she knew you would be . . . so long away. She did not know that Germans would come and take so much time. You see?"

Erin looked glum but nodded.

"And you want to get home? You say your pony misses you, *ja*?" Even as she spoke, she wondered how long her time with this kind family would last. This thread of uncertainty kept Mariel tied to the miserable past.

Erin brightened at the mention of her pony and nodded. "I miss Sundown. You'll like him. We will get you a horse, and we'll go riding every day."

A horse for Mariel? No, there would be no horse for a servant. "Oh, Erin, I never ride horse."

"Never?" Erin looked shocked.

Mariel shook her head. "Never. My family did not own horse."

"Then how did you get around?"

"We walk and sometime ride boat." Facing the inn with her back to the street, Mariel sensed Carson returning to them. She recognized the sound of his spurs and the gait of his horse. This was a dangerous realization. *I must not think of him so much.* Still, her disobedient heart skipped and hopped.

He dismounted and tied his horse to the hitching post just as Quinn came out and waved them all inside. "I have gotten us all rooms, requested baths, and have secured a private dining room for our supper."

Each word was instantly welcome to Mariel. And she wasn't disappointed. This must have been the best inn—*posada*—in San Antonio. It was surprisingly clean. Plus it was open and airy, not at all like the snug inns of Germany. Quinn had obtained a room for her, Erin, and Sugar across from theirs. The bathtub was brought in and filled almost immediately by servants chattering in Spanish, all sounding excited to see the Quinns again.

Mariel was a bit shy, but the maid was helpful, and soon all three of them took a turn in the tub. Mariel and Sugar scrubbed Erin's back and made sure that her hair was well washed and rinsed with water that smelled of rare lemons. But perhaps lemons weren't rare in this place.

Mariel felt gloriously clean and alive. Behind a screen, she slipped out of the large linen towel and donned her last clean set of underclothing. Before she could bear to put on her horribly wrinkled and shabby dress, a knock came and then a woman burst into the room. She spoke rapid Spanish. Mariel peeked around the painted wooden screen.

On one of the beds, the woman was laying out brightly colored embroidered dresses—a small one in red and two larger ones, a turquoise blue and a deep pink. Sugar and Erin were chatting in Spanish, touching the cotton dresses and exclaiming over them.

Erin turned to Mariel. "Look! From her shop across the street, Señora Ortiz saw us come to the *posada*, and she brought us new dresses."

Sugar smiled, suddenly looking happier than she had for days. "We always go to her dress shop. She is the best *Tejano* dressmaker in San Antonio. See how the dresses are in the Mexican style, loose and cool. Here." Sugar looked at the dresses and chose the turquoise blue one. "Try this on. It should fit you."

Señora Ortiz eyed Mariel and asked questions in rapid Spanish. Sugar replied for Mariel, who stood with the new cotton dress in her hands. She didn't know what the dress would cost, and she didn't need a new dress; she just needed to wash her old one. "I cannot afford—"

"This is our gift to you," Mrs. Quinn said, entering. She was already wearing a new dress, one in ivory with pink and blue embroidering around the neck and yoke. "Come." She clapped her hands. "Everyone put on the new dresses and come down. Dinner is waiting. We are nearly home, and we will not be camping on the trail again this year!"

Before Mariel's eyes, Erin and Sugar slipped new dresses over their cotton chemises and petticoats. The red dress looked beautiful next to Erin's dark hair and lightly tanned complexion. Sugar's waiflike charm made the pink dress even more striking.

Hesitantly, Mariel slipped into the turquoise dress, pulling together the gathered yoke and tying it high. The dress was very light, very cool. The feeling of being clean, wearing a new dress, one more vividly colorful than she'd ever worn, triggered unaccustomed self-confidence and joy. And the freedom she felt from not wearing a corset almost made her giddy. She couldn't help smiling. Or help thinking that she was happy that Carson would see her in this dress. A sad thought—that Carson was not for the likes of her—tried to snatch this joy away, but she refused, pushing it away.

In the private dining room, Quinn, Carson, and Emilio waited by the table. The master seated his lady; Emilio seated Sugar; Carson seated his sister. Mariel waited to be told where she should go to eat, her joy evaporating.

"Mariel," Carson said, "come here so I can seat you."

Mariel looked up. Everyone was looking toward her and waiting. Uncertain, she moved toward Carson, feeling jerky, like a puppet in the hands of an amateur puppeteer. Sitting around a campfire eating with this family was different from being invited to a table where she would be served as a member of the family. She let Carson seat her, and when his hands brushed her shoulders, her heart pounded.

The master said grace, then the inn's servants, who must have been of Mexican descent like Emilio, brought out large bowls of food the like of which Mariel had never seen. A bowl of beans in a thick sauce, sliced oranges sweetened with some liqueur, shredded beef and chicken in savory sauces, and curious flat cakes that everyone used to fold the beans and meat together. Mariel tried a bite of everything and found the food tasty but much spicier than any she had ever eaten. And such new flavors. Who knew that such food existed?

All through the meal, her eyes strayed to Carson, who sat at the foot of the table. Mariel did not speak except to reply to questions. Sitting here in the midst of this loving family made her suffer her loneliness more than ever. She glanced around the table and realized that Carson was as quiet as she was. Then she made the mistake of looking into his eyes. He was looking at her with an intensity that was at once both thrilling and overwhelming.

A man entered. "Señor Carson!" He carried a newspaper. "The newspaper you requested was just delivered. The courier from Austin was later than usual."

Mariel surmised that when Carson had left them earlier, he

must have gone to buy a newspaper. Mariel chewed a bite of chicken, glancing around at the sudden change on each face. Evidently no one expected the newspaper to bring good news. She swallowed and put her fork down.

Carson scanned it. Then he looked up. "There's been fighting between the U.S. Army and Mexicans on the Rio Grande."

Emilio, Quinn, and Dorritt began discussing whether this would start a war. Carson, his face buried in the paper, made no comment unless asked a direct question. Mariel hazarded another glance at him. He looked deeply troubled, and her heart quailed. Would Emilio and Carson have to go off to fight? Would the peace of this loving family be destroyed by war?

These good people didn't deserve that. And she knew something of government's taking action: one was never the same. At home, there had been not a fighting war but a political one over freedom, of democracy. Her husband had been arrested for sedition and taken away. She had never seen him again; he had died in prison.

She hadn't loved Dieter, but she would never have wished such a lonely, shameful death on anyone. Now the image of Carson riding off and being killed far away in a war emptied the breath from her. *Mein Gott, nein, bitte, nein.* The rest of her grandmother's verses came back to her, "But the humble shall inherit the earth; and shall delight themselves in the abundance of peace. . . ." Abundance of peace seemed far from them. Could the war pass them by?

Nine

The midnight breeze was cool on Carson's face. With his head down and his hands in his pockets, he walked with Emilio through the dark, quiet streets of sleeping San Antonio. A sweet scent of oleander alerted him that they were nearing the *posada*, with all its flowers. The deceptive peace of the setting contrasted with the restless flame inside him. A war was coming. Or might have actually started.

"Will you go to war?" Emilio said, halting just inside the glow of the oil lamp burning in the large arched window beside the *posada* entrance.

Carson turned the question back on Emilio. "Are you so sure that the U.S. Army will want the Rangers or need us?" Remembering Blanche's brother's scorn added a layer of sarcasm to his words. "We're just Indian fighters. What do we know of war?"

"You know of war firsthand," Emilio pointed out.

Carson shrugged this dart away, trying to ignore the shifting currents within. "San Jacinto lasted around eighteen minutes. That's all I know of war." *All I ever wanted to know.*

"Yes, and why would the U.S. Army want me, who they would see not as a loyal *Tejano* but as a Mexican?" Emilio let his irritation color his tone. "I am sure I am not white enough for General Taylor."

Dampened, Carson said nothing. Eyebrows had been raised when Emilio, a *Tejano*, had joined the Rangers. But Jack Hays had been a fair man, who had let Emilio show him what he could do with a horse, lariat, gun, and knife.

Emilio asked, "Why did Señora Quinn ask the German widow to come to your rancho?"

Carson's whole body clenched, remembering those kisses he'd shared with Mariel. He did not reply.

For once, Emilio did not push for an answer. "We must get to bed," Emilio said, linking his arm in Carson's and drawing him into the inn. Carson let himself be pulled along—though he feared he might lie awake all night, thinking of war, thinking of Mariel.

The innkeeper sat nodding in a chair by the door almost asleep. Without a word, he got up and dropped a bar across the inn door. Then he lifted a lamp and carried it high as the three of them climbed the stairs. At the door of Carson and Emilio's room, he lit a candle in a pewter holder and offered it to them. They both wished him a quiet *"Buenas noches."* The innkeeper nodded and walked away with the lamp.

Lifting the candle holder high, Carson let Emilio enter first. He paused and cast a glance at the door of the room where his sisters and Mariel were no doubt sound asleep. Then he turned his back and entered the room. What would come, would come. Until events took shape, he would go home and forget the war. And think of the pretty fair-haired widow—if he dared.

* * *

On the third day since arriving at the Quinn home, Mariel still felt as if she was living in a waking dream. The Quinns' sprawling one-story log ranch house was a place filled with sunlight and laughter, so different from any she had ever known. She had noticed that now that Sugar was in her own home again, she had either forgotten or had been able to put away her distress over her unknown family. This didn't surprise Mariel. She too had trouble recalling how miserable her last few days in New Braunfels had been. Here, the past lost its sting. Still, something bothered her. Sitting at the large round table in the main room of the house at breakfast this warm May morning, she had to ask the question she had been worrying about since she'd arrived here. She wouldn't feel right until she did.

"Emilio should return around noon with his parents," Sugar murmured, interrupting Mariel's thoughts. "They will want to . . ." Her voice faltered as she blushed.

"As is the Spanish custom, he'll want to formally ask for your hand," Quinn finished for her.

Mariel finished the last bite of her scrambled eggs, which had been served with a spicy red sauce. She wondered if she'd ever get used to how the food tasted here. It was good, but so different. Just as it had been at the inn, she was expected to sit at the table with the family at meals. A maid came forward and whisked away Mariel's plate. As she had expected, there were many servants here. *Why am I not counted among them?*

Mariel wondered at the haste of this wedding. Of course, the war to their south explained all. Something shriveled inside when Mariel thought of lighthearted Emilio and gallant Carson going away to face a faraway battle. Would they?

The meal was nearly over; the plates were being taken away, and everyone was sipping one last cup of coffee. Mariel must somehow persuade her new mistress to give her some duties so she didn't feel so beholden. She had tried to broach this subject many times, but Mrs. Quinn always brushed it aside. Perhaps her mistress wouldn't dismiss her question if she approached her when everyone was assembled. Mariel gathered her nerve.

When there was a lull in the conversation about the upcoming wedding, Mariel murmured, "Ma'am." Too low. She cleared her throat and tried again. "Ma'am?"

Mrs. Quinn turned to Mariel with a smile. "Yes, Mariel?"

"I begin Erin's lessons today, *bitte?*"

Erin jumped up. "It's summer! I don't have lessons in the summer!"

Mariel was shocked at the little girl's lack of decorum. To set a good example, Mariel sought to discourage such behavior. "Erin," she scolded in a whisper, "you must not speak that way to your mother."

Quinn chuckled, as did the other men. Mariel blushed. How could she teach this girl how to behave when the other adults allowed her so much freedom? Of course she could not say this. That would be disrespectful of her.

"Mariel, we allow our children to speak and to express what they are feeling," Mrs. Quinn said, laying her napkin beside her plate. "However, you are quite right that Erin shouldn't speak with such heat. Erin, you may question us, but politely, please."

Mariel kept her lips pursed together. She had always been taught that children were to be seen and not heard. Certainly that had been how she had spent her bleak childhood.

"I'm sorry, Mother, Father," Erin said in a sweeter tone. "Will I be having lessons?"

Mariel said nothing. She was not Erin's parent. What was it like to have parents who wanted to know what a child was thinking, feeling?

"Not regular lessons," Mrs. Quinn replied. "But we want Mariel to teach you German as you go about with her."

In light of all the Quinns had done for her, this seemed such a paltry duty. Mariel tried to think how to put this into polite words. And failed.

"That sounds like fun," Erin said with a little hop. "I want to ride Sundown again today, and I want Mariel to go with me this time."

Mariel nearly held up her hand to silence the child, but she didn't. "I do not ride, Erin. I told you before."

"Then you must learn," Carson spoke up. "You will come out to the corral, and I'll teach you how to ride a horse. Sugar, please loan Mariel one of your riding skirts."

Mariel sent an appealing look to her mistress, but Dorritt nodded her approval along with Quinn. Though queasy at the thought of mounting such a large animal, Mariel forced herself to smile also.

The maids whisked the last of the dishes and linens from the table. Sugar led Mariel and Erin to her room, where she offered Mariel a dark navy blue heavy cotton skirt that had been split and sewn into two very wide legs. Mariel had never seen the like of it before.

"Mother came up with this idea." Sugar grinned. "We wear riding habits if we ride off our own land. Just at home, these make more sense. And besides, if you haven't ridden before, learning to ride sidesaddle would make it all much harder."

Feeling numb, Mariel said nothing; she just exchanged the dress she was wearing for the white blouse and strange dark riding skirt Mrs. Quinn had designed. She also put on a leather hat and gloves. Yesterday, Mrs. Quinn and a seamstress had taken Mariel's measurements, and another new dress—this time in the Anglo style—had been ordered. Mariel had offered to sew the dress herself, but she had been ignored. A cobbler on the ranch was also making Mariel a pair of short boots and a pair of sandals. Sandals—she'd never even seen or heard of this kind of shoe before. And now they expected her to ride a horse. Her nerves jittery, she took Erin's hand and let the little girl lead her out to the corral.

Carson was there, waiting for them, leaning against the railing. He pulled at his hat brim politely, then motioned toward the horse on the other side of the railing. "I chose our gentlest mare. She won't give you any trouble."

Mariel knew that his encouraging tone and smile were meant to ease her fear. Their gentlest mare looked enormous even from this side of the fence. Mariel's heart seemed to expand and contract. Erin tugged her around the side of the corral, and Carson lifted the bar holding the entry closed. The three of them entered.

"Erin, why don't you go and saddle up Sundown?" Carson urged.

"But I want—"

"Go saddle up Sundown. Miss Mariel needs to learn this on her own. Without spectators."

Erin grimaced but trotted toward the adjoining barn.

Mariel had noticed that while Erin was permitted to speak freely, she was not allowed to disobey an elder. That was good.

"All right, then, let's get started," he said as he led her into the corral. "You always mount on the left side, or 'near side,' of the horse. Gather the reins in your left hand, put your left foot in the stirrup"—he paused to touch the piece of metal hanging down from the saddle—"and be careful not to hit the horse with your right foot as you swing on."

Mariel nodded, her mouth growing dryer by the moment.

"You only need to remember to sit straight and tall in the saddle, hold your reins steady and low, put the balls of your feet in the stirrups, and keep your heels low. All right?"

Mariel nodded again. Her ability to voice words had ended.

Then he lowered his arms and knit his fingers together like

a stirrup. "Put your foot here and I'll toss you into your saddle. It will make it easier for you at first. Be ready to swing your leg over."

Mariel's jaw had locked. She could not change her expression, so she nodded a third time, beginning to feel like a porcelain doll with a painted smile. She put her foot on his hands and— swoop—she was up and on the horse. The mare didn't behave as if she'd even noticed that a person now sat astride her.

Light-headed, Mariel took deep, calming breaths. She felt very high up and very precarious perched in the saddle. Still, she tried to follow Carson's instructions, straightening her spine, relaxing her arms so they were low and steady.

Carson went about tightening something around the horse and setting Mariel's feet into stirrups. Then he adjusted them. "To start the horse walking, gently squeeze her with both legs." She obeyed and the horse moved, making Mariel's pulse jump ahead of the horse. Carson walked the mare around the corral a few times. He showed Mariel how to turn the horse and how to stop it by pulling—gently and evenly—on the reins.

And then he insisted that she do it on her own. The mare still felt huge underneath her, though her initial terror was giving way. The mare's even pace and instant obedience were pumping up Mariel's confidence.

Her heart slowed some, along with her breathing, though still not enough to make her comfortable. Then Carson whistled for his horse. Soon the three of them were riding at a walk—for Mariel's sake—away from the hacienda. Soon Erin, on her pony, jogged ahead of them. As Mariel's mare moved slowly and surely, she tried to get accustomed to the gentle rolling motion.

"You're doing fine," Carson said.

Mariel did not look directly at him. "I must seem stupid to you, sir."

He grimaced and shook his head at her slip. No one here

wanted to be called sir or madam. "I'm sure if I went to Germany, there would be things that you would need to teach me."

She tried to imagine a man like Carson striding down the streets in Stuttgart. He didn't fit that setting at all. Lately he had begun to tie his hair into the beginning of a tail at the back of his neck like his father. Why? It made him look more dangerous somehow. And different from the other Rangers, Tunney and Emilio. She gave up trying to guess his reason for this. "You would not like it in Germany, I think."

"You mean they would not like me there, don't you?"

She looked into his face then—a mistake, because he had such an endearing, teasing look in his eyes. She looked away quickly, her heart bouncing again. "There are good men in Germany too."

"But not like me."

She glanced at him. "This place . . . this Texas . . . this ranch . . ." She found it hard, in her limited English, to find words to express how she felt. "It is all so big." These phrases were so inadequate. She hung her head.

"Yes, people from the East always say that. But I'm used to the open sky and the land without people for miles and miles. They also say it's a lonely place. But it's home to me."

More than his words came through to her. "You love this place."

"Yes, but . . ." He fell silent.

His hesitance broke her insecurity. Words that she had held back for many days came bubbling up to the surface. "I have never known a place like this, a family like yours. Your mother has been so kind to me. I want to help her, but she . . . tell me not what to do." She closed her lips. She had said too much.

"My mother wanted you here to keep Erin company and teach her German and about Europe. That's enough for you to do."

"I can do more than that. I am used to working—"

Carson reached out and touched her arm. "We have plenty of other people who work in the house and in the fields or with cattle. My mother wanted you to do what they cannot. Erin is lonely, and soon Sugar will leave home."

Before she could respond, he urged his horse forward. She nudged the mare to keep up with him. She still couldn't feel right about doing so little for people who had done so much for her.

Then, without warning, he turned to look at her. "It's best you put Germany behind you. And just take us as we are. You're not a German woman anymore. You're a Texas woman now."

The truth of his words shimmered through her. Finally she comprehended this fully. She had told herself she was a Texas woman, yet she had still been expecting this place to be like her past. Texas was her future, so unlike her past, and she must fit this future.

Erin called over her shoulder for them to catch up. And Mariel felt herself beginning to grin. *It is a beautiful day and I am riding a horse here in Texas. With Carson Quinn.*

* * *

Wearing his best suit of black broadcloth, Carson stood on the front porch of his family's hacienda, sheltered from the baking sun that hinted at the summer, now so near. Today was the final ceremonial visit to formalize Sugar's wedding ceremony, only a week away. His starched white collar circled his throat, tight. Somehow worry had clotted in his throat beneath the constricting collar. He swallowed with difficulty. When would he and Emilio, the bridegroom, be called back to Ranging, back to fighting, back to war?

Followed by a black carriage, longtime family friends Scully and Alandra Falconer dismounted at the bottom of the porch steps. Alandra Sandoval Falconer, her dark hair crowned with a black mantilla, threw her arms around Carson, kissing him on both cheeks. Before she moved away, she whispered in his ear, "When will *you* take a bride and make us all happy?"

Fortunately for Carson, Scully, tall and blond, was there, shaking his hand. "This is a happy day, a very fine day."

Carson nodded but couldn't stop himself from glancing over his shoulder at Mariel, who stood by the door, wearing the turquoise Mexican-style dress from San Antonio. Her pale hair and skin, large blue eyes, and neat figure beckoned him irresistibly. Alandra followed his gaze and then had the nerve to cast him a knowing look.

Dorritt hurried out and hugged Alandra. "It is so good to see you on this special day. Both of you, I want you to meet our friend, Mariel Wolffe."

Mariel curtseyed as the Falconers welcomed her to Texas. Carson noticed that as usual Mariel appeared embarrassed to be treated with what he considered common respect. It sparked his anger. He wanted to slam his fist into someone, but who? Who beside Heller had made her think less of herself than she ought?

Then from the carriage poured the Falconers' five children. They rushed forward, giving and receiving and welcoming hugs and kisses. Carlos was eight, Dorritt was six, Desmond was four, Houston was two. The baby, Flora, only a few months old, was carried in her nurse's arms. A cheerful hubbub reigned over all for a few minutes. Then Erin, the Falconer children, and their nurses drew away to play with all of the rancho's children, who had gathered near the corral. The adults moved to the large great room.

Carson noted that Mariel tried to leave with the other nurses. His mother intercepted her, drawing her into the room. When his mother was distracted, Mariel slipped away to sit in a chair far from the center. Was that due to her unfamiliarity with his family's unusual blending of *Tejano* and Anglo ways?

If so, he was experiencing a similar feeling of disconnection from what was taking place. He belonged here but, anticipating the dreaded war, he already felt called away. He withdrew from the knot in the center of the room and sat down beside her. She looked horrified. "You must go there, by family," she whispered, nodding toward his parents.

Carson slid into a comfortable position, his long legs out in front of him. Concentrating on Mariel distracted him from his growing sense of alienation. The fragrance of roses wafted to him. He breathed it in, along with Mariel's fragrance, and imagined that—in all of Texas—only this wedding mattered, only sitting here beside this pretty woman mattered. His hand itched to smooth away a tendril of her hair that had slid from her bun and now hung below her small, pale pink ear.

"You should go," Mariel whispered, motioning toward an empty chair closer to his family.

"This is about my sister, not me. I'll just be a groomsman." He had wanted to ask Emilio what he would do if they were sucked into the war. The words had eluded him, his tongue wooden at the thought.

Emilio's father, the Falconer foreman for years, had just risen. Carson turned his attention to him, hoping to be caught up in the festive spirit. "We are happy that our son Emilio Manuel Jesus Ramirez has been accepted by Sugar Quinn and her parents as her future *esposo*. We are doubly honored that our Doña Alandra and Don Scully have agreed to act as *madrina* and *padrino* for our son and his intended *novia*. My heart is full." He stopped to wipe his eyes, as his plump wife, dressed in black bombazine and sitting nearby, was already doing. "A father hopes much for his children. This is more than I ever hoped for my son."

"What is *madrina*, *padrino*?" Mariel whispered.

"The best man and matron of honor," he whispered back, wondering if they had counterparts in German wedding customs. She nodded, not letting on if this too was strange to her.

Quinn rose and took the elder Ramirez's hand. "We are honored that such a fine man as Emilio has wooed and won our daughter. We already love him as our son. I have no reservations about giving my daughter into his care." The two fathers shook hands, then slapped each other on the back.

Carson listened, still feeling a thousand miles removed from the tears, the hearty back-slaps. Would this all be for naught? If a Ranger came to summon them, would Emilio refuse to return? Within, Carson's emotions tangled into knots.

At a nod from Dorritt, the two fathers sat down. The servants came forward with a drink of coffee mixed with chocolate and a variety of cookies and sweetmeats. When all had been served, Scully cleared his throat. "My wife and I are happy that the Ramirezes have included us in the wedding and the feast. We have watched Emilio and Sugar grow up. Our hearts are also full. May the Lord bless them in their life together."

The *Tejanos* made the sign of the cross and the Quinns murmured, "Amen." This brought Carson an unexpected swell of pride. Being the son of Quinn and Dorritt often brought him notice he didn't relish. Though they were deemed Anglo, not *Tejano*, their lack of prejudice against dark skin, combined with his father's Cherokee blood, meant that they didn't fit into Anglo society neatly. Now he was reminded of how different his family was. In the very best way.

Emilio went out to his parents' wagon and carried in a large, ornate wooden chest, which held the *muhlul*, the Mexican or *Tejano* wedding gift. He set it on the stone floor, then brought his bride to open it. "For you," he murmured and kissed her forehead, then her hand.

Sugar knelt by the chest and opened it. She lifted out a gold chain of two loops, two gold wedding rings, hair ribbons, silk handkerchiefs, several yards of fine cotton, a bag of silver, and a bag of chocolate. Sugar exclaimed her pleasure, then kissed Emilio. Everyone made sounds of approval, and some even clapped their hands.

Carson felt Emilio's pride as his own. Rangers weren't paid much. Evidently Emilio had saved most of his wages over the past six years. Carson blinked back sudden tears. He tried to shake off the startling melancholy closing in on him.

Then Quinn cleared his throat. "To my daughter for her dowry, I give five hundred acres of land, a bull, a cow, and two horses." Again this was met with loud but polite approval. And then the discussion of the marriage ceremony and feast began.

Unable to bear hiding his feelings any longer, Carson slid to his feet and took Mariel's hand. She looked shocked but followed him outside.

"Where are we going?" she asked. "Is there something I must do?"

Carson halted in the shade cast by the hacienda. Her words gave his anger a target. "Why do you always sound worried? Or afraid?" He gripped her arms. "Do you think any of us would hurt you?"

Mariel looked even more uncertain. And he cursed himself for holding her so tightly. "Come." He drew her behind the house into his mother's carefully tended herb and medicinal garden, with its high fence. In spite of the hot sun, the garden was filled with healthy green plants that somehow cooled the heat of the day. "Mariel . . ." Words failed him. He didn't know what to say to her. He kept her hand in his. She gazed up at him with such worried eyes.

He stroked her soft cheek. He had to somehow soothe her fear. "You are safe. You are wanted here."

Her face crumpled, and she turned away. Why? He clung to her hand. "Mariel, you are safe here. You are wanted here. Why does that make you cry?"

Ten

You are safe. You are wanted here.

Overcome with emotion, Mariel swung back toward Carson. And then she was in his arms. Never had she felt as she did at this moment. She couldn't speak; her heart had been touched too deeply.

You are safe. You are wanted here.

No one had ever said those words to her before. And certainly no one had ever made her feel as if those words were true.

She lifted her face and offered him her lips. He claimed them as a thirsty man drank water. Warmth flowed down her neck and through her body. She hadn't realized how cold and dead she had felt until this moment when warmth and life burst over and through her—flesh and marrow.

Finally, their lips parted and she gasped for breath, her heart racing. "Why do you kiss me?"

Her words came out without her permission. And she regretted them immediately. Carson started to pull away. She clung to him. "Do not leave," she implored. *Don't take the warmth away.* She looked downward, her face burning.

"I . . . ," Carson started and then stopped. He tugged her close and folded her in his arms. He kissed her hair and stroked her back. The white oleander fluttered nearby, sending its sweet scent over them. He began another coaxing kiss, and she gave her lips to him. Words were too feeble to express her feelings.

Her knees weakened and he drew her to a garden bench. They sat facing one another, so close. Desire Mariel had never known blossomed. She slipped her hand inside the collar of his shirt and thrilled to his smooth skin and muscled shoulder. She offered him her neck, and he nuzzled her sensitive skin. Heaven—more than she had ever dreamed possible.

Then the sound of children running and laughing brought them back to reality. They parted just in time.

With both hands, Erin hit the wooden gate; it flapped back on its leather hinges. She led the running children into the high-fenced garden. "Oh!" Erin shouted. And halted.

"Yes, oh," Carson repeated with an austere look and tone. "Since when are children invited to gallop through our mother's herb garden?"

"I-I—," Erin stuttered. Peering around Erin, all the other children gawked at Mariel and Carson.

One of the two Falconer nurses hurried over. In a flurry of rapid Spanish and waving arms, the children were rushed out of the garden. The gate was slammed closed. And Carson and Mariel were alone again.

"We should go back to the house," Mariel murmured, straightening her skirt.

"No, not yet. They won't miss us."

Mariel thought this was wrong. Surely Mrs. Quinn would have noticed their leaving.

"Mariel, you asked me a fair question."

She went very still. She needed to know why he had kissed her. Yet she feared that the answer might destroy her. But how could this man who had shown her only kindness and concern since the day she'd met him do her harm? She turned to him. "You would never hurt me."

He took her hands between his. "I would never hurt you." He stroked the side of her cheek, his rough palms rasping her skin. She turned her face into his palm. Oh, the wonder of his touch. *I have never truly lived before this moment. Never.*

"Mariel, you are very special."

Her first inclination was to contradict him. Mariel was not special. She had never been wanted, never valued. But his words had shattered and then re-formed something deep within her. *I will put the past away. I will. I am a Texas woman now.*

"I asked my mother to invite you home with us. I couldn't leave you behind."

The marvel of these words made it impossible to speak. She kissed his palm, unable to utter a word.

He also looked as if he was struggling with some inner question. "There is much I wish I could say, but the times . . ." His voice faltered. He drew her to her feet and offered her his arm. Then he walked her through the garden, murmuring the names of the plants, what they were used for—seasoning, or healing, or both—and if they were native or imported to Texas. She listened to the pleasant flow of words in his deep voice, felt the sunshine on her shoulders, and was filled with the most exquisite contentment she had ever known. Not even thoughts of war could break through.

* * *

A week later Sugar and Emilio's wedding day in mid-May glowed sunny and warm. Mariel had decided that the constant sunshine must explain why people here were consistently happy. And on this particular day, spirits were higher than ever. Laughter was heard everywhere Mariel went.

Right now she was in Sugar's room helping her dress. The room was crowded with Dorritt, Emilio's mother, Erin, Mrs. Falconer, and a few maids. Mariel was really just watching everyone else dress Sugar. Mrs. Quinn was arranging a strand of pearls around Sugar's neck, and the groom's mother was weeping into her white handkerchief. Now Mrs. Falconer, who appeared to be an old family friend, was placing the high comb in Sugar's hair that would hold up the white mantilla.

Sugar was dressed in a new blue-sprigged dimity dress with delicate white embroidery and tiny pin-tucks, obviously made with deft skill and a desire to show regard for this bride. Mariel herself wore her new Anglo-style dress in a deeper blue. She no longer wore the black mourning for the husband whose loss she had never really mourned. She could hardly wait to see Carson's face when he saw her in this fine new dress, the finest she had ever worn. She had never thought such an idea before, how a dress would please a man. Her face grew quite warm. And she looked down and pretended to straighten her skirt to hide her blushes.

Then came a collective sigh of appreciation, and Mariel glanced up. With the white lace mantilla in place, Sugar looked . . .

"You look like a princess," Mariel breathed.

Sugar smiled and looked at herself in the mirror. "You think Emilio will like the dress?"

The women chuckled, and a torrent of Spanish followed. Though Mariel understood few of the words, the meaning was clear. Yes, Emilio would like the dress—if he bothered to look past his bride's face.

The women led Sugar out of the house toward the white canopy where the ceremony would be held. Mariel hung back toward the rear of the procession. The priest from a nearby mission church had come and would give his blessing to the couple in this unorthodox open-air ceremony. Since there were still few churches in Texas, the families felt fortunate to have a man of God present.

To Mariel's surprise, the two fathers would actually be the ones performing the wedding. Mrs. Quinn had said that this sort of "family" wedding was common on the frontier. Often, so far from any town or any church, a wedding consisted of a man and woman declaring that they were husband and wife and writing of their union in a family Bible.

Such a contrast to the formality of marriages and church records in Germany! But what really mattered was the commitment of the couple to each other. She had been married by law but not by love and devotion, as Sugar and Emilio would be.

Everyone waited under the canopy, leaving an aisle open for the bride's procession. Leading it was Erin as flower girl and Carlos Falconer as the page at her side. Then came the *damas*, or bridesmaids, and the *chamblanes*, or other grooms-men (Emilio's cousins), all in their wedding finery. At the front of the canopy waited a beaming Emilio with Scully Falconer and Carson as best man—both in black suits—at his side.

Mariel noted Carson's serious expression in contrast to all the shining, happy faces around him. What was making him sad on such a joyful day?

Finally Sugar, on her father's arm, reached Emilio, who wore a Spanish-looking suit of brown. Mrs. Falconer put something that clinked in Emilio's hand.

In the back of the gathering, standing beside Mariel, was the black man called Ash, with his wife, Reva. They were as close as family to the Quinns, more evidence of the Quinns' difference from other Anglos. Ash's curly hair was thick with white, and he had that thin, rangy build that masked unexpected strength. Reva was lighter complected, very pretty and plump.

Ash leaned close to Mariel and murmured, "Emilio will give Sugar those thirteen gold *reals* later in the ceremony. The coins you heard clinking into Emilio's hands symbolize that he is trusting her with all his worldly goods." Mariel nodded and smiled.

The priest began speaking in Latin, often making the sign of the cross and obviously praying for the couple. Then he stepped away, joining the wedding guests. Mrs. Falconer, the *madrina*, placed one chain of flowers, which circled both the bride's and the groom's necks.

Ash leaned over again. "This is *el lazo*, which symbolizes the love that has joined these two. They will wear it throughout the ceremony, then Sugar will wear it the rest of the day."

Mariel smiled. This wedding was so different from any other she had ever attended. Yet so filled with joy and deep meaning.

Carson spoke up then, first in English and then in Spanish. "Who gives this woman to be married to this man?"

"Her mother and I do," Quinn said, releasing Sugar and joining her right hand and Emilio's. Emilio's parents also gave their blessing in English and Spanish. Quinn read out the marriage vows from a small black book, and the bride and groom exchanged rings. Then Quinn said, "Emilio, you may kiss your bride."

Spontaneous applause broke out. Mariel thought it very strange. No one had applauded at her wedding, least of all her. Yet this seemed appropriate here. She joined in. After the formal kiss, she watched Emilio give Sugar the thirteen gold coins, which Sugar placed in a box that she handed to her brother. Then the newly married couple turned to face the guests.

Quinn said, "These two have become one for life. Please greet Mr. and Mrs. Emilio Ramirez." He repeated this in Spanish, and there were shouts of joy and more applauding. Mariel heard sprightly music and glanced around to see a grinning man playing a violin. Of course, there had to be music for the dancing later.

Many tables had been set up around the yard in the shade of palms and other trees. Now everyone chose a place and sat down to a sumptuous meal. Mariel found herself shunted by the movement of the crowd to a table of people she didn't know. Then Carson was at her side and all was well.

Under the cover of all the rapidly spoken Spanish, Mariel said, "Your sister made a lovely bride."

Carson nodded. "You look very pretty today."

She could not keep herself from showing her pleasure at his compliment. "You look . . . you look very . . . handsome."

In reply, he squeezed her hand. And she blushed again because of her own boldness and his touch. The gaiety around them buffered her and Carson, as if even though surrounded by many, they were really alone. The focus was on the bride and groom, and Mariel was glad for them. And glad for herself as Carson made it plain that he wanted only to be near her.

She wondered at the easy way she was accepted by everyone here. In contrast, a newcomer to her village in Germany would have been kept at arm's length for a long time. But here everyone acted as if she was a welcomed friend.

The meal went on for hours into the warm evening. They ate, joined in toasting the happy couple, then Carson led Mariel into the dancing. The fiddle player was joined by a few *vaqueros*, who played guitars. The sun lowered slowly, tardily on the horizon; it was summer now and the fiesta would continue far into the night.

In the shadows, Carson drew Mariel away. As they stood side by side, he put his arm around her. This made her feel painfully exposed. "Carson," she murmured, "you must not show . . ." *Show what? That you care for me?* She could not say that.

Carson responded by pulling her closer. "Don't act the coy young woman." He had the nerve to grin at her. "I have kissed you, remember? And more than once."

How could she forget? And when would these embarrassing blushes ever stop? Then he drew her back to the dance and she began to laugh and smile and become one with everyone celebrating the union of two fine people. She danced and danced, following Carson's every move easily and with an abundant joy that only expanded with each glance or touch.

At first, Mariel did not notice anything. Then people around her stopped dancing. The musicians fumbled. And then fell silent. Carson stiffened beside her. She turned and gasped. A large group of armed men—unshaven and rough-looking—had ridden into the yard in front of the Quinns' hacienda.

As one, the guests drew back. The buzz of so many people speaking at once surrounded Mariel. Quinn walked out to the leader, who had slid from his saddle.

"Sorry to interrupt," the tall man said loud enough to be heard over the few lingering voices, which then dropped away, causing a sudden silence. "Didn't know we'd be breaking in on a fiesta."

Quinn shook the man's hand. "Our daughter Sugar has just married Emilio Ramirez, Ben."

"Well, I'll be!" the man exclaimed.

Emilio led Sugar and presented her to the stranger.

"Who is he?" Mariel asked, looking up into Carson's face.

"He's Ben McCulloch."

She continued to look up at him. Who was Ben McCulloch?

Carson frowned. "He's my captain in the Rangers."

Mariel tried to say something, but her tongue had frozen in her mouth. Before she could regain the power of speech, Ben McCulloch was calling for Carson.

Carson went forward, leaving her standing alone. Each step he took diminished Mariel. She felt herself shrinking, shrinking. Then Reva, Ash's wife, was there putting a plump, comforting arm around Mariel's shoulder. Reva said nothing, but her kindness kept Mariel from giving in to tears.

"Carson!" McCulloch slapped him on the back. "I hardly knew you dressed so fine."

"Couldn't wear buckskins to my sister's wedding," Carson answered shortly.

"Well, I can tell that my turning up here is as welcome as a toothache. Nonetheless, we're on our way to the Rio Grande. Walker needs us to scout for the army. I thought I'd get both you and Ramirez. But I guess he's busy getting himself married."

Hearing these words, Mariel knew her beautiful time had come to an end. She had known it would, yet this interruption had come too soon. Did she dare hope he wouldn't go? *That he would stay for her?*

Carson folded his arms in front of him. He wanted to slam his fist into McCulloch's jaw. He stared into his captain's blue eyes, trying to make him back down. Leave without him. But McCulloch had said what he'd come to say, and Carson knew he'd say little more.

"Hey! Carson!" Tunney ambled forward on his horse.

"Tunney! You joined up again?" Carson wondered what the German widow had thought of Tunney's leaving for war.

"Couldn't miss the show. A real U.S. general and army with uniforms and everything."

Tunney's festive tone clashed with Carson's dark mood.

McCulloch stared hard at Carson. "We're not stopping till after midnight. You been on furlough for months now. Get your gear and saddle up."

Carson tried to pull together the words for a denial. He did not want to leave. Still, the call to arms stirred inside.

McCulloch interrupted his silent turmoil. "Carson, you know you're the best scout I've got. I'll not go south without you."

The pull of duty wrapped itself around Carson like a lariat. He wanted to deny that he was the best scout; however, he felt the eyes of all the men he'd fought side by side with for over six years. No one contradicted McCulloch, and the gazes said they were counting on Carson. Lives depended on him. Texas depended on him.

Glancing back, he saw that Reva was with Mariel. He gazed at Mariel a long, silent moment, barely aware that every eye had followed his gaze. Then he looked back up at McCulloch and nodded. "Eat a bite while I get my gear."

Carson turned, went directly to Mariel, took her hand, and pulled her along as he headed for his room. She ran to keep up with him. As soon as he shut the bedroom door, he wrapped his arms around her as if binding her to him forever. "I don't want to go, but I have to. You see that, don't you?"

Mariel nodded, barely meeting his eyes.

He hugged her to him, breathing in the fragrance of roses, memorizing the feel of her in his arms. "I will come back to you. I will."

"*Ja,*" she whispered, clutching his shoulders, lifting her face to be kissed. His lips touched hers.

A knock came at the door. "Son?"

"Come in, Pa!" Carson tore himself from Mariel. "Mariel, I must change into my buckskins. Go to my mother and sister."

Quinn entered; Mariel left. Carson let his gaze follow her till she shut the door behind her. Then he stripped off his wedding clothes piece by piece, tossing them onto his bed.

His father said nothing, merely watched Carson pull on his buckskins and pack his grooming pouch with his traveling mirror, razor, soap, and towels. When he finished looping his bow and rifle over his back and shoving his pair of Colt .45s into his belt along with his Bowie knife, he turned to his father.

Quinn put a hand on his shoulder. "I know why you are going. I will say nothing to halt you, for you are a grown man, a warrior. Do you care for the young German woman?"

"Yes." Carson felt as if the answer had been wrung out of him. It was true. He scarcely knew when he'd let go of the bitterness Blanche had planted in him. Mariel had filled that void of rejection and ridicule, with something much more real than anything he'd ever thought he'd felt for Blanche.

Quinn nodded solemnly. "We will keep her safe till you return."

Carson embraced his father, grateful for this assurance and that no other questions had been asked. He was glad his family had adopted the *Tejano* ability to show emotion without shame.

They walked through the quiet, dim house, which felt deserted with everyone outside. On the front porch, his mother, Erin, and Sugar waited for him. He hugged them all. Erin looked flushed. "Carson, I don't want you to go—"

"Your brother is a Ranger," Dorritt said, cutting her off. "He knows that the Mexicans must be defeated or we will have fought the Revolution for nothing. Whatever my opinion of slave-owning Americans, I do not want to be ruled by a dictator like Santa Anna. Good men must always fight such scoundrels."

Erin hid her face in her mother's skirt, sniffling. "We'll be praying for you," Sugar said, her face drawn and serious.

"I'm sorry to spoil your wedding day with this," Carson said, attempting to grin and failing. His heart was throbbing and he felt a little light-headed, disconnected already from his family, from this place. From Mariel.

"War spoils everything," Alandra Falconer, Sugar's *madrina*, said, pulling him into a fierce hug. "Be careful."

Carson nodded, then shook hands with a gruff Scully, who'd fought with him and his father in the Revolution a decade ago. He turned, and there was Emilio leading Carson's horse forward, announcing, "I saddled your horse, packed your ammunition and bedroll."

Their cook came running from the rear of the house and handed Carson a cloth bag of food and two full canteens. Carson thanked her. He shook hands with Emilio, then swung up into his saddle. He scanned the somber crowd for Mariel. He could not find her face. Perhaps that was just as well. Perhaps he wouldn't be able to leave her if he saw her now.

The Rangers had eaten what they could from the wedding tables and were mounting up all around again. McCulloch rode forward.

"Ramirez, I'm not bothering to ask you to leave your bride on your wedding night." The other Rangers chuckled at this. "But I expect to see you south on the Gulf within a month. Shouldn't be too hard for you to find the whole U.S. Army."

Emilio nodded soberly. Carson's throat was too tight for speech. He waved to everyone, then rode off into the growing darkness, not looking back. He always did this so that he wouldn't feel like he was seeing his family's rancho for the last time.

This time he had another reason not to look back. He didn't want to see Mariel's heartbroken face. He brought up the radiant image of her as she had looked today during Sugar's wedding. When this became unbearable, he concentrated on his horse's hoofbeats and the others around him, letting the rhythm block everything else out of his mind.

Eleven

On the bench in Mrs. Quinn's herb garden, Mariel sat very still, listening to the sounds of the wedding reception breaking up for the night. Instead of laughter and music, there were subdued voices and the sounds of cleaning as people carried away the makeshift tables and benches. Unable to hide her feelings or speak of them, she remained hidden by the tall mesquite-pole fence. She would wait until everyone had finished and turned in for the night. Only then would she seek her own bed.

Tears ran freely down her face. She did not try to stop them or wipe them away. She had at last found a place, the Quinn Rancho, where she was allowed to let her emotions flow. If she did leave the garden now, no one would snap at her, "Why are you crying? Stop it."

Being allowed emotions was good. How much better if Carson had not gone. The lovely wedding, the attention Carson had shown her, his tender embrace and teasing smiles as he had taught her the dances tonight. How wonderful, like scenes in a play, part of someone else's life.

Still, she clung to the truth. *This has happened to me. People are different here on this ranch. I am different here.*

At long last, all human sounds ceased; all light but moonlight and starlight was extinguished. In spite of the heat at noonday, the night grew cool. Finally, when the darkness threatened to chill her to the marrow, she rose and crept out of the garden. Then she tiptoed into the hacienda. She halted inside the door. Not everyone had gone to bed.

Mrs. Quinn sat beside a low fire in the hearth of the great room. Mariel stifled the urge to run to her room and lock the door. But Mrs. Quinn had been kind and was her mistress. Mariel bobbed a curtsey and tried to slip away to her room.

"Mariel, come sit beside the fire. I'm sure you must be chilled from sitting out in the garden."

"How did you know—" Mariel halted her question.

"You weren't in your room or anywhere else." Mrs. Quinn did not sound perturbed with her.

Mariel flushed with guilt. "I should have helped. I am sorry—"

"Come sit beside the fire. We need to talk." Mrs. Quinn motioned toward another comfortable rocking chair opposite her. "Come."

Mariel wanted to refuse; of course she could not. She walked to the chair and perched on its edge. "Yes, mistress?"

"I am not your mistress, Mariel. Or I don't want to be. I want to be your friend. I invited you here as a companion and teacher for Erin as the most acceptable way to keep you near my son. Till he realized what I knew—that he is in love with you."

Mariel heard the words, but they did not fit into her head. "I do not . . . understand."

"Carson is a complex man, a very intelligent and worthy one. At a very young age, he assumed and has carried great responsibility with dignity and honor. Quinn and I are very proud he is our son."

Mariel could not stop herself from speaking up. "You should be. Never have I known such a man. A true gentleman."

Mrs. Quinn nodded. "These are hard times. That is common on the frontier. Men can't always do what they want. They must do what is demanded of them for survival, to keep their freedom. Not only their own but their family's."

Mariel eased back into the curve of the rocking chair. Mrs. Quinn's voice was low and pleasant, and the fire was warming. Why was Mrs. Quinn telling her this? On the one hand, the lady sounded as if she approved of Mariel and Carson falling in love. On the other, she was showing Mariel how superior Carson was to her. And Mariel could not argue with that.

"It was very difficult to let him go tonight," the lady admitted.

That Mariel understood perfectly.

"I choose to believe and to pray that God will bring my son safely home to us. Will you believe that too? And pray?"

Mariel found she couldn't speak. Her heart, her emotions swayed inside her like water carried in a bowl. She felt herself drawn to Mrs. Quinn, and the pull was irresistible. She rose and knelt before Mrs. Quinn and laid her head on the lady's lap.

Mrs. Quinn stroked her hair. "My son wants to be a man of peace, not war. And we will pray that he returns to us. 'Mark the perfect man, and behold the upright: for the end of that man is peace.' That is my prayer, Lord. And, Mariel, your strength is in your endurance. Endurance is very important. We must keep our hope and strength. Or when good comes at last, we will not be here to savor it. Keep faith, Mariel. Keep believing."

Mariel could never remember feeling so torn between peace and despair. Mrs. Quinn must be a woman of great faith. Mariel wanted to be like her, but perhaps Mariel should not pray or hope too much. Little she had prayed for had ever come to pass. Why would this time be any different? Yet so much had changed in her life over the past few months, so much good had come to her. How could God not be here in this vast, wild land? Mariel whispered the same prayer. "Mark the perfect man, and behold the upright: for the end of that man is peace. That is my prayer, Lord." *I will keep hope and endure.*

* * *

Carson had been out of the saddle too long. When the order to camp for what remained of the night finally came, he slid from the saddle and stood stiffly beside his mount. It would take them nearly two weeks of hard riding to reach Matamoras, Mexico, where Taylor and his army might be. By then, Carson would be fully back in shape. He hobbled his horse and untied his bedroll.

No fire had been lit. That meant they were trying to slip unnoticed by Comanche or any other hostile tribe. Two Lipan Apaches rode with McCulloch. The Comanche were just as fierce enemies to them as to the whites.

Carson kicked away stones and sticks from an area and unrolled his bedding. He slid into the wool blanket, which smelled of leather and horse. Had he really just hours ago been at his sister's wedding? Images from the wedding felt unreal; he felt unreal, too, as if he might vanish into the night air.

A large man came up beside him, unrolled his bedding, and slid inside. "So how's the pretty Mariel doing?" It was Tunney's low voice.

Carson wanted to ignore the question and feign sleep. But that wouldn't stop Tunney. Carson said grudgingly, "She's fine. You saw her."

Tunney chuckled. "About to get leg-shackled like Ramirez?"

Nettled, Carson again thought of denying his interest in Mariel—for what purpose? "War interrupted me, and it looks like it interrupted you too. How's the German widow?"

"I left her in good health and she's not going anywhere. She'll be there when I get back. I can't be sitting by the fire when I know my friends are in the middle of it all."

Carson grunted, "Go to sleep, Tunney."

Tunney grunted in reply and said no more.

Carson lay there, listening to other men sleep. He'd had a few weeks of sleeping in his snug bed at home, and the ground felt hard and disagreeable. Refusing to move around to find a comfortable position, he thought over Tunney's words about wanting to be in the middle of it all.

I don't want to be in the middle of it all. Nor will I be. I'm just coming back to scout. This isn't like San Jacinto. I'm not a soldier this time. I'll just be doing reconnaissance, nothing more.

He closed his eyes, ignoring how unconvinced he was of his own words. And how much leaving Mariel behind still stung.

* * *

Thirteen days later, on June first, McCulloch and his Rangers reached the Gulf Coast. The hot, moist gulf air blew soft against Carson's face. Seagulls screeched overhead. By now, he again felt as if he'd spent his entire life in the saddle. The memories of the pretty Mariel had not faded but remained hidden behind an exterior that increasingly reflected the men around him, unshaven and rough-looking, nothing like Emilio's groomsman.

While it was still morning, they rode into the American camp at Point Isabel, north of Matamoras, Mexico. Indeed, it had not been hard to find the U.S. Army, with its thousands of sweating, wool-clad men. Carson, as always, rode beside McCulloch. Today they would report to the U.S. general and find out what he needed scouts for.

The regular U.S. soldiers in their blue uniforms gawked at them; some pointed, some stepped back. No doubt they had never seen Rangers or their like before. Carson heard a few say, "Indian fighters. Texans." Being called "Texan," not "Texian," sounded strange to Carson. Was that what they would be called now that Texas was not a sovereign nation but a U.S. state?

McCulloch halted and looked down at one of the men. "Where's Taylor?"

The soldier opened and closed his mouth a few times. "You mean the general?"

McCulloch nodded.

"Command's over there . . . sir."

"Much 'bliged." McCulloch touched his brim, then led his men to the rough building that had been pointed out. McCulloch slid from his saddle. "Carson, you come along."

Carson followed suit, tossing his reins to Tunney. McCulloch tried to enter the door, but a sentry stopped him and asked, "Who are you . . . sir?"

"I'm McCulloch. Tell the general the Rangers are here."

The soldier saluted and went inside, leaving Carson and his captain waiting outside. "I've had less trouble getting in to see Sam Houston," McCulloch muttered.

Carson didn't reply. No doubt a general was picky about whom he talked to. With a disagreeable twist, Carson recalled the West Point graduates at Blanche's wedding. Would Taylor be like that? All shiny brass buttons, white gloves, and a ramrod-straight back?

The sentry returned and directed them inside.

McCulloch led Carson in. Carson doffed his hat. When McCulloch didn't, Carson set his back on his head. He didn't want to show up McCulloch. Two men were in the office, a young man and a short, older man. The older man was very plump and was dressed in rumpled civilian dress—an old green coat and trousers and bedroom slippers. He was standing beside a cluttered desk. This couldn't be the general, could it?

The man ran a keen eye over both of them. "I'm Taylor," he said and held out his hand.

McCulloch grasped it. "I'm McCulloch, and this is Carson Quinn, my best scout."

Before it was Carson's turn to shake hands, he glanced more closely at the only other man in the room. He was obviously a young officer and in every regard the complete opposite of the scruffy old gentleman who had turned out to be the general. His high-necked, buff-colored uniform was pressed and freshly brushed, and his boots gleamed with black polish. He had familiar-looking, blue-black wavy hair clipped close to his head, white skin, and dark eyes.

Carson got around to looking at the young man's face. A spike of shock plunged through his chest. Of all the people in the world, his cousin had to be here?

Carson's face remained impassive. He was his father's son and could be inscrutable when needed. Why was it that when there was one last person in the whole world that you didn't want to see, that person popped up? And when least expected?

While his mind raced, Carson remained still and expressionless. *I should have expected him to be here. He bragged to everyone at the wedding where he was going and why—loudly and repeatedly.* But so much had intervened since then that Carson had put it, and him, out of his mind. And what had been the chances that in an army of thousands they would be thrown together?

Carson looked the young man in the eye.

Stark horror glistened in the younger officer's eyes. Evidently this cousin didn't want to own Carson—unshaven, dressed in buckskin, and grimy from weeks in the saddle—as kin. Carson stared coolly into those brown eyes, trying to decide whether to embarrass his "refined" cousin or not. It was tempting.

"Glad you got here," the general was saying to McCulloch. "This is my aide de camp, LaCroix."

McCulloch nodded to him; Carson continued to watch his cousin Remy LaCroix sweat. In the spring, Remy's sister Blanche had demonstrated what kind of woman she was and what she really thought of Carson in the most painful way possible. She hadn't done it in private. No. In front of strangers invited to her wedding, she'd snubbed and ridiculed him and his family. She'd done it subtly—whenever speaking about the Quinns, she'd added an arch or mocking facial expression. When she'd addressed them, she'd added sneering tones that had belied her polite words and elegant behavior. She'd given no direct insult that any Quinn had been able to react to. No direct insult, only a thousand tiny darts of contempt.

LaCroix also had relished snubbing Carson. So now, tit for tat? If Carson made their connection known, Remy would be embarrassed not only by having a cousin who dressed in buckskin and wore his hair like an Indian but also because he hadn't shown that he was family, as he should have. It was a unique situation. Carson tried not to take too much perverse enjoyment from it.

"How many men did you bring with you?" Taylor asked McCulloch.

"Seventeen. Another one will join us soon. He was busy getting married and couldn't leave right away."

The general nodded. "You know why I requested Rangers? You men know the land here. I don't. General Arista and the Mexican Army are somewhere west of here. Well, that figures, because he couldn't be east of me, could he? He'd be swimming in the gulf."

Carson liked Taylor's calm, sensible talk so far. Would it last? McCulloch just nodded.

"Anyway, I need you to find Arista without exposing yourselves to him and his army. And then, when you find out where he is, string out your men over the distance between his force and ours. We must keep a line of communication open. I need to know marching conditions—"

"What's that?" McCulloch asked.

Remy sneered.

Carson looked at him hard. LaCroix tried to look as though it didn't bother him. And failed. The young man's cheeks turned red.

"I need to know if the land will accommodate an army marching over it," Taylor explained without chagrin. "You probably don't ever have to worry about that, I take it."

McCulloch grinned. "Nope. Rangers don't march."

Taylor matched his grin. "Well, I can't mount my infantry of nearly six thousand. They march. And to do that, they need ground that gives them space to march abreast, the more even the terrain the better, and with water along the way and cover if possible."

McCulloch nodded. "Doable."

"What's the inland like?"

"Low plains. Grass. Then mountains. Pretty dry this time of year," McCulloch said.

"What about natives? I hear you've got some real hostile ones." Taylor sat down on the edge of his cluttered desk, waving a hand toward two straight-backed wooden chairs.

McCulloch lowered himself into one. "Two Lipan Apache always ride with me. The Comanche scare everybody, including most other tribes. Sam Houston supposedly signed a peace treaty with the Comanche end of last year. So you might not be bothered with them. You're pretty far south."

"My father and I met with the Penatekas a couple of months ago." Carson settled on the chair next to his captain. "We went to make a treaty with them for the new Germans settling north of San Antonio."

Both older men turned to look at Carson. Taylor asked, "The Penatekas?"

"Comanche band. Means 'honey-eaters,'" Carson explained, one eye still on LaCroix.

McCulloch stretched his legs out in front of him. "Sam Houston has used Carson and Carson's dad, Quinn, to make treaties with the different tribes. Quinn's a half-breed Cherokee. Knows how to handle Indians. Quinn's own dad scouted for Pike."

"Did the Indians make peace, these honey-eaters, with the Germans?" Taylor asked, a shrewd eye on Carson.

Carson watched LaCroix sit down and begin writing at a desk made out of two barrels and a slab of pine. "Tunney says yes."

Taylor cocked his head in silent question.

"Another Ranger with me." McCulloch supplied the answer.

"When can you start scouting?" Taylor asked.

McCulloch shrugged. "Today, if need be."

"Rest a day and let your men walk around so my men can see them. I don't want anyone shooting one of your men thinking you're Mexican."

McCulloch looked to Carson, then to Taylor. "Some of my Rangers are of Mexican blood. Some Mexicans fought on our side in the Revolution. They hated Santa Anna as much as we did. They're Texians too. They're called *Tejanos*."

"I'll have to give you something for them to wear so they are marked as Americans." Taylor looked like he was chewing his tongue, trying to come up with a solution.

"I think that we're dressed distinctively enough as we are," Carson spoke up, glancing ironically toward LaCroix and back to McCulloch, and then down at his own buckskins. LaCroix tried to act as if he hadn't heard, but Carson noticed that his ears had turned red.

Taylor looked at Carson and gave a dry chuckle.

I shouldn't be enjoying this, Carson told himself.

"Carson's right. Don't worry about my men. Anybody turns a gun on one of us, they'll regret it real fast." McCulloch grinned.

"Real Mexican soldiers have fancy uniforms too," Carson slipped in without looking at the younger officer. "Tell your men only to shoot Mexicans in blue-and-white uniforms. And only at Indians aiming weapons at them."

"I'll put out the word, then," Taylor replied dryly. Then he rose and held out his hand.

After shaking it once again, McCulloch said their farewells and turned for the door. Then another one of those startling coincidences happened. Or Carson's mother would say providences, God-arranged meetings.

Anthony Niven—Blanche LaCroix's new husband—walked in. Carson halted in his tracks, surprise quivering through his nerves. But Niven evidently didn't know Carson well enough to recognize him dressed as a Ranger. Carson watched LaCroix suffer the further torture of wondering if Niven would recognize Carson and reveal Carson's identity and, thereby, their relationship. And it would be all the worse for Remy, since Taylor appeared to be without pretension. Though the puffed-up young rooster deserved the torment, since it was all due to vain pride, Carson almost felt sorry for LaCroix. Almost.

Within a few moments, McCulloch and Carson left. When they reached their horses, his captain turned and asked, "You know that young fella?"

Carson nodded. "LaCroix's my first cousin. Our mothers are half sisters."

McCulloch made a sound of disgust. And said no more.

Carson agreed wholeheartedly. He almost preferred that this family connection not be revealed. His cousin was such a greenhorn. No Texian should be that green. Would their blood relationship come out? Not from his mouth.

Niven was the wild card. He might recognize Carson and let

it slip. And if Niven did, what would LaCroix say or do in his embarrassment?

Carson tried to settle back and listen to McCulloch tell the other Rangers the plans. But once distracted, his mind wouldn't cooperate. Drifting from LaCroix to Niven to Blanche, it finally settled on something better; the image of Mariel as she'd looked during Sugar's wedding stole him away, taking him back where he longed to be. At home. With her. In his arms.

* * *

Almost two weeks after the wedding, during the mellow time at the end of supper in the Quinns' great room, Ash cleared his throat. "I got something to say."

Dorritt looked up. Mariel sat beside her. The fragrance of roast beef spiced with black pepper still hung over the table. Carson's empty seat remained as a silent reminder of his absence. Emilio sat beside Sugar, holding her hand; he would be leaving soon to join Carson and the other Rangers. And Dorritt grieved for Sugar already. And worried over her son in a war so far away. The worry was like a brick she carried inside, a constant weight that sapped her strength, muted, blunted everything.

"What is it, Ash?" Quinn asked.

"Reva and I are going south." Ash leaned forward, resting his elbows on the table.

"Have you heard from Antonio?" Dorritt asked, placing her hand on Quinn's thigh for comfort.

Staring down at her plate, Reva answered, "Yes, in a way. One of our cousins from San Antonio traveled to Laredo and saw him there."

Dorritt wondered why Reva wouldn't meet her eye. The latent worry she'd carried since Carson had left began to grow larger, heavier in her middle.

His dark, lined face drawn down, Ash looked back and forth

between Dorritt and Quinn. "You know that things are going to change now that Texas is U.S. territory. We all settled farther west to keep clear of the Anglos because they have no use for people like us—half-breeds and free blacks."

"And that's why our son left Texas." Reva sounded like she might start crying. "He couldn't feel safe in a place where some people treated him like he wasn't a free man."

Dorritt wondered what was causing Reva such distress so long after the fact. Antonio had left Texas around the same time Carson and Emilio had joined the Rangers—probably because Antonio, a black man, hadn't been allowed to join the Rangers with them. It had been hard on Reva and Ash. Hard on all of them.

"It will only get worse now." Ash folded his large, work-worn hands in front of his face. "Texas is a U.S. state. And sometime in the near future, slave catchers will come and try to make trouble for free blacks. For Reva and me."

"You think you'll do better under a Mexican dictator?" Quinn asked.

"I don't like dictators, but I plan on staying clear of Mexico City, and Amos and Nancy want to go with us."

The mention of Amos and Nancy, freed slaves who had once belonged to Dorritt's family, brought understanding, electrifying understanding. It hit Dorritt what they were talking about. This wasn't about going for a visit. Disbelieving, she stood. "You're leaving? For good?"

Reva burst into tears, putting her hands over her face. "I don't want to go, but we can't stay."

Ash patted her shoulder. "Antonio has been working as a *vaquero* at a rancho southwest of Laredo. He's taken a wife and has an adobe house big enough for us to join him. I'm getting on in years. We need to be with our son."

Reva wept into her handkerchief.

Her knees failing her, Dorritt sat down.

"I want to go with Emilio," Sugar's voice cut through the emotional haze Dorritt was in.

"What?" Dorritt looked up, fresh shock sluicing through her.

"Sugar, you cannot," Emilio said in a low, firm voice.

"Yes, I can. Mother, you and Alandra went along with Father and Scully and Carson to the Revolution. And when they were wounded, you were needed. I can't just sit home and worry what might happen to Emilio." Tears sprang to Sugar's eyes. "I can't. I won't."

"Your mother and Alandra didn't intend to go to war. It just happened that way." Quinn laid a restraining hand on Dorritt's arm.

"Has everyone gone loco?" Dorritt asked, sitting forward. "Sugar, you can't go to war. This isn't like the Revolution—"

"Yes, it is." Sugar leaped to her feet. "It's just like the Revolution. Mexico wants Texas back. And the man I love is going to the war. I want to go with him . . . in case he needs me."

Emilio tugged Sugar's hand until she sat down, frowning.

Dorritt reached for Quinn's hand. She looked into his face, the face she loved above all others. Her heart was beating so fast that she wished she hadn't eaten. She felt a bit sick. "What do you say, Quinn?"

He lifted his cup and took a deliberate swallow of coffee. Everyone waited, looking toward him. "Ash, I know you want to be with your son. Some men have many children. You and Reva have only one son. I'm happy that Antonio has done well and taken a wife. I'm glad he's sent for you. It grieves me and Dorritt to see you go"—Quinn gripped Dorritt's hand—"but you must be there to hold your future grandchildren."

Dorritt knew everything Quinn said was true, but still her heart cried out, *Not Reva! Don't go, dearest friend.* Reva had been a slave of her family and then had married Ash, Quinn's oldest friend. Dorritt and Reva had never been separated. Nevertheless, Dorritt was Reva's best friend, and Quinn was right. She stiffened her resolve. Reva had mourned Antonio's settling so far away. What if Carson went far away? Dorritt couldn't make herself smile, but she made herself nod. "You should be with your son. It's only right."

"When I think of leaving you . . . all those years ago, you're the one who gave us hope, hope that we'd have good lives in Texas." Reva wiped her large brown eyes. "We were babies together."

Dorritt nodded, her lips trembling. Long ago Reva had been her only friend, her only true family.

Quinn cleared his throat and looked to Reva's right. "And, Sugar, I understand your wanting to go with Emilio," he said even as he raised both hands in denial. "But this war will be fought much farther away than San Jacinto."

Ash sat up straighter. "We can take her south with us. We'll go to the coast first along with Emilio. Then we can leave after Emilio settles Sugar with the other women who've come along with their husbands. After that, we'll just follow the Rio Grande west till we get to Laredo. Then we'll find Antonio."

Silence. Dorritt's ears rang as if someone had just sounded bells too close to her. Sugar? Go to war? *No.*

"You can't tell me, Dorritt, that having Emilio and Carson off away in the middle of a war hasn't worried you," Reva spoke up, her voice strengthening. "I know because you told me and we been praying. Maybe Sugar supposed to go along, and be ready in case either boy needs her."

Dorritt shifted uncomfortably in her seat. She couldn't deny what Reva had said. And there would be some women in the army camp, wives and laundresses and cooks. But Sugar? Did she have the stamina to stand up to the rigors of war?

"I already went through one war," Sugar said, as if reading Dorritt's thoughts. "I was just a little girl, but I understood what was going on. And I know how your nursing and care saved a lot of lives, more than just Father's and Scully's. I went through it once, I can go through it again. You think I'm too weak. I'm not. I'm not."

"I will go too."

Mariel's soft voice startled Dorritt. She swung her attention to Mariel. "You what?"

"I will go too," Mariel repeated, her voice still faint.

Everyone stared at her, yet she did not back down. Instead, she rose. Her heart thundered in her ears. "Ever since Carson left, I want only one thing." She swallowed, her mouth so dry that her lips were sticking to her teeth. "I want to see him again."

Before she could lose her nerve, she plunged on. "He . . . Carson told me I was not a German woman anymore. I am now a Texas woman. I did not think there was a way that I could go to him but . . ." Her courage gave out and she let herself drop back onto her chair. Where had she found the courage to speak?

"In that case, I guess we'll have to take Erin to stay with Alandra at Rancho Sandoval and then go—," Quinn began.

"No," Ash said. "We sat out the Revolution ten years ago. It wasn't our fight, and we weren't interested in giving slaveholders more power, more independence. Mexico has its problems, but there is no slavery there. Peonage, yes, but no slavery. So we stayed here and with Emilio's father's help, we kept this ranch and Alandra's safe while you went to fight."

"If what you say is true, then I should be there fighting again." Quinn's voice was prickly.

"This is your turn to stay home," Ash declared, looking ready to fight. "Let me do this for you, *mi mejor amigo*." His voice softened. "We will pack a wagon and drive to the coast and stay with Sugar and Mariel until we know they will be safe. Then we will go west, keeping our distance from the armies. I don't think I would miss a full army coming our way. My eyesight isn't that poor."

There was a silence filled with thinking, filled with strong feeling. Mariel did not even take a deep breath. She still could not believe that she had spoken what was in her heart. Now she must wait and see what would come of her boldness.

"We will think on this," Quinn said as he looked at his wife. She nodded, but she was holding her lower lip with her teeth.

* * *

That evening, at the end of a steady string of hot days, Carson took a bath in the river and changed his clothing. Being clean made him feel fresher, better, more himself. Now he sat at the Ranger campfire set apart from the main body of the U.S. Army bivouac. In the river, he had decided not to shave. They would be off scouting tomorrow, and he would wait and shave when he was nearing home again. Why bother here? He didn't have to look like a fashion plate. Like his dear cousin.

One of the *Tejano* Rangers was playing the guitar, making Carson think about dancing with Mariel and wonder how long it would be before Emilio turned up. The rest of the Rangers were just relaxing. Earlier, some had hunted, and they had dined on roasted prairie hens and some fish bought from a local fisherman. Carson hummed along with the tune being played. Then he saw the raised eyebrows on the men across from him and turned.

"Quinn! Carson Quinn!"

It was Niven, Blanche's husband, calling his name. Carson considered whether or not he should reply, but he decided to take the direct approach. He had nothing to fear. He rose. "What do you want, Niven?"

Niven halted and stared at him.

Carson returned the favor. Niven was taller than LaCroix, almost as tall as Carson. He was dressed in the same buff-colored, high-necked uniform as LaCroix. He had sandy brown hair that curled around his head in a short cut. Since the spring, since this man's wedding to his cousin Blanche, Carson had let his own hair grow till he could tie it back. If he was going to be deemed a half-breed by Anglos, he might as well look the part.

"Well, first of all to apologize for not recognizing you in Taylor's office. Pardon me, but you do look a bit different there than you did at my wedding."

Carson considered this. It was true. Niven had not looked as if he had recognized him.

Niven offered his hand.

And Carson shook it. "What can I do for you?"

"I've gotten the general's permission to ask if I can come along on your scouting trip."

The request left Carson speechless at first. The Rangers around him sat up and turned to gawk at the man. "You what?"

Niven grinned. "May we talk a moment in private?" He motioned for Carson to come with him toward the nearby creek.

Carson nodded. His curiosity was piqued. What was this man up to?

Niven led him to the creek bank. The evening shadows were long now. "I'm sorry that my brother-in-law gave you the cut direct today."

Carson raised an eyebrow.

"He recognized you and snubbed you in public. It's a serious social faux pas. I hope you weren't too insulted."

"It took me by surprise. Quite frankly, I would rather it wasn't generally known that this dandy and I are family."

Niven laughed aloud. "Good one. LaCroix is younger than we and he still has that tender pride. I heard at the wedding that you were a longtime Ranger and that your father was a notable scout, just the kind of men I'd hoped to meet in the West. I wanted to have time to get to know you, but my duties as the happy groom didn't give me much time. And then you took off early."

Carson continued walking along the sluggish creek with Niven.

"No doubt you're wanting me to get to the point." Niven halted. "So here it is. I intend to make the military my career, and I intend to go as high as I'm able. This war with Mexico is fortuitous, since it gives me a chance for quick promotion but—"

"What?" Halting, Carson propped his hands on his hips. So this newlywed thought that this war was "fortuitous"? Hadn't he been unhappy to leave his bride? For Carson, leaving Mariel had been . . .

Niven nodded, continuing, "As I have looked further into the U.S. future, I believe it will be dominated by Western expansion. Therefore, I think that primarily I will be given commands that put me in conflict with the native tribes. So in order to stay alive and continue to climb through the ranks, I need to know as much as I can about them and how to fight them."

In the lowering light, Carson looked at the man. He had never met the like before. "So you are a man of ambition?" Carson commented dryly.

"Yes. I am."

Carson started walking again along the creek bank, thinking about what Niven had just revealed about himself. Niven kept in step with him. What was he to think of a man with such ambitions? And was Niven right about the future? "So this war is fortuitous?"

"To me, yes."

"What did your bride think of it?" Carson watched Niven. His cousin Blanche wouldn't like a husband who wouldn't make her the center of his life.

Niven shrugged. "She married me knowing she was marrying a military man. I didn't ask her what she thought. It was a stroke of good fortune that my wedding in Texas coincided with this war's start. I might have been left out of it, but I actually came west with Taylor and got leave for the wedding. Yes,

I'd say things have worked out better than I could possibly have hoped."

I didn't ask her what she thought. Carson wondered if Blanche was still savoring her social coup of marrying the son of a U.S. congressman. Carson had rarely met such blatant ambition and arrogance as this man possessed. "Well, I'm so glad you didn't have to come to Texas *just* to get married." Carson couldn't resist a touch of sarcasm. He stopped and turned toward Niven, then folded his arms. "So you think you need to learn how to fight Indians."

"I do. Will you teach me?"

Carson rubbed the back of one hand over his new beard. "I'm a man who likes to think things over if possible."

"You will be leaving tomorrow. I need a decision before then."

Carson sidestepped the issue with, "Ben McCulloch is in charge, not me."

Niven remained undeterred. "If you are convinced I can go along, you will ask him in a way that leads him to look on my request with favor."

Might as well be honest. "You're a tenderfoot, a greenhorn to the West. There are so many things that we've all learned as children that you lack. How can I teach you things like that when I'm trying to do my job and stay alive?"

Niven inclined his head as if ceding the point to Carson. "All I can say is that I will be at your and McCulloch's command."

Carson drew his lips back in a silent snarl. *I don't want you with me.* He breathed in cool night air. "Look at your clothes. You couldn't come along dressed like that."

"I've already had a buckskin outfit made."

"You what?" Carson's shoulder hunched up.

"There are still some Cherokee in the hills near my home in Virginia. An old woman made me buckskins of deer I brought down. So will you ask McCulloch if I may go with you?"

Twelve

Carson chewed the inside of his cheek. Then he started walking. Why should he think this over? It would be McCulloch's decision. Carson headed back; Niven hurried after him. They reached the low campfire, and Carson led Niven right to McCulloch. "Ben, this is Niven. He just married my first cousin Blanche in San Felipe. He has something he wants to ask you." Carson moved out of the scant firelight.

Niven stepped forward, a smile on his face and his hand out. "Good to meet you again, sir."

McCulloch shook Niven's hand but said nothing.

"I'm a career military man and want to gain some experience in scouting and dealing with native tribes and Mexicans. General Taylor has given me permission to request you let me go with you tomorrow."

"So?" McCulloch challenged.

"So may I go with your scouts?"

Carson had to give Niven credit. He knew what he wanted and wasn't afraid to go after it.

"Looking to make your bride a widow fast, are you?" McCulloch's voice was harsh.

"I know I'm inexperienced in frontier warfare and that's why I want to go with you."

McCulloch stared into Niven's face. "No."

"That is your final word?"

Carson tried to be fair, but he sensed the men around him weren't impressed with Niven's request either.

McCulloch half-turned away. "Yes, a tenderfoot could get us killed. This war is too important to the safety of the people of Texas, and that's what we care about."

Niven bowed his head. "Perhaps another time?"

McCulloch grunted.

Niven turned to Carson, a smile still on his face. "Nice talking to you. Good luck." They shook hands. Niven walked away into the darkness.

Carson was surprised and uneasy. He hadn't expected Niven to give up without argument. He looked to McCulloch and shrugged.

"You got some interesting kin, Carson," McCulloch observed.

Carson could only agree with him. As he settled down by the campfire, he hoped he wouldn't turn around and find any other interesting relatives popping up with strange requests.

* * *

The next afternoon, Mariel walked beside Mrs. Quinn on their way to the corral. The bright June sun dazzled her eyes. She had slept very little last night. Images of Carson had kept her awake. She had not realized that she had memorized his every expression, every movement. His low voice repeated in her mind. And the memory of his tender kisses had become an ache within.

"I'm glad you were free to ride out with me," Mrs. Quinn said, sounding strained. "I'm restless. I had a hard time sleeping."

"I need practice riding," Mariel said.

"Does that mean you are serious about leaving with Reva and Ash?"

Blessedly interrupting them, a *vaquero* led two horses to the ladies and helped them mount. Mariel took a deep breath and settled herself into the saddle. Being up so high off the earth still bothered her. She stiffened her spine and her determination. She pressed her legs inward, and the well-mannered mare started off at a gentle pace. If only she could gentle her own nerves. She sensed that Mrs. Quinn had invited her along to question her.

They had barely left the rancho yard when Mrs. Quinn said, "I want to discuss you and Sugar going south with Ash and the others."

Mariel rippled with alarm. Did she have the courage to speak with honesty to this lady? She did. "I want to go to Carson. I have never want anything more in my life."

"We were all so happy," Mrs. Quinn murmured.

Mariel had an idea of what Mrs. Quinn was referring to. Life was like that. A person just started to think that she could bear life as it was. And then it got worse. And one had to learn to deal with it all over again. She once again recalled her mother's advice: Life is what it is.

Of course, that wasn't exactly what Mrs. Quinn was referring to. Somehow the Quinns had carved out a different kind of life than other people. In Mariel's experience, most people—unlike the Quinns—were busy trying to gain wealth or social standing or political power. "You have a happy family. It is just war has come."

Mrs. Quinn drew in a long breath. "I don't want Reva and Ash to leave us for good. I don't want my daughter and Emilio to go to the war. I don't want you to go. But I will not stand in the way of any of you. What right do I have? All of you are of age. And free."

That was true, but . . . "I do not want you to think I do not appreciate what you do for me."

"What I did for you was for our benefit too. Just watch over Sugar for me. She is still fragile. I don't want . . . I don't want her hurt more."

"I will." The promise welled up from deep inside. Mariel longed to repay this lady for her kindness.

"Now let's practice your riding skills. Pick up the pace." Mrs. Quinn nudged her horse, and it jogged forward.

Heart quickening, Mariel followed her example and tried not to take fright as the horse under her moved faster. Her stomach skittered. Would she really be able to ride a horse all the way to where Carson was stationed?

But she had no choice. She knew she could do anything, would do anything to be with Carson again. And her heart raced faster than before.

* * *

The day after Niven's request, Carson and the rest of the twenty Rangers headed out to find the Mexican Army and choose the best route for engaging them. The Rangers left camp just as Taylor's army was bedding down for the night. The grasslands of Texas and Mexico offered very little cover, so they would travel by night. And riding would be cooler under the moon.

Within the first mile of camp, Carson, riding beside Mc-Culloch, tried to ignore his feeling of ill ease and irritation. Something had cropped up that neither of them had expected.

McCulloch glanced at Carson, asking silently for his opinion about what to do with their uninvited guest. Carson made a face but gave one barely noticeable shrug. And then it was just the riding, covering miles till daybreak. They guessed the Mexican Army under Arista was probably miles deeper within Mexico.

As they rode through the moonlight, he took in the lay of the land. Over most of it, soldiers would be able to march abreast. Carson wondered what an army of thousands marching would look like. Memories of the brief battle of San Jacinto didn't help much. The Mexican Army had fled that day, not marched forward with bugles blaring. As Carson and his horse moved as one creature, he forgot everything else but the job at hand.

Finally, the dawn gleamed golden pink eastward behind them. McCulloch directed his horse closer to a creek they had been following, a tributary of the Rio Grande. Amid the trees and low green growth at the creek bank, they all dismounted and then turned as one to watch the presence every one of them had been aware of throughout the long night.

Carson's exasperation spiked inside him. Evidently, Blanche's husband matched her in egotism. Carson would enjoy watching McCulloch's reaction. He folded his hands and hooked a thumb over his belt buckle.

Niven rode up to them.

McCulloch said not a word, only motioned for the soldier to dismount and come to him. Niven did so, his expression a mixture of apprehension and cockiness.

Again, McCulloch said nothing, just waited. Then he slammed his fist into Niven's jaw. The American went down. "You disobey me again I'll cut off your right earlobe, got it?"

Carson waited to see what the American would say. The sound of the knuckles against jawbone had been sharp and painful-sounding. And very satisfying to hear.

Niven remained on the ground, rubbing his jaw and studying McCulloch. "Got it, sir."

"We don't do much 'sir'-ing. Stick to Carson and do what either of us tells you to. And if you get killed, it's on your head, not ours. We didn't invite you to come along."

Carson stared down at Niven, then, sliding from his saddle, offered him his hand. Niven took it. Niven had sense enough not to say anything in self-justification. Maybe the greenhorn wasn't a total loss.

* * *

Waiting in front of their hacienda in the morning sun, Dorritt stood beside her husband of over twenty years. His strengthening presence was the only thing keeping her from sliding limply down to the dry, sandy earth. *I will not cry and make this harder for Reva.* But if Amos and Nancy didn't arrive soon, her good intention might not be possible.

Erin had hidden her face in Dorritt's skirt, refusing to look at or speak to anyone. Reva had been a second mother to Erin. And today Erin, who had already lost Carson, would now lose Reva, her sister, and Mariel too. Dorritt's sympathy for Erin, her last chick still in the nest, irritated her like nettles. And made this parting all the harder.

Everyone who lived on the rancho had come to bid farewell to Ash and Reva. They'd also come to see off Amos and Nancy, who'd settled at nearby Rancho Sandoval; they would be leaving with the party. Mariel and Sugar, wearing the dark split skirts, long-sleeved white blouses, and Western-style full-brimmed hats, also waited, also ready to leave for the war. Emilio stood next to his bride, and his family had come too. Everyone tried to break the heavy silence with smiles and hope-filled expressions. But every face spoke of the pain of parting.

Ash beside her, Reva stood near Dorritt. "I will write you," Reva was saying. "Ash's cousins often go between San Antonio and Laredo on business. They will stop here and take messages south. They been doing that for us and Antonio."

Dorritt nodded. "I'll write too." The words hurt her throat but had to be said.

Ash stared at the ground, his hands in his pockets.

Quinn looked to the eastern horizon.

Then the wagon came into view, and everyone turned to look at it. Dorritt felt relief. The agony of parting would soon end, though the mourning of loss would follow . . . and linger.

Soon, Amos and Nancy halted their wagon beside Ash's and climbed down. Now two wagons loaded and covered with brown canvas stood in front of the ranch house. Now the farewells would begin. Coming in turn, men shook hands and women kissed cheeks. Everyone embraced those leaving. Finally, all the exchanges of affection had been fulfilled. Save one.

Quinn, who had held back, stepped forward. *"Vaya con Dios, mi amigo."*

Large tears slid down Ash's face, down the folds in his weathered skin. *"Vaya con Dios, mi amigo."* The two men embraced, slapping each other's backs.

Watching Quinn say good-bye to his oldest friend, the man who had helped raise him, nearly took Dorritt to her knees. Erin was weeping harder into Dorritt's skirt. The sound shredded her heart.

Ash turned and helped Reva onto the buckboard seat. Amos and Nancy climbed onto their wagon. Emilio helped Sugar and Mariel mount, then swung into his saddle. Waving and calling more words of farewell, they all turned away and started off at a quick pace.

Erin broke away from her mother. "Sugar! Be safe! Miss Mariel, keep safe! And come back! I want you to come back! Soon!"

Sugar turned her horse around and came back to Erin. Then Sugar bent down and touched her little sister's cheek. "I will, sweetheart. Don't worry. We'll all come back and bring Carson as soon as we can." Sugar spurred her horse, and the travelers headed toward the southern horizon.

Dorritt and Quinn pulled Erin close and hugged her, holding in their own grief as they comforted and reassured her. The crowd began to drift away. Emilio's family said their good-byes and headed home. The somber mood still hung in the dry, bright air.

Dorritt once again marveled at the life God had blessed her with. And she prayed silently for Reva and Ash to reach Antonio, for her children's safety and quick return. *The humble shall inherit the earth; and shall delight themselves in the abundance of peace.* Peace, what a wonderful promise. Yet so elusive in Texas, in this place that was home.

* * *

On the third hot, miserable night west from Point Isabel, just after nightfall, Carson saw a band of armed Mexican civilians ahead. An unlucky meeting. His pulse leaped in his veins. McCulloch glanced sideways to Carson. The glance said: "Attack." Carson nodded once, bracing himself for what he'd come south to do, to fight and kill.

The approaching adversary was also primed and ready. They rode straight at the Rangers. *"Quien vive?"* they shouted as they charged, "Who will live?"

McCulloch roared without words, spurring his mustang forward. Carson slid his rifle down. He shot one Mexican off his horse. He let the rifle dangle, slid one Walker Colt .45 into his hand. The fighting was hand to hand. The gritty smoke of gunpowder. Grunts as fists, lead hit flesh and bone. Shrieks of fury—pain. More gunfire.

Carson emptied one Colt and slid his other out of his belt. He got off two more shots. Then the remnant of Mexicans was galloping away. Some Rangers gave chase. Carson suddenly thought of Niven. Where was the tenderfoot?

Reining in his horse, Carson spun around. Niven was down near the rear, though, still holding the reins to his horse. Carson rode over to him and slid from the saddle. "Are you all right?"

Niven turned his head and vomited.

Carson turned away and let the man recover himself. Carson was accustomed to this kind of skirmish. He didn't even think anymore of the way a bullet could rip flesh and uncap a dam of blood. He didn't even think. He just shot and kept shooting till it ended. *I don't have to think anymore.* The thought went down like swallowing cactus.

Finally Niven rose, drawing his mount closer.

His movement caught Carson's eye, and he turned back. "First time?" *In battle?*

Niven nodded as he mounted.

"Most vomit or get the shakes." Carson kept his voice low, but frank. He wondered if Niven would have a change of career plans after a few more of these bloody clashes.

Niven looked away, as if wishing to divert attention from himself. "Who were they? I mean, they couldn't be the Mexican Army."

"Let's find out." Carson led his horse and began looking at the downed men. Most were Mexicans past help. A few Rangers were cleaning and bandaging their own minor wounds and those of other Rangers. Carson stopped, knelt to help a few tie bandages and get the Rangers back on their feet.

McCulloch met Carson. "It was Blás Falcón."

"Who's he? A Mexican vigilante or mercenary?" Niven blurted out the question.

"He's one of the largest ranchers in this part of Mexico."

McCulloch looked in the direction the Mexicans had retreated. "I'm sorry he got away."

"You mean a wealthy landowner just attacked us with his men?" Niven sounded astounded.

McCulloch looked down his nose at the Easterner.

Carson couldn't figure out why this would startle the American. He tried to view it through Niven's eyes. Niven wouldn't know about Texas. Carson explained, "We've been fighting a border war for the last ten years. Some Mexicans held title to land on both sides of the Rio Grande. And they have refused to part with it. And some just hate Anglos. No Mexican has ever accepted the Rio Grande as the boundary between Mexico and Texas."

Tunney came up beside them. "Yeah, so they raid and burn out Anglos. Steal cattle and horses. Trying to drive us back."

"And some Texians repay them in kind," Carson added.

"I had no idea." Niven gazed around and shook his head. "What should we do for the wounded?"

"Nothing for the Mexicans." McCulloch swung back up into his saddle. "Their people will come and get them after we're gone. They know that though Rangers will kill any Mexican who's aimed a gun at us, we don't torture like the Comanche or Mexicans themselves." McCulloch's lips pulled back in a snarl.

Carson knew that every word McCulloch said was true. The Anglos hated those who tortured. And had no qualms about killing them.

Noting that the remaining Rangers had helped their wounded companions onto their saddles, Carson urged his horse forward too.

Niven hesitated there, looking around, obviously disoriented.

"Time to move on," Carson told him. "This was just a quick skirmish. We need to cover more miles tonight. We're trying to find Arista and the real Mexican Army, remember?"

* * *

The long night in the saddle finally ended. Near daybreak, McCulloch led the Rangers to make camp near another creek bank. Most were so tired that they unsaddled and hobbled their horses, then threw themselves down on the ground onto their saddle blankets. Carson had survived another skirmish. Flashes of memory kept taking him back to other gory clashes with Kiowa, Comanche, Mexican *bandidos*.

Taught by his father, Carson always took care of his weapons first before sleep. He did not tamper with this habit. His father had told him that it would save his life many times. And his father had been right.

Tonight it served too as a way to distract his turbulent, fractious thoughts. He laid all his guns in a row beside him. This year, this war had stirred him up somehow. He remembered his mother teaching him about volcanoes and earthquakes, great forces from deep in the earth itself that could rip cities apart and leave them in ruins. He felt that had happened to his insides.

Amidst the cover of low bushes and high grass, he sat cross-legged under a popple tree and began cleaning his guns. First the rifle, then the two Colts.

Niven lumbered over, looking saddle-sore and exhausted.

"How do you like being a Ranger?" Carson murmured.

"Not much." Niven leaned against the tree, looking as if he didn't dare sit down. "How long have you been at this?"

"Six years."

"Is the pay good?"

"We get paid sometimes. When Texas can afford to."

Niven stared at him. Finally, he said, "I've never seen pistols like those. What are they?"

Carson went on reloading. "Only a few of us have these. We could use more. These are Walker Colt .45s. Samuel Colt designed the first one. Our own Ranger Walker saw that it was just what we needed here in Texas, but it required a few changes to be more practical. So a few years ago, Walker went back east, found Samuel Colt and showed him what we needed."

Carson held the gun in his palm. "Before, see, I would have had to take the gun apart to reload. Plus, the trigger kept disappearing into the gun, and it was too clumsy to get out easy."

Wobbly, Niven leaned over, inspecting the gun. "Why haven't I heard of such a weapon?"

Carson shrugged. "It's been a boon for us. Before we got these, we were at a disadvantage fighting the Comanche. We had single-shot rifles or pistols to their arrows. And a Comanche can shoot a full quiver of arrows into a man while he tries to reload."

"You wear a bow and have a quiver," Niven pointed out.

"Yes, I'm good with a bow." *I'm good at most ways of killing men.* This thought shriveled inside him. "And I use it sometimes if the raid goes on where I need to reload and don't have time."

"I have a lot to learn. And I want one of those Colts. How do I get one?"

"Well, why not ask Taylor?"

"I will." Niven wavered on his feet.

"You better go lay down before you fall down."

Niven nodded and staggered a few feet away. As soon as his head touched his blanket, he fell asleep.

Carson put his reloaded guns beside him, lay down, and tried to sleep. Impressions from the skirmish flowed through his mind. He couldn't remember if he'd killed anyone or not. The Mexican faces were blurred in his mind. And then they became Comanche faces. Carson shook his head, trying to bring the recent skirmish into focus.

He'd seen Niven throw up. He remembered that clearly. And he'd seen that kind of reaction happen before. Killing made

people sick. Or made them cry. Or shake. It was probably from
God. Violence should make a person sick. Shake them up.

It doesn't make me sick. Not anymore.

Grimacing, he made himself bring back soothing images of
Sugar and Emilio's wedding, of Mariel in her blue dress. Mariel.
At least Mariel and his family were far away from this war.
Safe.

* * *

After a week traveling southeast of the Quinn Ranch, Ash's
party halted early in the afternoon, camping near a deep creek
bank. They were tired and hot in the mid-June summer heat.
And the closer they ventured toward the rising sun, the more
moist and unpleasant the air became. Ash's dogs lay panting in
the sparse shade, their tongues out.

Sugar had appeared lost in thought and, worse, near tears all
day. Mariel talked to Reva for a few minutes and turned around
to find that Sugar had disappeared. Where was she?

Mariel left Reva and Nancy resting in the shade of a stunted-
looking tree. She walked past the men who were fixing harnesses and checking the horses and wagons for any signs of
weakening from rolling and jolting over the rocky, uneven, vast
landscape.

Mariel had almost become used to the continuing spectacle
of miles and miles of land without trees, streets, houses, people.
When, back in Europe, she had thought about America, she
had envisioned forests and savages. Where were the forests?
Galveston was as different from New Braunfels as New Braunfels was from San Antonio and as different as San Antonio was
from the land she was gazing at now.

Sometimes she closed her eyes, unable to look any more at
the measureless, untouched, uninhabited miles. How did people
confront such a limitless landscape, such loneliness? She gazed

around once again, impressed by the people around her. They faced this land and lived their lives. Bravely. Like Carson Quinn.

"Mariel!" Sugar was calling her and waving from the brush near the creek bank ahead. "Grab a basket or bucket for each of us! Mustang—"

The breeze caught the rest of Sugar's words and carried them away unheard. Mariel hurried back and dug in a wagon to find two water buckets. She picked her way through the wild shrubbery that lined both sides of the creek.

"Oh, good!" Sugar called out. "Come! I found wild mustang grapes!"

Mustang? Horse grapes? Mariel approached Sugar and offered her one of the buckets.

"Be careful. Snakes will be lying beneath the shade of the brush out of the sun," Sugar cautioned.

Snakes. Mariel halted in her tracks. Carson had described to her all the deadly snakes in Texas. The memory of the little Heller boy losing his finger made her freeze with horror.

Sugar shook her head at Mariel, who was petrified in place. Then Sugar came forward and led Mariel by the hand. "This path is safe. I checked it on my way to the grapes. Look."

Mariel looked around at the mass of twisted vines. She had never picked any grapes, much less wild ones.

Sugar opened her hand, revealing large, round grapes with glossy, dark purple skin. She squeezed one of the grapes and exposed what looked like a white eyeball inside.

Pressing her thumbnail into the flesh, Sugar exposed a double seed core. "You eat them like this—put a grape in your mouth and press it with your tongue and out comes the fruit. Then spit out the skin." A little purple juice leaked out at the corner of her mouth. She sucked it in and giggled.

The giggle turned into a sob. Sugar turned away and began to pick grapes and drop them into the tin bucket. Plop. Plop.

I was right. Something is tormenting Sugar.

Mariel began picking grapes, trying to come up with a way to ease Sugar into sharing a confidence. The fresh, sweet scent of the ripe fruit tempted her. She couldn't resist slipping a grape into her dry mouth, squeezing it with her tongue and letting the sweet, tangy juice flow. How she had longed for fresh fruit on the voyage to Texas.

As she picked the fruit, she tried to decide whether she should act as if she had not noticed Sugar weeping. But Mrs. Quinn was counting on her. Mariel said in a low, yet firm, voice, "Sugar, I will listen. And not talk about what you say."

Sugar audibly drew in her tears, but she did not look at Mariel. "I know about the letters. The letters Carson found in that . . . place."

Startled by this reference to something that had happened almost three months ago, Mariel considered it. "I wondered. I saw your eyes open in the dark that night. Why did you not say anything? I looked at you."

"I know." Sugar's voice sounded constricted. "But the fear had come over me and I couldn't say a word."

Mariel thought about the times she had faced overwhelming fear. Maybe Sugar needed to know that everyone was afraid of something. "I have been afraid too. Many times. Fear can have great power."

"What have you been afraid of?" Sugar asked in a serious tone.

Mariel would not give less than Sugar. She would be as honest as Sugar. Mariel reached down and brought up the worst, most fearful day of her life. She had to force out each word. "My wedding. I did not have a good one like you and Emilio. I barely knew the man who was to be my husband." She felt drained, as if each word bled her.

Sugar looked over her shoulder. "You mean you were like my cousin Blanche?"

"Blanche?" Mariel repeated, startled. "Who is she?"

"We went to her wedding before we met up with you at . . . Montezuma." Sugar's voice faltered.

Mariel wondered if mentioning the town made Sugar recall the old woman, the one who had recognized Sugar, and if that was bringing fresh pain, like pulling a dried bandage from a healing wound.

Her back still turned, keeping a wall between them, Sugar started talking again. "Anyway, Blanche started writing letters to a man whom her brother met as a student at West Point."

Mariel had heard of courtships like this even in Germany.

Sugar continued picking grapes, dropping them into the bucket and telling the story. "This man, Anthony Niven, visited earlier this year, and Blanche decided that she would accept his proposal. Blanche made it sound so romantic, but I don't think she fell in love with him. He is very good looking. And he was in uniform. I'll bet that impressed her—all the gold braid and brass buttons."

This Mariel could understand. Scheming to make a good match in this dirty world was as common as mud. "Oh? A marriage of . . . gain?"

"My mother called it a marriage of two self-seeking hearts," Sugar said, sounding a bit calmer. "Is that why your parents arranged your marriage? They wanted you to marry someone who would impress others?"

Mariel drew in the hot moist air, trying to draw strength from it, and failing. "My marriage was not like that. I did not marry to gain wealth or rank. The marriage was arranged by my parents. My husband was a teacher like my father but more interested in politics." The old bitterness seeped in and around her heart. She had been treated more as a maid than a wife in her husband's apartment. "My husband devoted his time to radical politics instead of providing for his wife." He would have lived longer if he had kept to his teaching. Politics had imprisoned and, in the end, killed him.

"Why would your parents think he was a good husband then?" Sugar sounded confused.

How could Mariel explain to Sugar that her parents had not had much of a dowry and had no longer wanted the burden of providing for her? "I do not know."

"And you couldn't say no?"

"No." Mariel left it at that. Of course, Sugar wouldn't understand the way marriages were handled in Germany. If a girl had loving parents, her lot was better. If not, . . . "*Grossmutter liebte mich.*"

"What?"

Mariel realized that she had murmured this last aloud. "Sorry. I said my grandmother loved me." And she said that God loved Mariel, too. She looked down at the lushly fruited vines. She had barely picked a fraction of the grapes there. This land had such untouched abundance. She recalled the widespread want in Germany. Perhaps God did love her. He had let her come here to these good people in this bountiful land. She returned to Sugar and her dilemma. "This is not about me, but about you and the letters. Tell me. I will try to help."

Sugar went on picking grapes. A mockingbird sang on a tree nearby. The sun was hot where it sifted through the leaves overhead. One of Ash's dogs barked at something.

Finally, when Mariel was about to prompt her again, Sugar said, "This year has been full of changes. I didn't want to go east to Blanche's wedding. I knew what it would be like. All society and everyone trying to impress each other and everyone looking down at me, the orphan without any family. I went to the wedding only to please my mother."

Sugar stopped picking and turned to look at Mariel. "I think . . . I think that Carson had a *tendre* for Blanche. I hadn't real-

ized until I saw them together at the wedding. There, whenever Carson was near her, she behaved strangely. And she said
such rude things to him, and in a way that he couldn't say anything back to her without being rude to a lady. Something he
wouldn't do, of course. I was so angry with her." Sugar pressed
her lips together. "I thought you should know that, know what
had happened to him this year."

Mariel didn't say anything, but yes, she had observed women
like this Blanche. *A stupid woman to scorn a man like Carson.*

Sugar began talking in a brisker tone, "And then on the way
home, that old woman in Montezuma recognized me. And now
this war has started." Sugar looked skyward. "Most of all, getting
married made me begin to feel differently. I mean I'm a woman
now, not a girl. I'm a wife, and soon I may be a mother. Do I want
to be an 'afraid' mother? That isn't good for children."

Mariel stopped picking too and gazed at the pretty woman
standing in the midst of the wild, tangled vines. Did Sugar
know how lovely she was? Mariel chose her words with care.
What would Mrs. Quinn want her to say? "*Ja.* You must not be
a mother who makes her children afraid."

Sugar's face lifted. She put a grape in her mouth. After she
swallowed the fruit and discarded the purple skin, she said,
"You see what I mean then. I think I must read those letters.
And not let whatever is in them frighten me. I have to stop
being afraid of . . . how I came to lose my first family. Of bad
memories."

Mariel rested her juice-stained hand on Sugar's arm, carefully avoiding her sleeve. "You will be a good mother. And you
are already a good wife to Emilio."

Sugar pressed a hand over Mariel's. "I want you to marry
Carson."

Mariel couldn't speak. Hearing her deepest desire spoken
aloud for the first time here in the sunshine made her heart

clench. She tried to smile, failed. She squeezed Sugar's hand. Then, along with Sugar, she went back to picking the deep purple fruit, hiding her thoughts behind the chore just as Sugar had. Mariel continued to eat as she picked the tangy fruit. Merely something fresh to eat gave her a lightening of spirit. And that brought Carson to mind.

Not much farther and they would reach the army. Would Carson be happy to see her? Or had she put herself forward by coming without an invitation?

* * *

A little more than two weeks after they had left the Quinn Ranch, Mariel pulled up on her reins, awed. Spread out before her was an army. After endless and empty miles, the sudden sight of thousands of blue-clad men made Mariel blink. The thousands didn't disappear. So it wasn't a mirage of water ahead, a trick the sun had played on her over and over on the way here.

The seven of them all paused to stare at the spectacle. Then Amos and Nancy, Ash and Reva, all on the benches of the buckboards, and Emilio, Sugar, and Mariel, all on horseback, ventured into camp. They rode on and on through men, many shirtless due to the heat, who rose and gawked at them. How would they find Carson in this mass of people?

Finally, one soldier who had gold stripes on his rolled-up sleeve waved them down. "Who are you? And what's your business?"

Emilio pulled up his reins. "We are looking for the Rangers who came about a month ago."

The man squinted at Emilio. "Are you one of the Mexicans who ride with the Rangers we heard tell of?"

"*Sí*, I am Emilio Ramirez, a *Tejano* Ranger."

"*Tejano*? What's that?"

"It means what you have said, a Texan of Mexican blood. Mexicans who prefer liberty. Are Ben McCulloch's Rangers here?"

The man rubbed the side of his nose with his index finger. "There are Rangers here. You go on up to near the command. That's ahead about a mile or so to your right."

"Thank you." Emilio pulled the brim of his hat. Ash and Amos slapped the reins to each team, and they moved ahead through swell after swell in the sea of gawking soldiers.

Mariel felt each man's attention burn, as if it were hot sunlight directed on her. She tried to behave as if she did not notice. Yet she felt exposed, defenseless. Her heart tugged her to move faster, to find Carson, who would protect her from this impolite ogling.

If Emilio, Ash, and Amos had not been there glaring at the soldiers, Mariel sensed it would have been much worse for her and Sugar. They were venturing into a place where women of their sort weren't expected and might be mistaken for camp followers, prostitutes.

At long last, they came to a few larger canvas tents with an American flag flying from a nearby pole. Mariel scanned the surrounding area, looking for men in buckskin, hoping to see Carson's face. To see him striding toward her and smiling. But she could see no men in buckskin.

Then, just as another soldier with more gold stripes was approaching them and looking disagreeable, two men—one old, one young—came out of a large tent.

"Remy!" Sugar called out, "Remy LaCroix!" The younger man looked up and his mouth dropped open.

At Sugar's exclamation, Mariel jerked her reins. Now she had to soothe the mare, who fidgeted beneath her. She stroked the horse's neck and spoke in soothing tones.

"It's me, your cousin Sugar. Help me down, Emilio, please."

Emilio dismounted, lifting Sugar from her saddle. She hurried forward, holding out her hand to the young man. "Remy, we've come to find Carson. Do you know where he is?"

The young man reluctantly took Sugar's hand and bowed over it. He did not look happy. Emilio followed right behind her and looked stiff and uncomfortable.

Mariel already didn't like this cousin LaCroix. She slid out of her saddle, ready to do whatever she could to protect Sugar from any impoliteness.

"Remy, we're looking for my brother, Carson," Sugar repeated and motioned behind them. "Some man told us that there were Rangers in camp near the command tents. Is Carson here?"

Remy looked chagrined and pained. "Carson left almost two weeks ago. We've been expecting his Ranger squad to return any time now."

"Lieutenant, introduce me to this pretty lady," the older man said. "Is she really the sister of that Ranger? And your cousin?"

Mariel caught something in the older man's tone that told her there was more to this question than the simple request. She studied the older man's face but could not tell if he was amused or mocking. And if mocking, whom?

Remy bowed to the older man. "This is Miss Sugar Quinn—"

"Oh, I'm not Quinn anymore, Remy," Sugar interrupted, smiling and reaching for Emilio's arm. "This is my husband, Emilio Ramirez, another Ranger."

Remy's face glowed red. Mariel read his expression with ease. Sugar's cousin was embarrassed to have it known that his kin had married someone with Mexican blood.

The older man stepped forward. "Mrs. Ramirez, I'm General Taylor. I met your brother with Ben McCulloch." The older gentleman bowed over her hand. And then he shook Emilio's, welcoming him. He sounded sincere.

Mariel did not like the way LaCroix was looking at Sugar. And what was worse, Sugar was beginning to notice his lack of welcome. Her pretty face was turning pink. And Emilio's eyes were stormy.

"And who is this other charming young lady?" the general was asking LaCroix.

Mariel stepped forward, shielding Sugar and Emilio. "I am Mariel Wolffe, Carson's fiancée." As the words left her mouth, shock exploded like ice inside. Why had she said that? Her mind racing, she focused on curtseying to the general and to LaCroix.

"You sound European, miss," the general commented.

"Yes, I come recently from Germany. I met Carson. He led my people from Galveston to land north of San Antonio."

"Your English is very good for someone so new to America," the general said.

Mariel lifted her chin, recalling Sugar's explanation of how LaCroix's sister had insulted Carson. "My father taught modern languages, English, French, and Spanish. I used to listen to him when he tutored students in languages." *From outside the door where he couldn't see me.*

"Well, well, I was quite impressed with your fiancé." The general rocked back and forth on the balls of his feet.

"Carson is not here, sir?" Mariel asked, still breathing fast from lying about her relationship with Carson. Had she done it just to turn attention from Sugar?

"That's correct," the general said. "He went with the other Rangers under McCulloch. Is there a family emergency? Is Carson needed at home?"

Ja, he is needed. Mariel didn't say this aloud. "No, but we, Mrs. Ramirez and I, decide we might be nurses."

"Yes, my mother helped the doctors after the Battle of San Jacinto." Sugar spoke with a lift of her chin and a challenging look toward her cousin. "I thought we might be useful."

"Commendable. Commendable," the general said. He turned to Emilio. "The other ladies of the temporary garrison here— the officers' wives or dependents—are along this lane of tents ahead. I'm sure you two ladies will be welcomed warmly. And Ramirez, you'll find some Rangers in the same direction. Hays is here with his men."

Mariel and Sugar curtseyed. Emilio nodded. General Taylor and LaCroix bowed and walked away. LaCroix did not look back.

The three of them did not remount; they merely walked their horses in the direction the general had indicated. "Mariel, I didn't know that Carson had proposed to you," Sugar said in an undertone.

"He did not. I do not know why I said that," Mariel admitted, feeling the burn of shame.

"It was a good idea," Ash said, breaking his silence. "You need to let them know that you're not just riffraff like the rest of us."

Mariel did not argue with Ash's impression. Neither the general nor the cousin had taken any notice of the four darker-skinned people on the wagons. Since coming to know the Quinns, Mariel now looked at people, at life, differently. Now she didn't view people according to their rank or color, as she had in Germany. Now she looked at their behavior, their character. This realization expanded inside her and gave her new freedom. This was the most important change in her. And she owed it to the Quinns, who lived their deep faith. And most of all, to Carson.

Thirteen

Two days later, even though the June sun had only recently emerged on the eastern horizon, it was already blazing. Escaping its heat, Carson and Ben McCulloch ambled into General Taylor's current office in a large canvas tent to report what they'd found. The U.S. Army had moved inland, some westward along the Rio Grande. Niven trailed into the tent after the two men, uninvited. Carson looked around, noting that LaCroix was not to be seen. *Good.*

After greeting Taylor, McCulloch gave a three-sentence account of the results of the scouting trip. "We had a dustup with a few Mexicans under Blás Falcón. Arista has fallen back to Monterrey. We got a marching route mapped out for you."

"What took you so long?" Taylor asked.

McCulloch gave Taylor a look that asked, *What's it to you?* Yet he only said, "Tried to find General Canales and settle a long overdue score with him. Couldn't run him to ground, so we headed back to you."

Taylor lifted an eyebrow. "A score?"

McCulloch nodded. "Canales has a habit of raiding Texan settlements, killing and looting."

Carson watched the general take this in. His face looked like he was sucking on a lemon. He didn't look happy, but that wouldn't change the Rangers' goal of paying back Canales. Easterners didn't understand that on the frontier, honest men had to enforce right and wrong or be erased from the land. Carson's jaw hardened. No one was going to erase him from this land. Or those he loved.

"I see." Taylor stared into McCulloch's eyes.

"General," Niven said in a respectful tone, "with your permission, sir. I'd like you to look at the Walker Colts these men carry."

The general turned his attention to Niven, and sounding amused, asked, "Did you learn what you wanted by going along with the Rangers?"

Niven bowed his head, grinning. "I learned a lot. And one of the main things I learned is that I want a pair of these Walker Colts. Have you ever seen a gun that can fire six times before being reloaded?"

Taylor frowned. "I may have heard of one. But I've never seen one."

"Carson, would you show the general how yours works?" Niven asked.

Carson didn't want to oblige. He just wanted to find the other Rangers and go to sleep. No matter. He dragged in air. "Need to go outside to do that."

The four of them moved back outside under the heat of the sun. There they gathered a large crowd of gawkers. Even though he was bleary-eyed, Carson fired a few accurate rounds into a log pulled from a woodpile near the command post. The gunshots drew more attention. Then, feeling sweat trickle down his back, Carson went on to explain the improvements that Walker had helped Colt, the inventor, make. Every soldier watched him. Some looked skeptical, others interested. Carson swallowed a yawn.

Niven took one of Carson's Colts into his hand, displaying it on his palm. "You can see the advantage, General. In hand to hand or a cavalry charge, a man can keep fighting longer."

Taylor made a face. "I doubt we will be doing much hand to hand, and I don't have a cavalry."

"I beg to differ." Niven silently demonstrated how easy it was to bring out the Colt from a belt or pocket. "The Rangers are already performing the duties of a cavalry."

Taylor tilted his head, as if thinking. "It doesn't hurt to have the latest in weaponry," he said, though with obvious reluctance. "History has taught us that the army that has the best weapons wins. I'll order a thousand for my officers and the Rangers. They'd be of no use to my infantrymen."

Carson didn't quite agree. He believed in having more than one weapon going into battle. He wasn't in charge here, though. And more Colts for his fellow Rangers might save their lives.

"Thank you, General." Niven grinned.

Taylor thanked McCulloch and Carson. "You two take a few days' rest and recover."

Carson turned, just wanting this done. This having to report to someone else didn't set well in his gut.

The general continued, "And Carson, your ladies are here. Go to the right up ahead to the family camp and you'll find them there with the servants they brought along."

Carson's custom of keeping his face expressionless, learned from his father, came to his aid. Not letting his surprise show, he merely turned his head to look at the general.

"Yes, your lovely sister and your fiancée," Taylor said, suddenly grinning. "I can tell you that among my officers, you are looked upon with general envy."

Carson merely nodded. He wouldn't jump to any conclusions. But he thought there was something else in the American's face. Was there something else Carson didn't know?

And then Carson and McCulloch walked away, leaving Niven behind with the general. It had occurred to Carson that perhaps Niven had been sent along not only to learn about frontier fighting but also to report on the Rangers to the general. He didn't like that, but he could understand it. Taylor had put a lot of trust in the Rangers, men he'd just met.

However, at the forefront of his mind was the news about his "ladies" being in camp. He didn't like the sound of that at all. Was it a mistake? *I left Mariel safe at home. What's going on?* Then the thought that something might have happened to his family, that there might be some bad news, made Carson move quicker.

McCulloch hurried away to rejoin the Rangers who'd come with Jack Hays, while Carson headed off to find the women from home. He was walking through the area of tents evidently occupied by the officers.

Without planning to, he found himself walking toward his cousin LaCroix, who was standing outside his tent, speaking to his Negro valet. Carson recognized this young man Jonah from his visits to the LaCroix plantation.

Just as Carson was trying to figure out how to go around his cousin and not have to speak to him, LaCroix backhanded his manservant. The sharp crack of the blow ripped Carson's temper wide open. Within two strides, Carson reached his cousin. He spun him around. And with his fist slammed him to the ground.

Mariel had been washing the breakfast dishes outside a large canvas tent where several of the officers' wives were billeted or stationed. One of the other wives had rushed to Mariel and told her that the Rangers had returned and were reporting to the general. Drying her hands, Mariel had taken off, hurrying toward the command tent.

Ahead, she glimpsed Carson coming toward her. She picked up her pace. Then he stopped and hit a man.

Mariel halted in her tracks, close enough to see and hear, wary of drawing nearer. Women were not supposed to be anywhere near where men were fighting. That she knew. Memories of Heller's attack on her and Carson fighting him made her a little light-headed.

When the man Carson had knocked down rose, Mariel recognized him as the puffed-up cousin Sugar had recognized when they'd arrived at camp. In spite of herself, she drew nearer.

"What did you do that for?" the cousin demanded, rubbing his jaw.

"A lot of reasons. The main one right now is that you struck your servant, something I won't stand by and let happen. A cowardly thing to do, since you know he can't hit you back."

The confrontation was of course drawing a crowd of onlookers. Mariel edged forward. The cousin's face flushed red. "Are you calling me a coward?"

"Yes." Carson raised his fists, obviously showing his readiness to finish the argument.

Something in the cousin's bearing told Mariel that he was afraid of fighting Carson. The cousin sneered aloud, "A gentleman doesn't indulge in fisticuffs."

The slur was flagrant. He had just insulted Carson.

"You're a gentleman, then? Is that what you call yourself? Is having a servant and being able to abuse him at will—is that what makes you a gentleman?" Carson taunted, his contempt for the other man obvious in his every word.

"Yes, I am. You're just a half-breed mongrel—"

With that, Carson reached over and snatched the gloves tucked into his cousin's belt. He slapped the man's face with them. "Isn't that how a gentleman challenges another?" This time Carson sneered.

"You're challenging me?" The cousin sounded as if he was trying to hide his shock and fear.

"Yes, I am. I won't stand by and watch a servant mistreated. And it's time someone taught you about being a man, not a spoiled, self-important boy."

The cousin stiffened, reddening more. He kept his lips pressed together, mute.

"Well, since you can't stomach an honest fistfight, it's for you to choose the weapon." Carson tossed the gloves into the dust. "So what is it?"

The cousin's face twisted. "Swords. The weapon of gentlemen."

"Fine. Tomorrow just before sundown outside the Ranger camp. My second will be Emilio Ramirez. Have yours speak to him."

Carson stalked away from the flushed and angry young man.

"Carson." Mariel looked at him, then lowered her eyes.

"You're here."

His unhappy tone drenched Mariel like an icy wave. "Yes, sir," she whispered.

He took her by the arm. "Don't call me 'sir,'" he said in a low, heated voice. He began to hurry her away from the men around his cousin. Everyone was gawking at them. Mariel felt her face burning, and she hurried to keep up with Carson. She had never seen him like this, so angry. Finally, they reached the area near the family camp. Carson stopped. He let go of her arm and stood there, staring at the dust around their feet.

"I'm sorry you had to witness that," he said, sounding strained. "A lady shouldn't be exposed to violence."

His calling her a lady bolstered her spirits, so she asked, "You will have to fight that . . . man? Your cousin."

"You've met, then." Carson made a sound of irritation. "I don't want to fight him, but he needs to have the stuffing knocked out of him. I will not stand by and watch a man abuse a servant."

Mariel remembered when Carson had come to her aid, yet the scene with Heller felt as if it belonged to someone else's life. The soreness of the experience lingered, though it had been diminished by all the changes this year had brought to her, to everything in her life. And Mariel did feel different, stronger than she had all those months ago leaving Germany. At least she had till she'd come face-to-face with this scowling Carson. *I shouldn't have come.*

At the forefront of her mind, however, was her concern for this man. A fistfight was different from fighting with swords. Did men still fight duels here?

Carson took off his hat and slapped it against his thigh, freeing it from its coating of dust. "Why are you here, Mariel? Has something happened to my family? How did you get here?"

His obvious unhappiness with her made it hard for Mariel to marshal her thoughts. She had just seen Carson hit a man, and now he didn't look happy to see her. It was all too much to take in. She tried to form words, failed.

"Carson!" Ash's voice hailed from behind them.

"Ash? What are you doing here?" Carson moved forward. Away from her. She stayed behind, her hands folded. *I shouldn't have come.*

Ash hugged Carson and said, "Glad to see you, son." Then Reva, Amos, Nancy, Emilio, and Sugar came hurrying to him. Mariel stayed in the background. There were greetings and much excited talk. All Mariel could think of was Carson's lack of welcome and the upcoming duel.

Reva led Carson to their camp, set apart from where Sugar and Mariel had been billeted with the officers' wives.

Carson didn't look happy to see his sister either. "I know that I'm just your brother now. But why did Emilio bring you here, of all places?" He glanced at her as if to add, and why Mariel?

Mariel lowered her eyes. Was this the source of his unhappiness with her? Was it just because they had come here—where he didn't want them to be?

"I'll remind you that this isn't the first time I've been to war," Sugar said with a warning in her tone.

"This is much different. I wanted you . . . Mariel . . . safe at home, not here in this awful place." He swung an arm around and made a sound of disgust.

Mariel understood then. He wasn't angry with her and his sister, just angry over their coming.

Emilio put a hand on Carson's shoulder. "Amigo, I know just what you are feeling. I also wanted my wife to stay at home—safe. But your sister was raised by Señora Quinn. How could I expect my wife to be less a Texas woman than her *madre*?"

Mariel watched as Carson took this in. He still didn't look happy, but he gave his friend a reluctant grin and shook his head ruefully at his sister. Reva came forward with a cup of coffee and a biscuit left over from breakfast, which she handed to Carson. Then everyone moved to relax around the low fire. With his coffee cup in one hand and the biscuit in his other, Carson sat on the ground while Mariel perched on a three-legged stool behind him. In spite of his displeasure with her, the urge to touch him was nearly overwhelming. She folded her hands in her lap.

Carson spoke to Ash. "So you're going to go live with Antonio? And he's taken a wife. I'm happy for him." Carson yawned. "Sorry," he apologized. "We rode all night. Every night."

"You should rest," Mariel murmured.

"I will. Soon." He glanced her way, then lowered his eyes. That made her wonder. Why wouldn't he want to look her in the eye? Was he regretting that he had not welcomed her here?

"The four of us were just waiting for you to get back before we left," Ash replied. "But now, since we hear you're going to put on a show tomorrow evening, we'll stay till the following morning. Antonio will enjoy hearing how you whupped Kilbride's grandson."

Mariel tightened her lips to keep from begging Ash to do something, say the right words to stop this duel.

"You heard about that already?" Carson did not sound any happier.

"Hey, I watched you knock Remy down," Ash said. Amos chuckled.

"Stay if you're of that mind, Ash," Carson replied. "But there's going to be trouble ahead with this war, and I don't want you to run right into it. Get to Antonio's as fast as you can and hunker down there."

Ash was standing, leaning against one of the wagon wheels, his ankles crossed. "You think you'll be doing much scouting?"

"McCulloch left a string of Rangers between here and Major Brown farther inland. We ran into him in our scouting. McCulloch also wanted someone to keep an eye out for Arista." Carson blinked his eyes, as if trying to stay awake. "A few scouts are ranging nearer Monterrey, where Arista and his army are. If they see anything, they'll head to Brown and send word."

"I don't know much about Arista." Ash hooked one boot heel between the spokes of the wheel and folded his arms. "I'm glad General Santa Anna was kicked out of Mexico and won't be in the mix this time. No one needs a butcher like him around."

Carson rose. "I'm dead on my feet. I got to go sleep."

He glanced down at Mariel, looking as if he wanted to say something but couldn't decide what. After a round of "Get some sleep" and more teasing, Carson loped away. Even though she felt unwanted, Mariel couldn't help watching him. He moved with that long stride she admired. He was such a tall man, long and lean. Yet strong.

He'd gone off with only a backward glance. Had he forgotten

the kisses they had shared in his mother's garden and the words he had said to her just before he had left with the Rangers? Or was he still trying to accept her presence here?

Sugar came beside her and put an arm around her. "He's glad to see you. It's just that we didn't mind him. We didn't stay where he left us."

Mariel nodded, thinking Sugar was right. They turned around to go to the wives' camp. With her first step, fear leaped into her. "Sugar, how can we stop this duel?"

"We can't."

Mariel had no doubt that Carson was a better fighter than his cousin, but she wondered about the choice of weapon. Carson did not seem like a man who would know how to fight with a sword. Is that why the rude cousin had chosen that weapon? Mariel couldn't put this into words. *This duel must be stopped somehow.*

* * *

Waking, Carson sucked in hot, sultry, late afternoon air. He was bombarded with noises—men marching to a drum, a voice singing off-key somewhere, and gunfire sounding like target practice. He rolled onto his back and gazed up at the clear blue sky, remembering where he was and why. *All I have to do now is survive another war. There's the duel. And Mariel here, not safe at home.*

He grimaced and rose. His horse was hobbled nearby. He went over and picked up a saddlebag. Then he sauntered the half mile to the river, followed it far above the camp and found a lonely spot with bushes protruding out into the river. After cleaning up, he'd go borrow what he needed for the duel.

Wading into the slow-moving, tepid water, he soaped his buckskins while in them, then stripped them off to rinse them and spread them on a bush to dry. Using sand from the river-bed, he scrubbed two weeks of dust and sweat from his skin and hair. He finished with a final wash with soap. He wanted to go to his first duel looking the gentleman, not the frontiersman. Climbing from the water in the cover of the bushes, he dried off and drew on black trousers. Then he decided to shave for the occasion. And for Mariel. His cheek tingled when he imagined her soft palm touching it. Hanging his traveling mirror on the branch of a willow tree, he lathered his face and began shaving off a month's beard.

Approaching, Niven called to him a few minutes later, "I find you at last. I hear you challenged my dear brother-in-law to a duel."

Carson wiped his clean-shaven face with his damp linen towel. "Yes," he said, facing Niven, who was carrying two swords on his shoulder. "Someone has to teach Remy the difference between being a man and a boy." He pulled on his heavily starched white cotton shirt and began buttoning up. As he studied Niven, memories of Blanche's wedding grated on Carson. "Remy forced the duel on me. I hate slavery, and, in any event, I won't permit any man to abuse a servant in my presence."

Niven held up a hand. "I don't agree with you about slavery, but in regard to abusing servants, we are of the same mind. And by the way, General Taylor asked me why I hadn't told him you and LaCroix and I were all related."

"What did you tell him?" Carson wondered if Niven was ashamed to call him family too. He and his whole family had been given the cut direct at this man's wedding, and this man had done nothing to change that.

Niven gave a wry smile. "Well, if you recall, you said you'd just as soon the connection not be made public. And frankly, I concur. Not many other officers are siding with my brother-in-law over this duel. He hasn't endeared himself to others here. Most think he'll do better with a set-down."

Buttoning the final shirt button, Carson said nothing. He didn't know Niven well enough to trust him. But he would take any help he offered.

Niven displayed one of the swords. "Anyway, I thought you might want to borrow a sword. And do a little practice."

Leaning against the tree on which he'd hung his traveling mirror, Carson folded his arms in front of him, smirking. "Don't you mean *teach* me how to fence?"

Grinning back, Niven handed Carson one of the two sabers he'd brought. "No, something tells me that you know how to handle a sword. I get the feeling you know all the ways there are to fight a man—or kill one."

The casual words sliced Carson, left him bleeding. This greenhorn had just demonstrated how little he still understood of war. Carson lifted his chin. "I've never used poison."

Niven gave a bark of a laugh. "You Texans and that dry sense of humor."

Carson moved away from the tree. His whole body, his entire mind, snapped to attention.

Without another word, Niven took up the classic fencing stance. Carson hefted the borrowed saber a few times in his right hand first. It had been a long time since he had held a saber. He tossed it back and forth from hand to hand. When the feel of it came back, he mimicked Niven's stance.

"*En garde.*" Niven lowered his sword. "Where did you learn how to fence?"

"From my father." Carson lowered the saber, his eyes on Niven's point alone.

Niven tapped Carson's sword to initiate the contest. "And where did your half-Cherokee father learn swordplay?"

Carson blocked the first thrust. "A young gentleman who explored with Zebulon Pike taught my father so he'd have someone he could practice with."

"Ah." Niven thrust again and again, but in slow beats, as if letting Carson warm up.

Carson answered each thrust with a parry. Yet he kept back, not letting Niven advance past his guard. "I've been wondering about something myself. Mind if I ask?"

"Ask away, man. We're alone here."

Carson felt the rhythm learned so long ago returning. And the question he'd longed to ask this uncommon man popped out. "Why did you marry my cousin?"

Niven grinned broadly. "You've seen her and you have to ask that?"

"You married her for her looks?" Carson couldn't keep the disapproval and disbelief from his tone. Tap. Tap. Tap—the sabers touched.

Niven chuckled. "You obviously had different reasons for becoming engaged." Then, though continuing the steady beat of blade against blade, he held up his free hand. "Not to say that your fiancée is not widely reputed to be lovely."

His fiancée. The idea did not anger him. Carson inhaled the warm air. Mariel was beautiful, as Niven had said, but he didn't want her exposed to a whole army and a war. He didn't even care for Niven's words. "Careful what you say." Possessiveness gripped Carson. "Want me to call you out too?"

"Decidedly not."

"I hope no one has or will make the mistake of bandying my lady's name about." Carson's words came out cool, but molten steel coursed through his veins. "If any man accosts my sister or my fiancée—" *I will hunt the man down. And kill him.*

"Never fear. Your reputation as McCulloch's most feared and respected Ranger has instilled a universal respect bordering on fear. "

"Good." Why had Emilio let Sugar and Mariel come along?

Mariel was too frail, too fine for an army camp. Both of them were.

Niven tried to feint.

Carson blocked him with a straight thrust. Now was his chance to try to get some more of the truth. "While we are still talking privately of ladies, I want to understand why you married Blanche. I already heard about the romantic letters and your visit. That's Blanche's reason for marrying you—"

"Blanche's reason for marrying me is that I am the younger son of a U.S. congressman from Virginia." Their exchange of metallic beats punctuated Niven's words. "And an honor graduate of West Point. And a man ambitious to gain higher rank. Marrying me, she gained prestige. It is a step up in her mind."

How could Niven put such snobbish behavior into words and treat them so lightly? Carson's mother had raised her children to behave toward every person with courtesy and regard, to have one set of manners for everyone. But Blanche had been raised by pretentious Jewell. "My east Texas relatives always have had a strange way of thinking," Carson muttered, his arm muscles warming.

Niven laughed out loud again.

Carson became a bit more adventurous, advancing, trying to put Niven on his guard. "So Blanche is willing to have you gone all the time in the army as long as she has your prestige to keep her warm?"

"Exactly. I'll tell you the truth. When I heard that Remy LaCroix had a lovely sister and his family owned a large cotton plantation in Texas, I struck up a friendship with him." Niven stepped up the rhythm. "Her situation was just what I was looking for in a wife. So I started writing to her, and then when the army came west, I took leave for a visit and proposed."

"Her situation?" Carson's heartbeat sped up in time with the tempo.

"Yes, she is of a wealthy family in the West. Until I have a post of my own, she can live at home. And since she's still at home, she costs me little now—when I am not making enough to keep a fine wife."

"So you gain a wife, not the expense of a wife?" Carson turned back each thrust, his confidence rising, along with the cool relief that stuck-up, social-climbing Blanche had rejected him. *Why was I ever attracted to her?*

"Exactly. And in the future, if she doesn't want to live at a frontier military post, I can visit her more easily than a woman on the East Coast. I need to visit often enough to make sure we have a family."

His pulse pounding at his temples, Carson grimaced at the man's words and his quickening pace. "Grandchildren whom Henri LaCroix will support and raise while you're away?"

Their blows were a constant tattoo now. "Just so. He looked to me to be an admirable man, and he will make a doting grand-father, I'm sure."

Carson felt sweat trickling down his face. He had never met the like of this man. "Have it all planned out. Didn't anyone tell you that life doesn't always go as planned?" *War doesn't always end in victory or even survival.*

"I've heard rumors like that. But that doesn't mean a man can't make plans. What are your plans for your future?"

The question made Carson miss a beat.

Niven, no doubt sensing distraction, finished with a flourish and touched the point of his saber to Carson's chest. "I win."

"You do." Carson straightened and bowed. Niven's lightly pronounced question pricked Carson. He wanted Mariel in his future. But first he had to survive another war. And this nuisance with Remy. And what if Remy got lucky at Carson's expense?

Niven also straightened and bowed. "Shall we have another try?"

"If you don't mind," Carson said with a polite nod. "Then I have a fiancée that needs my attention."

"Just so. You'll have to take me and introduce me. I'm always most eager to meet my *beautiful* relatives." Niven grinned, even his eyes laughing.

Unable to dislike the man, Carson grinned. *"En garde!"*

* * *

Mariel turned and saw Carson walking toward her. The dusty bearded Ranger had been replaced by a clean-shaven man no longer dressed in buckskin. Even so, he still moved with that masculine grace that seemed natural to him. She walked toward him, unable to resist his pull.

He had come back safely from scouting and fighting. She didn't want to think about his leaving again. But the thought of this man, the best she had ever known, fighting a duel chilled her. Her steps faltered.

He approached her. "You look upset."

Niven let out a crack of laughter. "Her fiancé is going to fight a duel tomorrow and you don't think that should upset your lady?"

Mariel bit her lower lip. She was not a little girl. She knew better than to call a man's judgment into question in front of another man. This only added to her tension.

Carson touched her sleeve. "Mariel, this is Anthony Niven. He is married to my cousin Blanche in San Felipe. Niven, this is my fiancée, Mrs. Mariel Wolffe."

She looked at him then. He had called her his fiancée. Why? And Blanche? His cousin? She recalled Sugar's words when they had been picking grapes together. So this was the man that Blanche, the foolish girl, had married not out of love but a desire for gain. Niven bowed to her and she curtseyed, murmuring a polite greeting.

"I will leave you two lovebirds," Niven said. "I see my pretty cousin-by-marriage Sugar ahead. I can't pass by without paying my respects and kissing the bride."

Carson shook his head and warned, "The man with my sister is Emilio Ramirez, another Ranger and her new husband. Don't make him jealous. And thanks again for the saber and practice session."

"No problem, dear fellow. I look forward to your trouncing our young relative as he deserves. And even after our brief acquaintance, I perceive that *West* Texas women choose men, not their fortunes," Niven said, grinning. "They choose them by how well they deem the man will be able to protect them. I see by the look of her husband that your sister has evidently made a wise choice." After tipping his hat to Mariel, the man hurried toward Sugar and Emilio.

Mariel stared after him.

"Niven is an interesting man. I don't like half of what he says, but he's so honest I can't dislike him."

Mariel turned to Carson. She wanted to ask, *Are you angry with me?* Instead she said only, "Must you fight a duel?" She flushed at her questioning him.

"I do, but I understand women don't like fighting." Then he glanced around, no doubt at all the officers' wives who were so obviously watching them. "Let's walk."

She wanted to say more, but she had been struck dumb by her reaction to Carson's nearness. She let him lead her away. When they were out of earshot of the others, Carson asked, "When did we become engaged?"

Mariel's face blazed hotter, and she pressed a hand over her mouth, as if this could take back the words already spoken.

"I know you had a good reason for saying that we're promised."

Mariel tried to look at the ground; he lifted her chin with his hand. "Mariel, I won't be angry. Tell me."

She didn't want to tell him that it was because the cousin whom he had just struck had been rude to Sugar when they'd arrived at camp. She wanted to stop the duel, not make the relationship between the cousins more difficult. "It just came out when we arrive here. Then Ash said it was right I said it. That I would be better treated. Treated the way you wanted me to be."

Carson stood, obviously thinking this over. "Ash is right, as usual."

She wanted to ask him more but did not. Sometimes it was better to let matters rest. She walked with him toward where Ash and the rest were eating the evening meal around their cook fire. Everything within her cried out for his touch, but he did not take her hand. And it was her fault. Her unusual and momentary boldness had led her to claim a relationship she did not have with this man. Shame was her just reward for rash speech.

* * *

The next uncomfortably hot evening near the river, Sugar stood beside Mariel, fanning herself with a woven palm fan. She and Mariel watched Remy LaCroix strut toward Carson. A slew of young officers trailed him. A duel, which normally should have taken place in private, had proved an irresistible draw.

The other army wives had told Sugar that an army kept waiting was plagued by boredom; therefore, they should expect a large crowd to come watch the duel. Sugar didn't think Remy could beat Carson at anything, but accidents happened. Emilio had escorted her and Mariel here, away from the main body; he'd told them to stay within the dogwood trees. After kissing Sugar's hand, he'd left them and gone to act as Carson's second.

"I have never seen a duel," Mariel murmured, sounding worried and tense.

"Neither have I," Sugar admitted, craning her neck to gauge the gathering crowd. Fortunately, Emilio hadn't expected her to stay away completely, but she had to remember to remain here, away from what the other ladies had termed "the boorish crowd."

"Carson is good with a sword, yes?" Mariel's voice quavered.

"Of course," Sugar heard herself lie. The truth was she'd rarely seen Carson with a sword in hand. Surely he wouldn't have consented to fight a duel with swords if he didn't do swordplay well. However, men did things that seemed foolhardy to her. She noticed a man ahead of them, collecting money from other soldiers. No doubt bets were being placed. Sugar shook her head. She'd also noticed that Carson was still keeping Mariel at arm's length. Men could be so stupid at times.

As Carson's second, Emilio was standing talking to that Easterner Niven, who'd married Blanche. They shook hands, then Niven said loudly, "This is not a duel to the death. Merely a duel to settle a question of honor. The gentleman who manages to touch the point of his sword to his opponent's chest will be deemed the winner."

This announcement didn't reassure Sugar. Fighting could always spiral out of control. She worried her lower lip.

Then Carson and Remy moved into the open area in the midst of the crowd and faced each other, their sabers upright in front of their faces.

"*En garde*," Remy said stiffly.

Both men lowered their swords and began prowling in a circle like two cougars looking to spring. Just as Sugar was silently predicting that Carson would not make the first move, Remy thrust his blade toward Carson's. It was easily turned aside, the blades making a scraping sound that went through her. And the contest began in earnest.

Remy continued to be on the attack. Carson kept his guard up, not letting Remy succeed in getting past his sword. The metallic sound of blade upon blade tightened and tightened Sugar's nerves. Soon she and Mariel were gripping each other's hands.

Remy's fair face had turned red. From embarrassment or exertion—Sugar couldn't tell which. Carson remained cool, but Sugar could tell he was giving his all to hold his own. The contest wore on. Finally, Remy appeared to lose his temper. He lunged forward and thrust his sword, trying to break through Carson's unwavering guard.

Carson caught Remy's sword in midthrust and parried, making a circle with his wrist. This threw Remy off balance, and Carson managed to force the saber from Remy's hand. It all happened so fast. It was over before Sugar could gasp.

Remy stared at his sword on the ground. Blanche's husband said, "LaCroix, your opponent has disarmed you—"

Before the man finished, Remy lunged at Carson's throat. Carson tossed down his sword. He leaped backward, out of reach. Remy stumbled, caught himself, and swung a fist.

Carson dodged him and maneuvered out of Remy's reach. This pattern—Remy attacking, Carson eluding him—went on for several moments. Finally, Niven said, "Finish it, Quinn."

What did that mean? Sugar pressed a hand over her mouth.

Carson nodded and launched a flurry of blows.

Remy staggered and fell to one knee.

"Do you concede?" Carson asked.

"Never."

Shaking his head, Carson lowered his fists and turned. He made a sound of disgust.

Remy sprang up and hit Carson from behind.

Sugar shrieked.

A gasp sounded—an overwhelming one—as if every man watching had gasped as one person. And then there was shocked silence.

Fourteen

Carson felt the blow. But he didn't quite believe it. Had it happened? To hit a man from behind—there was no more dishonorable behavior in the eyes of a gentleman than this. Prickling all over with icy shock, Carson turned back. He stared at his cousin. Remy's horrified expression confirmed that he indeed knew he was guilty of extremely disgraceful behavior, the kind that could brand a man for life.

Carson tried not to feel sorry for the boy who appeared to grasp the fact that he had just dishonored himself. And he had done it in front of everyone whose esteem he wanted most. Remy was breathing fast and shallow; his face was drawn, his eyes were wide with shock.

As darkness drew down over them, Carson tried to think of a way to save Remy's face. There wasn't any way. Perhaps honesty would be best. "Remy, you don't like me. I don't like you. I hate slavery; you own slaves. Our mothers are half sisters, and that ties us by blood. Nothing will ever change that. But you're not just my kid cousin from east Texas anymore. You're an officer in the U.S. Army. It's time to put away childish things."

Remy looked as if he would have liked to retort. And though his mouth moved, no words came out.

Carson shook his head. "I hope you have learned from this. And won't repeat it anytime soon." Then Carson glimpsed his sister and Mariel standing in the nearby knot of trees. After returning Niven's sword to him, he walked toward his family and didn't look back. The silence followed him.

Then, from the corner of his eye, he watched as bystanders began melting away into the darkness. Niven was standing near Remy, talking to him, looking earnest. Carson would leave it to Niven to try to soothe Remy's anger and humiliation. *That's not my job.*

When Carson reached Mariel, he took her small hand and drew her away with him. He didn't want her here, but he was glad she was. Seeing her thawed his tension even as it vexed him. Emilio had followed, leading Sugar, and the four of them left the scene of dishonor. They all went back to the fire near Ash and Amos's wagons. Carson's muscles were warm from the sword fight. He took off his black coat and hung it on the end of one wagon.

The ugly expression on his cousin's face tonight broke through Carson's bemusement, muting it. Carson had never wanted this fight he'd been forced into. He had won; and his cousin had disgraced himself. That might bear fruit. Nasty, poisonous fruit.

Suddenly sensitive to Mariel's sweet presence, he drew her hand up to his mouth and kissed it. He could think of no other way to express his gladness that she was here. She looked surprised but said nothing. He recalled how brusque he'd been with her yesterday. Still, he couldn't bring up any words. He was a dry well. What could he say now—with the war and

Remy hanging over them? He would have to make certain that
Remy didn't try to hurt him through Mariel.

He'd already made very sure that soon every man in the U.S.
Army would have heard by word of mouth that Mariel belonged
to him alone. And tonight's duel should add to the protection he'd
tried to put around Sugar and Mariel. Now he just had to stay alive
to take her home with him. He couldn't say that to this woman,
couldn't speak of the specter of dying. So he said nothing, just
accepted a hot cup of coffee from Reva by the fire. And started
reminiscing about the childhood days spent with Antonio.

* * *

The next morning dawned too early for Sugar. After the awful
duel, her brother had spent the night near his family. Now they
were all making sure that nothing belonging to the two families
about to leave them would be left behind. At the same time,
she knew that everyone was trying not to show how much Ash
and Reva's departure saddened them.

Sugar clung to her husband's broad hand, pressing into it all
the sadness that buffeted her in waves. For as long as Sugar
could recall, Reva had always been there just like the dawn
every morning. *This is best for them, for Antonio. I will see them
again*, she said to herself, yet deep down she knew that life
was uncertain and she might never again see these two beloved
friends this side of the Jordan.

Finally the voices trailed off as no one could think of another
item to pack. Ash offered his hand to Emilio and then Carson.
Reva kissed them each, saying nothing. Her sorrow at parting
was expressed in her forced smiles and teary eyes. Just as Ash
turned to help Reva onto the buckboard, a familiar voice hailed
them through the morning mist. "Hey! You there, stop!"

Sugar could not believe her eyes. Remy LaCroix was striding toward them with several armed infantrymen behind him. Shock radiated up her spine.

"You, people! Halt!" Remy shouted.

Sugar tightened her mouth. What was Remy doing here? Had her cousin lost his mind?

Carson stepped forward and growled, "What do you want?"

Remy did not look at Carson. "My slave is missing. I just heard that your people were leaving. I'm sure that my man is hiding in one of their wagons, running away. I'm going to search their wagons for him." Remy pushed forward.

Sugar watched as Carson and Emilio's hands suddenly and almost magically held Colts aimed toward the infantrymen. She blinked and then demanded, "Wasn't last night enough for you, Remy LaCroix?" When she heard her thoughts aloud, she surprised herself. Her voice shook. All this morning she had dammed up tears of loss, refusing to shed them. Now she found she could not hold back anything else.

LaCroix ignored her and moved to Ash and Reva's wagon.

Carson's cold, tight voice halted him. "Ash, what do you want to do? Shall I start shooting?"

From the corner of her eye, Sugar noted that the infantrymen, who were clutching their rifles, were staring in horror at the Colts aimed at them. Sugar had heard the other army wives parroting what was being said of the Rangers in camp. The regular army thought of them as they would a wild cougar, dangerous and deadly. Would they think themselves in danger? Would they try to shoot first?

Remy turned to look at the men with him. It was obvious from his sudden flush that he had not anticipated Carson's being here and ready to fight. No doubt he'd thought that Ash, Amos, and Emilio wouldn't be hard to overpower. How stupid. Sugar shook her head.

"Oh, go ahead," Ash drawled, "and let the boy have his way. His man isn't in our wagons."

Remy was foolish enough to try to backhand Ash. Ash knocked Remy to the dusty ground. When he tried to come up, Ash pushed him back down, planting his boot hard on Remy's chest. "You are your grandpa all over. Anybody ever tell you that?"

Remy lifted his shoulders, trying to get up, but he stopped. Grinning, Ash wouldn't remove his boot from his chest. No doubt realizing how foolish he would look, Remy refused to struggle. He stared into the distance. Ash folded his arms, chuckling softly.

Why would Remy put himself through this humiliation? Sugar had overheard her parents discuss Remy's grandfather, and this foolish behavior matched his, just as Ash had said. Just like his grandpa.

One of the infantrymen cleared his throat. "What should we do, sir?"

"I'm glad you asked me," Ash said, grinning wider with ironic humor. "Why don't you come over here and lift the canvas on both wagons and find out if a man is hiding in them?"

Again, Remy tried to get up, but Ash's foot was planted on his chest. All Ash had to do was step down hard and Remy's ribs would snap.

The infantryman who'd spoken before moved forward, giving Ash a wide berth. He used his rifle barrel to raise the canvas a few inches on both wagons.

"What did you find, young man?" Ash asked.

"No one is hiding in the wagons, . . . sir."

"Thank you. You're a mighty polite soldier. Your mama taught you right. You might live a bit longer than Kilbride's grandson."

The infantryman hesitated.

"Don't worry, young man." Reva patted the soldier's sleeve. "My husband isn't going to kill anybody this morning."

"Honey, that sweet streak of yours always spoils my fun," Ash winked. Then he removed his boot from Remy's chest. "Get," he snapped. "Now."

Remy got up and dusted himself off, looking ridiculous. "I know you have lured my servant away from me."

"You know that, do you?" Ash scratched his chin.

"Go away," Sugar said, her face warm. "We're tired of you embarrassing yourself and us. I'm ashamed to admit that you're blood kin. Go."

"*Vaya*," Emilio added.

His ears bright red, Remy stalked away, the infantrymen trailing after him, hiding grins.

Ash shook his head. "We needed a good laugh this morning." He lowered his voice to a whisper. "Because the fact is his servant cut out last night and is waiting for us ahead. I visited him last night during the big nasty duel. And found he was not *happy* with his situation."

Sugar whooped with laughter, then smothered it with her hands over her mouth. This was why she would miss Ash and Reva. They brought a lightness of spirit that was so welcome in this world of trials. She threw her arms around Reva. This wasn't the last of her seeing Reva and Ash. "When this war is over, Emilio will bring me to see you and Antonio."

Reva squeezed her close, as she always did. "You bet he will, my sweet child."

Then Ash was helping Reva onto the wagon. He slapped the reins, and the two wagons trundled off, heading westward. Carson leaped onto the back of Ash's wagon, obviously to protect the two families as they made their way through the thousands of surrounding U.S. troops. Emilio kissed Sugar's cheek, then ran to his horse and swung on bareback to trail after the wagons too.

Mariel came to Sugar's side and put an arm around her shoulders. *The Lord giveth and the Lord taketh away*, Sugar thought to herself before turning and pressing a bittersweet kiss to Mariel's cheek, grateful for this sweet woman who would be her sister—if Carson ever got smart and proposed.

* * *

Late in September, Carson rode between Emilio and Mc-Culloch on the Saltillo Road, approaching the fortified city of Monterrey. After they'd spent a steamy July and August scouting for Taylor, a battle was at last to begin. The army and Rangers had left behind the coastal plain and were approaching low mountains far inland in Mexico. The troops behind them, swollen with the new volunteers to over ten thousand, were sweating under a golden sun. Ripe corn fields—amber and green—crowded up against the rising land. Impending death dominated Carson's mind, making every sight and sound more intense.

Just yesterday a few Rangers had neared this pass between two peaks. The fort on Monterrey's Independence Hill battery had barked and roared as the cannon fire warned the Americans away. General Taylor had made his plan of battle, which included General Worth's leading a diversionary attack at this pass on Saltillo Road. General Taylor had put the Rangers in the front of that attack. Would the diversion work, permitting the main body of the army to breach the city's defenses to the north?

Carson went through his usual preparation for going into a fight. He'd slowly divested himself of everything except his purpose—to kill and not be killed. It was a narrowing, flattening feeling, as if one became as thin as a face on a paper. It was a paring down, paring down until one hit the bone of existence—survival. Would Carson Quinn still be breathing at the end of today?

With the constant sound of marching boots behind, Carson was very aware of Emilio beside him. Sugar had embroidered a large white star on the back of Emilio's buckskin jacket. She had tried to make it seem as if she'd only wanted to decorate her husband's jacket, but Carson had divined that she'd really been marking him with the Texas Lone Star in hopes that he wouldn't be killed by some less-than-discriminating U.S. soldier. Still, Carson would keep one eye out for his friend and brother-in-law.

He suppressed the urge to glance backwards, as if he could see Sugar and Mariel, miles in the rear of the main army, over the vast expanse of blue-clad infantry and the plainly dressed state volunteers marching behind them to the drum.

Busy with scouting and fighting, he'd had almost no time to be with Mariel and no chance to speak to her privately after the duel. *I should have apologized for the way I acted when I found out she had come with Sugar.* He still didn't want to think about what could happen to two women if for some reason the U.S. forces lost. He'd seen how some warriors gave in to the worst behavior in the flush of victory. *We can't lose.*

With the army wives and the troops protecting them, Mariel walked beside Sugar. She saw that Sugar's lips were moving, probably in silent prayer. At dawn, when they had moved out, the word had come that today the army would try to breach the defenses around Monterrey and enter the city. Mariel dabbed at the perspiration gathering at her hairline under her bonnet. She wanted to pray, but her lips, as well as her heart, were paralyzed by fear. *I will lose him. He will be taken from me. I know it.*

Farther along the Saltillo Road, the Rangers rode at an easy jog in front of the infantry. With his rifle lying across his lap, Carson rode round a bend. And there was the Mexican Army.

Or some of it. Carson gasped, his nerves tingling. Emilio let out a Spanish curse. The Mexicans were ranged in and around the road and in the ripe cornfields on both sides of the road. Thousands of soldiers. A blue-and-white Mexican haze among the golden fields.

In the front line, the sunlight gleamed on the Mexican lancers, with their silvered domed feathered hats, blue-and-white uniforms, and their lances polished to shed human blood. Their green-and-white flag fluttered over them.

For a few moments, there was silence as each soldier on both sides faced the enemy. Faced the moment of decision. Faced coming death.

At a shouted command, the Mexican infantry in the cornfields raised their muskets and opened fire. The brightly colored lancers spurred their horses to a gallop. The high battery on Independence Hill roared down, promising death.

McCulloch shouted. Carson and Emilio charged forward with all the other Rangers. The lancers surged toward them, wielding their long metal-tipped wooden lances, aiming to spear human flesh. Carson rifle-shot the nearest lancer, the sound lost in the din. Then he drew his bow and sent arrow after arrow into the oncoming lancers.

From behind, the U.S. cannon barked, answering the Mexicans' above. The noise shook its way through Carson. The lancers and Rangers slammed into each other—two twelve-point bucks ramming heads.

A melee crowded around Carson on the road. Fully engaged, he gripped a Colt and his knife, one in each hand. Emilio was slashing with his long dagger. Carson shot and hacked at any body that came within reach.

Something seared his forehead, and warm blood drooled into his right eye. He wiped it with his sleeve and, with his Colt, brought down another Mexican. He glimpsed the handsome lancer officer, still shouting orders, encouragement, going down under the onslaught. American infantry poured into the gap the Rangers had hewn. Suddenly, Carson found himself with other Rangers in the midst of the Mexicans, cut off from the U.S. line.

Carson slashed, sliced with his knife. Sliding the spent Colt into his belt, he slipped the fresh one into his ready hand. He heeled his horse around, still firing, and charged back to the U.S line. Out of the corner of his eye, he saw Emilio slide off his horse, sucked into the surging current of men. Carson attempted to turn back, but the other horses were tight around him. *No room! No room to maneuver! Emilio!*

Mariel heard the distant cannon and gunfire. She had never heard cannon before, yet the devastating, vibrating noise could be nothing else. Sugar gasped, a little moan escaping before she clamped her mouth shut. Mariel grasped Sugar's cold hands in hers. For a moment, all halted and turned toward the sounds of battle.

"It's started," one of the soldiers growled. "And we're stuck back here with women."

The soldier beside him cuffed him. "Be polite. We're needed here. Wouldn't you want to know your wife was safe?"

The first soldier bowed his head. "Sorry."

Mariel could only stare at the man. This was not how Carson thought of war. He hated it. *He would be with me if he could and take me home, far from here.*

One of the other wives began praying aloud. The party started forward again. Mariel recognized some of the woman's phrases from the Bible. The words seemed to wrap all the women together in their common misery and uncertainty. The bright sunlight crackled with silent prayers. Her mind had gone strangely numb. She could only hear the sounds of distant battle, and her own unspoken prayer repeated and repeated like a pale blue ribbon in her mind. *Let them live. Let Emilio, let Carson live.*

At high noon, with the sun blazing down on his head and shoulders, Carson stood beside his horse in this battle lull, looking up the steep rise to Fort Soledado. The slopes were covered with thick and thorny chaparral. Cannons from the hilltop fort were pointed down at them. The image of Emilio sliding from his horse taunted Carson, who—with the battle still on—could not look for him. He thought fleetingly, too, of Niven and Remy. He'd lost track of them today.

General Worth rode up and pointed his sword toward the heights. "Men, you are to take that hill! I know you will do it!"

The troops around shouted, "We will!" Carson said nothing; he merely checked his reloaded Colts and rifle and refilled his quiver with arrows from a saddlebag. His goal was to stay alive and find Emilio.

"Rangers, dismount and leave your horses!" ordered McCulloch, who was standing beside Worth. Carson took his canteen, hung it around his neck, and slapped his horse's haunch. The animal took off back down the Saltillo Road. He was as practiced as Carson in battle and would return when he heard Carson's whistle.

Still in the forefront, Carson and the Rangers led the infantry. They left the road and began marching through corn and sugarcane fields, which provided their only cover from the enemy's cannon sights aimed down at them. But the quivering of the tall green and gold stalks must have given them away.

The Mexican artillery opened fire, pouring down grapeshot—hundreds of small, hot balls like deadly grapes—onto the ranks, enveloping the crown of the hill with smoke. Fire as garish as the noonday sun flashed in the midst of the smoke. The man behind Carson shrieked and fell hard to the ground.

Carson didn't look back. Without any cover, he rushed toward the stream they had to cross.

He hoisted his rifle and two Colts overhead. He plunged into the cool current. Copper, iron balls hissed around him, hot metal hitting water, stirring up foam. *Keep moving. Stay alive. Keep moving.* Soldiers churned through the sweeping current under a shower of more grapeshot. Carson clambered up the rocky slope on the other side. *Safe.* He dragged in great gulps of air. The murderous artillery didn't pause. In spite of danger, the Texans and Americans all halted among the riverside shrubbery, letting the water drain from their clothing and boots.

Then they rushed to the base of the hill for cover. There they would be out of reach of the high cannon, too close, too low to be hit. Grabbing hold of the chaparral, Carson, the Rangers, and the infantry began to climb hand over hand, gaining rocky cliff after rocky cliff. They aimed and fired toward the fort on the hill. With deadly accuracy. Higher. Closer. Higher.

Carson scaled the final rise and fired straight into the opening around the cannon. The Mexicans shouted, *"Diablos! Tejanos!"* They panicked and ran, leaving behind their cannon. The Rangers approached a loaded and primed nine-pounder. A Louisiana infantryman pulled out a piece of chalk and wrote on the cannon TEXAS RANGERS AND THE 5TH INFANTRY. They turned it onto the nearby Bishop's Palace, achieving their immediate goal: These guns would no longer be aimed at them.

The U.S. soldiers around him relaxed; a few smiled. "Carson and Tunney," McCulloch ordered, "go back and find our wounded Rangers. The hospital tents will be set up now farther down the Saltillo Road. Take our wounded there."

Released dread and worry rushed, pumping hot blood through Carson. He began heading down the slope before McCulloch's order was finished. He heard Tunney sliding down the slope behind him. They made good time and soon were rustling through the corn and sugarcane. The ground was strewn with blankets, muskets, pistols, and more that men in their haste had tossed aside before plunging into the river. Carson moved without pause toward the road where Emilio had fallen. Only the battle had forced him to delay this search. *Emilio. Be alive.*

Day was fading fast, and roiling dark clouds lowered over the mountains and valley. For hours, Carson and Tunney had been searching for Emilio and other fallen Rangers. At the same time, Mexican and U.S. soldiers had been roaming, seeking their wounded. This was the informal truce to find wounded that always came after a battle. Carson had stopped many times to pour water from his canteen into the mouth of a wounded comrade. The ache to see Emilio's face and feel his heart beating strongly under his hand had kept Carson moving, moving. As they'd searched, he and Tunney had used their horses to ferry each fallen Ranger back to the hospital in the battle camp at the rear.

Finally, when Carson had about given up hope, he heard his name, Emilio's voice. He rushed through the shadows and found his brother-in-law lying hidden in the cornfield. He had come close to this place several times, but perhaps Emilio had been unconscious and had not heard Carson calling his name. Cold relief sluicing through him, Carson clasped Emilio's hand. "Where are you wounded?" he cried, and in the same instant he saw that someone had tied a tourniquet around Emilio's calf.

"I couldn't . . . get up. My leg." Using Carson's hand, Emilio pulled himself up to a sitting position. He gritted his teeth against the pain.

"I'll get you to the hospital." Carson helped Emilio up and slid his arm around him to support him. They began hobbling toward the road, Carson whistling for his horse. The sudden relief he'd felt earlier had made him feel the minor scrapes, bruises, and deep fatigue that had been nagging him all day. He breathed, and it sounded ragged to his own ears. He couldn't stop now, even though his own knees wanted to buckle.

The storm broke just then as night fell. Unable to take another step, Carson stood in the open, letting the cooling rain soak him, drag him into semiconsciousness. The hospital camp was still far away. He whistled and whistled, but his mount didn't return to him. The animal might have been commandeered by the hospital staff for another patient. Or stolen. Or shot by accident. And where had Tunney gone?

In the rain and gloom, a door miraculously opened ahead, and faint light glowed forth. Rain poured down Carson's face, and Emilio shivered against Carson. "*Ayúdame*," Carson called, but only a sad croaking sound came from his lips. "Help me!"

Then a Mexican, a farmer dressed in loose cotton, was there beside him, helping him and Emilio stagger into the jacal. The farmer and his wife quickly helped Carson lay Emilio by the fire. Shivering with the wet chill, Carson knelt beside his friend. He was about to ask for help with treating Emilio's wounds, but the wife, young and pretty, was already heating water over the hearth and opening a wooden box, which looked very much like his own mother's chest of remedies.

The Mexican husband put a pottery mug into Carson's hand. Carson mumbled, "*Gracias*." He downed the home-brewed ale in one swallow, then moved away from Emilio to collapse onto the earthen floor, leaning with his back against the mesquite wall. Even with overwhelming thunder overhead, he fell instantly to sleep. His last thought was that he was glad that on this day, he'd faced only the cannons of men, not God's thunder. God's thunder—like a thousand cannons pounded, vibrating through his very flesh.

* * *

At the next day's humid dawning, Mariel followed Sugar as they both staggered out of the hospital tent, where they had spent most of the night working. Dawn's light was sickly, pale, and wanting—just how Mariel felt in her every bone. Everything outside was drenched from last night's downpour. Mariel recognized a familiar Ranger asleep under the nearest wagon. She hurried toward him, bending down to shake him. "Tunney! Tunney!"

The Ranger moaned and tried to shrug off her touch. She increased her efforts. Finally, he rolled toward her, blinking. "You're Carson's woman." He got to his feet and rubbed his eyes with his hands. "How goes the battle?"

"All's quiet for now." Sugar had hurried to join Mariel. "Where are my brother and my husband?"

Tunney blinked some more and yawned largely. "I was with Carson looking for wounded Rangers. For hours. We brought back about a dozen to the hospital here. Then Carson's horse came up lame. I tied him up and went back to find Carson. But the storm came. Couldn't see my hand in front of my face. Or hear my own voice. I come back and got under the wagon. I was done in. Sorry."

Mariel wanted to rail at him for not finding Carson and Emilio. But he was just a man. And a man with silver in his mane of hair who'd fought a battle and then spent hours bringing the injured in for treatment. Mariel held back sharp words and chewed on them.

"Where was the last place you saw Carson and Emilio?" Sugar asked.

"We had worked our way along the Saltillo Road where Emilio was wounded—"

"My husband was wounded!" Sugar interrupted, gripping Tunney's sleeve. "You didn't say that—wounded!"

Mariel threw an arm around Sugar's shoulders as tears dripped down Sugar's face. Horror rendered Mariel dumb. She looked down at her bloodstained dress. She had helped clean wounds all night, preparing men for surgery or stitching them up. She had been left with gory images she doubted she'd ever erase from her memory. And now Emilio . . .

Sugar wiped her tears away with the hem of her skirt. "We have to go find them. I'll get my nursing chest."

"You two women can't go runnin' off. Monterrey hasn't been taken yet," Tunney objected. "You could run into Mexican soldiers—"

Sugar marched away without even replying. Mariel hurried after her, her heart beating in her ears. *Emilio hurt. Where is Carson?*

Soon Sugar and Mariel were striding down the Saltillo Road. General Worth's troops, still sitting and lying beside the road in the corn and sugarcane fields, watched them pass by. Many looked startled, but none tried to stop them.

Tunney rode up behind them and dismounted, falling into step beside them. "We'll need my horse when we find them," he said.

Mariel clung to his words—"when we find them."

Soon after they set out, the sound of battle started once more. Tunney trudged beside them, as agitated as a tethered dog that hears his master's call. He wanted to be back in the thick of the fight.

Mariel turned away from him, constantly scanning the horizon, watching the sun rise higher and higher. But vultures circling high above the Saltillo Road nearly broke her concentration, tried to make her captive to all her fears. *Emilio is alive. Carson is alive. They are alive.* If only her thoughts could make it so.

Finally, Tunney pulled up and stopped. "This looks like the place." He turned on the spot, considering and remembering. "Follow me." He left the road and worked his way through the cornfields, leading his horse. Mariel and Sugar followed him, swiping away the dried leaves of the tall corn. Tunney came to an abrupt halt. "Carson! Ramirez!"

Sugar and Mariel began calling the names too. And within minutes, a Mexican woman peered out between two corn rows. "¿Están buscando a Emilio Ramirez?"

"Yes!" Sugar shouted. "Sí, I'm looking for him! He's my husband. Mi esposo!"

The woman motioned for them to come with her. Tunney balked. "It could be a trick."

Mariel paid Tunney no attention, following Sugar and the stranger. Grumbling, Tunney trailed after them. Soon, at the woman's invitation, they entered a jacal. Mariel heard Sugar cry out and then saw her drop to her knees. Mariel glimpsed Emilio lying on the earthen floor in front of a low fire. Mariel hovered by the door while Sugar talked rapidly in Spanish to the woman and Emilio.

Fear kept Mariel from asking what, and how serious, Emilio's injuries were. Finally, Sugar turned and asked, "Is Tunney outside?"

Mariel nodded.

"Please ask him to come to the door so I can speak to him," Sugar said, still kneeling beside Emilio.

Mariel complied, and soon Tunney stood at the door, saying, "Yes, Mrs. Ramirez?"

"Emilio was wounded in his calf. The shot broke his leg. He can't walk. Juanita here has treated his leg well. Neither of us thinks he should be moved until his fever breaks." Sugar looked to Mariel. "Will you stay with me?"

"Ja," Mariel murmured, looking around for Carson.

Sugar went on, "We will stay here, then, till Emilio can be moved. Tunney, where do you think Carson is now?"

The man shrugged. "We all heard the shooting start again. I would think that he's gone off to fight again."

Numbness leaked through Mariel. Carson wasn't here; he had already gone back into the fight. He was still in danger.

Sugar sighed and shook her head. "That is what Juanita thinks too. You will have to go too, right?"

"I was just waiting to see if you needed me to help you get Emilio back to the camp and the surgeons. Don't you think he'd get better care with the U.S. surgeons?" Tunney asked.

"No, I don't." Sugar's voice was firm, inflexible. "They are only good at digging out shot and cutting off limbs. Juanita has already taken out the lead shot and is certain, as I am, that with careful nursing and fomenting the wound, Emilio won't lose his leg."

Tunney frowned, and Mariel could tell from his twisted expression that he didn't agree. But in the distance, cannons began barking destruction once more. "I got to go. If I find Carson, I'll tell him you're here." Then he was hurrying back through the cornfields, taking his horse with him.

Mariel and Sugar looked into each other's eyes and shared the same silent questions.

Fifteen

Another tense day and night had passed. Deafened by gunfire and choking on black smoke from gunpowder, Carson crouched beside McCulloch behind a corner of a stone building in Monterrey. Trapped. Thwarted. Taut.

Carson had hoped to return to the little jacal where Emilio lay. But the battle for Monterrey had him in its claws. He had been forced to entrust Emilio to the kindness of the Mexican couple.

He edged out, peering. Sniper fire pelted down, chipping the edge of the stone building. Carson pulled back, gasping. No food all day and no water left in his canteen. He gritted his teeth, forcing himself not to give in to the desire to rush out of cover, firing his Colts. Ending this.

For two days, the Rangers—still at the forefront of the U.S. Army—had moved forward. Inch by inch, painstakingly overtaking each of the four forts on the western peaks protecting the city. Now, after piercing Monterrey's defenses, the Rangers and U.S. infantry were fighting hand to hand, flesh to flesh. Street by street.

A few Mexican snipers had taken positions at high windows in the stone haciendas and buildings. Carson and McCulloch had been pinned down by a particularly accurate sharpshooter for nearly an hour. McCulloch cursed under his breath. "We need to get that one out."

Carson nodded, breathing fast in spite of the enforced immobility. He had been trying to think of a way to do just that for several minutes now. His hands were sticky with blood. The air was packed with the cloying odors of gunpowder, blood, and sweat. Leaning against the stone wall, he ached all over. All he wanted to do was go to Emilio.

Sudden silence. An eerie one. Carson and McCulloch traded questioning looks. An American voice called out, "Truce! There is a truce! Stand down!"

A second voice—Mexican—shouted, "*Tregua! Tregua!*"

Carson peered around the side of the building. "There's an American officer and a Mexican one. They are walking side by side down the street waving white flags and shouting truce."

McCulloch edged around Carson to get a better look. "It looks legitimate." McCulloch rose and shouted, "Rangers! Stand down!"

Carson rose, his knees rebelling. "Do you need me?"

"No, go check on Ramirez."

Carson had already turned and was jogging west. All around him, soldiers of both armies were coming out of buildings, out from cover, looking confused, some dazed. The fountain in the plaza stopped him. He tried to use his hands as a cup and was repulsed by the blood that drained from his fingers. Gagging, he scrubbed his gory hands. Then he washed his blackened face. He was able to draw in breath freely. He cupped his clean hands and sucked in the teeth-chilling spring water.

Nothing had ever tasted so pure, so good. Then he filled his wooden canteen. And he was off again, racing over the cobblestone streets to the corn and sugarcane fields outside the city, hoping he'd recall where the jacal was. And that Emilio would be there, alive.

It took him over an hour to cover the distance. And then another hour to find the lane to the little hut in the midst of the vast golden fields. When he at last glimpsed it through the tall corn rows, he gasped. She was there. His heart stopped and started with a jolt. He began running. "Mariel! Mariel!"

Mariel turned toward him, astounded. "You didn't die," she whispered, unable to raise her voice. "You did not die."

He came directly to her. He folded her into his arms and kissed her.

Mariel could do nothing but cling to Carson. The delicious kiss ended. He swung her up in his arms and whirled her around. No one had ever done this to her before. It rendered her speechless. Finally, Mariel was able to gasp, "Please, Carson, you must put me down."

Still, Mariel's heart surged toward Carson. Unable to speak more, she clutched him to her, and every part of her sang in welcome. His kisses continued to fall upon her like a blessed rainstorm. Finally, Carson took a deep breath and straightened, though he still held her in his arms. "Emilio? How is he?"

"Much better, *amigo*," Emilio replied, looking weakened. With his leg splinted and a crutch under one arm, he was leaning against the doorjamb. Sugar also supported him, and he was smiling.

"Carson!" Sugar exclaimed. "The gunfire has stopped. Is it over?"

"A truce. I don't know how long it will last, but for now, yes."

Though Carson looked exhausted, he smiled at Mariel, and her senses sprang to life. She wished she could prepare a bath for him, give him clean clothing and provide a feather bed for him to sleep on, but she had nothing to offer.

"Do you think the fighting's over, then?" Sugar asked.

"It's over for me," Carson said. He motioned toward Emilio. "As soon as my brother-in-law is able to travel, we're going home."

It was too much for Mariel to hope for. She looked up. "You can leave now? They will not make you stay?"

Carson's mouth became a straight line. "The Comanche have been acting up. Word came to McCulloch before this battle. Texas needs us to come home. We must let the Comanche know that we're back." He softened his hard words by pulling her closer, under his arm.

Did that mean that when they reached home, he would have to leave again to fight Indians? Mariel didn't ask. Ever since he had found her in the army encampment, matters between them had been strained, tense. She had tried to ignore it, because she'd known it had sprung from his desire to protect her. Now the truce had brought peace between Carson and her. And she would do nothing to upset this. She tried to hide her fear behind a smile. Would the dangers this good man was forced to face never end?

* * *

Later that day—just as if days of cannon and gunfire and bloodshed had not taken place all around his plot of land—the Mexican started harvesting his corn in the bright sunlight. Carson and Mariel joined him. Each one of them had slung a deep burlap bag over one shoulder to hold ears of dried corn. Mariel was happy to be given some way to thank the young Mexican couple for taking them in.

And Carson's willingness to harvest corn like a peasant was just another example that she wasn't in Germany anymore. Carson's father held vast acres, but his son could do manual labor without a qualm about his rank. "His foolish cousin wouldn't do this," she murmured.

"What did you say?" Carson asked, stuffing another ear into his sack.

"*Nichts*. I mean nothing." She looked down, twisting off another ear of corn. And hoping she had done nothing to disturb the peace of being together.

"You don't have to be afraid to say what you're thinking around me." He paused and tightened his lips. "I need to apologize to you—"

Uncertainty gushed within her. "No—"

"I do. When I found you in camp with my sister, I wasn't very welcoming." His tone was grim.

She twisted another ear from a stalk. The husks were brown, and they crinkled when touched. As flimsy and delicate as she had felt at his lack of joy upon seeing her that first day. "You had a reason to be angry with me. I did not stay with your family. And I said that you were . . . that we were—"

"Promised? Yes, you did, and I'm glad you did. I wanted everyone to know that you belong to me. I didn't want any man to think he could take liberties with you."

She brushed away a buzzing fly and nodded. *Ja.* Carson always protected her. Once that had been enough. No more.

"No, I didn't say that right. I didn't mean that I only did it for your protection."

She looked up, puzzled, hoping. "I do not understand."

Carson glanced around. Picking much faster than they did, the Mexican had disappeared into the tall amber corn stalks ahead of them. Carson lowered his voice, saying, "Mariel, I was just surprised, unhappy that you were there in the midst of an army, a war. But you know how I feel about you."

She paused, her heart jumping. She swallowed, moistening

her dry mouth. Did she have the courage to ask? *I must know the truth*. "No, I do not know. How do you feel about me?" Her heart pounded as if she had just been attacked.

Carson looked into her eyes. "I want you to be my wife."

Seven short words that could, would, change her life; she couldn't breathe. Fear made her afraid to look at Carson; it took her voice away. She turned her face and went on gathering ears of corn, as if running away. It was too wonderful to contemplate, too wonderful for her.

"I thought you knew how I felt about you." His voice sounded hurt.

This broke her hesitation. Striding forward, she brushed through the few thick stalks that separated them and laid a hand on his arm. "Do you want me for a wife? Truly?"

His broad, tanned hand covered hers. "Of course I do. That night I left with Ben McCulloch after Sugar's wedding, I told you that I'd come back to you, didn't I? Why would I say that if I weren't coming back to marry you?"

She smiled through the mist in her eyes. Men.

"I just . . ." He looked over her head toward the city, surrounded by mountains. "I just didn't want you to be here, see me in a war." He looked down at his hands. "Before I came to you this day, I had to wash blood away. I had blood on my hands." He looked down at his strong hands.

His crushed tone moved her. She threw her arms around his shoulders and held onto him, as though some force was dragging him away from her. "You are a good man. But the world is bad. You have done good, only good."

He drew her closer. She didn't demur but let him. When she pressed against him, a rush of pleasure evaporated all of her doubts. He brushed his thumb over the soft skin of her neck. And then pressed a kiss there. "You feel so right in my arms."

Her arms locked tighter around him. *"Ja."*

He held her and she was drenched with joy, abundant, abounding. Joy—such a rarity in this angry world. Peace too. Truly, today she believed that the humble like her and Carson would be blessed and harvest abundant peace.

This war had done them a favor in this respect. It had broken down her barrier of reserve and let each of them show their feelings for the other.

The Mexican called to them, laughing.

Mariel pulled away from Carson, blushing.

"Our host asks are we going to pick corn or kiss?" Carson teased, brushing the sensitive underside of her chin with the back of his hand.

She couldn't say a word. He kissed her nose. Then he pulled away and began picking corn and singing a song loudly in Spanish. She recognized it from Sugar's wedding. Smiling, she went back to picking corn, her heart singing along with Carson's lilting melody. *I am loved by a good man. He wants me for his wife.* And it was enough, more than enough, more than she'd ever dreamed possible.

* * *

Five days had passed since Carson had left the battle and found shelter at the little jacal. He didn't even feel like the same man. Battle diminished a man; peace lifted him. This golden September morning, he was packing his saddlebags, preparing to leave Mexico. He and the Rangers weren't needed here anymore. And frankly, he couldn't wait to put Mexico behind him. He yanked the saddlebag flap down and cinched it tight. If it only was that simple.

General Ampudia, who'd been in charge of the Battle of Monterrey, had requested a truce. General Taylor had granted it. With Taylor's permission, the Mexican Army under Ampudia had been permitted to keep their weapons. Carson shook his head as he remembered watching them march away to the south the day before. The deal had sounded untenable to Carson.

But he had already turned his mind back to Texas. Most of the Rangers had already left, heading north. In the Rangers' absence, the Comanche and *bandidos* had become troublesome again. Texas still needed him. That meant leaving Mariel with his family again. He tried to swallow down being parted from her. And couldn't. How could he—

Tunney rode into the small clearing around the jacal. He held the reins to Emilio's, Sugar's, and Mariel's horses. "Didn't have much trouble. Our soldiers had been collecting horses. I just picked out the three that belong to us."

Carson nodded and finished checking the cinch on his saddle. His mount fidgeted, neighing to the other horses. Then from inside came Mariel, followed by Sugar and then Emilio, on crutches. He still couldn't put much weight on his splinted right leg, but his calf was healing well even though the bone had been broken by the bullet. Still, it worried Carson to see how much weight Emilio had lost in such a short time.

Carson busied himself with attaching the travois behind Emilio's horse. Sugar came and helped him. She whispered, "I remember bringing our father home like this from San Jacinto."

Carson made himself smile, though the same disquieting memory had come to him. "And he's fine and has been."

She nodded, though she didn't smile.

Carson didn't blame her. They had many miles to cover, dangerous, rough miles. None of them would feel secure until they were home. Mariel was hanging a cloth bag of food the Mexican couple had given them onto her saddle horn. Carson had held himself back from speaking or touching her over the past few days. There was no privacy here.

Tunney and Carson helped Emilio onto the travois. As they

turned, a familiar voice hailed them. "Carson! I thought Tunney would lead me to where you were!"

Resisting, Carson slowly turned. There was Niven, leading a donkey that was towing a crude two-wheeled cart. Niven approached and offered his hand.

Carson shook but didn't take his eyes off the cart. "What are you up to, Niven?"

The man grimaced. "I'm afraid I must call upon the bond of blood in a very inconvenient way. Come." He motioned for Carson to follow him. In the cart, Remy lay unconscious or asleep, looking feverish, pale and thin, covered by a thin brown wool blanket.

Carson cursed under his breath. *No.*

"Exactly so," Niven agreed. "The very last person you wanted to see or to be saddled with."

"What do you want us to do?" Carson growled.

"You have to take him with you. I've done my best for him, and the doctors have done their work. But he needs careful nursing. And I don't know how. Nor do my duties permit me."

"Where was he wounded?" Sugar asked, coming up beside Carson.

"In the shoulder, a ball broke his collarbone and his right foot sustained injury, perhaps a horse stepped on it when he fell. I've been with him whenever I could. I haven't been able to rouse him very often or to bring down his fever." For once, Niven looked grim.

Carson felt his face assume the same forbidding expression. The call of blood was strong, but he didn't like it. He leaned close to Niven's ear. "He looks bad. He shouldn't travel in this weakened condition—"

"I know," Niven interrupted, "but if he receives good care, he'll have a better chance of surviving. Even traveling with you, he'll be better watched over than at the camp hospital."

"What if he dies along the way?" Carson whispered fiercely.

"Then at least he'll be buried on U.S. soil with family to speak solemn prayers over his grave. Not in an unmarked communal pit with strangers in a foreign land," Niven snapped back.

Sugar laid a hand on Carson's shoulder. "He's right. We have to take Remy with us. Mariel and I can nurse him as we go north. I have enough supplies with me." Without waiting for Carson's agreement, she touched Remy's forehead, shook her head, and bustled away to get her nursing chest.

Carson and Niven faced each other. Carson inhaled deeply. He knew there was only one answer. "We'll do our best for him."

"I know you will. I have already sent a letter to my wife in San Felipe, telling her that I've sent Remy home with you to your ranch. It will either take weeks to reach her or will be lost. The times are uncertain in the extreme." Niven stared into Carson's eyes. "And you realize this war isn't over by any measurement."

Shrugging, Carson turned to watch Sugar and Mariel hug the young Mexican wife good-bye. Sugar hurried toward the cart with her nursing chest.

Carson raised his arm to the Mexican couple. "*Vayan con Dios, mis amigos.*" The couple wished them the same.

Being taken in by a Mexican couple in the midst of a battle had confused Carson when he'd had time to consider it. But as the Mexican had confided, What were the battles to him? He had no part or say in the government, so why should he care? He wouldn't let a man die at his door just because the government in Mexico City said he should.

In farewell, Carson repeated his promise in Spanish to them. "If you ever need help of any kind, come to the Quinn Ranch or Rancho Sandoval southwest of San Antonio. We will not fail you."

The couple nodded and waved. Carson helped Mariel mount

her horse. Sugar settled herself in the cart beside Remy. Tunney led Sugar's horse, as well as Emilio's, with the travois attached. Carson swung his leg over his saddle and took the lead rope for the cart donkey. As the Mexican couple and Niven called farewell once more, he led the party through the narrow lane from the jacal to the Saltillo Road. With a final wave, Niven left them at the road, heading south while they turned north.

The addition of Remy to this difficult, slow journey galled Carson. But the call of blood ties could not be denied. And even though he knew that the journey home might prove perilous and exhausting, his spirit lightened. *We're going home. God grant us safe passage.*

Three days north of Monterrey, Carson sat in the silence of deep night. He was keeping watch as the rest of their party slept. His cousin Remy had finally gained true consciousness today. Sugar had spent most of the past two evenings fomenting his foot wound by the campfire. On the first night, Mariel had made broth, and then she'd spent most of two days walking beside the cart and spooning broth into Remy whenever he'd been lucid enough to swallow.

Tunney had also helped. From the rib bones and gut from a downed antelope, he had fashioned a splint to hold the collarbone still so it could knit together and wouldn't pain Remy so much as the cart bumped over the open country.

Tonight, Carson sat outside the glow of the fire, looking away from the flames, wishing that they could move faster. The night was still balmy, summer warmth lingering. But with the travois and two-wheeled cart and the uneven ground, they could not hurry. It would probably take them a month or more to reach the ranch. Carson could imagine the pain that Remy must be feeling, even with the new splint, whenever the large wooden wheels went over a bump. He cringed.

"Please," a thin voice quavered, "please."

Carson crept over to Remy, who lay under a wool blanket in the unhitched cart. "What do you need?" Carson whispered and leaned close to hear the reply.

"I need . . . to relieve myself."

Carson nodded. "That's a good sign. Your body's starting to work again. I'll lift you and then hold you up."

"Please."

Carson set his rifle down and gently lifted Remy like a sack of grain over his shoulder. Remy sucked in air, no doubt holding in a cry of pain. On the far side of the cart, away from the low fire, Carson lowered Remy bit by bit and then held the man nearly upright. The simple act exhausted Remy, who, afterward, trembled in Carson's arms. "I'll get you laid down again, cousin."

"The wagon bed is . . . hard," Remy said.

"I know, but we don't have anything to act as a cushion other than the corn husks in the sack we made for your bedding. We're out in the middle of nowhere, Remy. I'm sorry."

As Carson laid him gently back down in the wagon, Remy let out a strangled moan. "I never thought . . . I'd be wounded."

"No one ever does."

"You weren't." Remy didn't sound quarrelsome; he sounded embarrassed.

"Remy, we fought in a battle. Hot lead was flying everywhere."

"You—know—how—to fight." Each of Remy's words sounded dug out of him.

Carson stared down at what he could see of his cousin, a man he thought foolish. He could only pity him now. And Carson knew no man wanted that. "I know how to fight." His own voice now sounded forced. "But I hate it. Maybe now you see why."

"But—"

"Don't talk. You're wasting your strength, and you don't have any to waste. Sleep. We'll talk when you're better."

"Thanks."

"You're welcome. Sleep."

Then a totally unexpected, shivery wave of self-pity washed over Carson. This war wasn't finished. Carson might have to fight again. *I don't want to. I want to be done with fighting.* Would that ever be possible? Could a Ranger ever really quit?

After two uneventful weeks on their journey, tonight during his watch, Carson had become aware of something disquieting. He'd expected this danger might threaten them along the way. He hoped he was just plain wrong. As autumn progressed from September into October, night came earlier every evening, every increasingly chilly evening. And tonight, with the air dry and empty, only stars and a new moon tried and failed to illuminate the surrounding plain. Thick black velvet ringed the dim light away from the low fire.

Since Tunney would be taking the early morning watch, he had already lain down in the circle around the campfire. Sugar was helping Emilio get bedded down for the night. Soon the two of them settled down, wrapped together in their blankets. Remy was asleep in the cart. His fever had finally stopped recurring every evening. Carson expected him to live. Mariel lingered near Carson by the fire, as she did every night. This lull between waking and sleeping was their time alone together. He wished he could enjoy it tonight.

But his senses were on high alert. Mariel's nearness was interfering with his concentration. He grimaced.

"Is something wrong?" she whispered.

He shook his head as if waving away a fly.

The woman he loved lowered her eyes and stared into the fire. He didn't want to frighten her, but he also didn't want her to misinterpret his preoccupation. "I am going to tell you something," he murmured, "but you must not react to it. I need you to act as natural as you can. Understand?"

She looked at him for a long moment, then she nodded.

"I think that there might be Comanche close. Several times I think I've heard someone prowling nearby."

"Oh," she breathed, but she didn't start up or make any other outward reaction.

"Don't be worried. I think they recognize us as Rangers. They probably would have moved on if Emilio and Remy weren't wounded. They are wondering if they can get away with stealing one of our horses. I doubt they will attack us."

"They won't attack?" Her small voice sounded high and scared.

"I don't think so. There must only be a few of them or they wouldn't be prowling around, trying to see if they can slip away with a horse without us knowing till morning."

Just then there was a jangling of a low bell in the nearby brush. Carson leaped up. Tunney rolled to his feet, his Colt in hand. Both men charged toward the sound.

Mariel stood up, dropping her tin mug of coffee. From behind, a hand clamped over her mouth. A gun fired. Mariel was flung forward into the fire. She screamed, twisting and throwing herself beyond the flames. She lay, gasping on the dirt, remaining safe—outside of the circle of light. That much caution she had learned.

Carson came rushing to her. He grabbed her hands and yanked her up. "Are you hurt?" he cried. He pulled her close to the fire and began running his hands over her, checking for injuries.

She shook violently as she pressed her face into Carson's shoulder. His strong arms came around her, holding her close to his heart, which beat loudly in her left ear.

"What happened?" he demanded. "Who shot? Why were you nearly in the fire? Tell me!"

"One brave evidently wanted more than horses. He wanted Mariel," Emilio spoke up.

Mariel heard movement and Sugar's reprimand that Emilio should lie back down, that he couldn't go after the Comanche.

Emilio stilled and said, "While you were off checking on the horses, he came up as bold as polished brass and tried to make away with her. I winged him. And he took off."

At these words, Mariel's knees gave way. Carson carried her back to where they had been sitting and set her there. She couldn't stop shaking. Carson brought her blanket and wrapped her in it, settling her on the earth in front of him between his powerful legs.

He spoke to Emilio over her head, sounding gruff, agonized. "Do you think that's why they went for the horses—a diversion?" Carson rubbed her shoulders and her arms, chafing them, trying to warm her. He spoke to Emilio again. "Did you see anything about the brave? Are he or his band known to us?"

"I saw little, just Mariel being grabbed. Did they get any of the horses, Tunney?" Emilio asked.

"No, the old 'bell on a string in the brush' did the trick. I think they mostly wanted a horse if they could get one. One of them might have had his eye on your woman. I think that our being Rangers just made them want to see what they could get away with, you know? Be able to brag that they stole a horse or a woman from three Rangers."

After a few heated words in response to this, Carson urged "Go back to your blanket, Tunney. I'll finish the first watch."

Tunney grunted. Then Carson called Remy, who answered that he was fine. Carson said no more.

Before the commotion, Mariel had been sleepy; she was wide awake now. The thought that an Indian had wanted to make off with her hissed through her nerves. The night crept into the same quiet as before, disturbed only by the wings of night birds and the chant of insects. Her hands were fisted in her lap. She stared into the darkness, wishing somehow to recapture the calm she and Carson had been sharing before the bell had clanged.

"I wish I could take you someplace safe," Carson said, his lips right beside her ear. "I hate that there is always danger here. I hate it. Why isn't there ever any peace?"

His vehemence startled her out of her fear. She turned and rolled onto her knees. She threw her arms around his neck. She kissed him with all the love that she had for him. She didn't know or care whether the others were watching or not.

She clung to him. "When I am with you, I have peace, joy." The words came out of the deep well inside her that she usually kept sealed. "I never knew peace until I met you. I was wanted never. . . . No one ever cared. . . ." Her voice faded. How could she make him understand what his love meant to her? "You love me," she said, not able to say more. The fire had died down and the night was so dark that she could not see his face. She ran her fingertips lightly over his features, feeling his smooth skin and tracing his eyebrows.

"I don't want this frontier to be your life. I don't want you to always be in danger," he whispered, his voice disappearing into the black void around them.

"There is no real peace as you want," she whispered, "not in this world. There was no peace in Germany. And that is not a frontier. Germans fight, get murdered. There are thieves there too."

He stroked her hair as she tried to think how to confront him, still feeling his skin under her fingertips.

"All that you've said is true, but I wish it weren't. Now sleep. I'll keep watch."

She still held him, trying to think of a way to comfort him. No matter how much she loved him, she could not stop the war, could not make this a safe place. She was a Texas woman, but just one woman.

* * *

The last few familiar miles to the Quinn Ranch could not be covered fast enough to suit Sugar. After well over a month of travel, nearing the end of October, she wanted to gallop ahead and leave everyone behind. "It is hard to go so slow, *sí?*" Emilio said. "I see your excitement."

She slid from her saddle. Walking beside the travois, she took Emilio's hand. The sky was overcast, just as part of her was at this homecoming. "I don't ever want to travel again."

Emilio chuckled. "What about the trip to see Ash and Reva at Antonio's?"

"When the war is over." She turned her face north toward home.

Finally, the party reached the last rise, overlooking the gentle slope toward the hacienda. Sugar couldn't contain herself. She dropped her reins and ran. As she neared the house, people poured from the hacienda, from the barns, from the surrounding jacales. And everyone was shouting, "*Saludos!* You're home! Welcome home!"

Her mother ran toward her, and she was finally wrapped in her arms. "My darling daughter, my sweet child." Sugar wept with relief onto her mother's shoulder, but when she heard her parents call out Carson's name, she stepped back to let them welcome him and the others. She hugged her little sister Erin, who was jumping up and down in her excitement.

When Dorritt saw Remy in the cart, she exclaimed with dismay and began giving orders, devoting herself to giving him the attention he needed. Sugar turned and asked for help with

Emilio. She sighed and whispered to herself, "All I want and need is a long bath and clean clothes." Of course, that wasn't all she wanted. She wanted more.

Late in the day, Sugar found herself smelling of lavender-scented soap and sitting at her parents' large round dining table. She was wearing clean, pressed clothing and sipping a glass of fresh milk. She was also nibbling on the best food she'd eaten in months. She gazed around the huge room, with its large stone fireplace, and at the faces around the table—Carson, her parents, little Erin, Tunney, Emilio, and Mariel. *Home. I'm home.* In the midst of her peace, she recalled the letters from her past. Like a knife slicing through marrow, her peace was at an end.

Her mother was speaking to Carson. "I'll send one of our *vaqueros* to San Felipe with a letter, telling Jewell and Henri that Remy is here, recovering. I'll ask her to come as soon as possible. I think seeing his family would help Remy greatly."

Dorritt turned to Mariel and Sugar. "I'm sure your careful nursing saved Remy's life." Then she looked to Tunney. "And the splint you made him was excellent. I think you did better than any doctor could have."

"Thank you, ma'am." Tunney grinned. "I was glad to help. I could see he was in misery with everything, the moving around and bein' carried over rough ground."

Dorritt shook her head. "I shudder to think of the pain he's suffered. Are you sure you must leave us so quickly?"

"Yes, ma'am, I want to get settled in for the winter in New Braunfels."

"Still interested in that handsome-looking widow?" Carson teased.

Tunney only chuckled in reply and took another helping of everything on the table.

Sugar tried harder to hold back her request till she was alone with her parents. She found she couldn't. Somehow this must be spoken of in the open. No more secrets. "Mother, I know about the letters, the letters Carson found in the cabin."

Silence.

Only Tunney went on eating, trying to look as if he weren't there.

Finally, her father asked, "How?"

Sugar inhaled deeply. "I overheard you, mother, and Carson talking about them that night. I didn't say anything because . . ." She pressed her lips together and looked down at her plate. "I wanted to deny that they existed. I was still afraid."

"What changed your mind?" Dorritt asked.

The sounds from outside and muted laughter from the kitchen filled the silence around the table. How to explain? "I am not a little girl anymore."

Dorritt reached over and patted Sugar's hand. "No, you are a grown woman."

"And my wife," Emilio added, taking her other hand.

"I will give you the letters after supper," Dorritt said.

Sugar nodded and looked down.

Carson must have sensed her discomfort; he lessened the awkward silence by asking their father about a mustang he had been trying to break to the saddle before he'd left for the war. The conversation drifted back to everyday matters.

Sugar was grateful. It gave her time to calm down. Bringing up the letters had cost her. Nonetheless, she had spoken the truth, declared her willingness to face the truth. The road to Mexico and back had stretched her, strengthened her. She was not the same young girl she'd been this spring. Now she was a woman, a Texas woman, a strong woman, unafraid.

* * *

Emilio lay on their large bed in Sugar's room. With a wide white feather pillow at her back, she sat beside his head. An oil lamp found on the bedside table. On the bed coverlet lay five letters, faded and with one edge water-stained.

Emilio ran his index finger down her arm, causing gooseflesh to rise. "I am here, *querida*."

"I could not forget that." Sugar smiled and looked at the letters, trying to decide which one to open first. She finally chose one and unfolded it. She read aloud, "'Dear Ida Rose, I have dreadful news to tell you. . . .'" Sugar made herself continue reading her aunt Violet's letter aloud. "'My promised, Jacob Hinton, died of influenza last week. It has been a terrible shock. I feel as if my heart had been buried with him.'" Sugar's voice faltered. *What if I had lost Emilio?* She leaned over and kissed her husband.

He threaded his fingers into her hair. "*Mi amor*, don't be afraid."

In the early darkness after the evening meal, Mariel strolled beside Carson. The chill of late autumn made her lift her shawl over her head and draw it tight under her chin. A white veil covered the moon.

After the meal, he had whispered, "I have something to say to you alone."

The look that accompanied these mild words had ignited currents of pleasure flowing through her every vein. She had let him draw her outside. Now she could think of nothing but the kisses she hoped he would soon be giving her.

When he took her hand, she was pleased. They arrived at his mother's herb and medicine garden. He opened the door and let her in. Then they were behind the door, out of sight of all the people who lived on the ranch. Carson folded her into his arms. "There is so much that I want to say to you, but I have trouble putting feelings into words, words of love."

"I don't know why you would love me." The words embarrassed her as soon as she spoke them. She tried to pull her hand from his.

He wouldn't free her. "If I asked you the same question, what would be your answer? Do you love me because I can keep you safe?"

"You can keep me safe," she replied.

"Do you love me because I can provide for you?"

"You can."

"Do you love me because I am handsome?"

She caught the hint of teasing in his voice. She smiled and leaned over to kiss him. Then pulled away, putting her hands in the crook of his arm.

Carson led Mariel down the rows of dried plants, the moon lighting their way. "I remember when these plants were full and green."

"*Ja*, the little girls came running in the gate and . . ."

"And I was kissing you." He lowered his head and lightly brushed her lips with his—once, twice, tantalizing her.

She stood on her tiptoes and pressed her lips to his. Every nerve in her body sang.

Under the veiled moon in the dying garden, Carson whispered into Mariel's ear. "Before I go, I want to make you my wife."

She understood. He wanted to make certain she would be protected and provided for by his family . . . in case. She slipped her arms under his and clasped him to herself, trying to bind him to her. "Carson, I—"

"Hello, the house!" a man called out in the night.

Sixteen

Both Mariel and Carson stiffened, then Carson led Mariel out of the garden, into the moonlit open yard in front of the hacienda.

Carson halted, frigid shock icing his veins. Even though the full moonlight didn't reveal their faces to Carson, he could not be mistaken. The last people in the world he'd expected or wanted to see had just arrived at the Quinns' doorstep.

He knew why they had come, but he had not expected them yet. In front were two riders, behind them a buckboard with two dark people. A few feet behind the wagon, two Quinn *vaqueros* who had been on watch duty remained in the saddle, lingering, saying nothing. The *vaqueros* had permitted this party onto Quinn land. They obviously hadn't deemed these visitors dangerous.

How little they knew. Carson dreaded fully and deeply the aggravation that one of the visitors would cause.

In her blue flannel wrapper, his mother hurried out the front door into the chilly night. Quinn came right behind her, carrying a lighted lantern. She halted and gasped. "Henri! Blanche!"

Dismounting, Henri LaCroix moved to help his daughter down from her horse. A black couple, no doubt slaves, slipped down from the buckboard, remaining well behind Blanche and her father. Dorritt hurried down the steps. "Blanche! Henri! I can't believe . . . how did you get here so quickly?"

Carson hung back with Mariel anchored at his side, irritation grinding inside him. Indeed this was the first time that either Henri or Blanche had ever been to the Quinn ranch. Family visits had always been from west to east, not vice versa. Of course this time, the LaCroixs would have had to come to them. Carson drew Mariel closer to the light.

"How is Remy?" Blanche hurried forward stiffly, obviously fatigued. Henri and Quinn shook hands. Then Blanche looked toward Carson. She narrowed her eyes, as if measuring him. Or was she focusing on Mariel, beside him?

"Yes, he's here," Dorritt said, waving the visitors toward the porch. "Come in! My son and his party just arrived earlier today. Blanche, Carson said that your husband had sent you a letter—"

"We received Anthony's missive a little over two weeks ago and set out as soon as we could," Blanche complained, lifting her skirts as she walked up the steps.

Missive. Even Blanche's words flaunted her conceit. Carson and Mariel followed as his father with the lamp led the visitors through the large, dark room. Then they walked over the path through the open courtyard to the guest bedroom where Remy had been settled. In the glow of the lantern, Dorritt held her index finger to her lips and opened the door. Consuela, who was sitting with Remy, rose and stepped into the shadows. Remy was deeply asleep.

Carson was pleased that his cousin was looking much stronger in spite of the rigors of the journey.

"Don't waken him, Blanche," Dorritt murmured. "He needs

his sleep. Though our son says he's much better than he was in Mexico."

For a moment, Blanche looked subdued. Her chin dipped and her step faltered. She halted at the end of the bed. Henri came up behind her and put an arm around her shoulders.

Carson watched from the doorway. He could see that Blanche wanted to waken her brother. For once, however, she followed someone's advice. She turned away, putting her hands over her face. Dorritt motioned for them all to leave.

Henri led Blanche out. All of them followed, returning to the large room. The housekeeper had lit a warming fire in the large hearth and lit an oil lamp on the round dining table. She was laying out food and pouring new wine for the travelers. Carson dragged over more chairs, and the party sat down.

For a few minutes, the guests sat, nibbling the fresh cheese and flat bread and sipping the red wine. Then Blanche spoke up. "Tell me what's been done for my brother."

Carson answered, "After the battle at Monterrey, your husband brought him to us in pretty bad shape. He was feverish, weak, and nearly dead."

Blanche moaned softly.

Just talking about Monterrey battered Carson from within. Taking a hitching breath, he looked away from the lamplight, hiding his marked reaction. He continued, "But my friend Tunney rigged up a splint for his broken collarbone. And both Sugar and Mariel nursed him along the way. Remy hasn't had a fever for over a week now—not even at night."

Blanche looked at Mariel and then turned to Dorritt with a questioning look.

"I'm sorry. I should have introduced Mariel. She is new to Texas. From Germany—"

"She's my fiancée," Carson interrupted, taking Mariel's hands in both of his.

His mother and father beamed at him. Sugar stifled a happy squeal, and Emilio said, "*Felicitaciones*." Carson lifted Mariel's hand and kissed it.

Blanche stared at Mariel in a rude way. He steeled himself for the insult that would surely come. Blanche made a sound of exasperation and shook her head, turning back to Dorritt. "Mother was shocked that you allowed Sugar to marry—"

"There's no need to repeat what your mother says," Henri interrupted.

Both Emilio and Sugar had stiffened. Sugar glared at her cousin. Carson clenched his jaw, refusing to take the bait.

In the golden glow from the oil lamp, Dorritt stared into Blanche's eyes. "We are quite pleased with their choices."

Satisfaction warmed Carson. Leave it to his mother to be quick and undaunted. Neither Blanche nor her mother had ever been able to best Dorritt Quinn.

Blanche looked away, lifting her chin. "Has a doctor been summoned?"

Dorritt shook her head. "No, Remy's obviously on the mend. It's just going to take time to heal completely and regain his strength—"

"Father, don't you think Remy needs a doctor?" Blanche interrupted, ignoring Dorritt. "I think that's what my mother would want."

"After the battle, he was seen by U.S. doctors," Carson said.

Henri turned to Quinn. "Where's the nearest doctor?"

Quinn looked to Dorritt and said, "There's a few in San Antonio, but I don't know if any would come all this way."

"One will come if we offer him enough," Blanche said, sitting up straighter, her tone more snappish. "Aunt Dorritt, the full moon makes night travel possible. I'm sure you can send one of your men to San Antonio tonight—"

"No, I won't." Dorritt stood, sighing. "Remy is in no imminent danger tonight. Tunney, another Ranger who traveled here with Carson from Monterrey, is heading north tomorrow. He can stop at the doctor's office in San Antonio—if you still think that necessary in the morning."

Blanche was being herself, her conceited and demanding self. Carson wished propriety would allow him to kiss Mariel here and now for being the sweet, sensible, gentle woman she was. He suddenly felt exhausted. "Blanche, I'll take my gear out of my room so you can have it," he said, rising. "I'll bunk with the *vaqueros*."

"Yes, Henri," Dorritt said, "we'll have to make a bed for you in Remy's room. We're quite filled up now."

The housekeeper came back in and told Dorritt that the LaCroix servants had been taken to a jacal for the night and that bathwater was being heated for the guests. Dorritt nodded her thanks. "Blanche, a bath is being prepared for you and will be set up in Carson's room soon."

Henri murmured, "Before we turn in, we have news for you, too, Dorritt."

Blanche looked suddenly shaken, losing some of her starched-up posture. "Aunt Dorritt, you must not have received my mother's letter."

"Letter?" Dorritt echoed, sounding suddenly fearful.

Blanche nodded, looking downward. "Grandmother died eight days before we received news of Remy."

Dorritt moaned and wilted visibly. Quinn gripped her right shoulder. "We are very sad to hear this. Mrs. Kilbride was a good woman."

Sugar got up, went to her mother, and stood behind her. Dorritt reached up a hand and took Sugar's. Carson turned where he stood at the doorway. "This is sad news," he said and then left.

* * *

Mariel woke with a single resolve in her heart and mind—that this foolish woman Blanche would not disturb or hurt Carson, the finest man she knew. Mariel had met *her* kind before. Women who only cared for themselves and worked to make sure that everyone else put them first also. This morning's breakfast had been made miserable by Blanche's cutting but veiled remarks about Sugar's marrying beneath her. That alone had confirmed Mariel's assessment of this vain woman.

Now, after the unpleasant breakfast, Dorritt and Mariel accompanied Blanche through the inner courtyard, which opened at the back of the great room of the hacienda. The chill morning air made Mariel tighten her wool shawl around her. The walkway around the edges of the courtyard had an overhang to protect from rain, but not wind. In single file, the three of them were going to the room where Remy lay.

"I've never seen a house built quite this way," Blanche said. The words were not objectionable; the tone was.

"You have a very limited scope, having never traveled outside of Texas," Mrs. Quinn responded tranquilly. "We adopted the Spanish style, since it suits the climate here. Keeping the bedrooms open on two sides lets a free flow of air in the summer. And the courtyard is a lovely oasis most of the year. I prefer this arrangement."

"Yes, Mother has often commented about your . . . turning away from the ways in which you were raised."

Blanche entered Remy's room. Remy was sitting up in bed, feeding himself with a spoon. His movements were awkward because of his splint. At their entrance, he fumbled and spilled a little onto a large white napkin tied like a bib over the front of his striped nightshirt.

"Aunt Dorritt," Blanche snapped, "why isn't the girl feeding my brother?"

Consuela, standing by the bed, curtseyed. *"Señorita—"*

"I can feed myself," Remy growled. "She offered to feed me and I told her no."

"This is Consuela, a cousin of Emilio's," Mrs. Quinn said.

Blanche made a face, showing her disdain for everyone else in the room, save her brother. "We got here as soon as we could . . ." She let the sentence fade, saying without words that his care, before she had arrived, had been inadequate.

Mariel clamped her mouth shut to hold back hot words simmering on her tongue. If Blanche ventured to carry her insults any further, Mariel would speak.

Remy lifted another spoonful to his mouth, glaring at his sister. "Father came in early this morning and we talked. I've received the best care that Carson, his lady, and Sugar could give me so far from civilization." Remy set the spoon down into the bowl on the tray over his lap and looked to Consuela. "I'm just so tired."

His lady. The words filled Mariel's cup to overflowing.

Consuela approached Remy. "You need to eat, *señor.*" She picked up the spoon. "Just eat a bit more, and then I'll take the tray back to the kitchen."

"You speak English?" Blanche stared at the girl, who merely nodded and began feeding Remy.

"Yes, all our house staff speaks both English and Spanish." Dorritt moved to the opposite side of the bed and laid her wrist on Remy's forehead. "No fever. Good."

"I can tell you that spending a night"—Remy spoke between spoonfuls, grinning—"in a real bed felt wonderful, Aunt Dorritt." Then he looked to Mariel. "You see, all your efforts have helped me."

Mariel smiled in return. Evidently Remy had changed in his attitude toward the Quinns. Perhaps complete helplessness taught one humility.

After swallowing more food, he looked at Consuela and gave her a half smile. "*Señorita,* that is really all I can take in now."

"I will come back in a few hours with more. Rest." Consuela took off his bib, laid it over her shoulder, and carried out the tray.

Blanche sniffed and moved to the side of Remy's bed. "You've been through a horrible ordeal. I can't think why Anthony didn't leave you in the care of the U.S. surgeons."

"Maybe because he wanted me to live," Remy said with an infuriated expression. "You, sister, have no idea what an army hospital tent is like after a battle. It's a butcher shop."

Remembered revulsion raised the gorge in Mariel's throat.

"Remy, there's no need to be vulgar," Blanche said.

Her brother made a disparaging sound. "I'm tired, Blanche. Just eating is hard work."

"Father is sending for a doctor to see you," Blanche said.

Remy repeated the same disgusted sound. "I'm healing. What can a doctor do for me?"

"Well, he can tell them to take that ridiculous bone splint off you." Blanche's soothing I'm-a-caring-sister voice slipped, and her irritation at not being able to take control here gleamed unmistakably.

"The splint cannot be taken from him till he has healed," Mariel spoke up quickly. "You do not know the pain—"

"Thank you very much," Blanche said dismissively, "but this is my brother."

Trying to lean forward, Remy insisted, "Don't use that tone with her." Remy's face became flushed with the effort. "Miss Mariel took care of me as if I were her own blood, better than my own blood. Don't you dare—"

Dorritt gently urged Remy to lie down and adjusted his pillows for him. "You must not waste your energy. Rest, and Consuela will bring you more food in a little while."

Remy gave Blanche a scathing look, then closed his eyes. Dorritt turned. "I think we should let him rest. Consuela will check on him. She is a dependable nurse."

Mariel admired how Dorritt ignored her niece's annoying behavior.

Blanche hesitated, but Remy kept his eyes closed. Mariel didn't blame him. Did this girl care at all about her brother? It was hard to tell. If one considered just her words without judging her tone or motives, one could not find fault.

But the whole conversation had really been more about Blanche than her brother. Blanche wanted everyone to know that her family, and especially she, ranked above the others here. That came through every "concerned" phrase. Maybe that was why Remy was so cross. He knew his sister didn't really care about him.

Why had Carson ever been interested in such a woman? It made no sense. Mariel turned to leave the room and saw that Carson stood in the doorway. She blushed, as if he had read her mind.

He did not look pleased. "I came to get you ladies. Tunney is about to leave. I knew my mother and Mariel would want to bid him good-bye."

"Yes, thank you, son." Dorritt bustled past him.

Mariel heard her hurried footsteps on the flagstone path of the courtyard. Blanche pushed ahead of Mariel and halted beside Carson in the doorway. "So you've given your heart to this . . . *immigrant?*"

Carson looked down into Blanche's face. "I don't have time for your games. I doubt you want to bid Tunney farewell. So why don't you go to your room? I'm sure you're still fatigued from your trip."

Blanche halted, glaring at him, then marched off, her angry heels clicking on the flagstones.

"Tell Tunney farewell for me, would you, Carson?" Remy asked, opening his eyes now that his sister was gone.

"Certainly. You rest now." Carson offered Mariel his hand. She took it and smiled. Before she had taken more than a step, he paused and pulled her close. He kissed her.

She tried to object, but he ignored her, kissed her again, then drew her with him toward the front of the house. Mariel floated over the stone path and through the great room to the front door.

The late October sunshine was brittle and bright. Blanche had, of course, ignored Carson's advice. She was standing beside her father and pointedly ignoring Carson. Tunney was by his horse, looking the better for a few hearty meals and a night in a bed. Shaven and wearing clean clothing, he smiled at Mariel. "Do you have any messages for anybody at New Braunfels?"

Mariel thought for only a second. A backsplash of shame washed through her and made her angry. *I did nothing to be ashamed of.* "No." There was *no one* she wanted to be remembered to. No one there she ever wanted to see again. She gripped Carson's hand and shook her head.

"Remy says thanks again for the splint," Carson said to the big man.

With a wave, Tunney swung up into his saddle, calling farewells in English and Spanish. Soon he disappeared over the horizon to the north.

Blanche faced her father. "How long do you think it will take for the doctor to arrive?"

Mariel began to move away as the raw wind flared the ends of her shawl. Carson's parents drew toward the front door.

Her father turned away from Blanche. "I didn't ask Tunney to summon a doctor—"

"You what? Why not?" Blanche was instantly furious, red-faced and huffy.

"Because Remy doesn't need a doctor." Her father kept withdrawing. "He's improving—"

Blanche interrupted, "How can you know that—"

Her father swung back and bent his strained face to hers.

"Blanche, I have to take this kind of contention from your mother, but I won't take it from you. Go to your room." Her father stalked away from her.

As Carson's parents turned away too, Blanche brushed past them and stalked back into the house. Carson grinned. He hadn't expected his uncle to scold Blanche, but it was a welcome change. Carson drew Mariel with him. "Let's take a walk around the herb garden."

At the word "garden," Mariel's heart leaped. Walking in the garden had become her favorite pastime—if Carson was with her. She came with him willingly. Carson unlatched the garden gate and urged Mariel inside with a gentle nudge and a roguish grin. The gate had barely shut behind them when she found herself in his welcome arms. "Mariel," he breathed into her ear, "you're still going to marry me?"

She chuckled, thrilled at his teasing question. "I do not change my mind so much."

"Good. I do not change my mind so much either. But I'm afraid that we will postpone our wedding till my beloved relatives return home."

Mariel understood without any explanation. Who wanted Blanche spoiling the happiest day of Mariel's life? "I agree," Mariel said.

"Thank you. I expected you'd understand." The look that accompanied these mild words ignited her joy. Overwhelming gratitude swept over her, pure and heartfelt. *Gott, danke, danke*. The three words flowed through her with every beat of her thankful heart.

* * *

The Day of the Dead, or All Hallows' Eve, as Dorritt called it, dawned bright and clear, the sun warming them all. Mariel was fascinated by the festival, new to her, to honor the dead. Dorritt and Quinn did not permit the making of altars in the jacales to the spirits of the dead. But they had adopted the practice of visiting the family cemeteries and respectfully adorning the crosses and tombstones with flowers and other tokens of love. It was a day free from work, and it would end in a fiesta in the largest barn, which had been swept clean and decorated for the occasion.

Now Mariel and Carson walked in the solemn procession to the cemetery on Quinn land. Once there, the families spread out, visiting the graves of their departed. The Quinns had decided to use the day as a time to mark the passing of Dorritt's mother. Henri accompanied them, but of course, Blanche had blessedly declined. Quinn carried a small white cross with the name ELSPETH KILBRIDE, 1779–1846 notched into it. Now he pounded it into the earth as a memorial. Dorritt said a few words about her mother and then prayed, thanking God for her mother's life.

Then Sugar cleared her throat. "In all the rush of company and taking care of Emilio and Remy, I haven't said anything—to all of you—about my reading the letters Carson found."

Mariel felt the quickening of interest all around her. Carson gripped her elbow tighter.

"I feared reading those letters, but when I read them, I found that they contained nothing more than one sister writing to another. There were no startling secrets. I think that it was my aunt Violet who was angry with me. I think my mother wasn't with us when I was separated from my family. The woman in Montezuma said my mother had died. Maybe her sister Violet was left to take care of me." Sugar looked down, as if gathering composure. "I talked with Mother about that time. I remember it only in bits and pieces. I think that the letters terrified me because that was a terrifying year in Texas."

Dorritt murmured, "Yes, a dreadful year."

"Mother and I talked about my fear, and the memory of feeling as if I was being crushed by a crowd of people—"

"I saw those crowds," Henri LaCroix added. "People running from the Mexicans, who were looting and burning their way through Texas."

"The Runaway Scrape," Quinn said with a shake of his head. "Awful."

"I think the fear came from that time," Sugar said, lifting her face to the bright October sun. "It had been hiding inside me from all those years ago."

"But no more, *mi dulce*." Emilio, still on crutches, moved closer to her.

Smiling, Sugar took his hand. "And Emilio and I have discussed what to do about finding out more about what happened a decade ago." She turned to face Emilio. He smiled, encouraging her. "The past no longer frightens me. But what I am going to do is write to Sam Houston and ask him to see if my father, Ernest McLaughlin, appeared anywhere in the army records of the Texas Revolutionary battles.

"If any of my family is still alive, that could lead me to them. But I think that since no one ever came looking, something must have happened to them. No matter what I find, I am happy in my life, here, as a Quinn and now as a Ramirez." Sugar beamed suddenly and the sun lit her golden hair. "I am content and free of the past."

Mariel knew the feeling. She repeated silently, *I also am content and free of the past.*

* * *

The last of the November weeks had passed by. Now the inner courtyard walls protected Mariel from most of the brisk December wind. A stout clay stove warmed the center of the courtyard. With her feet close to the stove, she was stitching the hem of her pale blue linen wedding dress. She wanted to use the last of the day's sunlight to work the tiny stitches without interruption.

Tomorrow, Remy would be well enough to go home. Two days after he, his sister, and father left, Mariel and Carson would be wed in a simple family ceremony here in this courtyard. With the occasion so near to Christmas and Mariel's status as a widow, a quiet wedding was thought best.

Mariel wondered if she had ever been fully alive before. Ever since Carson had asked her to marry him, she had felt a vibrancy that was a completely new experience. Smiles came easily, and laughing did too. She paused in her careful stitching to smile up at the pale blue sky above her. This was the way life should be, relished moment by moment.

At times, her inner joy warmed her as it radiated outward like unseen sunshine only she could feel. The final words of her favorite psalm often slipped through her mind: *"But the humble shall inherit the earth; and shall delight themselves in the abundance of peace. . . ."*

Carson entered the courtyard. She didn't have to turn her eyes to know this. She knew his step. She closed her eyes, cherishing the moment as she waited for him to reach her. Footsteps stopped; lips brushed hers. "Wake up, sleeping beauty."

She laughed aloud. No one had ever called her beautiful, and Carson did so often. The thrill of it did not pall. She had given up arguing against his compliments. He loved her, so of course she was beautiful to him.

Finding herself truly loved felt almost like a fairy tale. Yet his love was real. She wouldn't reach the end of their story and close the book. Or wake up and find that Carson had just been a dream.

With eyes still closed, she reached up, found his stubbled chin, and stroked his smooth cheek. "Carson."

He sat down on the wooden settee beside her and drew her closer, his arm around her shoulders. "Is that dress nearly done?"

"If you do not interrupt me, I will have it done in minutes."

"Then I will not say a word." He punctuated this by kissing her left earlobe.

Delight shivered through her. Somehow she looked down and started setting stitches again.

Carson kept her against him. "The preparations for *Las Posadas* are about done. They will begin tonight."

Mariel had been very interested in the different customs here for Christmas. Evidently there would be no *Tannenbaum*. But Mariel had been intrigued by the excited children dressed in robes, practicing for the walk through the small village of jacales on the ranch, when the little Joseph and Mary would go door to door seeking shelter in a home for nine consecutive nights.

On the final night, the children, followed by all the people of the ranch, would come to the main hacienda and finally be invited inside. As there had been room for Mariel here, so would there be room for Joseph and Mary. A huge party, a *fiesta*, would then take place in this courtyard and all around the Quinn hacienda. Acting out the nativity sounded like wonderful, yet sacred, fun.

Into this quiet haven intruded loud voices. Mariel looked up from her sewing. Carson rose. A familiar but completely unexpected face appeared in the courtyard, followed by Carson's parents.

"Tunney!" Smiling, Carson called out. "What has brought you here?"

Seventeen

Tunney halted, then came straight to Carson. About halfway between the door and Carson, he stopped again and stood, holding his hat. His expression, his posture, all spoke of an unhappy man.

Mariel's whole body went cold. It was a feeling she'd never experienced. It was as if some icy, invisible hand squeezed her once. She tingled with chill foreboding. Something terrible had happened.

No one spoke. Her numb fingers let her sewing drop into her lap. No longer smiling, Carson stood like a tree. Tunney stared at them. Carson's parents had halted in the doorway behind Tunney and remained motionless, looking worried.

Mariel realized that she had stopped breathing. She drew in as much air as she was able, but the cold air did nothing to warm her. Slowly, she rose to her feet, trembling but ready to help. "What has happened, Tunney?" she asked.

The large man's face twisted. "I'd give anythin' not to have to tell you this—"

"The war's started again, hasn't it?" Carson asked in a strained voice. "Taylor wants the Rangers back."

"Yes." The man swallowed, then looked down.

Mariel reached for Carson's arm. *I don't want him to go. Not again. He's done enough.* And she couldn't go with him this time. Emilio was still recovering, and Sugar wouldn't be going. *I can't go by myself, can I? Yes, I can if—*

Carson turned to her and took her hands. As if he had read her mind, he said, "No, I don't want you there."

"We can marry and I will come as your wife. I must come—"

"No, you can't," Tunney broke in, "you can't marry."

Both Mariel and Carson swung around to face Tunney, who looked stricken. "What?" Mariel asked, though her dry lips were trying to stick to each other. "What are you saying? Why can't Carson and I marry?"

The big man shuddered. "Your husband just arrived in New Braunfels. Dieter Wolffe isn't dead."

It was as if the last four words had been written in red upon the cool dry Texas air in front of Mariel's eyes. The words shivered, then flew apart. Someone broke out in laughter.

They turned as one to the sound. Blanche had stepped out of her brother's bedroom. Though she put a hand over her mouth, her mocking laugh hung in the air over them.

Mariel's knees bumped the flagstone beneath her. She hadn't been aware that she was falling. Under her lay her wedding dress, crushed.

Carson turned and reached to help her up. Then he froze. The look in his eyes forced the last bit of air out of her. *He cannot help me, touch me. He must let me go. He must go.*

Carson tried to say something, but only a few garbled sounds came forth. He swung away from her and sped over the flagstones of the courtyard. Tunney raced after him.

Mariel could not move. All the life, all the strength had gone out of her. She fought against the pull of despair. It was like a dark river that wanted to drag her into its killing current.

She was familiar with it. Often in Germany it had pulled her under and drowned her hope. *No. No, Dieter can't be alive. They said he was dead and that I should leave Germany.* And New Braunfels—how could she bear to go back, to face the people who had thought ill of her? Spread false lies about her? The thought of Dieter touching her made her gag.

Dorritt hurried to her and reached for both of her hands. "Come inside. You could use something hot to drink. We have to make sense out of this."

Mariel tried to think of words but found she couldn't pull together, voice a rational sentence. She let Dorritt help her up. She left her wedding dress lying crushed near the oak bench. On wooden legs, she walked beside Dorritt, who kept up a flow of gentle words that Mariel couldn't focus on. Dorritt urged Mariel to sit at the large round table, gently pushing her onto the chair. Then, between her shock-numbed hands, Mariel was holding a mug of hot coffee with melted chocolate. She didn't know who had given it to her. She didn't have the strength to bring it to her lips.

Sugar had come and was sitting beside her. She lifted Mariel's cup and nudged Mariel to open her mouth. Mariel obeyed, and the warm, sweet liquid flowed into her cold mouth and down her tight throat.

"There has to be some mistake," Dorritt said, gripping Quinn's hand. "Your husband was dead and buried in Germany."

"That's what I was told." Mariel folded her hands around the pottery mug, trying to warm her hands, which felt as if they had been plunged into icy water.

"You were told?" Sugar asked. "Weren't you there when he . . . when your husband died?"

"No," Mariel said, speaking with difficulty, as if her mouth and jaw had rusted. "Dieter had gotten deeply into radical politics. He wanted Germany to become free . . . where men voted. He was arrested." She paused to gather enough strength to go on, oddly gasping. "Dieter's parents told me he had died . . . in prison before his trial . . . and he had been buried on the grounds . . . of the prison."

"So he wasn't with you when he died?" Sugar asked, her voice rising.

Mariel merely shook her head. Quinn lit the oil lamp in the center of the table. Mariel watched the tiny flame flicker in the air seeping in around the windows.

"Didn't his parents go to see him before his burial?" Quinn asked, sitting back down.

"No, they had disowned him for his . . . treason. My parents were already dead. Cholera." Mariel's words came haltingly, each one uncovering a mark, a scar from the dreadful past. "My husband's parents told me to go to Texas with the *Adelsverein*. They had no money or way to take care of me. So I came to Texas." *And when I met Carson, everything became better. I became a Texas woman, a strong woman, loved by a brave, good man.*

Early night dimmed the sunlight coming from the windows. A door opened and cold air rushed in. Without looking, Mariel knew Carson had come into the room. She'd recognized his footsteps, the way he breathed, the scent of him. . . . All eyes turned toward the door. Mariel rose. "Carson."

He came forward, near the pool of golden light over the table. He stopped before he reached her. Tunney hung back by the door, a sad shadow. "So you never saw your husband dead?" Carson asked.

"No," she whispered.

"So he could be alive?"

"*Ja.*"

"How?"

Tunney cleared his throat. "Someone at the prison made a mistake, sent a letter saying he had died when he hadn't. When he got out, he found that you had gone to Texas. He had to wait until the next *Adelsverein* party left Germany. He's at New Braunfels."

Carson sent a sharp look Tunney's way. "What does the man look like?"

"Medium height, brown hair and eyes, thin, of course, but that could be from bein' in prison and then travelin' all this way. He speaks good English."

"Yes, Dieter was a teacher of modern languages, like my father," Mariel murmured.

"Does that sound like your husband?" Carson asked.

She nodded, unable to form words.

"There has to be some mistake," Sugar insisted.

"No," Quinn spoke up. "Things like this happen, especially when there are a lot of prisoners at one time. Europe has been going through political upheavals. Your husband must have been one of many who were imprisoned."

Mariel nodded again, the old bitterness rearing its spiked head. Dieter had always, always been much more interested in politics than in her. He'd only married her because his parents had given him money to set up his household with her. They had thought marriage would give their son something more to think about than politics. He'd wed Mariel for this bribe and for her small dowry. But he'd barely ever behaved as a husband.

She let out a long, sharp-edged sigh. She had never wanted to marry Dieter. She'd been forced to, and now . . . *This cannot be happening.*

Tunney cleared his throat again. "Carson and I have to leave tonight. President Polk rescinded the truce with the Mexicans."

"That doesn't surprise me," Remy said quietly, speaking up

from the shadows near the doorway to the courtyard. "Polk's a Democrat. He doesn't want Taylor, a Whig, to politically benefit from this war in the next election."

Mariel ignored this. She'd never understood German politics, much less American. She'd never heard of a Whig or a Democrat. And what did this matter to her? Except that Carson had to go away, was being taken from her again—forever. She put her hands over her eyes, trying to hide from the awful truth.

"Anyway," Tunney continued, "things are heating up and we got to get to Mexico as soon as we're able. Polk allowed Santa Anna back into Mexico to broker a peace." Tunney growled, "Instead, the butcher's back leading the Mexican Army against us."

Quinn let out a sound of disgust. "Santa Anna always takes any chance to benefit himself. I don't think he cares a thing about Mexico except to rule it."

"Yeah, I agree," Tunney said. "But we got to get there. Taylor needs us for scouting. Bad."

Mariel uncovered her eyes. This might be the last moments that she would ever see Carson Quinn.

Carson took a step toward Mariel, his hands held out. Then he stopped and lowered his hands. "Good-bye, Mariel. I wish you the best." He turned and disappeared into the shadows, Tunney at his heels.

Mariel sank back into her chair. She clutched the edge of the table and tried to stay conscious. Gentle hands helped her up and led her to the room she shared with Erin. The same gentle hands helped her lay down, took off her shoes, and spread a quilt over her. Mariel lay without moving.

In Germany she'd had no choice but to obey her parents and marry Dieter. Here, she thought she had left that all behind her. How could the past reach into her present and utterly destroy her future? Destroy the woman she had become.

Carson rode without thinking much of the terrain or the cold wind on his face or the bleak moonlight. On the outside, a hard shell coated him; inside, he despaired. The desolate look on Mariel's face would haunt him for as long as he managed to stay alive. Until just hours ago, he'd thought that he had glimpsed his future, a future of being a family man, of being a man whose sole purpose in life wasn't fighting and killing but loving and building. He'd known that Taylor needed the Rangers, but he had hoped that he could, once and for all, put his Colts down and live a private life.

Become a man of peace. "Mark the perfect man, and behold the upright: for the end of that man is peace." His mother's repetition of those verses had become a part of him. He had tried to live an upright life. His word was his bond. He protected the weak. He respected God. Carson stopped that train of useless thought. *What is, is, and I can't change it.*

Tunney rode beside him, a man twenty-five years his senior. He wanted to ask Tunney why he was heading back to war, why he hadn't stayed with the German widow. What had brought Tunney back to the Rangers and now twice to war?

Was a man ever able to quit Ranging? Put down his weapons? Had Carson's path been set for him when he'd joined the Rangers at eighteen, before he'd ever thought about it? Had becoming a Ranger cast the lot of his life?

Dorritt paced her bedroom. Quinn had been called out to the barn to consult over a lame horse. His absence chafed her. She'd watched her son's heart being broken. She'd let him go to war again almost without a farewell. She ached to help Mariel, shield her some way. Was there anything she could do? Dorritt rubbed her arms against the chill.

Soon a servant would come and warm the sheets with hot coals in a long-handled copper pan. Winter was here. Dorritt noticed that she had not even lit the fire prepared in the small fireplace. She knelt and struck a match.

Quinn entered and shut the door against the cold. Shrugging off his wool poncho, he walked directly to her and wrapped his arms around her. He was cold from being outside. She snuggled against him, trying to warm him. Quinn announced, "We must plan to leave when the LaCroixs go."

She looked into the blue eyes she loved. His understanding of what she wanted lit a glow in her heart. "Truly?"

"We won't let Mariel go back to that New Braunfels without us. Face them without us."

Dorritt kissed him, savoring the familiar feel, taste, and smell of the man she loved more than any other. "Carson?"

"Yes."

"I'm frightened for him."

Quinn stroked her back. "You're worried he will be reckless?"

"Yes, dangerously reckless," she whispered. *Mortally reckless.*

"We will have to trust him to God."

Dorritt agreed by increasing her grip on him. "Mariel—I can't bear to see her go back to those people. They gossiped about her, and Sugar told me that Mariel was forced to marry this man by her parents. An arranged marriage. To a man who didn't, doesn't, value her."

Quinn kissed her ear and down the side of her neck. "I don't think that we can handle this alone. God must take care of them. All my life with you, we have prayed and believed that the Creator of all life hears us and works for our good. There must be a way of escape from this. Something we can't see."

Dorritt rested her head on Quinn's broad shoulder and stared into the dancing orange flames. *Lord, I believe. Help Thou my unbelief.* It helped a little. But her son's stricken face lingered in her mind. Carson had worn the expression of a man without hope. A man that didn't have much to lose. A man like that might take chances, risky ones, deadly ones. *Oh, God, keep him from despair.*

* * *

Two days later, Mariel stood beside Quinn and Dorritt near their horses. On the porch, Sugar, Emilio, and Erin huddled together against the sharp wind. "Why does everybody have to keep leaving?" Erin asked in a plaintive voice.

Mariel felt sorry for the little girl, but it was a shallow pity. She was still numbed inside. Losing Carson had killed all hope. She had believed that God had blessed her here. But it had been only an ugly joke. Everything she'd thought she'd gained was going to be taken from her again.

"Mariel was supposed to teach me German, but she went to war with Sugar, and now—"

"Erin," Quinn said, "we've been over this. We wanted Mariel to stay with us as . . . we wanted her to stay with us for as long as she wished. But she must go back to her husband. It's only right. She has no choice."

I have no choice. That was the way life had been, Mariel's old life in Germany. No choice but to obey.

"Why do you and Mama have to go? Can't Uncle Henri take her—"

"Erin," Dorritt interrupted, "we will try to be home before Christmas. Mind your sister and Emilio."

Quinn helped Dorritt into her saddle and then he helped Mariel. Remy was already mounted on his horse. He had finally healed enough to put away the splint. His shoulders were tilted slightly and his foot had healed misshapen, but he was alive and able to ride home in time for Christmas.

Blanche and her father were mounted. Their slaves sat wrapped in blankets on the buckboard. Many who lived on the Quinn

Ranch had gathered and now called out dispirited farewells. The party of riders and the wagon turned away and headed northeast.

Mariel tried to fight her way back to feeling. She made herself experience the brittle wind against her face, the rhythm of the horses beneath her, the chill that was creeping through all the layers of clothing she was wearing. *This is real. I am going back to New Braunfels. This isn't a nightmare. I won't wake up and find that I have been sleeping.*

Yesterday afternoon Dorritt had come into her room and had held her hand and prayed with her. She had told her that the Lord loved her. Dorritt had repeated some verses: "Delight thyself also in the LORD: and he shall give thee the desires of thine heart. Commit thy way unto the LORD; trust also in him; and he shall bring it to pass." She had tried to comfort Mariel that somehow God would intervene.

Mariel wanted to believe that God would intervene, but how could she? Dieter had come to Texas, and he was her husband. How could God change that? If God had wanted to intervene, couldn't he have had Dieter stay in Germany? She couldn't bring herself to wish Dieter dead. When she'd still been his wife in Germany, she hadn't prayed that he would die.

Remy rode up beside her. She tensed, afraid he would say sympathetic words and she might burst into tears. She kept her face forward, not glancing at him. He said nothing, just rode beside her. Slowly his sympathetic presence began to soothe her.

This man had changed over the past months. He was no longer a spoiled boy but a man who had suffered great pain with fortitude. And great disappointment with grace. He was a graduate of West Point, but with his body altered from his wounds, he would never be a cavalry soldier again.

After several miles of silent riding, Remy spoke, not looking at her. "If there is any way that I can be of service to you, Miss Mariel, you know that you can ask anything of me."

Tears moistened her dry eyes. "*Danke*, I . . . there is nothing anyone can do for me."

"I felt that way when I woke up in Mexico . . . such horrible pain. I thought I was going to die. But I came through it . . . because of my cousins' and your help. Just know that I am always yours to command, Miss Mariel. At any time. In any way."

"*Danke*." For some reason, German words were slipping from her more and more. Some part of her was preparing to go back to her own people—or at least the people that she had come from.

The two said no more. The chilly miles passed one by one. The wind played with the ribbons of her bonnet. It would take at least two days to reach New Braunfels. How far had Carson and Tunney gone since leaving? He had weeks to travel to reach Mexico. She closed her mind to the horrible memories of battle. Images of broken, bleeding, battered soldiers in the army hospital sickened her. If Carson was the one wounded this time, who would care for him? Emilio wasn't there to watch out for him.

This question moved her more than pity for herself. *Dear God, don't let him fall in battle. Bring him safely home.* She stiffened herself. She could not go with Carson, could not be there if he needed her. But she could pray.

Dorritt had said, "Commit thy way unto the LORD; trust also in him; and he shall bring it to pass." Mariel began to repeat these phrases, adding, "Keep Carson safe." Even though her freedom might be ended, it would console her knowing that Carson was alive. *This is all I ask. There is no hope for me. Preserve his life. Give him peace, a life filled with peace.*

* * *

Late in the afternoon two days later, Mariel hung back as their party rode into the valley of New Braunfels. The LaCroixs had gone east the day before, following the Colorado River toward home. Today Mariel must face Dieter and the people who had tried to destroy her with gossip. And she must not allow them to diminish her.

Reuniting with Dieter would not kill her; it would just make her hate living. She struggled against the despair that had sunk its ugly teeth into her spirit. *I am a different woman than I was in Germany. I am a Texas woman. I must not let Dieter take this from me. I will not be the frightened mouse hiding in the corner, hoping to be ignored. I am a Texas woman. The woman Carson Quinn, finest of all men, wanted as his wife.*

In the village, familiar people came out of their cabins and barns to gawk at them. How much of their vile gossip had they poured into her husband's ears? Recalling this ignited a blaze in the pit of her stomach. She straightened in her saddle.

I will not be ruled by any of these people and their mean-spiritedness. If anyone starts to speak against me, I will tell the truth. I don't care if they believe me or not. I will not be cowed by their gossip or Dieter's ill treatment. I am Mariel, beloved of Carson Quinn.

Finally, the Quinn party halted in the common green of the village. Herr Meuserbach came out of his large cabin to greet them. Other villagers were coming too. Quinn slid from his horse, and the rest of them followed suit. Mariel waited and was the last to dismount. Then she lifted her chin and walked straight to Meuserbach. A moment of silence splashed over all of them. Mariel felt every eye upon her.

Then the crowd parted, and a man with his hands in his pockets and his head bowed moved forward. His hat brim, pulled down low on his brow, hid his face from her. The clothing looked familiar, but . . .

Finally, he reached her and looked up. "Mariel?" His voice quavered.

Mariel, for a second time, felt the invisible hand crush the warmth from her. Why had no one told her? What could have happened?

Eighteen

Carson and Tunney had reached Taylor's command in Mexico, south of Monterrey, several weeks earlier, at the start of January 1847. They had ridden through the army encampment with thousands of blue-clad U.S. soldiers and volunteers, then camped and waited for McCulloch, Hays, and other Rangers to arrive. Taylor kept asking when they thought McCulloch would come.

Now, coming in from the blustery wind, Carson with McCulloch, who had just arrived, entered Taylor's office, a jacal some peasant had run from to escape the U.S. Army. Carson would finally find out why the Rangers had been called back. Still deep in a waking nightmare, he could not remember one detail he had experienced on the journey here. The numbness lingered on. He was barely aware of fatigue or hunger or thirst. Nothing seemed to stick.

"McCulloch, I've never been happier to see any soldier in my long career," Taylor said, then he cursed, startling Carson. "If you'd been here, this infernal situation would never have occurred."

McCulloch raised one eyebrow and looked to Carson first and then to the American general, who still wore scruffy bedroom slippers and the dusty green coat. "What's the trouble?"

"I sent out a courier and blast if he didn't let himself get caught. And with him all my dispatches about my plans, troop strength, and the new strategy from Washington. Polk is sending General Scott to land and attack Vera Cruz and then on to Mexico City. All of this information fell into Santa Anna's bloody, dishonorable hands."

For the first time in weeks, Carson felt something. He recalled Blanche's outburst of laughter when Tunney had said . . . Carson suppressed the same jarring, illogical reaction that Blanche had had. He must have shown some amusement, because Taylor scowled at him.

"That's a mite inconvenient," McCulloch commented and leaned out the door to spit. Cool air rushed in. "What do you want us to do?"

"I need to mislead Santa Anna into thinking that I am going to do what I had planned to do—to retreat. Then I must do the complete opposite—attack instead of retreating north. First, I need to know if it is a sound strategy. Or if I am, in effect, forcing my troops and all the volunteer companies to commit suicide."

With a steady gaze, McCulloch considered Taylor for many moments. "You need us to go in and see how many men Santa Anna has."

Carson comprehended how dangerous this mission was. This general wanted the Rangers to go where he didn't trust *his* own men—to go smack up to Santa Anna's army and get back, unscathed. Carson drew in air. Taylor had grit all right. And gall.

"Yes, so if Santa Anna tries to follow me thinking I'm retreating," the general continued, "I'll know if I can beat him. From what I've heard of him, attacking a retreating army is just what he's capable of. Here, look at the chart." He ruffled through the papers on his desk and pulled out a rough, hand-drawn map. "There's a place near an estate, called Buena Vista—"

Hearing that a Mexican estate had the same name as his mother's family's plantation made Carson think of Remy, of home, of . . .

When Carson jerked himself back to the present, Taylor was still speaking. "I hope Santa Anna will think he has us on the run. I studied that estate, Buena Vista, where it's situated in the surrounding mountains. He can't outflank me, and I intend to turn and beat him. Weaken him, make him retreat."

McCulloch grunted.

Sudden images from the bloody Battle of San Jacinto hurtled through Carson's mind. They jolted him. He blurted, "There isn't a Texian alive who won't do anything to beat Santa Anna."

Taylor rocked on the balls of his feet as if Carson's words had knocked him back on his heels. "You sound like you mean business."

Carson didn't bother to reply.

McCulloch did. "Carson fought Santa Anna at San Jacinto."

Taylor raised both eyebrows. "You must have just been a cub then."

"Fourteen," Carson bit out. The memories had awakened him now. His stomach roiled with anger over the past, over the present with Santa Anna's second attempt to best Texans, over this U.S. general sending the Rangers, not his men, on this dangerous mission.

"Maybe you're a natural born soldier. Some men are. I've seen that plainly over the years." Taylor clasped his arms behind his back and looked into Carson's eyes from under his own bushy gray brows. "I could offer you a lieutenancy in the U.S. Army, a battlefield promotion."

The words smacked Carson like the kick of a stallion. He

reeled with the blow, then glared. "I'm a Ranger because my people need protection. I'm no soldier."

Those same bushy eyebrows rose high. "McCulloch, pick your men and find out what I need. Send me the information I must have as fast as you can." Taylor held out his hand. McCulloch and Carson shook on it. Without another word, they left.

Outside in the chilly sunlight, Carson saw Niven striding toward him and inwardly groaned. *Not now. Not here.*

"How is my brother-in-law?" Niven asked without preamble.

"On his way home with his father and your bride. He probably won't serve in the army again. His shoulder and foot will never be the same."

"Sorry to hear that, but glad to hear that he's well enough to go home. How was my bride?"

"Just like you left her." Carson couldn't help adding a slight veneer of sarcasm.

Niven grinned. "Glad to hear that. Anything I can do for you?"

"No—"

"I hate to interrupt this cozy family chat, but the Rangers got to be moving out." McCulloch had arrived only a few hours before Carson and Tunney, and he looked peeved.

"Then I will let you go about your scouting." Niven bowed and said, "Godspeed."

Watching Niven walk away gave Carson a sense of relief. *She* hadn't been mentioned. He turned back to the scene around him and stalked after McCulloch to round up their band of Rangers. And head farther into enemy territory. Just where he wanted to go.

* * *

It didn't take weeks for McCulloch and his handpicked Rangers to find Santa Anna's army to the south. After night fell and the army slept, the Rangers crept forward through blackness. From a rise, they began counting campfires. On his belly looking over the cliff, Carson did his own count silently. And cursed Santa Anna. Where had the butcher dragged these poor fellows from? When McCulloch looked to him, the man's eyes glistened in the slight moonlight. Carson muttered, "I figure around fifteen thousand troops."

McCulloch's reply was pithy and coarse. Then he said, "Let's get some sleep, then we'll take another look in the morning."

Morning came, a damp foggy one. McCulloch tapped Carson on the shoulder. "I want a closer look before I report to old Rough and Ready in his bedroom slippers."

Carson just looked at him. Blankly. How?

"Let's take a ride through the camp. With the fog and the green-wood fires they'll light to cook breakfast, they'll never see us."

Two Rangers riding through an enemy camp of fifteen thousand? Carson's only thought was, *What do I have to lose?*

The two of them swung up into their saddles and walked their horses toward the camp. McCulloch was right. As they slipped between sentinels, the morning mist hid their approach. Once in the camp, the two of them moseyed their horses through the billowing white smoke of the breakfast fires.

Carson had been unmoved on his journey here and during the weeks of waiting, but this short jaunt prickled every one of his nerves wide awake. He quivered with awareness of danger on all sides. One outcry and they would be undone. Captured. Or killed.

As they moved on unmolested, occasionally a Mexican soldier would glance up, look shocked, and then blink. But by the time he opened his eyes again, they were cloaked once more in the white smoke. Just ghosts of Rangers—no doubt they were thought to be simply evil omens. *Diablos. Tejanos.* As one soldier gawked at them, he crossed himself. Finally, the two of them ambled out of the enemy camp and back to the rest of the Rangers.

Tunney looked up and shook his head in disbelief. Carson could hardly believe that they had come back alive. He felt like a bow string stretched too taut too long.

McCulloch said, "Fifteen thousand it is." No one replied, but all mounted up and headed back to Taylor. No one wanted to take this news to the General. The U.S. Army was outnumbered three to one.

* * *

McCulloch delivered the result of their reconnaissance to the U.S. general. Over the next few weeks, Taylor, with his reduced infantry less than a third of what he'd had to face Monterrey, fell back in a feint to draw Santa Anna to him. It worked. Santa Anna pursued them and caught them—right where Taylor had planned he would.

On the morning of February 21, 1847, Santa Anna's emissary, under a white parlay flag, suggested that the Americans surrender. Taylor told him to tell Santa Anna to go to Hades. The battle of Buena Vista commenced.

* * *

Near the end of the second day of battle, Carson and Tunney were backing up the Illinois volunteers, holding off the Mexican infantry. They fired their rifles, picking off Mexicans who broke through and pierced the Illinois line. The din of exploding canisters, whining lead balls hitting metal, dirt, and flesh, the yells and curses of the fighting men wrapped around Carson but did not stir him inside. He was a fighter. Habit took over.

A close outcry turned Carson's head. Tunney was falling from his saddle.

Carson didn't think twice. He leaped down and examined his friend. He froze, his heart flipping in his chest. A stray shot must have caught Tunney. Tunney was dead. The shot had severed an artery in his neck; the crimson flow had already gushed and stopped. Lifting his friend, Carson placed him facedown over his saddle and rode away, leading the horse to the rear. A constant roar filled his ears, but he wouldn't have Tunney's body trampled, desecrated by two armies.

By the time Carson reached the rear troops tucked into the mountains and ravines, the gunfire had ended for the night. Black smoke and early winter nightfall had halted the battle. Rangers started filtering back, joining Carson in preparing their comrade for burial. None of them spoke except in monosyllables. Within hours, Tunney had been laid to rest by his friends.

The sudden loss shocked Carson back to feeling once more. On the outside, he sat at the Ranger campfire, silent and morose, trying to keep down the bitter scalding coffee someone had handed him. On the inside, anger-hatred-disbelief-anguish-loss-friendship-shock cascaded through him in such vivid and brief blasts that he felt as though a volcano was working its way through him. Lava like currents seared him.

Why hadn't Tunney stayed with the pretty widow in New Braunfels? Why had Tunney, who'd retired honorably, returned to this war—twice? Had it been the pull of camaraderie, the call to protect? Carson had no answer. The person he wanted most to talk to, his father, was hundreds of miles north. His father had faced this kind of crisis long ago: whether to go on with the life he knew, rejecting God and his gift of Dorritt, or to turn toward God and accept life and love.

Memories of Mariel kept leaking through the barrier Carson had erected against her. Her flaxen hair whispered against his cheek. Her soft fingers stroked through his hair. Her . . . He forced himself to block out the impressions of her streaming through his senses. The battle would start again at dawn. Honor compelled him to stay and fight. He started in a war, he had to stay till the end regardless.

Despair washed through him, turning his thoughts stark and morose. *I will be the next to fall. What did Niven say about Remy when he brought him to us after Monterrey? Something about not being buried in a foreign land. "At least he'll be buried on U.S. soil with family to speak solemn prayers over his grave. Not in an unmarked communal pit with strangers in a foreign land."* Would Niven come when the Rangers buried Carson tomorrow?

* * *

The next day dawned misty as usual, but an unexpected sight greeted the Americans camped on high ground. The Mexican Army was retreating. A sound went along the lines, a single yell at first and then a murmuring, which became louder and louder until shouts went up, "Victory! Victory! The enemy has fled! The field is ours!"

Carson stood listening. Cool, bracing currents of relief and gratitude sluiced through him. Just as He had for Carson's father, God was providing a way out for him. The battle he'd thought he'd die in would not take place today. *And I won't be stubborn like Tunney.* When the general hoopla finally quieted, he walked over to McCulloch. "I'm going home. I'm done. With this war. With Ranging."

McCulloch stared at him. Then he offered his large hand. "You can leave with a clear conscience. You've served Texas and the U.S. with honor. Go home to that pretty widow."

The last few words staked Carson's heart. But he shook McCulloch's hand and rode through the celebrating troops, heading due north. Mariel's image flickered in his mind's eye. He banished it. There was no honorable way for them to be together. His hope for a life with her had been ended by circumstances beyond their control.

Still, he had family to return to. And he would try to find a way that didn't include war. If he wanted to walk the path of peace, he must find the start of that trail and begin tracking it. *I want to be a man of peace. God, you'll have to show me the way. I will study war no more.*

* * *

By the time Carson finally rode up to the porch of his parents' hacienda, chill March rains had come in full force. Rain poured from his hat brim and over his poncho. His horse stirred mud. The sun was low upon the horizon. Smoke floated upward from the many chimneys in the hacienda and jacales around the ranch. Numb from weariness and the loss of Tunney, he paused at the bottom of the steps to the front porch and waited. For some reason, he couldn't just get down from his horse and walk inside. He wanted to be welcomed first.

Finally a few people began coming out of the jacales to greet him, men tossing serapes around their shoulders, women within wool rebozos. It wasn't a joyous welcome. Perhaps they read his somber mood from the way he sat on his horse. Perhaps it was the dismal scene that depressed everything, even welcome. At last, the front door opened. He looked up, expecting his mother or father or sisters. Mariel stepped out onto the porch with a shawl around her shoulders. She opened her arms and said his name.

He slid from his horse, staring at her. Someone took his horse toward the barn. Carson stood, staring. Stunned. His very core blasted with heat, then cold. He couldn't take it in. *Why are you here?*

Without saying a word, she walked down the few steps and took his hand. "Come inside. It's warm there." He let her lead him up the steps and into the big room. Her small hand felt real. This wasn't a dream, conjured by his longing for her.

Inside, he paused to look around at the familiar room, the familiar faces. Erin ran and hugged his waist. Sugar came and helped him off with his wet poncho and hat. His mother and father embraced him. The housekeeper came out with food he loved, fragrant with chili peppers and coriander, and called for him to come and "Eat, eat!" Mariel led him to the table. There he began eating, each bite making him aware of how deeply hungry he was.

"Did you win the war?" Erin asked.

"The war isn't over," Carson said between bites, "just my part in it."

When Erin tried to ask another question, Quinn stopped her. He started talking about what had been going on at the ranch in Carson's absence. Carson was grateful for each piece of news, which knit him back into the life here. And he was content to eat and gaze at Mariel. Forever.

Finally, Emilio asked, "Are you home for good?"

"Yes, I've given up being a Ranger." He looked down, not wanting to see what the reaction to this would be.

"Why?" Erin asked and was hushed by Dorritt, who said, "There is a time for every season under heaven. A time for war. A time for peace."

No one said anything. He glanced up. They just nodded, as if they had expected him to say that. His eyes found Mariel again, and he couldn't drag his gaze from her. He wanted to ask, Why are you here? But everyone sat with them, and he couldn't ask how this miracle had happened.

His father rose. "We will leave you two alone for a while. Welcome home, son." And even Erin, though taken by the hand and twisting back to see him, left the room so Mariel and he could be alone.

"Why are you here?" he asked, the words flowing out. "I never expected to see you again."

"I will explain." She took his hand and held it to her cheek. "I have been so worried, worried you wouldn't, couldn't, come back to me. And here you are. You came through the valley of the shadow of death, back to me."

He tilted his head and kissed her, just lightly, so he could stop, because he had to know, must know how she had been given back to him. Still, the temptation to draw her into his arms pulled at him. "Tell me." *Quickly.*

She looked down at the white tablecloth, pressing it and smoothing it with the tips of her fingers. "Dieter was arrested for his democratic politics. Many were. In prison, he shared a cell with a man name Karl Meissen. He had been arrested for stealing. They learned that to lessen the crowding of the prison, Dieter was to be released—if he promised to leave Germany. The *Adelsverein* was offering to take political dissenters to Texas. But Dieter died during the night." She paused and looked up. "Dieter was never strong. He had a lung disease."

"I still don't understand." Her soft pink earlobes were enticing him now. He let his index finger brush the one nearest.

She blushed her nice rosy pink, just as he remembered. "Karl and Dieter looked much alike, so Karl took a chance. He put on Dieter's clothing and switched cots. When the guards came, he thought they must surely see that he wasn't Dieter, but they did not. They took his word that Karl Meissen, not Dieter Wolffe, had died. They carried out the body."

"They didn't recognize the difference?" *Your husband is dead, then?*

Mariel shrugged, gazing down. "Karl said it was a very large, very old prison. Some of it was still dungeons under the castle. The guards never took much notice of anyone."

"I can't believe it. But then why did they tell you your husband had died when they thought Karl was dead?" He lifted her chin with his finger, wanting to see her large eyes, so somber now. Yet he had seen them dance with mischief.

"No one officially told *me* anything. His parents told me about it. I think someone must have told my in-laws he was dead because so many were executed or died in prison. You know how gossip is. Everyone wants to think the worst and stories start and no one can find out who started the talk."

Carson listened to her musical voice. *Mariel, you're here.*

"I never saw any letter," she said. "Probably there was no letter. I was just told Dieter had died. I think his parents wished him dead. They made it clear he had disgraced their family. In any case, Karl as Dieter wasn't released right away. Another sweep of democratic meetings and more arrests had crowded the prison. Three more men were jammed together in the tiny cell he shared with Dieter."

Carson couldn't help it. He touched her pale hair, so smooth, so silken.

She caught his hand and kissed his palm, staring into his eyes. Desire broke over him. But he stopped himself. He must know the truth. "Go on." *Finish it so we can stop talking. I need to kiss you.*

"Finally, Karl as Dieter was released and was met by the *Adelsverein* at the prison gate, along with many others. As soon as enough people were assembled, he left with them on the next voyage for Texas."

"Still acting as if he were your husband?" He was more interested in Mariel, but the strange story managed to keep him listening. He must hear it all, understand it all so there would be nothing to keep them apart. He traced her eyebrows one after the other, just wanting to touch her, feel that she was real.

"No. He didn't know Dieter had been a married man. I can't blame him for switching places with Dieter. He says he wasn't guilty of stealing from his employer—that the man's wife was the guilty party, but he had no proof. After being in prison, he just wanted to get out of Germany before he was recognized and put back into prison." She shrugged and laid her hand on his, soft skin on weathered.

The lamplight gleamed on her pale blond hair. "When you arrived at New Braunfels, what happened? Didn't he try to say that he was your husband?"

"No, he didn't keep lying. As soon as I said that he wasn't Dieter, he told the truth. I think he must have been telling the truth about being wrongly arrested too. He struck me as an honest man, a desperate one to do what he had done. He said he was very sorry that I had been deceived. I believed him." She gripped his hand in hers.

"Why didn't he just tell the truth when he got to Texas? Certainly they wouldn't have sent him back." Finally, anger sparked, flickered within Carson. The man's lie had cost them both much pain, suffering.

"He was afraid, and no one mentioned me till he got to New Braunfels. He thought he would wait and see how I reacted when I arrived and do what I thought was right. I forgive him. Being in prison like that." Mariel shivered.

Carson shook his head, then forgot everything but Mariel. His desire for this woman, his love for her, overwhelmed, drowned every other reaction. He reached for her and dragged her into his lap. He kissed her. She clung to him, giving him her lips, her neck freely.

A throat cleared in the dimly lit room.

Irritated, Carson lifted his head. In the doorway from the courtyard stood his parents, sisters, Emilio, and the house-keeper and Consuela. His father carried the worn, small black Book of Common Prayer. Emilio carried the large family Bible toward the fireplace. "Carson and Mariel," Quinn said, "your mother and I have decided that we will marry you two here, tonight, in front of God and these witnesses. There is no reason that you shouldn't be together now—as man and wife."

Carson understood what his parents meant. His father was right. He and Mariel had waited long enough. He didn't trust himself to be alone with her after what they each had been through, and after weeks apart.

He sent her a questioning glance. She nodded almost shyly.

He let her slip from his lap. Carson led her to the fireplace, where his father had moved to stand with his mother and the rest of the witnesses. Carson led Mariel to face him and took her right hand.

"How can they get married?" Erin complained. "Mariel isn't wearing her wedding dress."

Dorritt answered for them. "We will have a party when the spring rains end. Then Mariel will wear her wedding dress and Carson his best suit. And we'll have a fiesta with dancing and a piñata."

"Promise?" Erin reiterated.

Their mother gave her a pointed look and Erin fell silent. His father began reading from the small book of prayer and Carson was relieved. The ceremony that joined the two of them till death seemed to pass in seconds yet last forever. Quinn's firm, low voice, the fire crackling on the hearth, Carson's own even heartbeat—everything was subdued, but as perfect as the feeling of Mariel's small hand in his.

At the end, he kissed Mariel, slid onto her ring finger the wedding ring Emilio had kept for him. And then his father recorded their names and the date in the family Bible. After subdued hugs, kisses, and many good wishes, Carson led Mariel through the dark courtyard to his room.

The staff had prepared a bathtub before the fire. Carson closed the door. He knew the bath was for him, but the thought of bathing with Mariel in the room gave him pause.

She smiled an understanding smile. "I'll go and get some of my things from Erin's room. I'll be right back." She left him alone.

He noticed that a dressing screen had magically appeared, and he smiled. He quickly disrobed, setting his soiled clothing outside the door for the laundress to take away, and sank into the hot bath before the fire. His exhausted, battered body slowly relaxed as the hot water loosened the knots in his muscles and soothed the ache in his low back. He tried to think over all that had just happened. He felt as if he'd walked out of the nightmare of the past months and had entered seamlessly into a pleasing dream, pleasing beyond anything he had hoped for. *This isn't a dream. Mariel is my wife now and no one can take her from me.*

Mariel slipped into the room and shut the door. Carson was facing away from her, looking into the fire. She saw that the cold breeze that had come in with her had made him, her husband, shiver. Her joy rippled up from deep within and poured through her, silent, rapturous and liberating. *My husband. Carson Quinn is my husband.*

How many times had she wanted to make this man more comfortable but had been prevented from doing so? Now he was her husband, and she could show him her love. She slipped off her shawl and went and knelt by the head of the high-backed tin tub. Picking up the bar of soft imported soap, she rubbed it onto her hands. Then she began to shampoo his hair.

He stilled at her touch and then relaxed in the shadowy room, lit only by the fire and one candle on the bedside table. In the low light, she took her time massaging his scalp and working out the tangles in his long hair. He had let it grow since she'd met him in Galveston. It was shoulder-length now. It suited Carson, son of Quinn. He had been a Ranger.

But no more; now he was hers.

"Will you always wash my hair?" he asked, catching her hand in his and drawing it to his lips.

"If you wish it." She kissed his ear. Then it came, the joy so abundant and the peace she had doubted would ever be hers. She, the meek, the humble, would live in the land. With her man of peace.

Epilogue

Sipping her last cup of morning coffee and wearing her best violet blue dress, Dorritt stood on her front porch and watched the bevy of activity in the sunny yard beyond. People were setting up tables, hanging the piñata for the children, decorating the tables with wildflowers, the bluebonnets and daisies. The spring rains had ended and the fiesta celebrating the marriage of Carson and Mariel would take place today. Guests would start arriving any time now. Dorritt looked out over their land, the land that belonged to her and Quinn.

God was good. When she had left New Orleans twenty-six years ago, she had hoped for only independence from her stepfather. God had given her more, much more than she had imagined. A loving husband, children, friends, and soon grandchildren.

Sugar and Emilio would be parents near the end of this year, 1847. Sam Houston had written to say that Sugar's father had been listed as one of those who had been killed in the massacre at Goliad. The family planned to honor Ernest McLaughlin during this year's Day of the Dead celebration.

The faraway war was grinding on. General Scott had captured the Gulf of Mexico port of Veracruz and, according to Carson, would march to capture Mexico City. Carson had decided to read law in San Antonio. He would protect his fellow Texians with the law, not his Walker Colt .45s. It would be hard to have Carson and Mariel settle a day's ride away, but he could have fallen like Tunney at the Battle of Buena Vista.

No, everything in Dorritt's life had fallen into place. God had given her the desires of her heart indeed. The only smudge on the page of her life was her sister's lack of love, combined with her vanity and her slave-holding. Texas had been admitted to the U.S. as a slave state. This grieved Dorritt, and she feared what this might cost Texas in the future.

Quinn walked out and stepped behind her. He slipped his arms around her waist and rested his chin on her right shoulder. "I love you," he murmured.

She lifted her palm and stroked his cheek. "And I love you."

Her mind roved over the past. A multitude of images flowed through her mind. Alandra's brother, Don Carlos's sincere expression the day he'd told her he had fallen in love with her, Sugar's pinched face the day they had found her, Alandra's smile when she had told Dorritt that she and Scully were expecting their first child. "We have so much to be thankful for," she said.

"Yes."

And no more words were needed.

Historical Note

So my Texas Star of Destiny Series ends here. What a wild ride of historical research this series has taken me on. I had never studied the history of Texas and am astounded by all that went on there in the years between 1821 and 1847. I also had never studied the Mexican-American War before and was amazed at Taylor's strategy, his victory over a much greater force, and the achievements of President Polk. Polk never got the credit he deserved in his lifetime or in history. And, of course, he was right. Zachary Taylor, the Whig, did beat him in the next election. Of course, one more major war was coming in just a little over a decade, the Civil War, as Dorritt predicted.

The scene I wrote in which Carson and Ben McCulloch ride through Santa Anna's army actually happened and shows you the real Ben McCulloch's grit. Also, I was happy to write about the large German immigration to Texas in this period. (The *Adelsverein* was created by many German noblemen to help the poor in Germany to immigrate to America, thousands of Germans settled in Texas in the 1840s.) John O. Meuserbach was modeled after a real man named Baron Von Meuserbach, though of course I embroidered a bit, not having met him in person. The German immigrants did strike a peace with the Comanche and lived as peaceful neighbors much longer than the Anglos or *Tejanos*. If you go to New Braunfels, Texas, in the Hill Country, you will find that the German heritage is still strong there today. Also, the Texas Rangers still protect the citizens of Texas—though now they are paid regularly. I want to thank librarians at the San Antonio Library for help researching this series. Thanks to all of you readers for joining me on this ride through Western history.

Discussion Questions

1. Why do you think Carson became infatuated with Blanche? Have you ever known a similarly mismatched couple who married for some reason other than love? How do you think a marriage based on ambition or something else would be different from one based on love and mutual respect?

2. Sugar had to face her past before she could reap the full blessings of her life with Emilio. Have you ever faced anything similar? How does the Bible tell us to deal with fear and remembered hurts?

3. I took the phrase "Texas Star of Destiny" from the Texas state song. Do Christians believe in fate, kismet, or providence? What are the differences between these three ways of looking at the events of life?

4. Carson Quinn had killed many in his job as a Ranger. How does this jibe with "Thou shalt not kill"?

5. What did Carson want most in life? What did Mariel want most in life? What did they have to learn before they could be blessed by God with the desires of their hearts?

6. Mariel recited scripture when she was frightened. Do you have a Bible verse that helps you face difficult circumstances? What is it and why does this speak to you?

7. Why do you think Tunney went back to the war?

8. Why did Ash and Reva go south to live in Mexico? How had the U.S. annexation of Texas affected them?

9. What new facts did you learn about American or Texas history from this book?

10. Who were your favorite characters from this book and/or the two previous? If you could choose one character to follow into a fourth book, who would it be? Which hero-heroine couple did you most enjoy, most identify with?

LYN COTE married her real-life hero and was blessed with a son and daughter. She loves game shows, knitting, cooking, and eating! She and her husband live on a beautiful lake in the northwoods of Wisconsin. Now that the children have moved out, she indulges three cats—V-8 (for the engine, not the juice), Sadie, and Tricksey. In the summer, she writes using her laptop on her porch overlooking the lake. And in the winter, she sits by the fireplace her husband installed with the help of a good neighbor during their first winter at the lake.

Lyn's inspirational novels feature American women who step up to the challenges of their times and succeed in remaining true to the values of liberty and justice for all. The story of America is one of many nationalities and races coming together to forge our one nation under God and Lyn's novels reflect this with accurate historical detail, always providing the ring of authenticity. Strong Women, Brave Stories.

Lyn loves to hear from readers, so visit her website at *www.LynCote.net* or e-mail her at l.cote@juno.com.